A Regency Christmas

Elisabeth Fairchild

Carla Kelly

Allison Lane

Edith Layton

Barbara Metzger

A SIGNET BOOK

SIGNET
Published by the Penguin Group
Penguin Putnam Inc., 375 Hudson Street,
New York, New York 10014, U.S.A.
Penguin Books Ltd, 27 Wrights Lane,
London W8 5TZ, England
Penguin Books Australia Ltd,
Ringwood, Victoria, Australia
Penguin Books Canada Ltd, 10 Alcorn Avenue,
Toronto, Ontario, Canada M4V 3B2
Penguin Books (N.Z.) Ltd, 182–190 Wairau Road,
Auckland 10, New Zealand

Penguin Books Ltd, Registered Offices:
Harmondsworth, Middlesex, England

First published by Signet, an imprint of Dutton NAL,
a member of Penguin Putnam Inc.

First Printing, November, 1998
10 9 8 7 6 5 4 3 2 1

A Regency Christmas

Elisabeth Fairchild

Carla Kelly

Allison Lane

Edith Layton

SIGNET
Published by the Penguin Group
Penguin Putnam Inc., 375 Hudson Street,
New York, New York 10014, U.S.A.
Penguin Books Ltd, 27 Wrights Lane,
London W8 5TZ, England
Penguin Books Australia Ltd,
Ringwood, Victoria, Australia
Penguin Books Canada Ltd, 10 Alcorn Avenue,
Toronto, Ontario, Canada M4V 3B2
Penguin Books (N.Z.) Ltd, 182–190 Wairau Road,
Auckland 10, New Zealand

Penguin Books Ltd, Registered Offices:
Harmondsworth, Middlesex, England

First published by Signet, an imprint of Dutton NAL,
a member of Penguin Putnam Inc.

First Printing, November, 1998

10 9 8 7 6 5 4 3 2 1

Contents

Three Good Deeds
by Barbara Metzger

1

No noise is louder to the ears of a boy than the sound of a window shattering when he is left holding the cricket bat. Unless, of course, the unfortunate pane of glass happens to have been in a church. At least this one was not a centuries-old stained-glass work of art. That noise would have made the crack of doom sound like a snowflake landing.

The boy could have run, as the other local lads had, disappearing through the village streets like so many leaves fading into the forest floor. This boy's sense of honor kept him in place outside the tiny chapel. Honor kept him there, as well as his bright red hair, which would make him visible for miles. Besides, he'd just left the vicar's study, his Latin lessons not ten minutes past. So he stayed, waiting, and his two brothers stayed with him.

"Oh, dear." The Reverend Mr. Davenport had been working on his Christmas sermon. That is, he'd been thinking of working on his Christmas sermon, which meant he'd been dozing when the glass shattered. He wheezed himself out of his comfortable chair and into his coat and muffler against the December chill, then joined the three boys outside in staring at the jagged

edges of the window. "Oh, dear Lord in Heaven, and the bishop is coming."

"I did it, Vicar," confessed ten-year-old Martin, the eldest of the Greene siblings.

"No, sir, I hit the ball." The middle boy, Jasper, adjusted the spectacles on his nose. "Mama told me not to play with my glasses on, and I couldn't see where I was aiming."

Benjamin, the baby of the bunch at five years of age, was not to be left out. "I made them let me bat, Mr. Davenport. Honest, I did."

"Oh, dear." The vicar huffed into the scarf around his neck. "What's to be done? Whatever is to be done? We'll have to go inside to discuss this; yes, we will." He turned to trudge back into his warm office, where Martin had so recently been reading his assigned passage of Vergil, and Jasper had struggled with Caesar through the Gallic wars. Little Benjamin had practiced his letters with first declension nouns. Now Benjy was the first to voice the dismal thoughts of all three boys.

"Do you think he'll cane us?" he whispered as the Greene trio followed in the vicar's wake, like felons to the gibbet.

"He didn't last time, when we left the gate open and Maude Binkum's cow got in and ate his roses." Still, Jasper handed the bat over to his older brother.

"No, but he told Mama, and she was that upset she cried." As one, the three slowed their steps, falling farther behind the vicar and their fate.

"Oh, dear, oh, dear," Mr. Davenport kept repeating as he lowered himself back into his study chair. "I'll have to call in the sexton and send him off to the glazier's with measurements, and hire a carpenter, and oh, my, I don't know what else. Paint, I suppose, if

they have to take the frame out, and caulking. Oh, and I so wanted St. Jerome's to look perfect for the bishop. We cannot very well ask him for the funds for an extension when we don't care for our little church now."

"We'll pay for the repairs, sir," Martin offered, emptying his pockets. His brothers did likewise. Soon a collection of stones and string and colored chalk rested on the vicar's desk, with a few coins buried in their midst. Mr. Davenport used his penknife to poke through the pile, separating two shillings and some copper pennies from the rest.

"We've been saving for Mama's Christmas present," Jasper confided.

Martin nodded. "We were going to buy her a dress length of velvet."

"Red velvet," Benjy put in, "so she'll have something pretty to wear to the duke's dinner for the bishop."

The vicar shook his head, whether at the alarming thought of Sabina Greene in red velvet, her with the same flaming hair as her three sons, or the unlikelihood of the young widow's being invited to Espinham Castle for the festivities. "It is not enough, boys. Glass is expensive, and the workmen need their wages."

The youngsters looked to one another, but it was Martin who spoke. "We'll work, sir, we'll do anything, so long as you don't tell our mother."

"No, no. The dear woman has enough in her budget without this. Why, I feel bad already, taking her money in exchange for your lessons, but she insists."

"We'll give up the lessons!" Benjy volunteered.

"No, that won't do. Perhaps I should go to the duke and ask him for the funds."

"No! Please don't," three desperate voices chorused.

"You can beat us, or . . . or take our pony, Chocolate. Just don't go to the duke." They all recalled the incident last spring involving a ram and a ewe and the Duke of Espinwall's garden party. His Grace had demanded Mama's presence, then thundered at her for a day, it seemed, leaving Mrs. Greene pale and shaking, weeping for a sennight. No, they would sell Benjy as a chimney sweep before they let the duke berate their mother again.

"Let me think, let me think," the vicar muttered, rubbing the penknife along his whiskered jaw. "I can take some money from the roof fund, and replace that with a bit of the choir robe budget. And, yes, I do believe you three can work to repay the cost. His Grace has generously offered the dead wood in Espy Forest to the poor of the parish, if we come and get it, of course." The vicar did not mention what he thought of such generosity. The fallen limbs would keep the poor warm this winter, no matter how cold the duke's heart. "You can go along with Wilfred Snavely and his son to gather the firewood, so the job will get done that much sooner and the parish can save a few pence there."

The boys grinned. "We'll pick up every twig, sir! In fact, we can climb the trees and knock down broken branches. Old Wilfred's too big to climb trees, and Young Wilfred's too lazy. And Chocolate can help carry, so you won't have to pay them so much to use their donkey." Martin slapped Jasper on the shoulder, and Benjamin bounced up and down.

"Ahem. That's not all, boys."

Three similar freckled faces turned pale again.

"No, you cannot learn to believe that money alone fixes wrongs. That would be a poor lesson indeed.

Why, they say that two rights don't even mend a wrong, so we'll try for three, shall we?"

"Three, sir?" The boys looked to each other in confusion.

"Aye, lads. Three rights to make up for the broken window. Three good deeds to repay the parish for the aggravation of having you three rapscallions loose among us."

"We don't understand, Mr. Davenport," Martin spoke for all of them. "Just what is it you would have us do?"

"I don't know, lad. Use your heads for once. It might be a good exercise. Look around and see who needs help this holiday season. And I don't mean using your pennies to buy candy for the needy children, or getting money from your dear mother to give to the poor. That's too easy. And helping each other with your homework assignments and chores won't count either. I mean you should perform three selfless acts, ones that aren't just for your own benefit, and do it anonymously, too. That means no one is to know who helped them," he added for Benjy's sake, "because this is not about winning praise for yourselves. It is about helping the Lord at His busy season. You look around the village and see who is unhappy and what you can do to ease their souls. And make sure you complete your three good deeds before Christmas, mind you, or I'll have to go to your mother after all, or the duke. Do you understand?"

The boys understood they'd be carrying firewood to stoke furnaces in hell if the duke got hold of them, so they nodded, but they weren't entirely sure they did comprehend the vicar's penance, nor what to do about it. So that night, when they were gathered around their

mother for the evening story, Benjy asked, "Mama, who is the most unhappy person you know?"

Sabina squeezed her youngest, there in the old worn leather chair at her right side. Jasper sat on her left, and Martin was perched on the stool by her feet. "Unhappy, dear? Why, I don't think I know anyone who is unhappy. Mrs. Cotter could use more milk for her children, but Jed Hanks said he'd lend her a cow. And Mr. Jordan at the inn is worried about his son off with the army, so we must remember to add young Tom to our prayers, along with the other brave soldiers."

"Gads, I hope Mr. Davenport doesn't expect us to end the war," Jasper whispered to his older brother, at which Sabina's brows came together.

"Now what is this about?"

"Oh, the vicar was just practicing his sermon," Martin quickly told her. "Something about windows to the soul, I think. What did you hear, Jas?"

"He definitely mentioned windows, all right. And . . . branches of knowledge. Isn't that right, Martin?"

Sabina shook her head. "Mr. Davenport must be preparing for Christmas Eve, hoping to impress the bishop if the children's pageant and the chorale don't sway His Eminence enough to loosen his purse strings." She only hoped the vicar didn't put everyone to sleep.

Seeing her frown, and worrying more over their thorny dilemma than over the bishop's visit, Benjy asked, "You're not unhappy, Mama, are you?"

Speaking of purse strings, Sabina would have been a lot happier if she did not have to worry about her finances all the time. She managed on her tiny income, but without the luxuries, nay, the comforts she wished

she could provide for her children, especially with Christmas coming. But her late husband's clutch-fisted man of affairs had no idea of how much three boys ate, or how quickly they outgrew their clothes. Still, she made do. "No, darling, I am not unhappy. How could I be, when I have the three finest sons a woman could wish?"

"Even if we are not rich?"

"Especially. Money doesn't bring happiness, darling. Just look at the duke. He never has to worry about paying the butcher or the wine merchant, so he overindulges himself right into the gout. Then he is even more discontented."

"But why is the duke so unhappy, Mama? He has the finest stable in the shire." Martin couldn't imagine anyone with such prime horseflesh not being delighted with his lot in life.

His Grace of Espinwall was the meanest, most ill-tempered old curmudgeon of Sabina's acquaintance. She believed he must have been born raging at the midwife, and he'd likely die swearing at St. Peter for interrupting his schedule. Sabina couldn't say that to her sons, of course, especially not if the vicar was trying to instruct them about goodness and mercy, along with their Latin. "Well, I suppose he is so downcast because his wife has passed on and his son never comes to visit. Think how wretched I would be without you and your brothers. Espinwall has that whole enormous castle to himself, with no one to talk to except his servants. Perhaps he is lonely." And perhaps pigs had wings.

"Why doesn't his son come?"

Sabina fingered the locket at her throat. "They had a disagreement a long time ago, before any of you were

born. And I suppose both have too much pride to mend the rift now. Viscount Royce makes his life in London, and his father stays in the country, so they never have a chance to reconcile their differences."

Benjy nodded somberly, but Jasper and Martin winked at each other. "What about Reverend Davenport, Mama?" Jasper asked before Sabina could resume her reading or announce bedtime. "Do you think he is happy?"

Sabina laughed. "Oh, Mr. Davenport frets himself to flinders, but I believe he enjoys worrying over all of us. I always thought he'd be better off with a wife to look after some of the parish duties for him and see that he gets a proper meal, but he hired Mrs. Hinkle to keep house for him, most likely with your Latin lesson fees, so I am even more pleased that he agreed to take you on."

Jasper nudged Martin with his foot, and the older boy nodded, already making plans. "Someone else in the village must need our prayers, don't you think, Mama?"

"Well, I suppose you could ask God to look after everyone in Chipping Espy, darling. That would be lovely, and wouldn't leave anyone out."

"What about Miss Gaines?" Benjy wanted to know. "Should we pray for her, too?"

"She doesn't even go to church, you noddy!" Jasper ridiculed. "You can't pray for a—"

His mother clamped her hand over his mouth. "Of course you may pray for Miss Gaines, Benjamin. She is one of God's creatures, too."

"And she needs it more, 'cause she has no friends. No one ever calls on her. Do you think that makes her unhappy?"

"How should Mama know, cloth-head? Miss Gaines ain't respectable. Besides, that toff from London used to come visit every few weeks. Ty Marshall says—"

"I do not think we need to hear what Ty Marshall has to say about Miss Gaines, Martin. In fact," Mrs. Greene quickly added, "it must be time for bed." She jumped up, nearly tumbling Benjamin out of the chair in her efforts to head off any more awkward questions. Giving each boy a kiss on the forehead, she said, "Good night, my darlings. Sleep well. And please try to remember to wear your old clothes tomorrow, and to be more careful near the briers. I am so proud of you for volunteering to help bring in the firewood for the poor families, I could burst. What would I ever do without my good boys?"

Sabina Greene's good boys stayed up for hours, plotting and planning. The next morning, before they went off to the vicarage for their lessons, the three red-heads detoured to the posting office, where they parted with one of their hoarded coins to see a letter delivered. They were not entirely sure of the complete address for the missive they'd spent half the night composing, but another tuppence convinced the post rider to discover Viscount Royce's direction. "Th'fella can't be that hard to locate," the rider declared, pocketing his fee. "Famous rakehell, ain't he?"

2

Connor Hamilton, Viscount Royce, rode as if the hounds of hell were snapping at his stallion's heels. Why he was in such a hurry, cutting across fields and taking barely remembered shortcuts through the home

woods, he was not sure. The demons that were urging
him on were nothing to the devils that waited ahead.

He hadn't wanted to come. He hadn't wanted to see
his father. Despite the lack of affection between them,
Connor certainly had no desire to see the old dastard
stick his spoon in the wall. He didn't want to be duke,
didn't want to live in Espinham Castle, with its foolish
turrets and crenelations, arrow slits and drafty halls
with rows of armor, where he and his best friend had
played for hours. He did not want to rule Espinham's
acres of fields and spinneys and ponds and forests,
where he and his best friend had rambled. Most of all,
he never wanted to see that best friend again. *Friend,
hah!* The jade had married someone else as soon as his
back was turned! By George, Connor didn't even want
to be in the same county as Sabina Martindale. No,
Sabina Greene.

He'd managed to avoid her for years—eleven, to be
exact. She did not attend his mother's funeral; she was
lying in, he was told at the time. And he did not attend
her husband's. He'd thought of sending his condolences, but that would have been the height of
hypocrisy. Connor wasn't the least bit sorry the old
lecher was dead, nor that Sabina was left alone with a
passel of brats to raise. She'd made her bargain, hadn't
she?

Now the duke was dying, but the memories never
would. Hell, even the urchins gathering kindling in the
woods reminded him of Sabina's bright hair and ready
laughter, blast her to hell!

He tossed Conquistador's reins to a slack-jawed
groom and pushed through the carved front doors.
"Am I on time?" he shouted to the startled butler who

hurried to see what manner of caller dared to open the massive castle doors by himself.

"On time?" The duke kept regular hours at Espinham Castle. Always had, always would. Watson glanced at the huge clock that stood in the entryway. It was barely five. "Dinner is not till six, my lord."

"Who cares about food at a time like this? Has the vicar come?"

"Tuesday, my lord." Watson hurried to catch the viscount's riding coat, hat, and gloves before the younger man tore up the wide, winding stairs. He shook his head at the retreating figure. "Same as always. That's His Grace's cribbage night."

Connor was already on the floor above, headed past the hanging tapestries and the battle axes on the wall, toward the modern wing of the castle. He burst into the duke's suite without knocking.

The duke had been enjoying a preprandial sherry and a salacious French novel in the privacy of his bedroom, where neither his busybody butler nor his meddling manservant could say him nay. His gouty foot was propped on an extra pillow on the immense ducal bed; his shirt collar was open, awaiting a fresh neckcloth. His Grace looked up at the commotion in his sitting room, prepared to tear the hide off any servant who dared interrupt his afternoon's repose.

There stood his son. In all his dirt, with a trail of mud behind him and the smell of horse wafting ahead of him, and a scowl on his face. The duke's glass tipped, dribbling sherry down his chin and onto his shirt. He dabbed at his mouth with his sleeve, then recalled the French novel and tried to stuff it under the bedclothes, which dislodged his foot off its pillow,

which sent pain shooting through him. He shouted in agony.

"Oh, my God, it's as bad as I feared! Thank goodness I got here in time!" The viscount strode to the bed and reached for his father's hand. "I came as soon as I heard."

When the pain subsided, Espinwall asked, "Uh, Royce, just what was it that you heard?"

"Why, that you were ailing, of course. Or did you think to keep it from me? That would be just like you, I suppose, dying all alone so your son could feel remorse for the rest of his life. Thank goodness your physician had the sense to send for me."

The duke took a moment to think. "You came to Espinham because you thought I was sickly—is that right?"

Connor's blue eyes narrowed. The duke's handclasp was surprisingly firm, and his eyes were as clear as the viscount's own. His Grace had always been a heavyset, robust man, and he hadn't lost a smidgen of heft that Connor could see. He took his hand back. "You don't look ill to me."

The duke gasped and clutched at his chest. He moaned a bit, too.

"Oh, Lud, I'm sorry. I shouldn't have burst in here like this, shouldn't have upset you or doubted the doctor. Would you rather I leave?"

For answer, the duke held out his hand, pleadingly. "Please . . . stay," he whispered.

"Of course, Father. Just tell me what I can do for you. Shall I send for your man? The doctor?" All Connor could see in the way of medication was a decanter of sherry. Perhaps it was too late for anything else but

solace for the pain. He poured a glass and held it to his father's lips. "What do you need?"

Groaning again, His Grace mumbled what sounded like air. Connor started fanning him with the French novel. "There, catch your breath."

The duke pushed the book aside. "I said, 'heir,' you dolt, not 'air.' I don't want to die without the succession assured."

Connor left the bedside to get help. His father was obviously delirious. The viscount shouted for the duke's man, then demanded he send for Dr. Goodbody immediately.

"But, my lord, His Grace's physician is Mr. Kennilworth, same as always."

"He must have consulted another doctor when the condition worsened. We'll track the man down later. Just get someone here, now!" He went back to the bedside.

"I thought you'd left," the duke whimpered, hanging onto Connor's coat sleeve.

"No, I won't go anywhere as long as you need me."

"And you'll look after Espinham and everything after I'm gone? You won't disappear back into London's stews?"

"You're not going anywhere," the viscount insisted, trying to keep his voice steady through the lump in his throat.

"Of course I am, you gudgeon. Everyone dies eventually, even youngsters like you, going off to wars and duels and madcap curricle races. Then where will the estate be? In the hands of some humgudgeon upstart fourth cousin, that's where."

"It won't happen, Father, I swear."

"You do? Heavens be praised! Now I can die in peace!"

"You're not dying," Connor insisted, but his father was already babbling about grandsons.

"Why, you could even marry that Martindale woman. She's a widow now, you know."

Connor took a step back from the bed. "What? You absolutely forbade me to marry her! That's why I went away in the first place."

The duke waved one hand in the air. "That was then, when she was my librarian's daughter, barely gentry. This is now. You haven't found anyone else to marry in all these years, and she's a proven breeder. Three sons, by George, and you have none."

"I wouldn't marry Sabina Greene if she were the last woman on earth."

The duke gasped and fell back on the pillows, his hand over his heart again. "Damn if you're not as perverse as ever. When I say nay, you say aye. When I say you can, you say you cannot. Thunderation, boy, I demand it!"

"And you are as pigheaded as always. I do not dance to your tune, sir, and never shall."

"Then I'll never get to dance at your wedding, will I?" The duke wiped a tear, or something, from the corner of his eye. "And I'll never live to dandle grandsons on my knee. Is that too much for an old man to ask?"

The Greene boys, meanwhile, ran to intercept Reverend Davenport. They'd followed the viscount and his flying stallion to the Espinham stables, where the grooms always let them watch the horses. They were there when messengers were sent for the physician and the solicitor and the vicar.

"We've killed the duke!" Martin cried.

"The groom says the shock of seeing his son sent him into heart palpitations. Or apoplexy," Jasper explained. "We were only trying to help, the way you said we should."

"We thought the duke was lonely," Benjy added. "Now, if His Grace isn't dead, he'll kill us for sure."

"Oh, dear."

So the reverend Mr. Davenport had to take the viscount aside and explain about the three poor fatherless children who were trying to do three good deeds for Christmas.

"Those redheaded urchins in the woods?"

"Yes, my lord, they are also doing charity work in atonement for a broken window. They are good boys at heart, and their mother tries her best. I thought this would teach them better values than a birching would."

The viscount shoved a paper under the vicar's nose. "You've taught them to be criminals instead! They've forged Dr. Goodbody's name, whoever the deuce he is."

The vicar studied the paper, recognizing Martin's handwriting instantly. "No, my lord, it is signed 'Dr. Goodboy,' not Dr. Goodbody. They must have thought that the end justified the means. After all, you are here, and the duke is pleased to see you."

"Pleased? He dashed near had a heart attack! He's too frail for such a shock."

"Frail? His Grace?" The vicar wondered if Lord Royce was the one suffering a brain fever. "The duke is the healthiest man I know, except for the gout."

"He has the gout?" Connor asked, only slightly embarrassed to be unaware of his own father's condition.

"Of course he does. That's why you found him abed at all. He stayed too long at Squire Marsden's last night, washing down Mrs. Marsden's lobster patties with the latest shipment from the Gentlemen Traders. Otherwise, he'd be out exercising one of those brutish horses of his."

Now that sounded more in keeping with Connor's memory. "So he's not dying?"

"Oh, dear me, I pray not. The bishop is coming to visit our little church in Chipping Espy for Christmas Eve services, and your father has invited him to stay for dinner. My lord, do you recall the pennant that is flown over Espinham Castle when the duke is in residence?"

"Of course I do. It's my family's emblem. The lion rampant on a field of blue."

"To be sure. Well, one of the footmen is assigned the task of placing a white cloth over one of the lion's paws when His Grace is having a bad day. That way everyone in the neighborhood knows when to stay away."

"Deuce take it—then I changed all my plans, nearly broke my neck and almost lamed my horse trying to get here, for nothing!"

"I wouldn't say nothing, my lord, if you and your father are reconciled. Why, the Greene children might have done a good deed after all."

Connor was having none of it. "I'll murder them, by Zeus. That will be my own good deed, ridding the world of those sneaky, scheming little bastards before they grow into embezzlers or extortionists."

The vicar pretended not to hear. "Of course, I cannot condone their methods, but their intentions were—"

"Their intentions were to feather their own nest!

Well, my father will not succeed in backing me into a corner, and neither will three future felons—nor their conniving mother!"

3

"I will not marry you, madam, and that is final."

Sabina was sitting with her mending, an endless task with three small boys, when the madman barged into her wee parlor, shouting. She took a firmer grip on her scissors. It wasn't much of a weapon with which to defend her sleeping babies, but the raving Bedlamite was between her and the fireplace poker.

Molly, the young parlormaid, was twisting her apron in her hands and wailing, "He wouldn't stop, ma'am, no matter what I said about the late hour and you not receiving. And he wouldn't let me announce him proper, like you taught me. What should I do?"

By now Sabina'd had a better look at the intruder, and decided he was better-looking than ever. His shoulders were broader under his well-cut coat, and his blond hair was styled in a fashionable crop. His eyes were the same angelic blue, but now they had tiny lines around them. Well, so did hers. A person could not live a score and a half of years without gathering some tokens of passing time. Of course her lines were from laughter and his were from depraved dissipation. And Sabina couldn't care for the new, sardonic sneer to his lip as he surveyed her with equal intensity. Oh, how she wished she wasn't wearing such a faded frock and such a dowdy widow's cap—not that she had any better in her wardrobe. And she really should have replaced the worn draperies ages ago. Most of all she wished she wasn't wearing her locket. Perhaps he

wouldn't notice, she hoped, and, while she was wishing, perhaps a great wind would swoop down and scoop him away. For whatever else Connor Hamilton was doing here, he was sure to disrupt her life.

"Ma'am? Had I ought to run to the castle and get help?"

"No, Molly. I don't think help will be coming from that direction. Nor heaven, I suppose," she added with a sigh.

The poor girl appeared confused, and Sabina couldn't blame her. She wondered if she was dreaming herself, or in the throes of some dire nightmare. "You may go to bed, Molly. I'll show our caller out."

Molly was uncertain about leaving her mistress alone with such a large, loud gentleman, until Connor tossed her a coin. "Go on, girl. I am not going to strangle your mistress, much as I might wish to."

"Should I be fetching the tea things, then, ma'am?"

Sabina had risen to her feet by now, to face him on his own level. Or to run. She took a step toward the door. "No, Viscount Royce will not be staying that long."

Molly's eyes widened. "Lord Royce? Him what's in all the London scandal columns? I'll be right outside the door, ma'am, iffen you should need me."

Sabina smothered the urge to smooth her hair or kick the boys' jackstraws under the sofa. And whatever made her think he'd be less formidable if she was standing up? He was casually leaning against the mantel; her knees were quaking. She'd forgotten how tall he was, that was all, Sabina told herself as she collapsed back into her chair. She would *not* invite him to sit. In fact, she refused to let herself be intimidated in

her own home, certainly not by this . . . this loose screw.

"Very well, Con—Lord Royce. You have five minutes. What do you want?"

He crossed his arms over his broad chest and glared at her. "I want you to call off your brats. I don't know when you and my father grew as close as inkle-weavers, but the plot you two hatched won't wash, no matter how many crimes you encourage your hell-born babes to commit."

Brats? Hell-born babes? Her precious darlings? Sabina jumped to her feet, hands on hips. "Whatever wits you might once have had have obviously gone begging, Connor Hamilton. I've heard a life of debauchery can do that. As for your father and myself, why, we have not had one halfway polite conversation since you left nearly twelve years ago. He barely nodded to me at Squire's house last night. If we were on the least of speaking terms, he could have warned me that the prodigal son was returning."

"He didn't know. But someone did." He raised his voice even louder. "Someone arranged the whole thing."

"And you think it was I, or my sons?"

"There was a note."

"Good grief. I can barely get them to practice their penmanship! How dare you accuse my boys of . . . of plotting against you? I cannot even begin to imagine how you might have seen them."

The vicar had sworn Sabina was ignorant of the forged letter, and her indignation seemed genuine. Connor decided he'd have words with the iniquitous infants himself on the morrow. "I've seen enough of

their handiwork to know they should be away at school instead of getting up to mischief."

"They are too young."

"They are too old to be tied to their mother's apron strings, especially the eldest. But like your father, you are keeping them around so you won't be alone. You'll make them into weak, puling cowards, afraid to leave your side, just as your father did to you."

He might say what he would about her, Sabina thought, but criticize her children? *Never!* "And you are mean and judgmental, just like *your* father. You dare come here to my own house to accuse my sons of heaven knows what, then declare they should be sent to some barbaric boarding school—and you don't even know them! You have become another Espinwall, a vile-tempered tyrant. And you shout just as loudly as the duke. If you wake my sons I shall skewer you with my darning needle."

"I am not shouting," he bellowed, causing the china shepherdess on the mantel to rattle only slightly. "And I am not like my father."

"No? It would be just like His Grace to appear, uninvited, at any house in Chipping Espy, and expect to be received. As though we lesser folk were not entitled to our privacy or our rest."

Connor shrugged. What else could he do, admit he was in the wrong? Hardly. "I did not come here to discuss the duke," he said stiffly. "Except that my father has the notion to see me wed. To you." A mouthful of lemons could not produce a more sour expression on Viscount Royce's face. "I came to tell you that it won't do. I will never marry you, Sabina Greene."

"You will not marry me? Well, I do not recall asking. And let me tell you, my high-and-mighty lordship,

that I wouldn't have you if you begged on bended knee. Nay, if you came crawling through broken glass. What, should I take up with a rake, a libertine, a womanizer? A fine example a wastrel like you would be for my sons, if you weren't killed in some war or a duel. And what kind of father would you be to them? A clamorous, cantankerous clunch who'd chase them off, as yours did. Why you . . . you'd likely have little Benjy running away to be a cabin boy in the navy and I'd never see him again!" Sabina realized she was shredding one of Jasper's mended shirts in her hands, so she used it to dab at the tears that were streaming down her cheeks.

"You still look like a roasted pig when you cry," Connor told her, taking out a fine lawn handkerchief. "All pink and puffy. And your nose is shiny."

"I am not crying," she sniffed.

Connor raised one eyebrow, but did not comment as he gently blotted the moisture from her eyes. "You seem to have lost your freckles, anyway. What was it that finally did the trick? Lemon juice? Denmark lotion?"

"I merely stopped traipsing about the countryside without a bonnet. I am a mother now, a respectable matron, not a ramshackle miss."

Connor had loved her freckles, all one hundred and seventy-nine of them. And he'd loved the girl who raced at his side through meadows of flowers. He turned away so she wouldn't see his pain at the memories, and he wouldn't see her tears. Damn, he knew he shouldn't have come back. Eleven years, and he was still mesmerized by the little witch. Looking anywhere but at her, Connor inspected the sitting room. At first he'd seen only Sabina; now he noticed the pinchpenny

parlor. His eyes took in the bare spots of the carpet, the chairs with more pillows than upholstery, the chipped vase holding a bedraggled sprig of ivy.

"You could have had a better life, Sabina."

Sabina took a deep breath, knowing they were to have an eleven-year-old argument, one she'd heard a million times in her head. "I could not leave my father, Connor, and you should not have asked me to. He was sickly; I was all he had."

"I wasn't asking you to leave forever, dash it, Sabina, only long enough to get to Gretna Green and back."

"You didn't ask me; you gave me an ultimatum. Either I flee with you to the border, or you'd go off without me. You could have waited."

"What for? An elopement was the only way. You know my father would never have given us permission to wed."

"He was right. I was far beneath you."

"I was willing to chance it. You were the coward who was unwilling to face society's censure."

"Society had nothing to do with it, Connor. That's your world, not mine."

"Your little society here in the countryside, then. You were quick enough to marry a man twice your age for the security of staying here."

"What was I to do? You left and never sent a word!"

"Thunderation, Sabina, I was with the army in Spain, fighting for my country. There was no way to—"

"You were there to spite your father, you nodcock."

"I had funds of my own to purchase my commission. I did not need his approval."

"The only heir to the Duke of Espinwall? They say

Wellington demanded your resignation himself, when His Grace protested."

"I sold out when I was injured, damn it! And this isn't about me, Sabina, it's about your marrying that old man before I got back."

"Don't you understand? I would have been alone, with no way to live. When my father died, his pension would end. There was nothing put aside for me, not even a roof over my head. Before he passed on, Father begged me to wed Mr. Greene so I'd be cared for. I agreed so that he could die in peace."

"So now you're a widow, with no one to look after you."

"Married to you, I could have been a widow thrice a year, if that were possible, with the life you've led."

"Who's to say what path I would have chosen if you were with me? You cannot know that we would have been unhappy."

"Connor, we were children! You were an irresponsible, daredevil boy then, and what are you now? I've been raising my sons, at least. You've been raising Cain."

Viscount Royce was pacing now, with barely enough room for five long strides in any direction. "Your opinion of me is gratifying, Mrs. Greene, especially coming from one who has never been out of Chipping Espy."

"I do not need to travel to London to hear the gossip. Besides, if you weren't a here-and-thereian, a care-for-naught, you'd be in Chipping Espy yourself, looking after the people who depend on you."

"No one depends on me, madam, and that is the way it should be. The duke is not in the ground yet."

"But he is too cross and choleric to reassure his ten-

ants. Why, you don't even understand how the people you've known all your life live in fear of him, and more fear of his passing. It's positively medieval, but the countryside depends on your family for its very life. What if the next duke brings in sheep, or raises the rents, or forbids fishing in his streams? What if he shuts down the racing stud and no more wealthy gentlemen come to purchase horses? What if he never resides at the castle at all, and the army of servants is dismissed? How will the village survive, Connor, and do you care?"

"Of course I care. That does not mean I need to be here holding the blacksmith's bellows and the pig farmer's pitchfork. Espinham has overseers, accountants, and land agents. No one has to worry."

Sabina shot him a look of pure disgust. "It is you who has no need to worry; your inheritance is secure. You can do whatever you like, go wherever you wish. The rest of us have no such luxury. Hired stewards have no loyalty to the land, Connor, or to the people."

"What would you have me do, then?" He'd already promised the duke to stay around, but he wanted to hear what Sabina had to say about his remaining in the vicinity.

"I'd have you be a son to your father. Help him manage the estate but, more important, assure the succession. That's what you were born to do, Viscount Royce, and I shouldn't be the one to have to remind you."

"You are not the first today, madam," he said through clenched jaws, heading toward the door. "But I shall not be forced into leg-shackles by any man, woman, or child, dying or otherwise. I suppose we shall continue to disagree about a son's duty to his par-

ent. Or a daughter's to hers. Good night, Mrs. Greene. I am sorry to have disturbed your pleasant evening." He turned before leaving. "And I always liked your freckles."

4

The viscount stayed on, as he had promised his father. And he stayed away from Sabina Greene, as he had promised himself. He also stayed away from discussing any controversial topics, in deference to his father's health. If the duke mentioned marriage and Sabina again in the same breath, Connor feared it just might be Espinwall's last, and not because of that counterfeit cough the cad contrived for his son's edification now and again. By mutual, if tacit, agreement, they did not speak of politics, the viscount's way of life, the succession, or the duke's miraculous recovery. There were some *very* long silences at the castle. Thank goodness for horses, a subject dear to both men's hearts.

To fill the awkward moments, the duke took to inviting company to tea or dinner, for cards or conversation. He entertained the neighborhood's first families, and any nobility or gentry or gentleman farmers near enough to travel to Chipping Espy. His Grace even invited a few of the wealthier merchant class who had bought property in the area. They all had one thing in common—daughters of marriageable age. Thank goodness for horses, which enabled Connor to put as much distance between himself and the company as possible.

Contrary to most people's surmise, Viscount Royce was interested in good land management. He'd at-

tended enough country house parties to accumulate farming techniques from every corner of the kingdom. He was knowledgeable and, now that his father seemed willing to turn over some of the reins, he was eager to bring modern improvements to Espinham. First, Connor had to survey the farms and fields. The more his father trotted young females past him, the more thorough his inspection. Returning from one of his long rides, he decided to while away another hour by scouting out a Yule log. Christmas was only a few weeks away now, and his father's old friend, the bishop, was to spend the holiday eve at the castle. The kitchens were already working overtime, and the housekeeping staff was recleaning spotless corners of unused rooms.

When he was a lad, bringing in the Yule log was a celebration in itself. Lighting the log in the castle's massive hearth was a tradition for the entire household, family, servants, and guests. They'd all gathered around as his father lit a sliver saved from last year's wood, then handed it to him to light the new. Everyone had toasted the prosperity of the house, the continuity of succeeding generations. Hell and tarnation, Connor cursed. Even his recollections were turning into nags. He spurred Conquistador along the path through the home woods, more interested in losing his memories than in finding a log to burn for the twelve days of Christmas.

Some kind of melee was going on in the clearing, he could hear. So Connor headed in that direction until he could see a group of boys, fighting. Now, he wasn't one to interfere in a good bout of fisticuffs nor a squabble among young hotheads, but this was different. Young Wilfred Snavely, who was nearly a man grown, had a much younger, slighter lad on the ground, and he

was rubbing the other's nose in the dirt. Old Wilfred was shouting encouragement while he held off a still smaller boy who was kicking and clawing to go to his brother's aid. A third red-haired sprig, the smallest of the lot, was dangling by his coat collar from a protruding tree branch, screaming for all he was worth.

"You cost me da a day's pay," Young Wilfred was shouting as he pushed the boy's face deeper into the ground. "You rich boys what can do charity work for nothin'."

"That's right, son, make 'im pay!" Snavely called out, cuffing the boy in his hands across the cheek to shut him up. The littlest lad had ripped his coat to get down, and ran toward his fallen sibling, but Old Wilfred grabbed him by his shirt front this time.

"I say it stinks," Young Wilfred taunted. "An' you stink, Martin Greene. Fartin' Martin, that oughta be your name. Go on an' say it, or you can eat some more dirt." He raised the boy's head so he could speak, and Connor could see blood streaming from Martin's nose. The other two Greene boys were bellowing, and one managed to bite Old Wilfred's fingers that were holding his arm. Snavely cracked the two boys' heads together.

"Enough!" Connor shouted, leaping off his horse. He didn't see a scuffle. He didn't see bullies tormenting helpless infants. What he saw was Sabina's face. My God, he thought, her children are being hurt! He would have gone to the aid of any outnumbered, outmuscled soldiers, but these, these were Sabina's life. A tiny voice whispered inside that they could have been *his* boys, his own flesh and his own blood pouring onto the ground. "Enough, I said, you bastards." Snavely did not release the little boys quickly enough to suit

Connor, so he planted the man a facer that would have made Gentleman Jackson take note. It made Snavely keel over backward. Then the viscount grabbed Young Wilfred by the scruff of his dirty neck, lifted him off Martin Greene, and shook him until he could hear his teeth rattle. "If you or your miserable father ever lays one finger on any of these boys again—one finger, mind you!—I'll have you thrown off my land, arrested for trespassing, and transported. After I tear you to pieces. Is that understood?"

Young Wilfred nodded. The viscount was holding his neck too tightly for him to speak. The father was stirring, so Lord Royce called over, "Do you understand me, Snavely, or do I have to show you again?" He received a grunt in return. "Then get out of here before I change my mind, and take this offal with you." Connor shoved Junior toward a donkey cart that stood nearby, overloaded with wood. Snavely Senior staggered aboard, then snapped his whip at the poor ass and was gone.

Blast, Connor swore to himself, looking around the clearing at the tattered, battered boys. Now he supposed he'd have to take the miserable maggots home to their mother. And she was sure to blame him for not protecting her progeny on his property. Damn!

The oldest boy's nose was still streaming, and Connor thought his lip was split, too, but it was hard to tell through all the blood and mud. The viscount hoisted him onto Conquistador's saddle, where he could hold Martin's head back to stop the bleeding before Sabina saw the lad. The other two boys mounted double on their pony. The middle boy, Jasper, he learned, was developing a magnificently colored black eye. The youngest, Benjamin, was delegated to steer the pony,

since Jasper's spectacles were broken and he could barely see the mare's ears, much less the path home. Benjy was missing all four of his front teeth, which made his excited babble nigh unintelligible, so Connor couldn't tell if that was a recent loss or a previous condition. The infant's clothing hung about him in shreds, so Connor wrapped his own coat around him, before mounting his stallion and leading the little caravan home to their mother. He thought of taking the halflings to the castle first, to clean them up, but the sun was sinking and Sabina would worry if they were late. Besides, the castle was filled with simpering young females who were sure to swoon at the first sight of blood. With any luck, he could sneak them into Sabina's kitchen before she caught a glimpse of them.

As luck would have it, Sabina was in her kitchen, ironing, a task Lord Royce had never seen a well-born woman perform. As he'd predicted, the first words out of her mouth were, "My stars, what have you done to them?"

"Drawn and quartered the lot of them. What else do you expect from the ogre of Espinham?" he asked wryly as he half carried Martin to one of the worn chairs drawn around a battered oak table. The boy's nose had started bleeding again from the walk to the kitchen door. Connor tilted Martin's head back, over the chair rung. "Deuce take it, Sabina, he's had his cork drawn, is all. You've seen worse, so don't turn missish on me now."

By this time, all three boys were nattering at her with the news of the fight, how the viscount had rescued them and threatened to have the Snavelys transported, and how Martin got to ride the stallion, but the others were promised a turn, too.

"And his lordship is going to teach us how to defend ourselves."

"He has boxed with the Gentleman himself, Mama. Isn't that marvelous?"

"And the viscount says that if the other chap is already fighting dirty, it's all right to kick him in the—"

"Quiet!" Connor shouted over the din, winning instant silence in the small kitchen. "Your mother's head is already spinning. What we need is some hot water and clean clothes, not all this racket. Where is the maid?"

"She's gone to market," Sabina replied, clearing the table of her clean linens and reaching into the laundry basket for towels. She filled a kettle with water at the sink and went to put it on the stove. Without thinking— and without the protective cloth she'd been using— Sabina picked up the flatiron that was heating there, to make room for the kettle. She screamed, which had all the boys and Connor at her side. Benjamin started whimpering. "It's nothing, boys," she reassured them. "I'll be fine. I'll just put some lard on it."

"No!" Connor yelled. "What you want is cold water, not grease to sear the skin worse." He picked up the kettle and poured it over her burned hand, and over her floor and her clean sheets.

"Now see what you've done," she cried, pulling her hand from his clasp. "Let me tend to my boys first."

"Deuce take it woman, I've seen burns fester and turn to blood poisoning. This one is already blistering, by Zeus. That's a lot more serious than a bit of spilled claret. Now sit down, Sabina, before you fall down! I'll take care of the brats."

Before she could protest further, he shoved her into a chair, with her arm resting on a clean pillow slip. In

short order, he had the two youngest boys running to fetch soap and salve, bandages and brandy. While the water was heating to mop up Martin, Connor found a glass and poured Sabina a drink. He poured himself one, too, swallowed it, and had another. "Gads, the war in Spain was nothing to this!"

Sabina watched, numb with shock, pain, and simple amazement, as London's premier rake tenderly dabbed at Martin's face and chin, until her son reappeared from the muck. "His nose doesn't appear broken," Connor reported, to her relief. The viscount had Benjy and Jasper lined up for inspection and repairs, then ordered them all into fresh clothes while he brewed the tea. He added a bit of brandy to the pot, too. "So they'll sleep better," he told her. "Otherwise the excitement would have them up all night, and they'll feel every bump and bruise. And you'll need your rest, too."

When the boys returned and had their tea, and Connor felt fortified enough himself, he gingerly spread some ointment Sabina had over her hand. The whole palm was burned, with the flatiron's handle imprinted on her soft skin. "Damn," he cursed as she drew in a breath. "I'm so sorry, Sabina."

"Why should you be sorry for my own stupidity?"

"Do you mean there is some evil in this world I am not responsible for? I was beginning to wonder."

She smiled at him, and now he had to take a deep breath. "Let's get this bandaged, shall we?" he said, trying to ignore the warmth he felt spread through him from the touch of her warm skin, the contact of her knees brushing his as he worked on the burn. And Sabina wasn't indifferent either, for her cheeks were as red as her hair. Or perhaps that was merely the brandy. He cleared his throat. "You'll have to keep this ban-

daged until it heals, and you won't be able to use your
hand much, you know. Will you be able to manage? I
could send a maid or two from the—"

"Oh, no. Molly will be back shortly, and the boys
are quite helpful, really."

"But, Mama, how are you going to play the church
organ for Christmas?" one of the helpful lads asked.
"The bishop is coming!"

5

"Oh, dear. Oh, dear." The vicar was predictably upset at
the Greene boys' news that their mother would not be
able to play the church organ. "And the bishop does so
love a musical service. He has always sworn that music
brings one closer to heaven. I was hoping to bring him
closer to releasing the funds for our extension."

"What if we could find someone else to play the
organ for you instead?" Jasper asked, peering at the
cleric through one cracked lens.

The vicar looked at the middle boy, then winced at
the lurid colors of his eye. Mr. Davenport had carefully
avoided asking about the split lip, swollen nose, broken spectacles, and missing teeth. What he didn't
know was better all around, he felt. "Another profi-
cient performer in this town? Why, if you could find
one, that would be more than a good deed, my lad.
That would be a miracle."

"What if this organist wasn't a usual churchgoer,
sir? Would that matter?"

"Such talent can only be a gift from God—that's
what the bishop said. So I would welcome Beelzebub
himself, if he could play the *Messiah*. But—"

"And it is all right for us to invite this person to come play for you?"

"Of course, of course, but there is no one, lad, no one at all. Perhaps the choir can be encouraged to sing louder." He waved them off, so despondent he forgot to give them their homework assignments.

Once they were away from the manse, the other boys turned on Jasper. "Why did you say we'd find him an organist? We'll never, and then he'll make us do more good deeds."

"I know someone who can play," Jasper claimed. "Miss Viola Gaines."

Martin opened his cut lip again, laughing. "She can't play the church organ!"

"I heard her playing the pianoforte one day when Vicar kept you on after lessons."

"Is she as good as Mama?"

"Almost," Jasper answered loyally. "And she's almost as pretty."

"She smells almost as nice," Benjamin added. "I helped her get her cat out of a tree once, and she gave me a biscuit."

"She dresses better than Mama," Jasper said, and no one could contradict him. They all sighed, wishing they had some way to earn enough to buy their mother that length of velvet.

"But just because she can play the pianoforte doesn't mean she can play the organ," Martin reasoned.

"There's still ten days before Christmas Eve. Mama can teach her. She taught Georgina Marsden to play *Greensleeves*, and Georgie's just a dumb girl."

Martin was beginning to permit himself to be convinced. "But Miss Viola never goes to church. Why should she do it for us?"

"She'll do it if the vicar asks her special."

"I'm not writing any more letters," Martin announced. "Two jaw-me-dead lectures were enough. 'Sides, we made up Dr. Goodboy; copying the signature of a man of God has to be a sin."

"You don't have to write another letter, 'cause Mr. Davenport said we could invite her, plain and simple, he did. Only he didn't know her name."

"And if that doesn't work," Martin said eagerly, "we can get Benjy to cry. That always works with Mama."

Benjy was way ahead of them. "And she and the vicar can get married! Then we'll have all our good deeds done!"

Even serious-minded Jasper had to laugh. "The vicar isn't going to marry Miss Viola, noddy! She's a Bird of Paradise. I heard Squire Marsden say so once."

"So what? Mr. Davenport is always going on about paradise, too, isn't he?"

While the boys were at their lessons, or so he supposed, Connor called at Sabina's cottage. He told himself it was just polite to see how she was going on, and to deliver in person the tin of soothing salve.

"You shouldn't have bothered your kitchen staff at a time like this," Sabina said when she answered his knock on her door. "They must be frantic with the Christmas preparations and the company coming."

"Actually, I didn't bother the cooks at all. I had my head groom mix up the stuff from a recipe I had in Spain. It won't smell as good as the kitchen's, but ought to help heal the burn faster."

After such a kind gesture, Sabina had to invite Connor in, as much as she wished to keep her distance. She gestured him to follow her to the little parlor, which

was strewn with fabric, trims, sewing supplies, and a sheepskin.

"Dash it, Sabina, not using your hand would help more than any ointment. What the devil are you doing, anyway?"

She gathered some of the material into a pile to make room for him to sit. "It's the costumes for the children's Christmas pageant. I thought that, since we will not have organ music, perhaps I can improve on the Nativity."

"With your hand bandaged? I suppose you're still cooking and cleaning besides."

"Oh, no. Molly is doing everything. She's in the kitchen right now making gingerbread while the boys are away." She would not let on that the gingerbread was going to be almost the only Christmas delicacy for her sons. With new clothes to replace those damaged in the altercation and new spectacles for Jasper, her meager stock of coins would be nearly spent.

"Is she making gingerbread men?" Connor asked, his blue eyes lighting up. "With currant eyes?"

"Of course," Sabina said with a laugh, remembering how much he'd always loved the treat. "They'll be ready in an hour or so. You could come back then for a taste."

"Or I could wait here . . . ?"

Sabina bit her lip, not knowing how to answer. The man was definitely not healthy for her equilibrium, but, oh, how sweetly he smiled at her now, flashing a well-remembered dimple in his right cheek. She nodded, then picked up some gold braid to pin on one of the Magis' robes. She was awkward in his presence, and the bandage didn't help. The pins kept falling.

"Why are you the one doing this?" the viscount demanded as he retrieved them from the floor at Sabina's

feet, then took the fabric from her and proceeded to fasten the braid on, all higgledy-piggledy, but on. "Surely one of the other women in the congregation could help."

"Who? The village women are too busy with their cooking and cleaning and helping their husbands at work. The farm wives have animals and gardens to tend. And the vicar has no wife, Mrs. Marsden has the rheumatics in her fingers, and the castle has no lady bountiful to oversee the needs of the community. I at least have help with the chores."

This last, pointed reminder destroyed Connor's good humor and determination not to argue with her again. Besides, he was pricking himself with every pin he put in. "Thunderation, Sabina, do you have to take on the responsibility for the whole town now?"

"I find that more estimable than not taking responsibility for anything, even one's own actions, my lord. The life you've led . . . and you are pinning the trim to your coat sleeve."

"Blast!" He tossed the wretched mess aside. "I have a seamstress at the castle who does nothing all day that I can see. I shall send her down with a wagon this afternoon to pick up this whole jumble, and your instructions. And no argumentation for once, miss, if you please. Now let me see your hand. It would be just like you to put the medicine on an injured rabbit rather than use it for yourself."

He sat on the floor next to her chair and unwrapped the bandage. While he worked, he told her some of his plans for the castle and its holdings. He thought he might start a small hand-weaving guild, or a pottery, to employ more local residents. And he'd see a dam built along the stream, so the workers' cottages wouldn't

flood come spring. Sabina thought he ought to move the whole lot to higher ground and start anew, since some of the houses were no more than ramshackle huts. Soon they were talking like old times, passing comments back and forth, building on each other's ideas and opinions. If he could have wrapped a mummy in the time he spent rebandaging her hand, Sabina did not complain.

This was madness though, she told herself. He was bored in the country without his opera dancers and actresses, that was all. That was why he was spending time with his estate managers . . . and with her. Connor was flirting with her, she decided, trying to seduce her with his newfound respectability. Then he'd leave. He always did.

"Oh, I forgot," he was saying, reaching into his pocket. "I brought a pair of spectacles a guest left behind at the castle. I don't know if they'll do for Jasper until you can have another set made up, but these were going to waste."

Sabina smiled. "Between the boxing lessons and your offer to let the boys ride Espinham's cattle, they already think you are top of the trees. Pulling new spectacles out of thin air should convince them you can walk on water."

And their hearts would be broken when he left, too. "You . . . you won't disappoint them, will you?"

"What? Go back on my word? Such an accusation would be cause for a duel among gentlemen, by Jupiter. I have been waiting until their bruises are healed, is all. But, thunderation, do you really believe me to have so little honor as to lie to innocent children? I keep my promises, madam."

Except for the ones that hung between them: *I'll love you forever. I'll be back.*

Connor got up from the floor and strode to the mantel, where he stared at the framed miniature of Jessup Greene. "Did you love him, Sabina?"

Sabina could have taken umbrage at his familiarity, but she felt she owed him an honest answer. "I . . . I respected him. He was kind."

"Kind? Is that all you can say about the man who fathered your children?"

She shrugged. What more was there to say, except that Mr. Greene was not used to children, not used to women having thoughts, and not used to his steady, bachelor life being continuously disrupted. She'd always wondered what he thought would happen, taking a young wife. And she still resented his giving the trustees absolute control over her finances, as though she could not balance her bank accounts. "I did not know him well. He kept himself apart. But I was not unhappy," she quickly added. "And I had my sons. Other women fare much worse in their marriages of convenience."

"Yet you wore my locket."

Sabina's hands flew to her throat, where the locket usually rested on its chain. She'd removed it after Connor's first visit, hoping he hadn't recognized the only piece of jewelry she had on, other than her wedding ring. Silly notion, that. "I don't have much jewelry," she tried to explain. "Mr. Greene was a frugal man."

"So he was a nip-farthing besides a lecher. But to wear another man's token, Sabina?"

"He believed it had come from my mother. I saw no reason to disabuse him of the thought. And, very well, if you must know, I wore the locket to remind me of

those other times. Days when I was neither caretaker for my father or for my children, nor a necessary inconvenience to my husband. I wore the locket to remind me that once, very briefly, I was loved for myself, and in love with the world. It was a magical time."

"Just like Christmas."

She ignored him. "And I took it off because I am not that girl anymore." And because she did not want him to think she'd been wearing the willow for him all these years. She'd never say that, though, so she told him, "I have a rich, full life, with people who love me and need me. That's enough."

But was it? she asked herself. Had it ever been enough? Could it ever be again, when he was gone? Sabina had no answers.

6

Viola Gaines almost burst her stays, laughing, when the little boys asked her to play the church organ. What a chuckle the girls back in London would have over this. But she wasn't back in the city; she was in a tiny, respectable town, and she was bored with her own company. Besides, Viola was used to being the center of attraction, not being treated as if she had the pox. What she had was the lease to this cottage from her last protector, and no desire to go back to her old way of life. So why shouldn't she perform at Christmas, especially if that prim and proper young Widow Greene was sending her boys over to second the vicar's invite? Miss Gaines had played for merchant princes and members of Parliament. What was a bishop or two? Viola was fairly confident she could master the pipe organ, too.

Viola did not need a great deal of convincing. Neither did the vicar—he needed smelling salts. Oh, dear.

When Mr. Davenport found his breath again to speak, he addressed the three red-haired imps grinning up at him, instead of the woman by the door. "What trouble have you wretched children gotten into now?"

"Remember how you said you'd welcome Beelzebub himself if he'd play the organ?" Jasper asked. "We couldn't get the devil, but we did get Miss Viola."

The next worst thing, to the vicar's thinking. "Oh, my. Can she play?"

"Like an angel," Martin told him. "Like the one you sent us to find."

"Like an angel in Paradise," Benjy chirped. "It's a miracle, isn't it?"

'Twould be a miracle if lightning didn't strike the little church during Christmas Eve services. And bring the rotting roof right down on the bishop's bald head.

With two good deeds accomplished, the boys were stymied. They couldn't think of anyone else who needed their help, and Christmas was coming. Bad enough their mother was injured; her holiday would be ruined beyond hope if the vicar told her about the broken window. She'd feel obliged to pay for the replacement, and the trustees would never deem that a necessary expense, the old nipcheeses. Heaven only knew where she'd get the money.

"Maybe we could teach Chocolate to count like that horse at the fair last summer." Benjy was taking his turn riding the old pony while his brothers walked alongside. They were on their way to Espinham Forest to finish gathering the deadwood for the poor. "Everyone paid tuppence to see him add."

"We can hardly teach you to count, gudgeon. How are we going to teach Chocolate?"

"The viscount is richer'n Golden Ball," Jasper pointed out. "I heard Molly telling the egg man."

"So? We can't ask him to lend us the money, 'cause we couldn't pay him back. That's not honorable."

They each got to thinking on the rest of the walk, about good deeds, good incomes, and their good-as-gold mother. No one wanted to be the first to voice the obvious connection, for fear the others would only laugh.

There was no laughter when they reached the meadow, where Wilfred Snavely was supposed to have his donkey cart ready for loading. Wilfred and his son were there, and the cart, but the donkey had fallen over, dead. Old Wilfred and Young Wilfred were cursing and shouting at the beast, cracking the whip over her head, but she was beyond caring. The Snavelys cared, for they'd have to pull the cart all the way back to the village themselves. And the donkey foal, nuzzling its dead mother, cared. The baby donkey was braying for all it was worth, trying to waken its mother. Young Wilfred kicked out at the thigh-high creature, which ran, still shrilling its distress, into the woods.

"Good riddance to it," the elder Snavely snarled. "Damned noisy nuisance'll be no use to me for over a year, eating its ugly head off at my expense. Bad enough I'll have to come back with the cart and a winch to haul the mother off. I ain't feeding and cleaning up after some useless creature. I already got my boy for that." He cuffed his son on the ear and laughed.

"You mean you're just going to leave the baby out here alone?" Martin wanted to know.

"At night?" Benjy asked, jumping off Chocolate. "In the dark?"

"With nothing to eat or drink?" Jasper peered into the woods.

Snavely eyed Chocolate, and the empty traces of his laden cart. He calculated the odds of the viscount killing him if he took the boys' pony, then shook his head. It was a sure bet. "Makes no difference. The beastie'll be dead by morning anyway less'n it learns to eat grass quick-like. Ain't weaned yet, and I ain't wet-nursing no ass."

Jasper said, "We'll take him, Mr. Snavely."

Both of his brothers turned to him. "We will?"

"We can't just let him die, can we?"

Benjy shook his head. So did Martin, after a momentary hesitation. "We'll take him home with us, then. Mama will know what to do for him."

"If not, Viscount Royce is sure to. He knows everything about horses, and donkeys can't be all that different."

"Hold on, Carrot-top. Afore you go making plans for the spawn, what are you going to give me for it?"

Martin tried to be reasonable. "Why should we pay you for something you were throwing away? If you wanted the baby, you'd put it in the cart and take it home with you."

" 'Sides, you said it was going to die," Jasper added.

Snavely scratched his armpit. "But the little bugger just might surprise us all and learn to eat grass and stuff. It's mine till it dies or I say different, understand? So how about we makes us a bargain, eh? How about if I trade you the asslet for use of your pony there? It'll just be for a few days so I can deliver the wood for the reverend, and get the jenny out of here. His Grace won't like no dead animal littering his property."

Benjy started sniffling, and Jasper said, "He'll never give Chocolate back, I know it."

Martin eyed the heavily loaded wagon, the whip in Snavely's dirty hand, and the dead donkey. "No, sir. We can't let you have Chocolate, even for a day. Our Mama wouldn't let us, even if we wanted to. But we can find the viscount and tell him how you beat your poor donkey to death and left its baby in his woods. He was calling on us this afternoon, wasn't he, Jas?"

"Viscount Royce said he was bringing Mama some medicine. They're old friends, don't you know, Mama and Viscount Royce," Jasper contributed, deciding it couldn't hurt to invoke their powerful protector's name a few times.

"The jenny died of old age, and don't you go spreading no tales, hear? And the viscount's too busy to get himself in a swivet over no orphan ass, so we'll leave him out of this. Iffen you won't lend your pony, I figure I'll have Young Wilfred go put the spat out of its misery. You got the axe there, son?"

"We've got some money. You can have all we've got," Martin offered in a rush.

Snavely rubbed his chin. "Well, that's more like. You brats cost me some wages, so it's only right you hand over some blunt. How much've you got?"

The boys did not have enough for a church window, and not enough for a dress length, but it seemed they had just the right amount for a useless, dying baby ass. Snavely took all of the boys' coins, along with Jasper's pocketknife and Martin's handkerchief, which was of finer fabric than any he owned. And if you held the thing upside down, the embroidered *M* could be a *W* for Wilfred.

"Better'n nothing, I guess," he said. "Enjoy your

purchase, brats, while you can." He gestured to his son to hoist the wagon pole, and they started off, leaving three pale-faced boys in the meadow, with no coins, and no little donkey, either.

The boys dove into the woods where they'd seen the baby run. Jasper tripped over a protruding root and landed in a mud puddle. Benjamin thought he'd climb a tree to get a better view, and tore his pants. Martin listened quietly till he heard the baby's whickers, then he located the beastie where it was all tangled in briers, panting. He took off his jacket, remembering Mama's laments over their clothes, and pushed through the prickers to free the infant. His shirt, of course, was torn to shreds, but he got the donkey. The small creature was shivering, so he wrapped his jacket around it and tugged it back to the clearing.

Chocolate took offense at the baby's nuzzling attempt to find milk, and was not having any hoofed creature ride on her back, either. The baby was too heavy for the boys to carry, and protested too much anyway, so all three removed their belts, cinched them together to make a collar and lead, and half carried, half dragged the donkey along the path toward home.

With such slow going, they had time to reflect on their new acquisition.

"Do you think this counts as a good deed?" Jasper wanted to know.

"We couldn't let them kill him!" Benjy wailed.

Having looked beneath the donkey, Martin reported that Baby, as they were calling the donkey to encourage it along the trail, was a girl. "And the reverend always said we are all God's creatures, big and small."

The three boys looked at the sorry specimen, all big ears and sad brown eyes and skinny legs.

"God must have been getting tired by the day He created donkeys," Jasper pronounced. "But I suppose we just helped the Lord out a little, right, Martin?"

"Right. Now all we have to do is keep Baby alive."

Benjy's toothless grin faded. "Mama will know how."

Which reminded the others of the further consequence of Baby's purchase. "Now we'll never be able to buy Mama the velvet for Christmas."

Jasper sighed and expressed the thought none of them had wanted to put into words, for fear of jinxing the wondrous notion: "And the viscount is used to fancy ladies in satin and lace. That's what Molly said."

They glumly marched on. Then Benjy asked, "Do you think he'll take up with Miss Viola?"

Martin squared his shoulders. "If he does, then he's not the man for Mama anyway."

They put Chocolate in her stall next to their mother's gelding, and tried to get the donkey to take some water. Soon they were all sopping wet. They gave up and sent Benjy to sneak the trim from the wreath Sabina had placed on the front gate. In a few minutes they all trooped in to the little parlor, three bedraggled, dripping boys and one ribbon-bedecked, dazed, and half-dead donkey.

"Here, Mama. Look what we bought you for Christmas. Her name is Velvet."

7

Sabina used to wish her husband's cottage wasn't so isolated, being nearer to the castle than the village. That evening she was relieved no neighbors were kept up long into the night the way she was, listening to the

new arrival's complaints. Her own babies hadn't set up such a racket. They hadn't cried *ee-aw* either.

She'd done what she could for the poor thing, mixing up some mash and trying to teach Velvet to eat from a dish. More of the concoction was on her, Sabina knew, than in the donkey. Then, with the boys' help, she'd made a warm nest of straw in the corner of the little stable, with bales of hay to keep the creature penned. She'd tried barricading their old hound, Beau, in with Velvet, but after licking up the spilled mash, Beau headed back to his warm blanket next to the kitchen stove. Sabina couldn't blame him; she felt too old for this, too.

Now she lay awake, wondering how she was going to feed this new mouth—and clean up after it. In a few years, she supposed, she might teach Velvet to pull her light rig, so the boys could ride her gelding. Martin was ready for a full-size horse now, and Jasper would be by then. They should each have their own mount, she believed, angry all over again at the miserly trustees and her dead husband for not deeming her capable of knowing what was best for their sons. Connor Hamilton would never make his children share one old pony. Whatever else his faults, he was generous and kind, offering to take her sons skating as soon as the pond froze over, if he was still here. He remembered that childhood should be fun. He'd likely spoil his progeny dreadfully, Sabina thought, especially if he had a little girl, a dainty little charmer with dimples—and red hair.

Now that kind of thinking would never do, Sabina told herself. The donkey's plaintive braying was bad enough without her own maudlin musings. Then she realized that the noise from the barn had stopped. Velvet had exhausted herself, finally. Unless she was too weak

to cry anymore. Perhaps she was sick, or worse. Good heavens, the boys would be distraught. Sabina put on her heavy robe, then her cloak over that. She pulled on her boots, awkwardly wrapped a scarf over her head with her bandaged hand, and lit the lantern by the kitchen door. She had no idea what she could do if the little jenny was expiring, nor what she could tell the boys. If ever there was a time she wished for another to share the burdens of life, this was it. Someone who knew about horses and such, and wouldn't mind leaving a warm bed to go traipsing across the yard in frigid December temperatures. Instead, old Beau wasn't even around to accompany her on the dire mission.

Sabina hurried to the barn as fast as she could without jeopardizing the lantern's light. She pushed open the door, dreading what she might find, and held the light aloft, so she could inspect the makeshift enclosure. She couldn't even see the donkey, surrounded as Velvet was by three sleeping boys, two barn cats, and one comfort-seeking hound. Her sons were tumbled together in the straw with quilts from their beds and, yes, that was her old shawl that she saved for cleaning stalls. She straightened the covers as best she could, feeling her throat tighten at the sight of her beautiful, big-hearted boys. They were perfect, no matter what anyone in the village said, or what certain toplofty aristocrats accused them of. She wouldn't change a hair on their red heads.

Beau lifted his muzzle from the pile of arms, legs, and donkey, then went back to snoring. All was right with the world.

Some women could stay up all night, worrying over donkeys and bank deposits, and still look beautiful in

the morning. Sabina was not one of them. She looked haggard, in fact, with her complexion as dull and gray as the faded, shapeless gown she wore. A limp cap covered every inch of the red hair that would have enlivened her appearance, but she hadn't had the energy to brush it out and pin it up on her aching head. Her hand was paining her, and Benjamin was covered with a rash from the straw. At least she hoped it was a rash and not flea bites from the barn cats.

Since she did not have to work on the pageant costumes, Sabina had taken up her mending again this morning, trying to see what she could salvage of her sons' adventures yesterday. Not much. At this rate, they'd be running around like half-naked savages by spring. At least the weather would be warmer. Sabina moved her chair closer to the fire and huddled into her shawl, hoping she wasn't sickening for something. Who would look after the boys then, or the baby jenny? Her thoughts were as dismal as her dress.

Altogether, she was not pleased to see Viscount Royce that next morning. He was looking bang up to the mark, as Martin would say, with his Hessians shining brighter than any surface in her house. Not a dog hair clung to his burgundy coat, not a scratch or worn spot marred his buckskin breeches. Well, she thought, ten minutes here, and Connor would be embarrassed to be seen at his clubs, since that was about how long clean clothes seemed to last in her household.

Connor's first words were not what a female wanted to hear from an attractive, affluent, aristocratic gentleman. "Gads, you look like last week's laundry. What has you so blue-deviled?"

"The ass," she snapped back.

"Snavely? Is that bounder bothering you or the boys

again? I warned the makebait that I'd toss him off the property next time. I hadn't wanted to evict him yet, because his wife seems a decent sort."

"No, Wilfred is not bothering me. It's Velvet, my ass."

She couldn't be saying what Connor thought he was hearing—or thinking. "Excuse me?"

"I own a donkey, you gudgeon. Her name is Velvet, and my sons gave her to me for Christmas."

He tried to hide his smile since she seemed so moped about it. "Odd, I always gave my mother a box of comfits."

"I don't like comfits," she said, lest he think poorly of the boys' choice.

"But you do like donkeys? I'll make a note of that for my Christmas list."

"Oh, stop teasing, do. They meant well."

Connor inspected his sleeve for lint. "I do believe I have heard that phrase before, in reference to the threesome. More harm has been done in the name of good intentions than Satan himself could imagine."

"So you are still blaming my sons for your arrival at Espinham? You are not faring so poorly, that I can see. You and the duke must be rubbing along well together, else you would have left days ago, once you saw he was not truly ailing."

"We manage. His Grace and I play games. Chess, backgammon, and pretend. He pretends all the silly young chits he invites to the castle are not there for my inspection. I pretend he is not an interfering old matchmaker."

"Then your coming was not such a bad thing, after all."

"I haven't decided yet." He didn't want to talk about it, either. "Tell me about the ass."

Sabina frowned. "She's an orphaned infant that won't eat properly and cries all night. She might have colic for all I know. I understand babies, not big-eared beasts!"

"I'll take it up to the castle, then. There's bound to be a mare in milk. Some will let another foal suckle. My grooms can stay up with it, otherwise. I don't know much about asses myself." He couldn't help grinning.

"No, I want to keep her here. The boys would be heartbroken, and they'd think I didn't like their gift."

"Then I'll send someone down to see what's needed."

"I cannot be so deeply in your debt. You have already done enough for us, Connor—my lord. Why, having Sophia Townsend to sew the costumes was a godsend. She's at the vicar's right now, taking measurements for new choir robes. It seems she always wanted to help, but could not feel comfortable offering her services whilst in your father's employ."

"She should have asked. Father would have let her—" He paused at her raised eyebrows. "Well, perhaps not. Still, he is mellowing, which is one of the other reasons for my call. I have actually come to beg a favor of you, so you need not feel indebted at all if I provide assistance with the donkey. Tit for tat, don't you know."

"What is the favor? If it involves the duke, I am not in good odor with him, you know. He always blamed me for your leaving, and has taken his ire out on my boys. I believe he referred to my sons as mannerless mongrels the last time we spoke."

"And you called him a stiff-rumped old stick. Yes, I've heard. But calling on you for aid was his idea. The

thing is, he wishes to reinstate the old Christmas festivities at the castle, in honor of the bishop's visit. Remember how the Great Hall was thrown open to all the villagers and tenants and everyone else for miles around, with feasting and dancing? His Grace is afraid this will be his last Christmas, and wants to see it done up right."

"Nonsense, he wants to show his son off to the countryside, is all. He just won't admit it."

Connor laughed. "Either way, he's put me in charge. The problem is, I'm no hand at decorating and such, and no one at the castle remembers how it should be. The housekeeper is new since the last grand celebration, before my mother moved to Bath for her health."

"She moved to Bath to avoid His Grace, and everyone knows it."

He shrugged. "Theirs was an arranged marriage. Her Grace felt she'd done her duty by producing the heir. Of course, no one else would dare to mention the family's dirty linen, Sabina. I cannot tell you how refreshing it is to find a woman who speaks her mind, after the simpering debs my father keeps finding. But to return to my difficulty, the attics must be filled with all the old ornaments and stuff, but I have no idea where to begin. I am begging you to come help."

Sabina remembered how the hall was festooned with ribbons, and candles lit every corner. Tables had been spread along one wall, piled high with food, and there was still room for anyone who wanted to dance. She and Connor had watched many a fete from the minstrels' gallery before they were old enough to join the company. The servants had smuggled cakes and punch to them. Such sweet memories . . .

"You'll be staying, though?" she asked. "You don't

mean I should decorate the castle so you can go back to
London?"

"No, I am staying, through Twelfth Night, at least.
After that, who knows? There are two factors that need
to be decided. It's too soon to tell. For now, I want to
stay to see how the duke goes on, and the party will
give me a chance to meet the rest of the tenants and
local gentry. I'm sure that was His Grace's plan, but
how can I deny him when he claims to be hearing
Gabriel's trumpet?"

"Shall you mind?" Sabina wanted to know.

"Mind? I've always loved the country. But Espinwall
never let me *do* anything, not even hold an opinion of
my own. Do you know that the first time I defeated His
Grace at chess last week, and he complimented me on
a good game, that was the first bit of praise I have ever
heard from his lips? I was as useless here as the arrow
slits on the castle turrets. That was one of the reasons I
had to leave then, to find something to do with my life.
I had thought the army might be it. Now I discover I am
busy every moment with some estate matter or other,
and I am enjoying it. Which is not to say that I would
be content to spend every last one of my days immured
in the countryside."

"Of course not. A gentleman cannot be without his
tailor for long."

He flashed the dimple at her. "Must be à la mode for
the milch cows, don't you know. Seriously, though,
even if I do not stay year round, I won't be gone entirely again. I see nothing wrong with enjoying the theater, the galleries, and one's friends betwixt the beets
and beef. Have you ever considered visiting the city?"

The opera, the shops, the book-lenders! She'd considered it many times, in her dreams. Sabina sighed.

"London has always sounded marvelous, and the boys would be in alt to see Astley's Amphitheater and the Tower Menagerie, but can you imagine loosing my sons on the streets there? Why, I'd never have a moment's peace, worrying that they'd be kidnapped . . . or arrested."

"But if they had a competent tutor?"

"Ah, then London would be a delight. And educational, too. But if wishes were horses, my lord, I wouldn't have a baby donkey in my barn."

8

Sabina could not spend the necessary hours at the castle if it meant leaving her sons unsupervised. So the viscount had to do some hard bargaining.

Having heard about Snavely's dastardly extortion of their Christmas money, Connor offered the Greene boys a fair wage if they would come to the castle with their mother and assist her in decorating. They'd also have to help him gather the branches and such she'd want, and climb trees after the mistletoe required for the kissing boughs. In addition, they just might be drafted to help exercise the horses if the stable grooms were too busy to ride. In return, he promised them enough blunt to purchase the velvet for their mother's dress.

"And if you stick close by me, so I am never left alone with any of the young misses, I'll even get Sophia Townsend to sew the dress, so it will be a real surprise. Your mother might be too busy, and her hand is still bandaged. That way she'll have her new velvet gown to wear for the party."

"Red?" Benjy wanted to be sure. "It's got to be red."

With Sabina's hair? She'd look like a forest fire—or a wanton. "I'll try, but the shops just might be out of red, what with the holidays and all. How would you feel about a nice dark green, to match her eyes?"

Martin and Jasper allowed how their mother would look beautiful in anything. Benjy wasn't so easy to convince, until his older brothers kicked him. "The viscount knows all about ladies' clothes," they whispered. "You heard Molly."

So they solemnly shook hands all around. "But, my lord," Martin felt compelled to tell Connor, "we would have helped for nothing, you know."

"I know, lad. And I would have bought the dress for your mother whether you helped or not, so we are even."

Sabina worked feverishly to transform the Great Hall from a great barracks to a grand ballroom. She also worked hard to keep her darlings out of mischief, which meant out of the duke's way. They wanted to play with the ancient weapons on the walls, slide down the banisters, try all the antique instruments. Coming to the castle was a mistake, she began to realize. Then the viscount came to help. He was all thumbs at braiding swags of pine boughs, but he was a marvel at entertaining small boys. He took them with him to fetch the mistletoe and the Yule log, to deliver hampers of foodstuffs to his tenants, to visit the stables and the kennels and the dovecotes. This was the best holiday her sons had ever had, and it wasn't even Christmas yet. What a good father Connor would make—to some other woman's children. Coming to the castle was a dreadful mistake.

But the place was beginning to take on a festive ap-

pearance. They'd found filigree candleholders and gilded pinecones in the attics, along with boxes of bows and bells and blown-glass icicles. Sabina found places for everything, as well as the forest of greenery Connor and the boys brought in for her to wrap around newel posts and knights in their dented armor. Soon each old warrior had a wreath around his neck, or a clove-studded orange skewered on his sword, or a red ribbon on his arm, like a lady's favor. The duke grumbled about the sacrilege to his ancestors' memories, but also reminded Sabina that at least four kissing boughs were needed.

"Four, Your Grace?"

"Aye, to ensure I get to kiss all the pretty ladies without having to walk too far."

So Sabina made four balls of twined vines and ribbons, with clusters of mistletoe hanging from each. The enormous chandelier was lowered so she could hang garlands of holly and ivy, with red and green and gold silk streamers trailing to the edges of the vast chamber. Between times, she looked over the menus with the chef, inspected the silver serving pieces with the butler, and assigned guest rooms with the housekeeper. All the servants were deferring to her opinion, and even the duke allowed as to how the place was beginning to look like Christmas the way he remembered it.

Sabina left the castle—in the viscount's carriage—only to rehearse the village children for the pageant. Then she went home to her cottage that was looking tinier and shabbier every day, by comparison, and fell into her bed without ever hanging one ribbon or sprig of holly in her own parlor. Ah well, she thought in the instant before falling asleep, the boys will have enough of Christmas at the castle. What more could they ask?

"What are you going to wish for on Christmas Eve, Martin?" Jasper inquired of his brother as they were making paper chains to decorate the little barn for Chocolate, Velvet, and her new foster mother, a placid bay mare. "A horse of your own?"

Martin knew that was an impossibility. As the eldest, he was more aware of their straitened circumstances. Besides, now that they could ride the viscount's cattle sometimes, having a horse of one's very own wasn't quite as important. Or so he told himself. "I suppose I'll wish for a book. That way I won't he disappointed. Mama always buys us books for Christmas. Then I can tell her my wish came true."

Jasper nodded. Their mother was working so hard, helping the duke get ready for his party, that she'd have no time to buy them toys, even if she could afford them. But Viscount Royce had given them the run of his old nursery, so they had tops and darts and balls aplenty, for once. "I s'pose I'll wish for new mittens, then. I saw her knitting them last month."

Perhaps Benjy was too young to understand nobility and sacrifice. Perhaps he was simply more honest, or more hopeful. "I'm going to wish for a castle!" he announced.

"Don't be a cake, Benjy. You might as well wish for a piece of the moon. You might get it sooner than a castle of your own."

"I didn't say it had to be my own, did I? I want the duke's castle. I want us to live there, forever."

"Maybe if we all wish for the same thing . . ."

Everything was as ready as it was going to be. The castle looked like an enchanted kingdom, waiting for a fairy princess. And Sabina almost felt like the eldritch

being in her green velvet dress. The boys proudly presented it to her on the afternoon of Christmas Eve so she could wear it to church, and then to the duke's party. The gown was simple in style, with long sleeves and a slim skirt that fell from a fashionably high waist. But there was nothing simple about the fit, or the neckline. No little boy had selected this dress, she knew. It was the work of a man, a connoisseur of women.

Sabina felt indecently exposed. Decadent, in fact—deliciously so. Never had she worn so daring a décolletage. Never had she had more of her out of a dress than in it. Never had she felt more beautiful, more womanly. She spent almost an hour with her hair, gathering most of it onto her head with a coronet of ivy, but leaving a few long tendrils to trail down her nearly bare shoulders, against her pale skin. And she wore her locket. The gown needed some ornamentation, Sabina told herself, to distract the eye from the obvious evidence that she'd nursed three infants. She'd have her cloak over it anyway, during church at least. But she wouldn't feel like a country dowd later, at the castle, among Lord Royce's elegant friends. She'd feel almost . . . seductive, she thought, her hand rubbing against the soft nap, as if she'd dressed to please a man. Which she hadn't, of course. Furthermore, those were not proper thoughts for a widowed lady on her way to church for this holiest of times. She was a mother, for heaven's sake, not in the muslin-company. If she needed any reminder of her place, Sabina was brought back from her daydreams by Jasper's announcement that he was feeling poorly. He was anxious about his part in the play, and Lord only knew what they'd been feeding him at the duke's kitchens. Marzipan pigs for luncheon, most likely. "Mama, I am going to be sick."

"Not in the duke's carriage, you won't," she firmly ordered. "Not on my new gown."

The Espinham carriage was coming to fetch the entire Green ménage to church, then carry them on to the castle, where they were to spend the night. That way the boys could enjoy more of the festivities, and Sabina could stay till the end of the party, in case there was a problem with provisions or proceedings. Of course the duke's household had managed very well without her all these years. Sabina was certain the competent staff was well enough trained to cope with any difficulty. They'd been managing the irascible duke for years, hadn't they? Still, they seemed to be counting on her.

She was counting on seeing Connor's blue eyes light up when he saw her in, and partly out of, her new gown later, when they reached the castle and she removed her cloak. Then she'd see if her secret Christmas wish had any chance of coming true. No, she told herself, almost as firmly as she'd commanded Jasper not to be sick— she would limit her wish to one dance, one dance with him to remind her of the girl she once was, and how it had felt to be cherished. That ought to be enough for the long winter, without chasing after moonbeams.

The enormous coach, with the Hamilton family coat of arms emblazoned on the side panels, brought them to the church early, by design. Sabina and Molly joined with Sophia Townsend, the seamstress, to help the village children into their costumes, smooth ragged nerves, and repeat forgotten lines.

Then it was time for Sabina to take her seat in the church, as nervous as Jasper over the coming performance. The little chapel was so crowded with townspeople and farmers filling every pew and aisle that the rear doors had to be propped open, so those left outside

could hear the service. Surely, the bishop would be impressed that Chipping Espy needed a new church. Mrs.
Marsden slid closer to her husband, making a space for
Sabina in the second row. The only other empty seats
were in the first row, the Duke of Espinwall's family
pew. All Sabina could see in front of her were two
broad backs in midnight superfine. The bishop was
seated at the altar, looking out of place in his fine robes.
Sabina prayed for the vicar's sake that he approved
their service.

The children's Nativity pageant went first, so the
children did not have to wait on tenterhooks through
the sermon and hymns. Martin walked in from the rear
door first, moved to the lectern, and began to tell the
story of the infant's birth. Sabina felt tears well in her
eyes.

Next came Joseph and Mary, riding her ass into
Bethlehem. Mary, Georginia Marsden with a pillow-
stuffed stomach, was having a fit of the giggles because
redheaded Joseph's spectacles kept sliding down his
nose. And she wasn't actually riding the ass, either.
Jasper was tugging on Velvet's lead, begging the little
donkey to come along and stop embarrassing them all,
between muttered threats to squire's youngest daughter.
An angel, one of the tenants' girls, recited a short verse
and danced across the altar with her paper star, urging
everyone to come worship the newborn babe. The
shepherd followed the star. Benjy led poor, patient
Beau with a sheepskin tied around his neck up to the
makeshift manger. The hound threw himself down on a
bale of hay with an exhausted sigh and began snoring.
Luckily, everyone was watching the three kings with
their gilt-trimmed robes and crowns march in, their
hands filled with gifts. Even Young Wilfred Snavely re-

membered to lay his chest at the foot of the manger.
He'd refused to be an ox again this year.

When all the children, innkeeper, animals and angels, were present, they stood together to sing "Gather
ye, Shepherds, Gather ye, Kings." Surely, Sabina
thought, heaven was a little closer to all of them this
evening, as the pure, sweet voices rejoiced.

While the children were singing, Mary was supposed
to reach behind her and put the hidden infant Jesus in
the hay-filled manger. But the manger was already occupied. Velvet had climbed into the soft crib and was
half asleep there. Georgina was about to bash the little
donkey over the head with her doll, while everyone,
even the bishop, laughed. Jasper took the doll away and
tucked it next to Velvet in the creche. Martin impro-
vised: "And the donkey made a pillow for the infant."

Sabina was weeping during the last children's hymn,
and could barely see the handkerchief Connor handed
over the back of the pew to her. Then the children all
scurried to seats on the floor or on parents' laps, and it
was time for Vicar Davenport's reading and sermon. He
said all the right words, Sabina was certain, but she
couldn't concentrate on the message. Was everything as
it should be at the castle? Would the duke approve her
efforts? Was her gown too coming? Perhaps she ought
to change when they dropped Beau and Velvet back at
the cottage.

Sabina wasn't the only member of the congregation
paying scant attention. Benjy had his head in her lap,
and Squire Marsden was sliding farther and farther
down his seat, while his wife poked him awake. Even
the bishop seemed to be nodding off. At last it was time
for the choir, with their familiar hymns and traditional
carols. The entire congregation joined in. This was the

real Christmas, Sabina thought, wrapping Benjy in her cloak and smoothing back Jasper's hair, then touching Martin's cheek—not the food and gifts and decorations.

9

As soon as the last note of the last hymn was sung, the organ sounded. All eyes turned to Mrs. Greene. Yes, Sabina was still in the second row, her hand bandaged. Then who . . . ? They all craned their necks to look into the organ recess, where exquisite music was being created that no one was listening to.

"By George, it's the Gaines woman," Squire exclaimed, slapping his knee. "In church. Ain't that a rare 'un!"

Such a performance was rare, indeed. Miss Viola Gaines was playing to perfection, and she knew it. She knew they were all whispering about her, and smiled over her shoulder at the congregation while her fingers found the correct keys.

Miss Viola's improbably blond hair was braided atop her head to resemble a halo, with enough feather plumes stuck in it to waft a small angel to heaven. Her gown was decorous, thank goodness, Sabina thought, not as daringly cut as her own, and in the same dark plum-colored fabric as the choir's new robes. The woman sincerely seemed to be enjoying herself and the music. Sabina closed her eyes to enjoy the masterful performance, too.

" 'Tain't right, I says," a voice from the rear of the church called out, "one such as her playing in our church on Christmas Eve. Sacrilege, that's what it is." Other whispers could be heard, along with foot shuffling.

Reverend Davenport mopped at the sweat pouring down his forehead, and it was still cold in the chapel. Some of his congregants were gathering their children and their hymnals, preparing to leave. "This is Christmas, time of forgiveness," he reminded them, shouting to be heard over the continuing organ music, "as the Lord forgave us."

Still there were mutters, and one starched-up matron did leave.

"Such talent is a gift from God," the vicar called out, but he was losing them, he knew, and his hopes for a bigger church.

Then Sabina stood up. "Mama, you can't leave!" wailed Jasper.

"No, darling," she said, tucking her cloak more firmly around Benjy, asleep on the bench. "I am only going to help turn Miss Gaines's pages for her." Sabina forgot that her new gown—and her bosom—would now be exposed to all eyes. She remembered when she heard Connor's indrawn breath as she passed in front of him on her way to the organ niche, and when she heard Wilfred Snavely shout out, "And there's another of the straw sisterhood. I don't want my wife being exposed to such blasphemy. If you won't throw 'em out, Vicar, I'll be leaving. Come on, Mavis."

The duke got up, too, and shook his head. "The man's a maggot, but he's right. Can't have Chatworth's castoff playing the organ in church. And the Greene gel will be tarred with the same brush. Too bad, but that's the way of it. Come along then, Royce." As usual, he spoke loudly enough that most of the assembly could hear him over the organ.

The viscount stood, and Sabina held her breath, but Connor put his strong hand on his father's shoulder and

pushed him back to his seat. "Sit, Father," he said. "We are staying. Or are you so righteous that you cannot bend a little on Christmas Eve?" The duke knew what his stubbornness had cost him in the past; he saw what he could lose in the future. He sat.

Connor turned to face the congregation. "Let him without sin cast the first stone," he told them, "and that goes doubly for you, Snavely. One more insult to either of these ladies and you'll have me to answer to. Miss Gaines has kindly offered to share her remarkable musical talent with us at the castle fete later, so let us permit her to finish here."

Everyone knew what he was saying—that if they walked out now, they weren't invited to the party.

"Oh, sit down and shut your trap, Wilfred," Mavis Snavely was heard to say. "There's already one jackass in church. Iffen I don't get my dance with our handsome lordship, you'll be eating cold porridge the rest of your days."

"And sleeping in a cold bed," another voice called out, laughing.

Sabina was grateful to the viscount, and proud of him for standing up to his father without a confrontation, but she had to worry about his reasons. He was a rake; his motives had to be suspect. He had to have known that her own standing in town could have stood the test, so Connor was really defending Viola Gaines, a beautiful, talented woman some five or six years younger than Sabina, and many years older in knowing how to please a man. Suddenly, Sabina felt that it wasn't fairy dust that had been sprinkled over her tonight, but the sands of time, running out.

Then Viscount Royce reached over the carved back of the pew and lifted sleeping Benjamin in his arms, her

cloak and all, and sat with him next to the duke. With
that one gesture he stated his intentions, made his
claim. Sabina's heart soared with the music.

A huge candle-lit procession wended its way back to
the castle, carriages and carts, farm wagons piled high
with hay and drowsy children, sturdy village men carrying torches. They all sang carols as they went, and
looked up to see if they could find the Christmas star,
or a snowflake. They all fell silent when they caught
sight of the castle, even Sabina, who'd known what to
expect. The whole pile was lit by candles in every window, and Chinese lanterns strung from the battlements,
and a bonfire in the front, where the moat used to be.
Inside looked just as magical. The wassail bowls were
filled, the tables were invisible under the platters of
foods, and the hired musicians were tuning their instruments.

The duke led off the first dance, a stately minuet,
with Lady Arbuthnot from the next shire. Then Connor
shouted, "Now let the real dancing begin!" and ordered
the orchestra to play reels and contra dances and fast,
frenzied jigs everyone could join in, from the oldest
grandmother to the youngest toddler. The swords on the
walls rattled with the music and the pounding of hundreds of pairs of feet. The castle had never been mer-
rier. Sabina had never been happier. Her sons were
playing snapdragon, watched by a hundred doting castle servants, and Viola Gaines was being drooled over
by Lord Arbuthnot. Sabina danced with the squire and
had her feet stepped on by the blacksmith. She went
down the lines with the baker and the banker and bald
Lord Quigley. Then the orchestra struck the first chords
of a waltz.

"This is my dance, I believe?" Connor was bowing before her.

"No, it's my Christmas wish," was all she could say.

He laughed and led her onto the cleared area set aside for dancing. "You are beautiful tonight, in case none of the two thousand other men you've danced with haven't told you. And you are quite, quite tipsy, I believe. No more lamb's wool for you, my girl." And no more words as she floated in his arms, her eyes closed.

When she opened them, they stood in an alcove, partially hidden by tapestries. She was suddenly shy, afraid to ruin the moment with a wrong word. "The, ah, duke seems to be enjoying himself. Having you here has done wonders for his health."

"The old faker will live to be a hundred, I'd guess, just to spite the devil. He'll be fine."

"Then you are free to leave again?" She had always known he'd return to his pleasure-seeking ways, his gaming and opera-dancers.

She must have spoken aloud, for he answered, "I find that my pleasure is here, Sabina, and always has been. Besides, someone has to be around to look after the boys so you don't coddle them too much. Will you marry me, Sabina?"

"What, so you can have my sons? I know you've grown fond of them, and they of you, but surely——"

"Don't be a peagoose, my precious. You are all I want, all I've ever wanted. The boys are simply an added bonus."

Sabina waved her hand around at the room, the opulence, the wealth beyond measure. "It would still be an unequal match. Everyone would talk."

"Very well, if you think your boys are worth more, I'll deed the London house to you, too."

"No, silly, you know very well what I mean. You have everything—"

"Except the one thing I need most. You can give it to me, Sabina, only you." His hands were stroking up and down her arms, setting fires in cold, dark places.

"You said there were two conditions to be met before you'd stay."

"You are the first. I wouldn't, couldn't stay here if you won't stay with me. I cannot see you without wanting you, don't you understand that, sweetheart?"

She was beginning to, as his hands reached higher, to the bare skin of her shoulders and the locket around her neck. "I never could, never will, no matter how hard I tried to forget you."

She sighed. "And I, too, never loved another."

She thought he'd kiss her then, but Connor wanted to explain more. "The other reason I could not swear to remain was the duke. I couldn't subject your sons to his choleric temper. That's why I wanted them around the castle so much this past sennight, to see if he could be livable with three boys in the house. If he couldn't, then I'd have done my damnedest to convince you—all of you—to run away with me. This time I would not have taken no for an answer, my girl."

"You wouldn't have had to." She gestured toward the nearby corner of the room, where the duke was holding court from his thronelike chair, his gouty foot propped on satin pillows. Martin and Jasper were leaning over his shoulders, rapt in the stud book he held. Benjamin was asleep in his lap, peppermint-sticky face pressed against the duke's previously pristine white waistcoat.

"So will you, my darling Sabina—will you finally be my wife after a very long engagement?"

"Of course I will, Connor. That's what I really

wanted for Christmas, you know," she confessed with a tender smile. "Not one measly waltz. I wanted your love, for all time, as you've got mine."

"And I really want a red-haired choir of my own," he said, before finally sealing their vows with a kiss that had waited more than a decade.

The enormous clock in the hall started chiming the hour, and the church bells in the village started tolling. It was twelve o'clock, and Christmas had finally arrived. Everyone had collected their wraps and their children for the trek back home, as soon as one more toast was made. The wassail cups were all refilled as the duke signaled for the company to gather near the vast hearth.

"The name of Hamilton is an ancient one," he began, loudly enough to wake sleeping babies. "Handed down from generation to generation, from father to son since the time of the Normans. With the names goes the title, and with the title goes the land and the responsibility for everyone on it."

"Hear, hear!" was heard from one who'd already had too much of the heady brew.

"Now I hand it to my son," the duke continued, turning to Connor, "along with this sliver from last year's Yule log, to carry on the tradition, to carry on the family into a long and happy future." Among shouts and cheers, he set flame to the bit of wood. "Just make sure you have someone to pass it to, while I'm still around to see."

Connor looked at the burning stick in his hand, then turned to Martin, bending to his level. "I am not your father in name or in blood," he told the boy, "but I would be your father in heart. Will you and your broth-

ers help light this fire, until your mama blesses us with
a son of our own? And then you'll help him be the man
he should be?"

Martin almost tripped in his hurry to light the Yule
log before the match burned out, and all their luck with
it. His hand in Connor's, together they lit the new log
from the old. When it caught, Martin called out, "To the
House of Hamilton, long may they prosper."

Jasper shouted to be heard over the cheers and clapping: "And all of us with them!"

And Benjy, from his mother's arms, mumbled, "And
to good deeds."

EPILOGUE

So the church had its extension, and a new roof, to boot.
The viscount had his choir, and the new viscountess a
new green velvet dress every Christmas. The donkey
was in many a Nativity pageant, with many a red-
haired Joseph and a few redheaded Marys. The duke
shouted at all of the children impartially, and the vicar
wed Sophia Townsend, the seamstress. Oh, and Viola
Gaines? She went home with the bishop.

Felicity's Forfeit
by Elisabeth Fairchild

Legs pumping, blood burning, cheeks stinging with the cold, Bingham Kirby, fifth viscount of Westbrook Hall, drew his coat close, shoulder capes billowing in the wind. Before his eyes flashed a blur of dark, leafless trees. Beneath the blades of his skates glittering ice crystals spewed.

Forfeit the wind seemed to whisper. All is forfeit.

It was late November, the weather unseasonably cold, snow on the ground, ice on the pond, Christmas plans to be laid and no holiday spirit in Bingham.

How to generate anticipation for a Season of giving when so much was soon to be taken from him? The loom of loss, the threat of debts, the weight of responsibilities proved too much for him. He could not see his way clear.

The day was appropriately clouded, the sky too gray. The trees along the pond's banks clutched close a shroud of fog. The ice beneath his feet, too, was clouded, its sheen marred by evidence of his own passage—cut up—like his direction. Where to turn? What to do? Whom to rely on?

For the moment he knew only that he must avoid the dark patch of thin ice at the pond's center. His feet car-

ried him, like his thoughts, in fast, endless, hissing circles.

So focused were his thoughts, so fast his circuitous **race** to escape the inescapable, he almost ran them down, four who braved the day's icy pinch. The vicar's daughters, apple-cheeked and round as robins, bundled in thick layers of tatty brown wool. They spilled onto the ice directly in his path, scattered, laughing, cheerful, halooing "Good day!" in every way contrary to his mood and direction.

"A cold day," he called to them, unwilling to deem it good.

What had they to laugh about so blithely? The Pendletons were of meager means, as thin of purse as his own was soon to be.

They were young women almost of an age with him. He knew them but little, remembered them as his sisters' pig-tailed playmates, one possessed of a beaky nose, another an overbite, the third a mass of freckles. He stood up with them on occasion at the odd holiday dance. There was a fourth female with them today. She wore a red cape. He did not recognize her.

Small surprise. He had been away from Westbrook most of his adult life. First to school, then to university, and finally in his three-year Grand Tour of Europe. And in all that time his father had never hinted at the true state of their affairs, had never once suggested he curtail his spending, or concentrate on making Westbrook economically sound. Circles—he skated circles, faster and faster, pulse pounding, no closer to answers.

Like the arthritic-limbed trees that flashed darkly before him, his father now lived in a state of fog, his mind slipping, glassy as virgin ice. It was rare that the old man's reason sharply surfaced, and he spoke for a

moment or two with a lucidity that left them all aching in the grim inevitability of its slipping away again.

The Pendletons, he whipped past again—their names remembered—hopeful names in this moment when he felt the loss of all hope—Faith, Comfort, and Charity they were—giggling and calling to one another, their cheer a rasp on raw nerves.

Perhaps there was a joy in never knowing what it was one did not have, a joy equal to the misery found in loss. Grief would soon be his—and want. He balanced bleakly on the thin blade of anticipation. How to survive? How to provide for his sisters?

The Pendletons offered no answers, only laughter. The sound skittered callously across the frozen pond.

The fourth among their number evidenced little acquaintance with the ice. They showed her how to don skates. Arm in arm, they helped her as she slipped, slid, and careened, red cape flapping, directionless and laughing in her first windmill-armed, stiff-legged attempts to master the ice.

They got in his way, together went down in laughing heaps, getting themselves up, only to fall down again—ungainly and giggling—bonnets bobbing.

He ignored them after the first shouted exchange. They seemed too interested in their own dearly bought progress to pay him much mind.

Around and around he went, head down, faster and faster, his mind on bills to be paid, repairs long overdue on the Hall, his sisters latest requests for new clothes and a Yuletide house party.

Money. He needed money, scads of money, a thick, substantive wad of soft to lift him from the icy waters of impending penury. He considered what to sell. Horses, vehicles, jewelry, art. The flocks? The land?

How much land would it take? And without the sheep, the land, whence came an income? They had always depended on fleece, rents, and investments to keep them afloat.

His progress a racing whispered hiss, his skates cut and recut the same track in the ice, the tips of his ears and nose gone numb with the cold, almost as numb as his mind with fear of the future. He was a gentleman well educated and well traveled, but had little to recommend him in the way of marketable skill. Without political prowess, not called to the cloth, in no way a fighting man, he might discourse at length about most subjects while being master of none.

The awkward solo progress of the newest of the skaters dragged his attention away from his troubles. Clumsy as a wooden doll, she took off without the assistance of the others. They scattered like sparrows from a hedgerow when she waved them away. He might not have paid her mind even then, but her clumsy progress took her closer and closer to the center of the pond.

Down she went. He skated toward her, his movements smooth, loose, assured. "Need help?"

She waved him away, head bent to the task of standing, single-mindedly intent on doing it herself.

A muffled, "No, thank you," emerged from the woolen scarf about her neck.

He left her to it, no more than a brief meeting of their eyes as up she rose, stalwart, indomitable, clumsy but unvanquished.

A gliding step or two and down she slid, her movements uncontrolled, awkward, ineptitude inching her ever closer to danger.

Bingham pivoted as he skated away from her, his

progress more backward than forward, that he might watch her direction. It worried him.

Red cape aflutter, petticoat revealed, limbs asplay, she laughed, unaware of peril except to her knees in falling. She studied briefly a tear in her stocking, brushed powdered ice from her skirt as she set off, a little more gracefully, managing a short stretch of choppy movement before down she plonked, this time with a cracking noise that alarmed Bingham into instant action.

From his throat he dragged the long hunter's green muffler, skates carrying him as swiftly as legs could move. She struggled once more to rise.

"Don't move!" he called, unnerved by an ominous creaking noise beneath his skates.

From the far side of the pond came a distant shriek, "Felicity!"

As if she did not hear, one mittened hand planted firmly on the ice, she struggled with her skirts, skates scrabbling for a foothold. "Oh, de-ah!" Her accent, the tone of her voice, was strange. "The ass is very wet here."

Ass? Good God! Ice! Surely she meant ice?

"Damn it, woman, do not move!" he shouted.

Again, beneath him, the ominous creaking.

Here were eyes, bright as a summer's day, robin's egg blue, a blue that spoke of spring and balmy breezes, a blue made brighter still by the cold-scalded scarlet of nose and cheeks.

She was not one of the Pendletons, who raced from the far side of the pond. Her cherry nose was neither Roman nor freckled, her even white teeth suffered no overbite, and yet she bore resemblance. The hair beneath the brim of her bonnet was the same mahogany

brown, of the same thick, curling texture, her brow equally deep, her chin identically cleft.

"The ice," he said irritably, his own troubled thoughts coloring the words. "Could you not see it is thin there?"

The blue eyes widened, gaze dropping first to study the ice, rising terror stricken to lock on his.

"You are tawlking to a greenhorn, mistuh," she said faintly, her voice startling—slow and sweet, softly blurred, warm enough to thaw ice. This singsong cadence was completely unfamiliar to him. An unexpected puzzle.

"Ah am open to suggestion."

Her drawl was sultry. American. She was American. No Englishwoman of unsullied reputation would put words together with such languid heat, such suggestion, without blushing.

He blurted gruffly, "Do not attempt to stand! Your weight is more evenly distributed if you remain as you are. Hold fast. I shall drag you free."

His muffler—he tossed an end to her. She stretched gingerly to take hold.

The ice, in wet silence, gave way as she grasped it fast. Shrieks again from the Pendletons, closer now as she fell, half in and half out of icy water. He dared not look away. Terror tightened the American's jaw, but she did not squawk or struggle or scream, merely said to him conversationally, mittened hands clenching green wool as the blade of her doused skate splashed up onto thin ice, boot, ankle, and knee dark with the wet, "Ah depend upon you, suh, nawt to let go."

Bingham had never looked into a young woman's eyes, her fate suspended in his hands. An unspoken and highly intimate language passed between them in

the fraction of a moment when life and death tested either end of a knitted scarf. The urgent intensity of her blue-eyed gaze willed him to succeed. She gasped. More ice gave way, the wet reaching for her. He dared not fall or slip. He allowed no thought of failure to enter his head.

Ice shattered in her wake, but he plucked her, dripping, from the jaws of danger. On solid ice again, he helped her to stand. She was not up to it.

Teeth chattering, lips blue, her ankles gave way. "De-ah Gawd!" she exclaimed as she hung unabashedly on his arm, as she slid into his chest, breathing hard, the fog of their combined exertion and fear clouding the air, her nose redder than ever, blue eyes moist with a freshet of tears.

"You saved mah laf!" she cried against his neck, the syrupy sweetness of her accent an odd contrast to the dry sob that tore from her throat, the stiff brim of her bonnet bumping his ear, as her breath—warm, cinnamon-scented—stroked his chin. "Bless you, suh. You saved me from certain dayeth!"

She clutched him, arms enfolding, not loverlike, but at the means of her survival. He squeezed her to him, held fast the living, breathing truth of a stranger brought close by the near disaster they had together avoided. The solid warmth of her felt good in his arms, evidence that his problems, in the grand scheme of things, were trivial. Here was a heart beating, a pulse throbbing, a breath misting the air before his cheek that might in an instant, have ceased to be.

She trembled. The rhythmic click of her teeth was strange music to his ears.

"We must get you out of these clothes," he said.

"Goodness, suh!" Her laughter was husky, deep and warm, as intoxicating as the mellow burn of whiskey.

He drew a hip flask from his pocket. "Care for a sip?"

She accepted, took a gulp, her teeth ceasing their chattering. She laughed, the laugh whiskey-scented. "You British boys"—she said the word as though it consisted of two syllables *bo-ays*—"work fast. Here we have just gone and met, and you mean to get me liquored up and out of my clothes."

He pushed her to arm's length, that he might study her face. "You jest?" he hazarded.

"Whut else?" She laughed again, the laughter warm. "Mah teeth are rattlin' too much to be seductive, don't you agree?"

"Remove your shoes and stockings," he insisted. "This sopping wet petticoat as well."

He bent to remove her skates, surprised when she offered him clumsy assistance.

"Muh fingers are a bit sti-iff," she drawled, cupping them to her mouth, blowing warmth on them.

"Of course. Silly of me."

He removed his own gloves, chafed her chilled hands between his palms, blew warmth on them from his own mouth, and tucked his gloves onto the icy digits.

"My, my but tha-at feels good." She flexed her fingers and smiled with delight. "Kind of you, but won't your own ha-ands get cold?"

The cadence of her voice was hypnotic—the slow drawl deceptively simple and unschooled, at the same time amused and intimate.

"Think nothing of it." His voice seemed hard-edged by contrast.

"Ah can think of nuthin' but your kindness at the moment, suh."

The Pendletons swooped down on them like pigeons come to roost, clucking and cooing, voices familiar, diction clipped and clear. Removing the young woman from his arm, they insisted that cousin Felicity must be hurried home at once to get her out of wet clothes and into a warm bath.

The image crossed Bingham's mind in a brief irresponsible flash—bared, blue-eyed Felicity lounging in a steaming bath. He shook away the uncalled-for suggestion, assisting the poor, rattled young woman in the more appropriate removal of her skates and shoes.

Charity remarked sharply at his cavalier familiarity with her cousin's clothing. Ignoring her, he squeezed frigid water from sopping hems, knotting the fabric of cloak and dress in small bunches that lifted them scandalously high, away from drenched stockings.

"You must have those off," he insisted brusquely, "and if one of you boasts an extra petticoat, please be so kind as to hand it over."

A gasp from Faith, but Comfort was swift to turn her back, and fumbling beneath her skirt, shook free the garment required—a flannel petticoat, much darned about the hem, but blessedly warm.

Faith and Charity, he took each by the shoulder and placed them either side of their cousin. "Spread your skirts," he snapped.

They did as he directed, discreetly shielding their cousin, listening with nodding heads as he shed his own skates, saying, "Remove everything that is wet and touching skin. Do your best to keep her warm. I shall run to Farmer Brewton's for a wagon."

The coat from his own shoulders draped across Fe-

licity Pendleton's back, he set off, only to look back and find them following at a distance, contrary to his suggestion.

Disgruntled, colder than he had anticipated without coat, muffler, or gloves, he retraced his steps, hands pocketed in the small warmth of his armpits. "Are you up to this?" he asked Felicity. "I meant to bring a wagon to you."

"Ah thought it would be better for awl concerned if the damsels in distress walked rather than sittin' about awaitin' the return of their knight in shinin' armor."

She saw him as a knight, did she? The idea warmed him. He admired her spirit, admired the amused twinkle in her vivid blue eyes.

"We did try to convince her otherwise, my lord," Comfort said primly.

From Felicity a fluid chuckle. "Ah am an American, suh. We are a rebellious lot, but ah would not mind dependin' upon the support of your arm the rest of the way to this Farmer Brewster's."

"Brewton."

"Ah stand corrected." She accepted his arm. He drew her close as much for his own warmth and support as for hers. His bare hand found comfort in the heat of her gloved clasp. Blue eyes met his a moment, the look one of admiration. "Or should I say lean. I do not stand corrected so much as lean at the moment."

And an invigorating lean it proved. He liked very much the sensation of clasping womanly warmth to chilled frame.

He laughed—he could not restrain the reaction. That she pressed herself to him without missishness or hesitation, her mind turned to humor so close upon the heels of disaster, pleased him immensely. Perhaps his

own problems were better met with a sense of humor and a warm woman to cling to.

"Are all Americans as witty as they are stubborn?" he asked.

"Witty? High praise, suh, from an Englishman, for ah consider your countrymen and women among the cleverest in the world."

"Clever in all things, perhaps, except the conquering of a rebellious American temperament. Do you miss America, Miss Pendleton?"

Her lashes covered any contradiction to be read in the blue eyes. "Ah make England mah home, suh."

"A rebel returned to her motherland?" He was surprised. There was much in the young woman that ill fit the English countryside.

"Mah family, suh, what little ah have left of it, reside here. Ah have settled my affairs in America. There is nothin' left in Georgia to howld me there."

"She is one of us now," Faith stated proudly.

"Indeed, she shares my room, my lord." Comfort seemed, if not pleased, entirely conscious of her own contribution in such an arrangement.

"We cannot think how we have managed without her." Charity patted her shoulder briskly. "Now, come along, girls. We shall warn Farmer Brewton to put the kettle on. A bracing cup of hot cider is what we are all in dire need of."

The muffled crunch of their footsteps as they ran, soon diminished. In the distance a dog barked, Farmer Brewton's Shep run out to challenge the girls.

Silence and isolation cocooned Bingham and his shivering charge, heightening his awareness of the sounds of their own tandem footsteps, the rattle of icy limbs above their heads, the rasp of their labored

breathing. Their position was undeniably intimate, arm in arm. The heat between them seemed suddenly wanton—willfully sensual.

He gazed into the brilliant blue of her eyes, wondering if her sensibilities were similarly affected.

She gazed back, unblushing, and made things right, saying in that honeysuckle drip of a voice, "Ah am indebted to you, suh. Or is it my lord ah should be callin' you, for you have proven an angel of mercy today, a servant of mah Lord in every way."

This mention of God, of his own goodness, quelled any thoughts to the contrary. He liked that she called him "suh," that she questioned the idea of addressing him as her lord. How very American.

"Call me Bingham," he said, "or Kirby, whichever pleases you. As you are not a British subject, I am, in fact, no lord to you at all, and should very much dislike being confused with any greater deity."

"A man at once humble and noble? Ah marvel at such a discovery!"

How flat her *a*'s, how like music that ribald flatness. "I hope some day, in some way, to repay your kindness, Bingham Kirby, for without your swift and skillful intervention today, mah laf was most certainly forfeit."

"Forfeits! We shall play at forfeits," Mary insisted, her voice echoing down the Long Gallery, where Bingham bent to the billiard table, while his sisters dashed the length of the room, playing battledore, forced to remain indoors today, by a nasty turn in the weather.

They kept cheerful and warm because of their exertions, though sleet tapped at the windows at either end of the gallery.

Bingham stared blindly down the shaft of his mace, his thoughts focused not on the ivory balls before him, nor on the suggestions his sisters lobbed his way as vigorously as the shuttlecock that flew between them, but on yesterday morning's rescue of Miss Felicity Pendleton.

An intriguing young woman. He could not remember a time when he had been more struck by the image of female courage and uncomplaining fortitude.

"Forfeits and charades." Joan sounded winded.

"And bullet pudding. Father loves bullet pudding." Mary's enthusiasm lent strength to her return as she whacked the shuttlecock.

Games. They talked games while he considered the deeper truths of life and death, and the meaning of near misses.

"Bingham, you must pick us out a good, fat Yule log."

"As Lord of Misrule, you must decide upon the games."

Joan struck an underhand swing. The shuttlecock soared high and long, over Mary's head, an arc that sent it fluttering directly onto the billiard table. It knocked two of Bingham's balls into motion.

"Really, Mary," he snapped. "I have more important matters to keep me occupied."

She fetched their errant bird. "More important than the saving of us, Bing?" she asked breathlessly.

Could he save them, as he had so recently saved Felicity Pendleton?

He stared at the mace poised in his hand. It was a work of art, an extravagance he never should have indulged in, never *would* have indulged in had he known the true state of their affairs. The stick was capped in

ivory, the butt inlaid with five different woods, a floral design that had cost extra, as had the ebon slate that made up the table. The hinged brass, hand-patterned ball pockets—extra as well.

The ball, when he hit it, did not go where he intended.

"We cannot afford extravagances," he said.

Joan replied briskly, "We cannot afford *not* to have this Christmas party. You know I am right."

"Indeed," Mary agreed. They were united completely in their efforts to convince him.

One hand braced upon his thigh, the other deftly guiding the mace head, Bing was struck by the idea that he, like the ball he set into motion, sank, not into a corner pocket but an icy pool of debt. His sisters held out not muffler but wedding veil to save him from certain debtor's prison. Was he a fool to scorn their assistance?

Their play began again with admirable vigor, and with it their attempts to sway him.

"You must compile a list of guests."

Whack.

"Gentlemen you would not mind calling brother-in-law."

Whack.

"Gentlemen of wealth and standing."

Whack. Whack. Bingham felt kinship with the poor, feathered object his sisters batted between them.

"We have compiled a list of ladies."

Crack.

The shuttlecock struck the ceiling and fell to the floor at his feet.

He interrupted his shot to retrieve the object. "Really, Joan, this idea seems most unwise!"

They would not allow him to object.

"Unwise!" Mary challenged.

"Nothing could be wiser," Joan insisted.

"One of us must marry into money."

"And if we have none to consider but wealthy candidates . . ."

"Then one of us is sure to make a good match of it."

There was an uncomfortable logic to what they said. Bingham tossed them the light, feathered object of their game, troubled by the sense he became just such an insubstantial plaything in this merry matchmaking scheme.

"Marrying for money is a shallow, ill-bred solution to our problems," he argued.

"A common solution," Mary interrupted.

"All too common. Lacking in strength of purpose or character . . ."

"Have you a better idea?" Joan asked. "Would you sell the house out from under us?"

Bingham's shot was locked in a corner. He moved to the far side of the table to try a fresh angle. They stood waiting. Mary tapped the shuttlecock against her racket.

"No, I should not care to sell Westbrook," he admitted, "and no, I have not a better idea."

Mary smiled grimly and tossed the shuttlecock into the air. "It is settled then."

He sold the billiard table. His father's old friend, Lord Heath, had always admired the thing. He called on Lady Heath in person and convinced her the table and cues were the perfect Christmas gift for her husband.

She leapt at the chance, after asking how his father did, of course.

Bingham stroked the feather of his freshly sharpened quill and scowled at the page before him—blank, like his mind. Who among friends and acquaintances to invite to the Christmas house party on the table's proceeds?

Rich men, Mary wanted.

He scribbled three names.

Men he would not mind his sisters marrying, Joan had said. He frowned and crossed off two.

Seven his sisters had asked for. *Seven!* Far easier to come up with dozens of fine paupers he would rejoice in them marrying than coming up with seven well-monied gentlemen he would not mind calling brother.

He shrugged, dipped quill afresh, and penned three names. He frowned, stroking the feather, considering what he knew of the men. Rich, yes, but family? Did he hold even one in high regard? Were they worth his precious billiard table?

He could not do it. His every feeling rebelled.

Fresh ink again to scratch out these contemptible contenders. A new list, the names coming faster, seven of them, one right after another. Fellows he admired. Good-hearted, bright-eyed chaps. There were among them one or two who could stand up to Mary's bossiness. And Joan? Joan would be easy enough to please.

He sat, pen poised. This list was not what Mary had asked for. His friends were ripe with promise, with potential prospects, and several stood in line to inherit, but none of them swam in ready at the moment, certainly not enough money to save Westbrook.

It was his responsibility to see his sisters happily

settled. If sacrifice need be made in marriage, it should
be he who made it, not they.

He doodled, as was his custom, on the blotter beneath the list—he had already this evening penned a
rough likeness of the money tree his father always referred to. Would that they had such a thing. Now an icy
pond took shape beneath his pen, surrounded by barren
trees, of which the money tree was but one of many.
From the center of the pond a hand rose. A man gone
down, as he was going down.

He studied the list again. Good lads all, guests he
would take real pleasure in welcoming to Westbrook.

His father shuffled into the room. At his heels was
his portly, nearsighted valet, Peel, both shadows of the
men who had once tossed him high in their arms, who
had taught him to ride, to hunt, to tie neckcloth and
polish boots—men against whom he measured all
other men.

"What's this, then?" His father tapped his scrib-
blings with a hand gone soft with inactivity. Peel
leaned closer, squinting.

"Names, sir," Bingham said loud and clear, the volume and tone he always adopted with his father, who
was hard of hearing, harder still of understanding. "We
mean to have a house party, Father, for Christmas."

"Do you?" The bushy brows rose. "Your mother
loves to bring in guests for the holidays."

"Indeed she did, sir," Peel said politely. He was ever
polite. "An excellent hostess, the late Lady Kirby."

Lord Kirby looked for a moment baffled, as if for
the first time hearing his wife referred to in the past
tense. "That's right," he nodded, then tapped the sheet
of foolscap. "Did slip me mind for the moment that she

was gone, your dear mother. Good lads, are they, these friends? Gentlemen?"

"Indeed. The best I know." It felt right to say so.

"Know any of them, do I?"

Bingham hesitated, the truth painful. "I doubt it, sir. But you will enjoy meeting them. Every one. And they you."

His father took up the list, held it to the light, laboriously pondering the names of lads he had known since they wore short coats.

Bingham, a lump swelling in his throat, dipped quill again. Upon the blotter, his pen produced a mighty sword clenched in the hand at the center of the pond.

"I've something important to ask you, Father."

"Hmm? What's the trouble, lad? Tell your old dad. Glad to help."

Bingham rubbed his forehead. His father had once guided him through all of the rough spots in his life. Old habits died hard. "What would you do, Father, if we needed money?"

Peel's head came up. He was surprised by the question.

Bingham pressed on. "Large sums of money, sir?"

"In debt? Overspent your allowance, have you?"

Bingham nodded. "I'm sorry to say we have."

"Well, don't be shy about asking, my boy. You've only to ask. We shall apply to Mr. Benson . . ." His expression clouded. "No, not Benson."

"Mr. Benson is little help these days, sir," Bingham said sadly.

"Don't trust the man!" his father announced with a firm volume that echoed the length of the drawing room.

"Not trust Benson, sir? Why ever not?" Peel asked.

Kirby touched the side of his nose, with a canny look. Bingham had not seen such look, or gesture, from his father in the three months he had been home.

"Money tree's the thing, lad," the old man whispered, shaking the list of names at him. "We must pluck a leaf or two from it, don't you see."

"If only it were that easy," Bingham murmured.

Lord Kirby set off, as if on his way to the very money tree mentioned. Bingham suggested to Peel, "Perhaps some laudanum?"

"As you say, sir." He drew a vial from his pocket.

Lord Kirby became distracted in his trek across the room. "What's this then?" he inquired blankly, staring at the page in his hand.

Bingham's heart turned over.

Polite and patient, Peel went to the old man. "A list of guests, sir."

Over the old man's gray head the gaze of master and servant met.

"A Christmas party, Father," Bingham said loud and clear.

"A pahty? Are we awl invited?"

It was, unmistakably, Felicity Pendleton who spoke with honeyed drawl—from the doorway—and at her back her cousins—a gaggle of geese following the American swan. At their heels trotted Hibbs, the butler, round face florid, his manner flustered.

"I do beg pardon, Master Bingham! The Misses Pendleton. I have rung for the Misses Kirby, but they insisted it was you they came to see. They were not to be gainsaid."

"It wuz nawt our intention to intrude, gentlemen." That voice again—warm, languid, and sweet. "Only to return your gloves and scarf, suh."

Bingham was pleased to get a better look at Felicity Pendleton, and to accept the return of the articles of clothing from her hand. She was an attractive and shapely female freed from her bundled woolens, her nose no longer scarlet with the cold. The cut and color of her dress, the arrangement of her hair, he found intriguing, decidedly different from that of her cousins, different from any Englishwoman's he would wager.

American.

Her walk, too, was different, her stride long and confident, as if she had within her not an ounce of hesitation. She was not shy in holding out her hand to him. No bobbing curtsy here, no hopes that he should kiss her knuckles. Instead, the outstretched hand of an equal.

Her eyes sparkled with pleasure, her hand took firm hold, gave a firm shake. The gesture was ordinary enough, between gentlemen. To receive such salutation from a female was decidedly unusual. Bingham's blood raced a little faster with the return of his scarf, still warm from Miss Pendleton's neck, his gloves pulled from the pocket of her cape.

Joan entered the room to find them thus engaged, Mary at her heels.

"Why had she your gloves and scarf, Bing?"

"Did he not tell you?" Faith squinted at them myopically.

"Tell us what?"

"Rescued Felicity from certain death, he did."

"What's that, you say?" His father took renewed interest in the conversation.

As confidently as she had crossed the room, Felicity took the old man's hand in hers. "Have you nawt been informed, suh, that your son saved my life?"

"Did he?" Lord Kirby's face lit up with delight.

"Stopped me from fallin' through some thin ice, suh. Stopped me from missin' Christmas, mah favorite season of the year."

"My favorite season as well, my dear. Extraordinary! As is your accent. American?"

"Ah ahm from Georgia, suh."

Peel sidled up beside Bingham and discreetly motioned to the bottle of laudanum.

"Perhaps not," Bingham mused, his attention focused on Felicity and his father. "I cannot remember when I have, of late, seen Father look half so animated."

"You mean to have a party?" Charity Pendleton asked.

"But you told us nothing of this unexpected prospect of delight!" Faith said to Mary. "Is it meant to be a secret?"

"Secret? What nonsense!" Her protest too loud, Mary darted a worried look at her sister. "By no means a secret."

"We have only just decided upon the plan," Joan said.

"And who is this?" Lord Kirby jovially welcomed the Pendleton sisters.

"But Father, you know our neighbors." Joan sounded embarrassed. "Comfort, Faith, and Charity."

Charity leaned forward and spoke very loudly. "You have known us since we were wee ones, sir."

"We are Vicar Pendleton's daughters, and live at the bottom of your park, my lord," Comfort reminded him.

"Yes," Faith chimed in. "It is only our cousin, Felicity, who is unknown to you."

"And how is it you know my son?" Lord Kirby asked blankly of Felicity.

Without the slightest sign of impatience, she announced, as if the news had never been revealed. "My deah man. Your son is a hero. He saved mah life, you see, when ah might have fallen through the ice on the pond at the bottom of your park."

"The vicar and his daughters live at the bottom of our park. Do you know them?" he asked.

"My cousins, suh." She gestured toward the girls. "The vicar was my father's brother. I wuz with my cousins at the pond when your son saved me."

She glanced up as she said it, her gaze locking briefly with Bingham's. He could have kissed her in that moment, for her words made his father beam with satisfaction.

"Mah first time on skates," she said, a smile on her lips. "Ah must admit, ah knew nothing of the dangers of thin ice."

"Balance is the key," Lord Kirby said with authority.

"Do you skate, suh?" She turned her attention back to the elder gent, endearing herself completely to Bingham.

Bingham's sisters carefully avoided all mention of the Christmas party during the remainder of the Pendletons' call. Bingham could not similarly avoid the topic. Would not.

"We are planning a house party," he announced as their neighbors stood to take their leave. "A fortnight of Yuletide frivolity. We shall have a houseful of guests, all of whom will be happy to make your acquaintance. You are invited to attend."

His news brought happy smiles and expressions of

gratitude from all but two, those two being his sisters, who took him to task as soon as their guests were gone.

"How could you invite them, Bing?" Mary asked.

"When we were so very careful to avoid doing just that," Joan said.

"And why should they not share in our fun? They have little enough in their lives to entertain them."

"They will spoil our numbers! We shall have far more ladies than men with four poor Pendletons added to the equation."

Bingham laughed. "Afraid they might ruin your chances with our wealthy guests?"

"No." Joan laughed caustically. "Afraid one of them will steal your heart. For then, without doubt, we shall all be paupers."

Frost starred the ground beneath the birch canopy, where dark-limbed trees caught the snow in dry-leafed aprons. The air was sweet, clear and crisp. The sky gazed back at him, blue-eyed beneath a topknot of high, white clouds. Everything glittered, diamond-dusted, as Bingham set out, horseback, in search of the perfect Yule log. A bittersweet joy, riding the park. The trees cut hard silhouettes, the fields lay barren and colorless, the streams lay locked in the gleaming bondage of ice. He found the land beautiful, comforting, a heartbreak.

The rocking gait of Tulip, his favorite saddle horse, pounded a familiar warming rhythm between his thighs. Steamed breath plumed from the bay's black velvet nose, from his own lips when he spoke to the gelding. Memories misted his mind. Many years he had aimlessly wandered these acres, secure in the belief it must one day be his. His birthright. His inheri-

tance. He had never considered all might be lost before he laid claim. Such thoughts ran contrary to the natural order of things.

As did thoughts of Felicity Pendleton, who filled his mind this morning.

He saw her first from a distance, the only brightness in the winter-dulled landscape, a bright red cape, cheerful and warm. His heart quickened to see it. Only one such red cape in the neighborhood, only one such long-limbed stride.

"Why Mr. Kirby," she called to him. "What a pleasure to see you again. A beautiful day to be outdoors."

Out-doe-wahs. Her voice was as vivid, as individual as the cape. Audacious—his sisters had determined the woman. Not only did she boldly walk the woods alone in her red cape, but she dared to address a gentleman she knew but little before he had opportunity to say a word in greeting. Bingham found her manner refreshing.

"A beautiful day on a beautiful bay," he quipped, gigging Tulip into a high-tailed high-step through the snow.

"An animal of exquisite conformation, to be sure," she said.

The bay brought him within a few feet of her. He reined in the gelding and clapped the glossy brown neck with affection. "I take joy in riding the solitude of these woods."

"Ah would nawt spoil that solitude, suh." She tugged at the brim of her hood, face hidden in its shadows. "You must simply pretend nawt to have seen me and ride on by on that beautiful bay."

He was certain she jested. "Think you I would behave so churlishly?"

She kept her face downturned, naught to be seen but scarlet cloaking.

"Do you mean to send me away as soon as we have met, Miss Pendleton?"

Pink-cheeked, red-nosed, bright of eye, she looked up from beneath the droop of scarlet hood, so abrupt her movement, Tulip threw his head up with a snort. The bay startled Miss Pendleton into a mirrored high-headedness. The bright folds of the red cloak slid back, so acute the angle of her head that a veritable flood of curls spilled free.

An unusual sight. Most young ladies wore their hair up beyond the age of their debut, a sign of their modesty. So much hair unbound was undeniably provocative. His own sisters let their hair down only when freshly washed or tucked into nightcaps.

Remarkably beautiful, this hair, heavy and dark as the limbs against the sky, and yet possessed of as much windblown vivacity and curl as its owner.

Bingham stared, and in staring realized that upon each cheek, beneath an uneasy flutter of dark lashes, glistened a trace of moisture. Had she been crying?

"Oh, de-ah," she said, cheeks flushing. She reached for the hood, hampered by the fall of the cloak, and the cascading weight of her waist-length locks.

"Here, let me help." He swung down from the saddle, despite the havoc frost and mud and wet brought to the high sheen of supple leather riding boots. Catching the tasseled end of her hood, one gloved hand came into brief contact with the sliding fall of unbound hair. He wanted to gather the glossy locks in both hands, to bury his nose in their faintly floral scented riches. He refrained, saying, "If you will be so good as to bunch

this up, we shall tuck it away, though it is a shame to cover something so beautiful."

"Ah thank you for the compliment. Ah know it is nawt the habit here to allow one's hair to fall free, but on such a cold day, ah thawt it would feel warmer upon mah neck."

He let go the fabric of her cloak with as much reluctance as he watched the glory of her hair confined.

"Tell me," she said, drawing the cloak close about her neck, "is it your land I trespass upon? I am in a mood to dress my aunt and uncle's cottage in the Christmas spirit. The chapel, too. But I would not strip your forest bare of holly and evergreens without permission."

"It is my land, at present," he said blandly. "I am myself in search of a Yule log. Perhaps we should pool our efforts."

"Ah should be glad of the company," she said.

He wondered if she meant it. Whatever her troubles, she had certainly come to the forest in order to weep privately.

"I believe we may find what we are seeking this way."

He tugged at the bay's reins. They set off side by side, boots blotting virgin snow. He hoped she might tell him what troubled her. It always seemed to settle his sisters' minds if induced to talk about their worries.

"Had none of your cousins fortitude enough to join you in your search, Miss Pendleton?" he ventured to ask.

"Ah slipped out without asking them to accompany me." She said it so quietly the sound of the horse following them almost drowned her out.

She cleared her throat, then said at greater volume,

"You will think me ungrateful, even selfish, but as an only child ah am accustomed to a great deal of quiet, and long moments alone to gather my thawts without interruption. Ah feel fortunate indeed to have such lovin' family to welcome me to this country. Mah cousins are lak the sisters ah never had. Mah aunt and uncle make me feel lak one of their own. But, their house is small, and within its confines ah do rarely find myself alone. There are times when my head gets to whirlin', when ah feel like bawlin' mah eyes out over Daddy . . ." Her voice broke.

"No need to explain. I lost my mother when I was twelve."

She peeped at him from the confines of her hood in surprise. "Ah am sorry to hear that. It must have been doubly difficult at such a young age."

"I do not think losing one's parent is easy at any age."

"No. You have the right of it." Her voice, that strange, mellifluous voice, now sounded fragile and brittle.

"You have lost homeland as well. I would imagine even the wind in the trees sighs differently here."

Her eyes sought his, the blue of them magnified, brightened with unshed tears. "How wonderfully you put things, suh. You are very kind. It's true. Ah ahm homesick. Ah did not realize how different the Season until Thanksgiving passed by as if just another day."

"Thanksgiving?"

"Yes. A day to count one's blessin's, a day to celebrate mah mother's New England forefathers. The Indians brought food, that they might survive their first winter."

"A lovely reason for a holiday."

"My father thought so. He always engaged in a day of feasting in Mother's honor. Wild turkey was the usual fare, with cornbread stuffing and New England cranberry sauce. Father always drank too much, especially when Mother was no longer alive to celebrate the day with us."

"How old were you when you lost her?" Bingham asked softly.

"Five," she said grimly. "She died in childbirth. The baby, too."

"I am sorry to have distracted you from the topic of Thanksgiving." He yearned to reach out to her, to smooth the line from her forehead, to lift the sadly downturned lips.

His redirection of their conversation did the trick. Her mood lightened. "The men would fire off their guns, and if there were firecrackers to be had, they were set off. Baskets of popcorn were roasted on the fire for the children. Ah would bake plum tarts from mah great grandmother's recipe, and Mammy Doe could be counted on to make a dozen or so of her wonderful sweet potato and Georgia pecan pies."

"Mammy Doe?" He was pleased to see her cheerful again.

"Our cook. She is . . . was a wonder in making up a feast to remember. She baked all mah favorites on the day ah left. Enough to pack up in baskets to take along on the ship. Ah did hate to leave her behind, but her folks are all livin' in America, and ah did not see much sense in uprootin' her that I might go to mine."

Though he had no luck in easing his own suffering, he felt within him a great urge to in some way ease hers.

"It is a pity nothing was done to celebrate your

Thanksgiving holiday, but perhaps something can still be done to make Christmas reminiscent? There are, sadly, no Georgia pecans or New England cranberry to be had, but plum tart is one of my favorites, and there will be sugarplums and plum pudding."

She laughed and seemed determined to put a brave face on it. "Do tell, suh! You make my mouth watah. Ah have been well fed in your country. There are delights and confections I have never tried at home."

"Such as? What have I been taking for granted?"

"Let me see. Gooseberries are new to me, and clotted cream, toffees and caramel sauce. Your cheeses, too, have been wonderful—Cheddar, Stilton, Wiltshire . . ."

He found he could not take his eyes from her profile as she spoke, could not stop thinking of the tumble of hair hidden away in her hood.

"Have ah a smudge on my nose, suh?"

"What? Oh! No. Forgive me. You have, as you say, set my mouth to watering, Miss Pendleton."

She looked past him, past his double entendre. "A Tannenbaum tree!" she cried. Stepping from the path, she stopped before an evergreen, blue berries clinging to blue green branches.

"A juniper," he said, tethering Tulip. "I do assure you all our trees are English."

She laughed. "Hessian mercenaries decorated little pine saplings about this size and shape during our Revolutionary War. They called them Tannenbaum."

"A sore point you touch upon—the American uprising," he said wryly.

"Oh, deah." She laughed. "Ah do beg your pardon. Is that what you cawl our war? An uprisin'?"

He was pleased to think he amused her. Anything to cheer her.

"Yes. That is what I cawl it."

"You're makin' fun of me."

"I am a dreadful tease. You must not take it to heart."

"So you find the way ah tawlk amusin', do you?"

"Fascinating. I could listen to you all day."

She blushed, turned her head that he might see no more than the edge of her hood, and said softly, "Ah keep thinkin' ah sound slow, stupid. Ah love to listen to the British tawlk. Your words are so crisp and clipped and . . ."

"Off-putting?"

She laughed again, a sound that brought a broad smile to his lips. "Owf-pudding? That is a term you would seldom hear used in Georgia. It was certainly nawt the word ah would choose to describe the sound of your voice."

"What then? Come. Give me your worst."

There was mischief in her glance. "Uppity." Her eyes twinkled as she said it.

He laughed outright. Tulip lifted his head curiously at the sound. In a whirring flurry two birds took wing.

"Uppity?" He chuckled. "Poor competition for a honeyed drawl."

"Suh!" She laughed, her breath a little cloud between them. "Are you flirtin' with me?"

Bingham sobered, considered. Was he? What mischief was he about? He had promised to make a good match, to save his sisters from a future as bleak as that which Miss Pendleton and her cousins faced.

"Not flirting," he said firmly, as much to convince

himself as her. "But I do have an uppity reputation to uphold."

She seemed to sense the change in his tone. Smile fading, she plucked a cluster of berries from the tree and lifted them in mittened hand to her nose. "Junipers always smell lak gin to me. Daddy's favorite drink."

He forced good cheer into his voice when he was feeling anything but cheerful. "The berries are used to flavor our local spirits. Shall I arrange to have it cut for you? This tannenbaum? Is there room for it in the vicar's cottage?"

"A shame to cut it," she said. "To end its laf when it looks so pretty all dusted in snow." Again the look of mischief. "Besides, Uncle, bein' a vicar, might not appreciate the smell of spirits hangin' about his parlor."

"It is candles they are decorated with. Is it not? The tannenbaum?"

"Little white ones. Ribbons, too. And small red apples."

"Like our kissing ball," he murmured. A mistake to have said so. His mind strayed immediately to the prospect of kissing Miss Pendleton's flushed face under such permissive auspices.

Brows raised, that sultry, suggestive voice of hers repeated, "Kissin' bawl?"

"Mistletoe. See, there is some hanging there, in that tree. Do you not have mistletoe in America?"

"Why, certainly. We hang it from doorways tied up with loops of ribbon."

"Exactly so." His voice was as rushed as his pulse, for he was determined not to think about kissing her. "Here the mistletoe bunch hangs in the middle of a wire ball trimmed in ribbon and a ring of candles and

red apples. My sisters make any number of them for the hol . . ."

"Is it true here, as back home, that when a woman is caught beneath the mistletoe she cannot refuse a kiss?" Her attention fixed on something above his head.

"Indeed, it is a quaint old custom."

"Ah am caught," she murmured.

He did not hear her, too busy rattling on. "Ancient, in fact. Nothing to do with Christmas really. I believe it was called the Golden Bough in classical legend."

Mischief in her smile again. He had to look up, knowing what he would find.

"The Druids held it sacred—believed it brought good luck and fertil . . ." A huge clump of mistletoe clung to the branch above their heads.

"We are in luck," she said quietly.

Once it was said, he could not refuse to kiss her. It really would have been rude, even insulting, to refuse.

He meant to give her a peck, just a quick peck, on the cheek. There could be nothing misconstrued in that.

She obligingly tipped up her chin, but the movement set her hood to slipping, and with it her hair cascaded loose, all in the instant that his mouth meant to meet her cheek, and in the distraction of all that beautiful, head-turning hair, he missed his mark, kissing her temple instead.

She laughed and said, "Oh, deah. Ah come undone!"

As before, he helped her with the hood, and once again she tucked away her hair. Clutching the red wool of her cowling, she tilted up her chin to say, "I think it only fair, you should be offered a second chance at that kiss."

Without so much as closing her eyes, she planted

her mouth squarely on his in a brief, friendly smack—
the kiss one delivered to a relative, a sister, a brother.
A disappointing kiss. A kiss so fleeting he had little
chance to so much as purse his lips.

The scent of her lingered, an impression of the red
wool warmth of her body pressed briefly to his, a sense
that a proper kiss would prove a pleasant experience.
But this was not a proper kiss. It was over.

She pulled away from his stupefied grasp on her
hood, saying, "Too much of a squeeze."

"What?"

"Fittin' the tree into Uncle's parlor."

"Tree? Oh. Yes, well . . . as you say."

They turned their backs on the juniper in silence. He
gathered up the bay's reins, as if nothing had happened, as if it were common practice to take mistletoe
kisses in the woods. Together they walked on, the wind
sighing in the bare limbs above, their footsteps loud in
the snow, the horse at their heels champing at the bit.

His mind fixed on the disappointment of taking so
little part in their kiss. His gaze fixed on the branches
above their heads in hope of more mistletoe.

Silence piled up between them like a snowdrift.

A thought popped into his head. He blurted, "I must
take you to see my favorite tree."

"A favorite, among so many?" She swiveled her
head to look at the trees, not at him.

"Had you not a favorite when you were a child? A
hiding place?"

"What had you to hide from?"

Sorrow, he might have said. The sound of his sisters
weeping, the sight of his father's haggard expression
every time he set eyes on something that had been his
mother's.

"Sisters," he said. "Rather like you running from your cousins. As the only boy, and the youngest, I did like to quit their company now and again."

"Ah would have liked to have sisters," she said. "Or a brother lak you, with whom ah might have tawlked about anything, as we seem to be able to tawlk about anything."

He knew not what to say to that. What would it be like to be an only child? An only child deprived of both parents?

"It is a chestnut tree," he said. "My pony, a canny, mean-spirited creature, unseated me by way of its lowest branch. Left this scar upon my forehead."

She leaned close to look, the hood lending her whole countenance an appealing pink cast, her breath misting before his eyes as she crooned, "Aw! Poor little boy."

Her lips, so close to his, were tempting, but he must not be tempted. He laughed away her concern and turned away from her to give Tulip's velvety nose a rub. "Foolish lad. I should have mastered the brute far better. Flat on my back he left me, staring dazedly up at a tree that became far greater friend than the animal ever was."

"He was friend enough to introduce the two of you."

Her manner, her way of looking at the world, words sliding sweet and wise from her tongue, made her every utterance a fresh surprise.

"So he did." He chuckled. "And carried many a bushel of nuts upon his broad back in the October months. I built a tree house in the lower branches, and sat for hours reading, dreaming, imagining my future."

"Has it turned out as you supposed?"

Her words gave him unexpected pain. His smile hid a grimace. "No."

"No," she echoed. "Does life ever follow the expected pattern?"

"A boring affair if it did," he said briskly, no inclination to go maudlin. "Ah, here we are. See how the ground is littered with nuts? Far more than usual." He bent to pluck up one of the spiny-balled seed pods that crunched beneath their feet.

"Oh, de-ah!" she said.

He knew, even before he looked up, that the tree was in trouble. Too many nuts on the ground. And bits of fallen bark and branches. There was even a volunteer sapling sprouted at the base of the trunk, nature's effort that though the parent tree died, its rootstock might bloom again.

His chestnut was dying, one side scarred, top burned black, bark peeling away.

"Lightin'," she said.

"Struck to the heartwood," he agreed.

The chestnut, he decided, must be chopped down and used for the Yule log. An honorable end to his old friend, though it pained him to see it topple under the blows of the woodsman's axe.

An end perfectly timed. If he must lose his hold on the land, then so too, it seemed, must his childhood companion, the tree.

On Christmas Eve, his friends Tom, Gareth, Timothy, Stewart, Brett, Howard, and George, warmly dressed and fortified with cups of hot rum punch, to the tune of the most ribald Christmas ditties the lads could think of, dragged the downed tree trunk into the Great Hall fireplace.

They were in rare form. The hall, as they came in singing, red-cheeked from the cold, was rich with the smell of oranges, cloves, and fresh-cut wood. The female members of the party had spent the afternoon decking the Hall with holly, ivy, and bayberry. Boughs of yew and juniper twisted into patterns enlivened the walls. Evergreens bristled like an old man's brows atop the picture frames about the room. A fine, rosined fragrance bespoke the Season.

A merry party, they rolled the log into place. A cheerful scene, bright as the brass andirons, busy as the placement of kindling, as brisk as the striking of the match. There were none to know the wrenching of his heart to see an old friend put to flames.

None but Felicity Pendleton. She sent a look of commiseration his way when the stick of wood from the previous year's log kindled flame about the old chestnut's ribs.

Between their eyes sprang a silent, heated language of understanding and compassion. His gaze lingered. He allowed his head a slight nod, his lips a slighter smile. And then he turned away.

His guests required his attention.

He did his best to devote time to his sisters' friends—Corisande, Anthea, Victoria, Glynis, Nola, Edwina, and Rose. He knew them each by name, sat with one on either side at dinner, chatted with a third as they moved to the drawing room after the fruit cake was served, and made a point of exchanging a word or two with the fourth when the men returned from their brandy and cigars.

They were nice girls, all—two of them quite pretty.

Glynis had beautiful eyes, spoke three languages fluently, and was dowried with an annuity of more than

five thousand a year. Edwina had an engaging smile, a winning way with servants, and an impressive inheritance from her dowager aunt.

Victoria was blessed with the profile of an Italian cameo, the voice of an angel, and thriving properties in Devon. Anthea, a delightful musician on both harp and pianoforte, was the only child of a wealthy spice trader.

Rose, a well-endowed widow, was a model of charitable thought and deed. He spoke to her at length about God over dinner, the topic close to her heart, second only to her fascination with the lucrative banana plantation in the West Indies that had claimed the life of her recently departed spouse.

Corisande kept disappearing into the library. She was enormously well read, with a thorough understanding and interest in politics, antiquities, and the noble lineage that made her father one of the wealthiest lords in England.

They were each of them likeable, laudable. They mingled with every evidence of good nature and cheer. His friends claimed they had never met a more charming bevy of beauties. His sisters took him aside to promote their favorites and to ask if he had formed any kind of preference.

He knew not what to say.

He could not tell Mary that all else paled when Felicity Pendleton stepped into a room. He could not announce to Joan that his eyes were drawn to a poverty-stricken Pendleton whenever she moved or spoke, that he longed above all else to be alone with her and her alone, that his pulse raced as tumultuously as if he were poised yet again to drag her back from the brink of a cold and watery grave.

A ludicrous notion. *He* needed rescuing, not she. A few leaves from a money tree, as his father suggested. The daily flood of bills for the expenses incurred in making this Yuletide celebration possible proved daily reminder.

He shoved aside all thoughts of debt when they settled by the fire for a game.

"Forfeits!" he announced cheerfully.

"Oh, lovely!" Comfort said.

"Are we not to play cards?" Glynis asked.

"Explain!" Felicity Pendleton called out. "Ah do nawt know this game of fo'fits."

" 'Tis nothing but wordplay," her cousin Charity said. "Silly words really."

"And silly rhymes," Victoria added.

"How does it begin?"

"Tell her, Bing." Brett poked him in the ribs.

"Come!" He held out his hand. "You shall be our first player."

She gave him her hand. He led her to a centrally placed chair, took another by the back, and seated himself knee to knee with her.

Her brows rose, her eyes twinkled expectantly.

"Listen carefully. I mean to recite a rhyme, which you must repeat to me without error."

"That does nawt sound so very difficult."

Chuckles sounded from the gathered party who knew otherwise.

Bingham raised his hand for silence. "If you should fail in the repetition, then I shall require some small article from your person as forfeit for your failure."

"Whut kind of article?"

"A pin. A smelling salts bottle. Your handkerchief or glove."

"And if you wish the return of it . . ." Joan leaned forward to say gleefully. "He shall require the forfeit of your pride in the doing of some small task—"

"Generally humiliating," George interrupted.

Bingham chuckled. "Justly so."

"I have the idea," Felicity said with a saucy grin. "Give me your rhyme or riddle, suh. I have a goo-ud ear."

He smiled at her before blurting: "A twister of twist once twisted a twist, and the twist that he twisted was a three-twisted twist; but in twisting the twist one twist came untwisted, and the twist that untwisted, untwisted the twist."

Laughter again. Her mouth had dropped open.

Bingham merrily expected her to fail, but with a determined expression she set off, pausing only once to search her memory, and to a round of wine-mellowed cheers and applause, carried the thing off without a hitch.

Triumphant, she beamed at him, and then, one brow raised, announced, "And whut must you fo'fit to me, mah Lord of Misrule, now that ah have successfully completed yowah tongue-twister? Will you attempt to repeat the one ah have for you in return?"

The gathering cried out their approval, teasing him into compliance.

Bingham nodded. "I am man enough for it."

Wearing the look of a cat who plays with the mouse, her rhyme galloped from her lips, as if any simpleton could say, "Peter Piper picked a peck of pickled peppers. If Peter picked a peck of pickled peppers, where's the peck of pickled peppers Peter Piper picked?"

Her words set them all to laughing.

He did his best to repeat the thing. It was more dif-

ficult than he had expected, and there was something terribly funny about the way his own pronunciation made the words sound. Pompous, he thought. No, *uppity*.

A few snickers, but in the end he had them doubled over with guffaws when he slipped, creating the amusing misnomer Peeper Piker.

Comfort called to her cousin, "You must take forfeit from him, Felicity. You are well due something for such a good show."

"Whut would you fo'fit?" She laughed as she spoke.

"What would you have of me?"

She seemed at a loss, and cast about among the group, fishing for advice, "What should I ay-ask for?"

"His stickpin. That diamond is worth a mint," Tim suggested. "He shall pay dearly to have it back again."

"A cufflink," Gareth said.

"A dance. He is not fond of dancing," her cousin Hope said.

Felicity stilled them with a wave of her hands. "I have it!" She beckoned him closer. "Yoah hand, suh," she said.

"Oh ho! Do you mean to marry our master of mischief?" George's quip set them all to laughing.

"Ah do nawt think he will have me," Felicity said wryly. "But ah will have, as fo'fit, the ring from your finger, suh."

Her hands warm against his, she slid the ring over his knuckle.

He caught her wrist. "My signet? I think not."

"Would you refuse me, suh?" She slid the heavy gold ring onto her thumb.

Her cousin Charity giggled. "He must beg to redeem it."

He knew she did not expect him to lower his head to her lap, facedown, the velvet soft against his cheeks, the achingly sweet odor of perfume strong.

She stiffened and moved deeper into the chair, legs clapping together as if to snip off his nose. "De-ah me! Whut are you doin', suh?"

The musculature of her thighs was enticingly firm as she poised for flight.

The party was loud with amused suggestions.

Corisande muttered to her chaperone in a voice loud enough to be heard by all, "I do not care for this vulgar country pastime," before the door closed on their exit.

"He must beg," Tom's voice, above him, explained. "Facedown in your lap. It is the rule of forfeiture."

"Strange ru-ule, ah must say." Felicity laughed gamely enough, but her legs, beneath the thin sheath of dress and petticoat, evidenced her readiness for the burden of his head to be gone.

Bingham mumbled, his words hot against the velvet, her lap uneasy beneath him, "I beg you will allow me to keep my ring, Miss Pendleton."

She laughed uneasily, asking of the others in that suggestive drawl, "Whut am ah to do with a man whose head plays lap dawg?"

Bingham could think of any number of suggestions.

One of the gentlemen, it sounded like Brett, gave a very ungentlemanly imitation of a dog howling.

"You must hold up the ring," Mary directed impatiently. "And say, 'Here's a ring, a very pretty ring! What must the owner do to redeem it?'"

Felicity's voice repeated the words above his head. He could feel every movement of her limbs in his odd position. She was nervous, gamely playing along, and

breathlessly trying to hide between clenched thighs a desire that could not be disguised.

"Make him balance on one leg in the four corners of the room," someone shouted.

"See if he can stand on his head."

"Make him your lapdog for the evening."

"Ahem!" The gentle clearing of a throat as Peel interrupted. "I do beg your pardon, sir."

Bingham reluctantly lifted his head, cheeks aflame.

Peel hovered in the doorway. At his heels was a dapper if rather rotund little man with a pointy mustache and beard, wearing a distinctive fur-trimmed coat.

"Mr. Benson, sir," Peel announced coolly as if he might not recognize the solicitor.

Humiliated to be caught in such a position, Bingham rose, bowed to Miss Pendleton, and said tersely, "Excuse me, mistress, but your lapdog has a bone to pick elsewhere."

"Is his nose wet?" Brett murmured wryly behind him.

"Any healthy cur's would be," Stewart replied snidely.

Felicity must have read some sign of concern in his eyes. Smile fading, she said, "Nothin' serious, ah hope."

He forced a smile and murmured something suitably noncommittal.

"No chasing the cat," George teased as he crossed the room.

"Does our lapdog have a bone?" Howie wore a mischievous grin.

"One can only hope he is house-trained," Gareth jested.

Bingham ignored the lot of them, eyes fixed on Benson, jaw set, all humor fled.

"I had no idea, sir, that you would have guests." Benson looked about him a trifle askance.

"Shall we retire to a quieter room?" Bingham, mock cordial, guided him away from the party.

"But of course. I do apologize for intruding."

They gained the privacy of the study, a room that never failed to remind Bingham of the keen reader his father had been. He waved his guest to a chair, shut the door, and leaned upon it, saying facetiously to this gentleman who had so poorly managed their affairs, "You came all the way from London, on Christmas Eve? You are too good, sir."

The man did not seriously expect to find himself welcomed, did he?

Benson smiled, as if they were the best of friends. "My wife's mother abides in the neighborhood. Once here I could not enjoy the holiday without calling on you to see how your father does."

"My father, sir, would have it that you are not to be trusted." Bingham's tone was as chill as the frost upon the windowpane.

Benson's round chin wobbled. "Indeed, sir. He said as much to my face, and in no uncertain terms, sir, on the last occasion we spoke."

"As our accounts stand empty, the money all flown, I am inclined to agree with him."

Benson licked his lips and cleared his throat. "I feared as much. It has preyed on my mind, sir. My honor had never before been questioned, and as my business relies on the trust of my clients, I felt it imperative we speak."

"Where has all the money gone?" Bingham asked coldly.

"But, sir"—Benson wore a dumbfounded expression—"it is noted in the ledgers. And quite alarming, too. Your father's massive withdrawals . . . in the last six months . . . I did send you word by post, sir, but the letter"—he drew a battered wax-sealed pouch from his coat pocket—"if you will study the postmarks, sir, having followed you the length of Italy, has since been returned to me as undeliverable."

Bingham took the pouch, troubled by the unsettling sensation that the world spun. "What do my sisters know of this?"

"Nothing, sir. It never occurred to me, sir, to consult them. The onset of your father's memory lapses was so gradual. I knew you were on your way home, sir. I knew your father had no intention of spending the money, simply of removing it from my care."

Bingham tore open the pouch, perused briefly the pages within, and muttered, "What did he do with it?"

"The money, sir? I was hoping you could tell me," Benson replied.

Joan held the lantern high in her mittened hand, the better to study Bingham's face. "Do you mean to say Father has hidden vast sums of money and no longer remembers where?" Her breath misted white against the darkness of the night.

"I do," Bingham said.

Mary bent to the basket at her feet, plucked up an apple on a string, and hung it from one of the bare branches. "You may rest assured he has not spent it. We are in need of a roof repair above the west wing,

and so I have told him on more than one occasion. More light, Joan," she begged. "I fall into darkness."

"What does Father say?" Joan, teeth chattering, ignored her.

"I have yet to ask him." Bingham stretched high to dangle a suet ball rolled in bird seed from his side of the juniper, Miss Pendleton's juniper. Suet stained his gloves. Fallen bird seed sprinkled his boots. "He was too tired, too muddled this evening, and we had the tree yet to do. I will ask him tomorrow."

"And if he does not remember?"

"He keeps mentioning a money tree."

"Dear God! Do you think he has hidden your inheritance in a tree?"

"The money tree means nothing else to either of you?"

They looked at one another bleakly and shook their heads.

"If anyone would know, it is Peel," Joan said firmly.

"And if he does not?" Mary pressed.

"We shall have a treasure hunt on our hands," Bingham said.

"Lud! And how many hundreds of trees do we have to search?" Mary asked, turning on her heel to stare into the tree-filled darkness.

"It would have to be a tree with a hole in it," Bingham reminded her.

"A pretty idea," Joan said.

They looked at her in confusion.

"*This* tree." She stood back to admire their handiwork. The little juniper was richly dressed in bright ribbons, red apples, clove-studded oranges, and bird seed suet balls.

"A festive surprise for our guests as they walk to

chapel in the morning," Mary agreed. "Whatever gave you the notion to do such a thing, Bing?"

Bingham gathered up the baskets he had carried into the night, and plucked up his lantern. "Miss Pendleton," he admitted.

His sisters exchanged worried looks. He did not miss their heavily shadowed frowns in the meager light of the lantern.

"Is this an American tradition? This Tannenbaum?" Joan brushed bird seed from his coat lapel.

"German, actually," he said. "The German soldiers—"

"You do not think it singles her out too much?" Mary held high her lantern, shedding fresh light upon his face. "I would not want the poor girl to get the wrong impression, the mistaken idea that you care for her more than you do."

"It is no more than a trifling kindness," he protested. "She mentioned herself homesick."

"I do hope you have not taken a fancy to Felicity." Joan, her back to them, set off toward the Hall, her lamp throwing uneasy shadows from the nearby trees. "After all, it would be cruel to give the girl false hopes."

"Indeed, which of our worthy guests *do* you care for?" Mary asked, for perhaps the twentieth time.

Corisande, Anthea, Glynis, and Edwina chose to ride in Gareth's carriage the following morning. The rest of their party braved the outdoors in the short, invigorating walk through the woods to Vicar Pendleton's chapel.

The sun was out, the snow asparkle, and to please his sisters, Bingham tucked Victoria Hansen's gloved

hand into the crook of his arm, that they two might converse a little as he eyed the glittering forest for likely money trees. She was a great talker, he discovered.

"I am a lover of horses," she revealed. "And a great fan of the races."

"Brett," he mentioned, "loves nothing more than a day at the track."

Overhearing, Brett broke away from a discussion with Stewart to join them. And when the pathway narrowed, it was Bingham who stepped back, while Brett thoughtfully held aside a branch, that Tory, as she liked to be called, might not bump her head.

Lord Kirby had stopped beside the Tannenbaum tree. His thinning, flossy white hair caught the morning light. It glowed about his face like a halo. With an expression of childish delight he stared at the suet balls and apples.

"Bingham, my boy!" He gestured with the walking stick that punched holes in the snow with his every step. "A lovely morning. A lovely thing, this tree."

"The deer seem to like it," Bingham said. "See the teeth marks in this apple?"

"Your mother would have loved it. Loved trees, she did. Always in the orangery when you were young, fussing with the lemons and pineapples."

"I remember," Bingham said, full of hope and yet troubled by guilt that he found hope in his father's mention of his mother in the past tense. His mind showed a keenness to match the bite of the wind this morning.

"Father, there is something I must ask you."

"What's that, lad? Ask away."

"The money you withdrew from Benson's care, Father. Where is it?"

"Withdrew?" Lord Kirby wore the baffled look that more often than not marked his features when questions were posed. "Why should I do such a thing?"

"I've no idea, sir. I was hoping you could tell me. We are in need of funds, my lord."

"Bills, is it, lad?"

"Bills, sir, yes sir. And repairs to the Hall."

"Why did you not come to me before?"

Heart sinking, Bingham rubbed at his forehead with a sigh. "I should have, sir."

"Never fear. You shall not want, my boy. I have but to inform Benson, and the money is on its way."

Bingham closed his eyes, defeated. "That money tree has lost its leaves," he murmured, tugging a frond from the Tannenbaum tree and wondering if the money might be hidden in the orangery.

Bingham sat with his father, his sisters, ten attendant guests, and five attendant chaperones in the family pew. Peel sat separately, as did the Misses Pendleton, who sang in the choir. Bingham shared a hymnal with Rose Grantham, while sharing stolen glances across the aisle with Felicity Pendleton, who sat quietly beside her aunt.

He admired the flush on her cheeks as she sang, admired the expression of peace on her features as certain passages were read, admired the new dresses the Pendleton sisters happily claimed as gifts from their cousin when their choir robes were removed.

He complimented the vicar on his sermon reminding them that this was the Season of giving in the purest sense of the word. He had promised himself, and God,

that he would give himself to the task of marrying well. A gift to his sisters.

And so, despite his heart's desire to spend the morning staring into blue eyes rather than brown, he focused his attention on Rose Grantham as their party walked back to the Hall.

"Goodness me!" Felicity won his attention in flying off the path to circle the decorated juniper, eyes bright. "A Tannenbaum for the birds. How chawming!"

Her gaze sought his—eyes bright, mouth merry.

He could not return the smile. His sisters' fears of fostering hope where there was no hope to be had, resounded. Another female clutched at his arm. He must not forget.

Mary said swiftly, "I am pleased you like it, Felicity. Joan and I heard you were homesick. We came out in the cold last night to decorate."

Bingham blinked with surprise that his sister would so pointedly leave him out of the endeavor.

Felicity Pendleton's gaze fell away from his. "How thawtful." She directed the remark to his sisters. "So very thawtful."

Bingham went alone to the back garden as soon as they returned to the Hall, his footsteps the first to pass along the path since the latest snow. He had let the head gardener and his lads go. The untouched snow made a still, white winterland of the grounds.

His guests went in to warm themselves by the fire. As he circled the house, he could hear Anthea playing "Good King Wenceslas" on the pianoforte. His guests, laughing, enjoying themselves, joined in to sing.

He was in no mood for music, for song. His mind

was again on the cost of Christmas, on the elusive mystery of where his father's money tree bloomed.

The orangery, no longer steam-heated, was bleak—frigid. Not perfumed now with oranges, lemons, and pineapples, the odor of moldy soil and decaying plants assaulted his nose. Rows of pots stood empty; others held the dry-leafed corpses of trees.

There was no hiding place for his inheritance in this sadly barren landscape, only reminders of what had once been taken for granted.

He did not realize himself followed until a shadow fell against the glass. The door to the orangery squealed open.

"Whut a shame," Felicity said. "They are awl dead!"

"Yes," he agreed. "A shame."

"Whatever made you come out he-ah?" she asked.

"I might very well ask you the same."

She ducked her head, the red hood hiding her from his eyes momentarily. He did not want her to be hidden, did not want to embarrass her.

"I'm sorry," he said. "I do apologize. It was rude of me to ask."

"It was rude of me to follow you, but ah did not think we would have opportunity for privacy otherwise, with so many guests at the Hall. Ah wanted to thank you for the tree. It wuz your idea and nawt your sisters, wuz it nawt?"

He was too recently reminded of the miserable state of his affairs to want to claim credit. It would not do, as his sisters had so baldly pointed out to him, to make himself too much the hero in this young woman's eyes.

"We three wanted to make you feel a little less homesick," he said, his tone and manner as chill, as brittle, as the leaves on the abandoned orange trees.

Few words between them, he walked with her back to the Hall, an uneasy tension building, one that she seemed determined to lighten.

She hummed "God Rest Ye Merry, Gentlemen" as they crossed in silence the flat, untrampled stretch of snow that made white the bowling green. A kissing ball hung above the door they were to enter. He could not take eyes or thought from it.

Her grip shifted. She broke off humming to suggest gleefully, "Temptin', isn't it?"

"Tempting?" Thought she of kisses, too?

"It is the perfect place, don't you agree?" She gestured to the bowling green.

"Perfect? In what way?"

"For makin' snow angels." She let go of his arm to break a fresh path, turned with a gleeful smile, and holding out her mittened hands, said, "Come! Lower me."

He could not refuse. Clasping fast her mittened fingers, he lowered her into the unblemished snow, watching, amused, as she moved arms and legs to create wings and skirt. Her cheeks were in high color, snow all over her red cloak when she held out her hand to him, laughing and saying, "Ah feel like a girl again! Yo-ah turn."

He helped her up. "I've no desire to make a cake of myself."

"A cake?" She laughed. "How very British. Come, suh. You cannot refuse to get a bit of Christmas icin' on your back."

She grabbed his hands, leaned back to brace herself against his lowering, and gave a happy little shriek when he landed softly in the snow.

"Now flap your wangs," she directed. "It will put you in a holiday mood."

He had to admit it was fun. The snow was a cold cushion, smooth and ready for his impression. A temporary mark to make on the world, yet it seemed fitting this year of all years, to cut snow angels in the bowling green he might never bowl again.

They made a row of them, wings touching, like paper doll cutouts. Covered in snow, blood racing, cheeks rosy, he laughed as hard as she, money woes forgotten. Not even the snowball she dashed atop his head could spoil his mood.

He chased after her, snow flying, chest heaving, and caught up to her as she gained the doorway, snowball ready.

"Oh, no!" She laughed, throwing up mittened hands to guard her face. "Ah ahm caught!"

It was not the snowball he launched then, but a kiss, moved not by temptation so much as by the glowing moment of breathless joy she had managed to make of the afternoon. Cold and wet, he pressed heated lips to hers, beneath the kissing ball. A proper kiss this time, full on the lips. Not at all brotherly.

She responded in a manner not at all sisterly.

But for the melting snow dripping from the rooftop, in that instant the world stood still, nothing in it but the shared heat of wind-chapped lips, the shared cloud of their breath, the smell of cinnamon and flowers filling his nose, while one hand traced the seam of her woolen hood and the other slid inside her cloak to find the heat of her waist.

An abrupt spill of warm air and lamplight cut short his bliss, parting them. The door opened to reveal Peel. He showed no surprise at seeing them standing there,

arm in arm, wearing guilty looks and a generous powdering of snow.

"The Misses Pendleton," he announced with his customary dearth of emotion, "are looking for their cousin."

"Are they?" Felicity's color was high. "We've been makin' snow angels, Peel. I cannawt remember the last time ah had such fun."

"Very good, miss."

She stepped inside. Peel gingerly took her cape and held it, dripping, at arm's length. "Your cousins, miss, are in the drawing room."

She paused a moment to shoot a look in Bingham's direction, before proceeding to the drawing room with an impish smile.

As Peel helped Bingham with the removal of his overcoat, he said in an undervoice, "There is a gentleman who insists on being paid, sir, in your study."

"The butcher?" Bingham asked, reality cooling the heat of passion. The butcher had dunned him three times.

"No, sir. The confectioner refuses to be sent away again, sir. I did try."

"Yes, Peel. And my father?"

"With your guests, sir. I did not think it prudent to bother him with such details."

"Yes. Quite right. Have you any idea, Peel, where he keeps a money box or safe I might not know about?"

"Sir?"

"Benson claims Father made withdrawals."

"And do you trust him, sir?"

"There is a certain logic to what he said, given Father's condition. Do you know of any such monies?"

"No, sir. Your father kept business matters private."

"Of course."

"Is that all, sir?"

"One more question. Has my father a favorite tree, Peel?"

"I believe he likes beeches, sir."

"Any one tree in particular?"

Peel shook his head, surprise ghosting across his features. "Not that I'm aware of, sir. Is it important?"

Bingham sighed. "Vitally so."

The confectioner paid, and a plan in mind to ride the woods, hunting money trees in the morning, Bingham played jovial host the rest of Christmas Day. He was, after all, Lord of Misrule, master of mischief, charming, attentive, most accommodating of hosts.

He would find a woman he liked. He would provide a solution to the family's monetary woes. He would do it with a smile, a glad heart, a merry countenance. It was a Season of merriment, was it not? A Season of happiness, hope, good friends, and good cheer?

He agreed to sell his traveling coach to Howie. Howard had long admired the vehicle.

"A fine Christmas gift that you should let me have it at last," his friend said.

Bingham smiled and refrained from informing him that his all-too-welcome bank draft kept hovering butchers and confectioners at bay, that even more pressing bills must be met, that the Boxing Day provisions for the local poor must be arranged, as was customary. That none of it would have been possible without the sale of the coach.

He smiled as he juggled money, smiled as he conversed with the female guests, and smiled through a

feast of proportion and variety he could no longer afford.

Cook had outdone himself in preparations for the table, every dish festive, irresistible, and expensive: boar's head, buttered lobsters, a roast duck, ham, lamb cutlets, and a huge roast beef. As centerpieces, a turreted gingerbread castle, a pinnacle of fruit, and a butter ship that sailed a sea of blanched endive. The side dishes were too numerous to be counted. Wine flowed like water. All begged to be tasted. All bespoke a wealth and prosperity Bingham had formerly taken for granted.

He was smiling still, cheeks aching, when the flaming, blue-lit, holly-topped Christmas pudding was brought into the darkened dining room.

He smiled in reminding his guests, "Be careful you do not bite too hard into your future."

He refrained from answering when Felicity Pendleton asked, with a glance in his direction, "What does that mean?"

Her cousin Charity explained that silver trinkets had been baked into the cake and that she must poke her pudding with her fork until she was sure there was nothing harder than the sauce in every mouthful.

He kept smiling even when he discovered his piece of pudding held the silver sixpence. A good sign, this omen of coming wealth, and yet, at what cost? He looked about the table at the young women who might give him wealth. And he smiled, though his heart wept for them.

It was only when his gaze settled on Felicity, whose trinket was not so happily portentous, that his smile faded. She quietly slipped into her pocket the silver thimble of spinsterhood as her cousin whispered its

meaning to her, while Victoria Hansen held high the silver ring of an upcoming wedding.

That night, the door to his bedchamber shut on the houseful of guests, all smiles and light extinguished, shutting out the sight of more bills, always more bills, stacked upon his desk, Bingham's thoughts turned again to Miss Felicity Pendleton.

It was her voice his ears were attuned to in every conversation. Her laughter lived in his memory, her perfume in his nose. Magnolia she had identified it when asked. An American flower, like a gardenia, big and white and sweet. Her lips he remembered upon his, firm and clinging, her hands in his as she safely lowered him into the snow, and he, trusting her grip, falling, falling, falling.

He dreamed himself drowning and her with him, then woke to find another morning come and his head yet above water. He spent the morning riding the woods. No money tree to be found. Before nuncheon was served, he negotiated the sale of a collection of Greek vases to Gareth. Over a plate of cold ham he planted the idea he might be willing to discuss selling his favorite hunting dog to Tom.

It was Boxing Day, the first day of Christmas, and as was their custom, he and his sisters, Rose Grantham at his side, set out that afternoon to deliver boxes of food, gifts, and coin to the servants and tenants. The Pendleton, alas, put in no appearance—engaged, he knew, in their own Boxing Day deliveries to the poor.

His houseguests reassembled that evening at his mother's huge and much admired dining table for another exquisite meal, and a game of snapdragon. It was a country pastime, involving a large bowl piled high

with brandy-soaked raisins, which in the darkened room were set afire and while they blazed, were plucked from the flames with bare fingers, and popped, still burning, into the mouths of all who dared.

Everyone enjoyed the evening but Bingham. He missed what he considered the greater fire of Felicity Pendleton's presence.

The second day of Christmas he once more rode the woods without luck. That evening he lost at cards, afforded no more than an occasional exchange of glances with Felicity, who sat at a separate table. He dutifully cultivated the acquaintance of Anthea Trent.

On the third day, following another fruitless morning in the woods, the sun brightened, the snow began to melt, and charades was the game of the evening. His whole life a charade at this point, Bingham took little joy in more pretense. His guests never suspected their host unhappy, especially Glynis McNab, with whom he amiably enacted a platitude or two.

On the fourth day of Christmas he and all potential brides and suitors went riding in the woods. Largely clear of snow, the ground was not yet soft enough to get bogged down in. The game was hunt-and-seek. They were, in pairs, to find as many trees with hollows in them as they could, marking each with a colored flag. Joan and Mary declared the game a stroke of genius. The Pendletons, who owned but one horse to draw the vicar's gig, were unaccustomed to the saddle. They begged off from the excursion.

Felicity sent him a note. She knew how to ride well enough, but would not abandon her cousins.

He spent the day in Edwina Drake's company.

The game successfully entertained his guests, who

competed fiercely to locate pockmarked trees. Bingham decided the day a miserable failure. No bags of gold or wads of soft were discovered, only three abandoned bird's nests and a handful or two of squirreled-away acorns. His father's money tree remained a mystery, and he longed for Felicity Pendleton's company.

On the fifth day of Christmas it rained.

Bingham sent his carriage to the vicarage. The Pendletons must join them for dinner and games. He instructed the coachman he would not take no for an answer.

They did not refuse him.

A cozy evening it proved, and festive. All gathered around the long dining table, their stomachs full of good food, their heads swimming with fine wine and finer brandy, the Yule log crackling on the fire.

To begin the game, seven tea carts were rolled in from the kitchen by seven footmen, resplendent in gold-trimmed livery. On each cart a silver serving dome, beneath each dome a large silver bowl, one for every four guests. They watched as the bowls were filled with finely sifted flour, dry drifts of snow coaxed into powdery white peaks in the middle of the bowl. Atop each flour hillock, the head footman gently placed a single shining bullet.

"What's this?" Nola Bettison asked, intrigued.

"Bullet pudding," Bingham announced to the tune of chuckles from those who knew the game. "The idea is that each of you must cut a slice from the pudding without causing the bullet to fall."

"And when it does?" Tom called out.

"Why then, whoever made it fall must attempt to retrieve the bullet . . ."

"Small challenge," George said snidely.

". . . using their teeth," Bingham clarified.

Mingled laughter and indignant cries of protest sounded.

"You jest!" George said.

"But our clothes!" Nola complained.

"Aprons are available." Bingham smiled as the footmen produced seven matching starched white aprons. "A word of warning before you begin. The one who goes facedown in the pudding had best not laugh. I would not have any of you choking on a lung full of flour."

Only Corisande refused to participate, at the behest of her chaperone, a maiden aunt by the name of Biggersley. "Green velvet would be completely ruined, my dear," she insisted. "Ladies must not make a laughingstock of themselves, or their clothes."

The rest of the company, chaperones included, merrily took part in the messy game.

Bingham started off his foursome with a successful slice, and sat back to watch the others' progress—most especially that of Miss Felicity Pendleton, whose slice came third among her foursome of players.

The flour tumbled, and with it the bullet. A shout went up.

Nola, who sat opposite, brought his attention back to the game. "Bingham, your turn."

He took up the cake slicer.

"Ah shall require an apron," Felicity drawled.

Distracted, he made his cut too hastily. The bullet in his bowl toppled, to the amusement of his pudding partners.

"Apron please!" he called out wryly.

Young, the footman, shook out fresh linen.

Felicity's gaze met his, eyes sparkling with merriment. In a tandem state of humiliation their tapes were tied.

"Here goes," she said. "No sniggerin', now. Ah don't want to die laughin', facedown in a bowl of what you folk call puddin'.'"

Brett elbowed him. "On with it, Bing. Stout heart, old man, and quick teeth."

Bing paused, head poised above the bowl, eyes locked on Felicity Pendleton's just long enough for her to shock him with a cheeky wink.

Smiling, he went chin first into the flour, laughter erupting on all sides as the real business of the game commenced. Cool and soft the flour upon his skin, dry and flat the taste upon his tongue. Flour tickled his nose. He shut his eyes, held his breath, and bit into the powder, waiting for the click of the bullet against flour-coated teeth. Gently grasping the thing, flour sticking to lips and tongue, flour falling from nose, lashes, and hair, he rose from the bowl, triumphant.

"Ta-da! He's done it!" Glynis crowed.

From Felicity's direction, as he wiped flour from his face, came a similar uproar.

"Good show, my dear!"

"She's got it, she has."

Blinking owlishly, swiping flour from mouths and noses, they gazed at the wreckage of one another's features, and burst out laughing, flour spraying in all directions.

Not so entertained, a flour-covered Anthea threw her apron over her head and dashed from the room, her chaperone at her heels.

"I told you a young lady ought not embarrass herself in such a fashion," Biggersley gloated to her charge.

Corisande, who laughed as heartily as anyone else, ignored her. Bingham liked her the better for it.

Waving his befloured fellows together, he announced, "Those of us who are unfit to be seen will remove ourselves for repairs while the rest of you are free to proceed to the drawing room."

Laughter drifted up from the chairs and away into the drawing room, while the pudding victims, trailed by fine white drifts and helpful, stone-faced footmen, giggled their way to the buttery. Steaming washbowls and fresh linen awaited them, along with the willing assistance of several maids equipped with brushes for clothes and hair, who did their utmost not to smile.

Felicity and Bingham were the last offered assistance. Bingham because he insisted his guests be seen to first, Miss Pendleton because she offered up the maid who came to her aid to fellow flour fiasco Glynis McNab, whose face and hair were in far greater need of attention than her own.

She and Bingham exchanged glances as they waited, eyes dancing, smiles blooming into laughter. They and their fellows were a sight indeed, all over white stuff, flour in their hair, brows, lashes, and mustaches. Flour in ears and noses and mouths, and yet the valets and maidservants moved about them as if in attendance at a funeral, sober-faced and attentive.

"I've a proposal," he suggested.

"On your knees, then," she said with a laugh that sent flour flying.

"I propose"—he sank to his knees—"to serve as your valet if you will play maid to me."

Flour-dusted brows rose. "What game is this, suh?"

His thoughts turned to the marriage game he played. It terrified him to think he would soon bend knee to an-

other woman. "No game," he said earnestly. "Between us we shall make one another presentable."

She took up a hairbrush and ran a hand through his hair, contact both soothing and provoking. Flour danced before his eyes along with the image of another woman's hand in his hair—Rose? Victoria? Corisande? He closed his eyes.

He wanted to kiss her, wanted to forget guests and responsibilities, debts and promises, wanted nothing to move him in that moment other than the sensation of Felicity's hands in his hair, and the brush, gently tugging.

He glanced up, flour stinging his eyes.

"Are you all right?" she asked.

"A complete mess," he confided, the words more earnest than he had intended. "I shall be much better when you are done with me."

"*If* ah am ever done with you," she replied. Her face, still ludicrously flour-powdered, might have provoked a laugh had not the expression in her blue eyes registered surprisingly serious.

The brush at his temple stopped. Her fingers slid from his hair. "Most gratifyin', havin' a man on his knees," she mused, setting aside the brush for a dry cloth. She bent to wipe his face, neck, and ears free of flour, paying special attention to the divot above his lips, the areas about his eyes and behind his earlobes.

He paid attention to the wonderful view to be had of her breasts and cleavage.

Cloth rasping against his skin, she seemed unaware of his interest, her own gaze traveling in tandem with the passage of hand and cloth, a sensual indulgence Bingham found both torturous and delightful.

He thought her finished, but she took up a steaming

wet cloth next. He closed his eyes to savor its warm passage, and listened to the rhythm of her breathing. He tried to convince himself that another woman, a wealthier woman, might just as easily fill him with desire, and failed.

"Yo-ah turn," she said.

He opened his eyes, disappointed she touched him no more.

She held out the brush.

He rose and took it from her hand, their fingers bumping, every small contact between them of greater import than it should be. The tortoiseshell handle was warm from her clasp.

Her gaze followed him upward. He was a good head taller than she.

"Shall I kneel?" she asked.

"No. You are perfect," he said.

She smiled ruefully and self-consciously brushed flour from her cheek. "Ah think you overstate the matter."

"No," he corrected her, and then felt foolish. The word hung baldly between them.

He dashed powder from a stray lock or two and gently brushed the hair at her temple. She inhaled abruptly as he cupped his hand beneath her chin, thumb brushing flour from her lips. Dark lashes fluttered downward when his fingers passed over her mouth. In the vein at her throat her pulse throbbed faster.

"A beard does not become you," he said lightly.

The buttery was emptying, but there were still one or two remaining to turn head and chuckle.

Cheeks flushed, she drew back, dragged her own hand across her upper lip, and with the dab and dash of both hands dusted at her own cheeks and nose, as if to

remove from her flesh all traces of his touch along with the flour.

"Can I help, miss?" Sue, a maid, stopped to ask as the others swept flour from the floor and carried away abandoned aprons and basins of milky water.

"Yes, please," he said before she could respond. "Will you be so good as to take away our aprons and leave a whisk broom. We are almost done here."

He reached around Felicity's neck to untie the apron's strings. She watched, unblinking, from the center of his odd embrace. He slipped his own, handed the aprons to Sue, and turned back to Felicity, whisk broom in hand.

He circled, brushing traces of flour from shoulder, sleeve, and the blue satin back of her dress. Low cut, white lace at the neck, a row of flounces at the hem. He wondered how she could afford it, worried that his invitation to the Pendletons' might have strained the vicar's purse, wondered if the shiver she gave indicated she enjoyed the sensation of the whisk as much as he enjoyed passing it the length of her back. "This is very pretty." He bent to work on the flounces.

"Thank you," she said. "Ah made it."

He looked up, amazed. Both of his sisters did needlework, but neither of them had ever attempted the making of a dress.

He stood. "There you are," he said. "One might forget you had just played Bullet Pudding."

"Ah, suh, shall not forget. Ah shall never forget this evening."

The room, empty now, gave echo to her words, which hung charged upon the air. She made the smallest move in his direction. In her beautiful blue eyes he read an inclination to take advantage of the moment.

She would not have turned away had he tried to kiss her.

It was he who remembered his place, and hers.

"Shall we join the others?" he suggested, politely offering her his arm.

On January 6th, Twelfth Night, an Epiphany feast was held after the whole party had descended upon Vicar Pendleton's chapel to assist in the removal of the shepherds for the wise men's arrival. The news of the royal delivery of frankincense and myrrh was read in the newspaper. A meal of royal proportions was enjoyed by all. And at last the twelfth night cake was delivered to the table in all its glory. Marzipan crowns, flowers, and dragons richly decorated the top.

"Who has the bean and who the pea?" Bingham called out as the cake, its heart dark with currants and fragrant with spices, was cut.

"Bean?" Felicity asked her cousin Charity as the slices were passed.

"The man who finds a bean in his portion is named twelfth night king and the woman with the pea is crowned queen until midnight," Charity explained, carefully cutting into her cake. "Take care not to swallow proof of your royalty if you should find it."

"Ow!" Felicity bit into something with a grimace, and pulling it from her mouth, whispered, "What if a woman should find the bean?"

"Felicity has found the bean," Charity gleefully announced.

"You are allowed to choose your king, cousin," Hope told her.

As a paper crown was placed upon Miss Pendleton's

dark locks, Bingham discovered the pea in his own slice.

"Choose a queen," Mary cried triumphantly as a second paper crown was set upon his head.

His gaze briefly met Felicity's. She was flushed with delight, the crown a regal addition to the height of her confidence in looking his way. She meant to name him her king, he could see it in her eyes, could see the beginnings of a *B* form upon her lips. Rather than further play upon her hopes, in that instant he called out the name of the young woman most withdrawn among the party—Corisande Faversham—who blushed scarlet and ducked her head. She was the last choice his sisters expected of him. He had, as yet, spent no time with her, so remote had she kept herself in his library. As she was crowned his queen, he watched over her shoulder Felicity's joy extinguished, and knew a pang that it was his breath blew out the light of her smile.

"Pick someone else!" Hope whispered in her ear, smile forced. Bingham read the words clearly upon her lips.

Felicity recovered; it took but an excruciating instant. Favor was bestowed upon a tongue-tied Howard, who bowed before his queen with laughing good grace.

In a flurry of donned wraps, hats, and boots, the party moved outdoors to the apple orchard, where kings and queens raised their glasses to the moon, to each other, to the trees, and at last doused the tree roots with splashes of cider, as those who knew the words, sang, *"Bear apples now, hats full, caps full, three score bushels full, and my pockets full too,"* before the jug was passed to fill cups again.

Twice, Bingham's gaze met Felicity's. The first time her brow furrowed, as if in confusion. Wearing that

puzzled expression she did not look away, but waited for him to do so. The second time, a shuttered look about her eyes, as if she meant to guard herself against any attraction she felt for him, she looked away first, as if disinterested.

She avoided his gaze; indeed he did not expect to share a glance or word with her again that evening. He was wrong.

"You'll take good care of the Tulip, won't you, old man? He is the keenest bit of blood and bone I have ever had the pleasure of riding," Bingham said gruffly, punching Timothy Egerton in the arm.

"Like the gem he is, Bing. You know I will. How long have I been asking you to sell the brute to me? And how long have you refused? I am all amazement that you would sell him to me now."

"Had to silence your begging, didn't I?"

"You have not had too much punch this evening, have you?"

"Not a drop."

"Good. Mustn't change your mind now. You shall not have him back again, not after that great wad of soft I have promised to pay you has changed hands."

"He is yours, Tim. No reneging. Just give me a moment to say good-bye to the old fellow."

The sound of his friend's footsteps fading, he offered Tulip the apple from his jacket. The gelding ate it with noisy enjoyment and snuffled wetly at his jacket, looking for more. "No, old fellow. You must ask another for them from now on."

Liquid brown eyes regarded him benignly. Bingham stroked the velvet nose, the satin neck. He buried his gloved hand for a moment in the horse's wiry mane,

felt strangely, like crying, and he was not one easily given to tears. He leaned into the gelding's warmth, hand passing along Tulip's withers.

Jaw set, he whispered. "I shall miss you."

A rustle in the straw.

"Ah am confused." Her voice came from the doorway. No question that it was Felicity Pendleton.

"Why in the world would you sell your favorite horse?" she asked.

How to answer? He schooled his expression, schooled the words into good order, then turned to peer at the darkness of her silhouette.

"Tim wanted him more than I needed to keep him."

She stepped into the circle of light, the red of her cloak cheerful.

"Ah would nawt have thawt you the sort to so easily give up the things you love."

She spoke of more than horses. He answered her in kind, gaze unflinching. "I never said it was easy."

A pained expression crossed her features, as if he reminded her of loved ones relinquished. "No," she agreed.

"Are you a woman of your word, Miss Pendleton?"

"Ah ahm."

"You would honor promises? Pay off your debts? Even if it meant giving up what was dear to you?"

"Always."

"So would I."

Silence gathered between them, broken only by the stamp of a hoof, the swish of a tail, the steady munching of hay.

"It is no accident all of the women invited here are wealthy, is it?" she asked bluntly.

"No," he replied, voice husky. "No accident."

"Your debts are great?"

"Debilitating," he admitted. "It would appear my inheritance has been mislaid."

"And you would marry into money?"

He sighed. "You find me contemptible?"

"No."

"I find myself contemptible."

"You saved my life, suh. What should ah find to condemn in your desire to save your own?"

He had nothing to say to that, only wished he might tell Felicity Pendleton how deep was his regard for her. At the end of the row a horse gave a low-throated whicker.

"Will you accept a loan?" she asked softly.

"What?"

"You saved mah laf. It is only fair that ah should be rewarded an opportunity to return in some small way, that favor."

"But Miss Pendleton . . . the amounts required to run an estate are large . . ."

"Ah know. Did you assume ah had no money because my cousins have little?"

"Am I mistaken?"

"You are. Daddy grew tobacco. Lots of it. The proceeds from the sale of the plantation leave me very comfortably provided for."

"I had no idea!" He stood transfixed.

"No. Nor do many. Ah prefer it that way. There are so many fortune hunters who would prey upon an unmarried woman of substance."

He flushed hotly.

"All the busybodies in Atlanta were set on marryin' me off to the first likely bachelor to come mah way. All he really wanted was the land."

"Were they?" His voice was gruff. "You had no desire to enter into the married state?"

She laughed. "It is nawt marriage that offends me so
much as marriage where there is no real affection or
affinity. A marriage to satisfy the neighbors' notion of
propriety, is, in mah opinion, no marriage at all."

"I agree," he said softly.

Her voice was low and husky in asking, "And do you
find one among your Christmas party to love?"

He could not look at her. "I do."

"And does she love you?"

"I don't know. I think so. But I cannot ask her to take
on a penniless husband."

"Wuz that nawt the plan?"

"It was. A plan I find most distasteful."

"You need not be penniless if you accept mah offer,
suh." Her voice rose. "You saved me. Why will you not
allow me to return the favor?"

He exhaled heavily. Never had he been presented
with such a quandary. "You are the most generous of
friends. We are friends, are we not, Miss Pendleton?"

Her lip trembled. She set her jaw, stilling it, then
lifted from her neck a gold chain, and on it his signet
ring. "You are forgettin' suh. You owe me fo' fit for the
return of your ring. And you did tell me you were a man
to honor your debts."

She held it out to him, palm up, the chain dangling
from her fingers.

"Yes, but . . ."

"Will you not reach out and take my hand, suh, before you fall into an icy black hole of debt?"

*I would take your hand, Miss Pendleton, if I might be
assured I need never let go again,* he thought. Taking
up the signet ring, unclasping it, he poured the chain

into her palm like silver rain. "I would not have you flee the grip of one sort of fortune hunter only to find yourself in the grasp of another, Miss Pendleton."

They returned to the house in silence. She wore a pensive look. His heart was filled with despair, for though she provided him with the perfect answer to his problems, his pride would not allow it. He loved her, yet she must never know. He wanted more than anything to marry her, but he could not be happy in it if she, even for a moment, believed he took advantage of her.

The intensity of unvoiced feelings reached explosive capacity by the time they reached the doorway and the weather-bedraggled kissing ball that would be gone with the morning along with the majority of his guests.

Knowing it was his last opportunity to do so, he pulled her into his arms and kissed her, a hard, demanding kiss that said all that words could not.

She responded fervently, pulling him closer, her mouth open beneath his. For a wonderful moment they clung to one another, then he pushed her from him as abruptly as he had taken her into his arms.

"No more," he said, his breath coming fast. "This is wrong."

"Why?" she asked quietly as they stepped through the doorway and instantly into the false cheer and crowded bustle of the party that he now considered a monumental fiasco.

He had no chance to answer. His sisters were at once upon them. This evening was their last, and though the hour was late, his party wanted to spend it singing. Miss Hansen had agreed to play songs on the pianoforte. The servants were preparing for departures in the morning. Had he made his mind up yet, they asked

with significant glances. Would Miss Pendleton mind very much if they stole Bingham away from her a moment? Important matters to discuss.

"Nawt at awl," said Miss Pendleton coolly. "I would not keep you from important business."

Her words came as if from a distance. Her hand slipped from his arm, and with it all chance of happiness, and Hibbs was at his elbow, like a troublesome fly as she walked away, asking, "How many leaves will we be requiring in the dining table tomorrow, sir? I understand a number of the guests will be leaving us after breakfast, which will be served in the morning room."

His gaze met Mary's. In unison they echoed Hibbs's question. "How many leaves?"

"Not a tree at all," Joan said.

Hibbs stared at them blankly.

"Once a tree. It is made of wood," Mary said gleefully grabbing him by the arm, propelling him into the dining room.

"How many leaves, Hibbs?" Bingham called.

"Sir?" Hibbs trailed after them.

"Leaves, Hibbs. How many leaves are there?" Joan's laugh bore a hint of the hysterical.

"Ten, miss. They are very heavy since your father had them modified." Hibbs wore an alarmed expression as Bingham shoved aside the epergne in the center of the long dining table, tossed back the tablecloth, and removed a protective felt pad.

"Modifications!" Mary and Joan were giddily dancing about. They clasped one another, then Bingham, chortling, "Did you hear, Bing? Modifications!"

"Give me a hand here, Hibbs." Bingham pulled ineffectually on the end of the table.

"One must release the spring mechanism, sir." Hibbs

passed his hand along the deep, inlaid lip at the edge of the table and the interlocking leaves slid apart with a sigh.

Hands shaking, Bingham removed one of the leaves, carefully turning it facedown onto the table.

"There!" Joan squealed.

A recessed container had been built into the bottom side of the leaf.

"Open it!" Mary cried.

Bingham ran his fingers over the metal-banded wood. "I do not see how one gets into the thing."

"Are there more?" Unwilling to wait her answer, Mary squatted beside the table and peered up underneath. "They are all this way, Bingham. All ten of them."

"The money tree," Joan breathed. "We have found it."

"Father. Fetch Father, Bing. He will know how to open them."

Bingham raced for the door.

He burst in upon the party in the drawing room, interrupting their full-throated song. "Your cousin. Where is she?" he asked Charity Pendleton.

"I thought she was with you," she said plaintively.

He sped from the room. His father stood alone near the foot of the stairs in his dressing gown and nightcap, his hair gone golden in the flickering glow of the candlelight.

"Bingham, my boy!"

"Where is she?" he demanded breathlessly, without real hope of an answer.

"The American?"

"Yes." Hope bloomed.

"Gone home." He waved at the door. "Looked peaked, she did. Going after her, are you?"

"Yes." Bingham paused buttoning his overcoat. "Joan and Mary are looking for you. Require your help, sir, in the dining room."

"Ought to ask the gel to marry you," Lord Kirby said stoutly.

"Sir?" Bingham was amazed by the suggestion.

His father tapped the side of his nose with a canny grin. "Clear as the nose on my face you fancy her, my boy."

Lantern in hand, he set out across the park at a run.

As fast as his legs could carry him, mindless of the dark, mindless of what tripped him on two occasions, Bingham ran, boots slipping in the mud, cold nipping at his nose, ears, and fingertips.

None of it mattered. Nothing mattered but finding Felicity.

He called her name as he ran, wind whipping the sound from his mouth. His lungs ached with the chill.

She stood, cape billowing, before the decorated juniper, her back to him, shoulders shaking.

"Felicity! You ought not walk home alone."

She whirled, red cape whipping in the wind, cheeks glistening with tears. "Why should you care?"

"Because my heart is forfeit without you."

He held out his handkerchief. She scowled at him, with bad grace snatched up the windswept offering, and dabbed impatiently at her cheeks. "Isn't there some other young woman you should be lookin' after?"

"None that I can think of," he said gently.

"Well, ah can look after mahself quite well, thank

you," she snapped, turning her back on him, setting off in the direction of the vicarage.

"Marry me," he said quietly.

She stopped, the back of her hood his to regard.

Slowly, she turned her head, the wind catching her hood, throwing it back from her face, revealing her stricken expression. "Whut did you say?"

He went to her, stood before her in the path, blocking the way, and sank to one knee among the damp leaves. The wind caught at her hair and sent it dancing about her head in wild, unbound tendrils.

"I asked you to marry me, Felicity."

"Oh, Bingham!" She threw herself into his arms, hands in his hair, her mouth seeking his. He rose, his lips still locked on hers, and crushing her close, kissed her again until both of them were sated.

"Am I to take that as a yes?" he asked with a chuckle, his breath a plume that was whisked into the night air by the wind.

She snuggled against his chest, lifted her head to look at him, and said with a twinkle in her eyes, "Fortune hunter, are you?"

"Indeed." He tucked her hand into his and gently kissed her forehead. "I have been seeking my fortune high and low," he admitted. "Only to find it right under my nose."

She stood on tiptoe and kissed the nose in question.

Second Chance
by Allison Lane

1

Tension churned Alice's stomach as the carriage rolled through Blatchford's familiar gates. Spending Christmas here was a mistake. Why hadn't she feigned sickness? More importantly, why had she accepted a position with the Westlakes, knowing that they always attended this house party?

But in the cold days of January, desperation had kept her from thinking this far ahead. Lady Westlake had offered her shelter, security, and the dignity of earning both. Even considering the consequences would have left her no choice. Returning to England had backed her into a corner with no other exit—hardly the first time that impulsive behavior had caused trouble. She had a long history of mistakes and poor judgment.

The worst consequence this time was Christmas at Blatchford. It had been ten years since her last seasonal visit. Ten years of anger, pain, grief, guilt, and loneliness. Returning brought her full circle, back to the scene of her first mistake—innocuous compared to later ones, but she dreaded meeting even these earliest ghosts. They could rip open deeper wounds.

"Don't wake William yet," she murmured, staying

seven-year-old Michael's hand as he reached for his young brother. "He'll just fuss."

"But—" Michael's voice died at the look in her eye.

"We will not reach the house for at least a quarter hour."

"There goes a fox!" ten-year-old Elizabeth exclaimed, distracting Michael's attention.

"Where?"

"By that wall."

It was already gone. Michael opened his mouth to complain, but his eye lit on another prize. "Look! There's snow in the ruins." His excited bouncing jarred William. "Do you think we'll get more?"

"Perhaps." William whimpered in protest, but Alice did not notice. She was trying to steady her breathing.

Snow in the ruins. The snow had been unusually heavy ten years ago, especially around the ruins. Few had ventured so far from the house, so the crypt had offered privacy impossible to find elsewhere.

Elizabeth's voice cut across the memory. "I love visiting Grandfather at Christmas."

"It is a wonderful house party," Alice agreed. "My family always spent Christmas here when I was a girl."

"I forgot." Elizabeth sounded uncertain for once, perhaps sensing her governess's distress. But she didn't remain subdued for long. "Do you think Uncle Frank is here yet?"

"And Uncle George? Maybe he'll let me ride his horse again."

Alice let them prattle. Anything was better than answering their questions. She hated Christmas. The pain was always worse then. Time had not eased it, for every time she began to heal, some new trauma would revive all the old ones. This year promised to be no different.

He would be here.

Masons and Caristokes had married often. Thus the Earls of Blatchford and Pembroke, who headed the two families, held combined Christmas house parties, so no one had to choose which tie to honor. It was a tradition that dated back more than fifty years. This year Blatchford was the host, just as he had been ten years ago.

She shivered, then cursed herself. Allowing her discomfort to show would draw the very attention she wanted to avoid. Few had known about that holiday flirtation, so there should be no questions. And surely she had learned how to fade into the background. Since leaving England, she had traveled thousands of miles, seen much, done much, endured far too much . . .

She stifled the newer memories, though the embarrassment of her last visit remained. Even at seventeen, she should have known better. Her mother may have been Blatchford's third cousin and her father the younger son of a baronet, but that placed them firmly in the gentry. So why had she taken the attentions of Pembroke's son seriously? He had merely been amusing himself with a harmless holiday flirtation—harmless in his eyes.

No one will remember, she reminded herself sharply. *Even he will have forgotten. Do your job and put the past behind you.*

The coach wheeled across the stone bridge that offered a spectacular view of the manor. They had met here more than once to talk, to admire the view, and to watch the water—it had tumbled too quickly to freeze, its motion one of the few signs of life in a snow-draped

landscape. The willow that had sheltered their first kiss still stood sentinel on the far bank.

Stop this!

She raised her eyes to the house that sprawled across acres of hilltop. A thousand years old at its core, it loomed like something out of a nightmare. But that perception arose from her own distress. Despite its piecemeal construction, the facade unified the whole into an image many found welcoming.

"Can I explore the tower this year?" demanded Elizabeth. The oldest courtyard was off limits to the younger children.

"Ask your grandfather."

Michael was again bouncing with excitement. She absently calmed him, but her thoughts remained mired in relentless memory. The carriage rolled past the ice-skating cove, where he had plied her with chocolate as they warmed themselves by the fire. Farther along was the grove that supplied Christmas greenery, including the mistletoe that hung throughout the house. That ancient oak had sheltered them from prying eyes. The lakeside folly, the sledding hill . . .

Shrieks of ancient laughter echoed in her ears. She could almost feel the cold wind in her face and his warm legs wrapped around her hips. They had overturned into a drift, where he had landed on top, his mouth a scant inch from hers . . .

Enough!

She tucked the rug tighter around William's legs. Reliving the past was pointless—and painful. She should have accepted his attentions in the spirit in which he had offered them. And if she had not been so stupidly naïve, she would have. It was time to put the past behind her. He was now nine-and-twenty, more

than old enough to have set up his nursery. Thus her
fears were groundless.

She ignored a wave of shudders, attributing them to
the cold that had long since invaded the coach. His
marital status was irrelevant. For her own peace of
mind, she would avoid him, but that would be easy.
Blatchford housed dozens of guests during the Christmas season. Even when she brought the children
downstairs, she could stay out of sight.

Unwillingly, her eyes returned to the window. The
setting sun lit the house with a rosy glow, but it still offered her no welcome. A lap robe warmed her thinly
gloved hands, but nothing could warm her heart. As always, the chill came from her soul.

William awoke as the carriage lurched onto the
steepest portion of the drive, but even his fussing could
no longer distract her. They were nearly there.

Please don't let him be in the hall.

Michael and Elizabeth jumped out the moment the
carriage rocked to a halt. She barely prevented William
from falling.

"Uncle George!" Michael shouted as Blatchford's
oldest son, Lord Rufton, appeared at the top of the
stairs.

"Uncle Frank!"

"Grandmother!"

The children's voices rang out as Rufton's brother
and parents appeared. Aristocratic reserve collapsed
under excited greetings. But not until Rufton's eyes
passed over her without pausing did Alice finally
relax. Rufton was *his* closest friend. If he saw only a
governess, then she was safe. Thank God that the aristocracy rarely looked at servants.

Yet pain tempered her relief. For the first time, she

admitted that seeing him again was not her greatest fear. It was seeing his eyes slide past her with no sign of recognition.

Jeremy Caristoke pulled his muffler tighter and swore at the snow swirling outside the carriage. Only a fool would press on in these conditions, but even a short halt would strand him. Christmas was in two days. It would be unbearably rude to miss the annual house party, especially since one of the guests was there by his invitation. He could only hope that continuing on would not prove fatal.

Where were they?

This predicament was his own fault. He should have started home a week earlier, but he had been enjoying his stay with Thomas's family. At three, his godson was curious as a cat—which often led to trouble—but Jeremy loved the boy like a son and could rarely stay angry at him.

He sighed. Would he ever have children of his own?

It seemed an odd question for a man many considered a prime catch, but while Lady Luck had often smiled on him, providing health, wealth, and a host of good friends, his most cherished dreams—a loving wife and family—remained beyond reach.

He had first fallen in love while still at Oxford, but the girl had played him for a fool, disappearing without a word. It had been a portent for his life.

Another sigh escaped as later interests paraded through his mind. Elizabeth had turned him down, wedding Wrexham barely a week after his own proposal. His next *tendre* had been for Thomas's wife, though he had hidden his attraction; in the four years since their marriage, he had transformed it into friend-

ship. Thomas's sister Eleanor had accepted Captain Hanson before he'd decided whether to offer for her. At least he was in good company over Millicent Avery, who had turned everyone down, preferring to remain scandalously single.

Which left Miss Victoria Havershoal. He had courted her during the Season and had added her name to the Blatchford guest list. But he could not make up his mind whether to make an offer—which was another reason he had dawdled. Did he care for her beyond casual friendship? Could he share a bed with her for the rest of his life?

Even more than marriage, he wanted a family. He had a score of nieces, nephews, and godchildren—and loved every one of them—but they could never compare to children of his own. Every year the ache grew stronger, but never quite enough to push him into a marriage of convenience.

So he was back to Victoria. She was intelligent, possessed a good sense of humor, and also wanted a family. Her breeding was equal to his, her training impeccable, her looks far above average, her interests compatible. She would make a perfect wife, so why had he not already proposed? Was cowardice holding him back, or was there a deeper problem?

Caroline and Thomas hovered before his eyes. They were so very much in love, often reading each other's minds and exchanging looks that were downright embarrassing to witness. He envied them, which contributed to his current dilemma, for he wanted that same connection with his wife.

Why had Lady Luck favored his siblings, yet ignored him? Even Harold, the oldest, who had entered

a marriage of convenience to secure the Pembroke succession, had found love with his wife.

He sighed. Five happily married siblings with eighteen well-loved offspring made family gatherings increasingly painful. No matter how much he enjoyed seeing them, he felt odd man out.

At least George was still single—the only person close to him who was. But that would not last long. As heir to Blatchford, George was under mounting pressure to secure the succession—which would give Victoria plenty of company. Lady Blatchford made sure that every gathering included candidates for George.

As the carriage skidded, he again berated himself for waiting so long. Blatchford might be more accessible in poor weather than Pembroke Park, but it was risky to remain on the road. Vicious gusts of wind were slamming into the door.

Tightening his muffler, he returned his thoughts to Victoria. Finding someone better could take years. Could he learn to love her? He must decide before he arrived. If he singled her out, he would have to propose. If he ignored her, everyone would assume she was another of Lady Blatchford's protégées. At least his family was not pressing him. Poor George.

The carriage again lurched, its lanterns briefly illuminating a folly. He let out a sigh of relief. They were nearly there. He would not die by the wayside after all. Pulling out a pocket watch, he was shocked to find that it was midnight.

"You made it!" exclaimed George when Jeremy staggered into the hall.

"Barely. I should have left Thomas's sooner. Rouse help for my coachman. He's been through hell since this snow started."

"Already done. How is our godson?"

Jeremy relaxed. "More mischievous than ever. He upset a vat of milk in the dairy last week trying to dip out some cream for one of the barn cats."

Laughing, George led him to his room. "Miss Havershoal has been here for two days. Are you still interested in her, or is she one of Mother's maidens?"

"I don't know," he admitted, sobering. "I've not seen her since July and can't make up my mind. Perhaps meeting her again will help."

"Or perhaps not. Have you eaten?"

He shook his head. "I dared not stop. As it was, we barely made it."

"Then I'll have something sent up. Most people have retired, though billiards and cards are still going."

"Tomorrow. A light meal, perhaps some warm soup, is all I need tonight."

George left him spreading numbed fingers above the fire. Now that he was safe, he was shivering harder than before.

2

"Did you see me knock off Uncle Frank's hat?" demanded Michael. His next snowball struck Mercury's ear, dropping fragments onto the statue's winged foot.

"You have excellent aim," agreed Alice.

"Maybe, but Uncle Frank won," Elizabeth taunted. "He threw you in a snowdrift."

"That's not winning. I wanted him to," said Michael stoutly, aiming at a bird's nest, then plastering a stone lion in the eye.

Alice smiled as she led the way back to the house. The storm had created a winter wonderland that few

could resist. Children and adults had tumbled out, launching a resounding game of snowballs that eventually included half the guests. And their exuberance was catching. For the first time in years, the sight of snow did not make her cringe.

But the easing of one painful memory had little effect on the others. Or perhaps it had been her breakfast with the Caristoke governesses.

"Mr. Jeremy made it after all," Miss Anders had reported. "Lord Welman had feared that the weather would keep him away, but he arrived at midnight." Welman was the woman's employer, Jeremy's older brother.

"The children will be pleased to see their favorite uncle," said Miss Norris. "Lady Wormsley was convinced that he would slide into a ditch and freeze to death."

So much had changed in ten years. Lady Wormsley was one of his sisters. Alice remembered her as a giggling twelve-year-old and had trouble picturing her five years wed, with two children of her own. Was Jeremy married? She had heard no disturbance during the night, but the Caristoke children were housed at the other end of the wing, so she could easily have slept through an arrival.

"He will be relieved that Miss Havershoal arrived before the storm," said Miss Highwater. "My lady was delighted that he invited the girl. It is past time that he wed. Of course, he should have made his offer last Season—he'd courted her long enough. Miss Havershoal was heartbroken when he left town without a word."

Miss Anders sniffed, dismissing Lady Tewsport's delight and Miss Havershoal's megrims. "Don't exag-

gerate. She had half a dozen suitors and favored none of them. But I expect we'll see a betrothal by Twelfth Night."

"Twelfth Night! Lady Wormsley anticipates an announcement at the Christmas ball. If it isn't all but settled, he would not have brought her here."

Alice ceased listening. Jeremy's plans did not matter. Whatever his intentions toward Miss Havershoal—and she was less credulous than these gossiping governesses, for she well knew his penchant for toying with female affections—she did not want to see him. But he was unlikely to visit the children's wing. His later arrival explained why he had not joined the company for snowballs. She had journeyed through blizzards often enough to know how enervating it was.

But even if he paid a visit to his nieces and nephews, avoiding him would be easy. As an invisible servant, she could slip quietly away. When the company gathered greens after breakfast, she would stay in the background. He would never even notice her.

After helping her charges into dry clothing, she escorted them to the schoolroom for their breakfast. A three-year-old scampered across the floor and bumped into her leg.

"Josh!" she gasped.

The room swirled as she stared down at a cap of brown curls so familiar she nearly screamed.

But when the lad turned his face up, it silenced her. *Foolish woman!* She willed her heart to stop pounding. Those blue eyes bore no resemblance to Josh's chocolate brown. This chin was weaker, the forehead wider, the lips thinner.

Josh was dead, she reminded herself, deliberately

repeating the words as she pulled composure around her like a cloak.

Idiot! You should have expected this.

Many children in this house would resemble him. She had often been mistaken for various cousins in her own youth, so she should have prepared for the likelihood. It was yet another consequence to accepting this position.

If only she wasn't a governess. Living with children kept too many memories alive. Three years hadn't begun to dull that pain.

Jeremy glanced out the window while Stokes readied his shaving water. A flock of snow-caked children was straggling back to the house, chivvied along by a gaggle of governesses. One of the boys zinged a snowball into a statue's head.

He grinned. It looked like he'd missed a whopping good time.

Breakfast could wait. Eighteen nieces and nephews would be wondering when he would arrive. It was past time to lay their fears to rest.

Shaving and dressing seemed to take forever, but at last he headed upstairs. Laughter led him to the schoolroom, where meals were always served during the holidays.

"Harry," he called, spotting his sister's oldest the moment he opened the door. The lad was hugging a lady's knees, but turned at the sound of his voice, then squealed and ran into his arms.

"Unca Je'my! What did you bring me?"

Laughing, he tossed Harry high into the air. "Greedy little devil, aren't you? But you must wait until tomorrow. No presents before Christmas."

The lady turned jerkily away and tripped over a chair. Still holding Harry, he lunged to catch her, then froze, unable to breath.

It can't be!

Without a word, she fled.

"I'll be back in a minute, Harry," he mumbled, absently setting the boy down. Her flight proved she was no ghost. Light-headedness weakened his knees. Someone should have warned him that she was back.

Yet who knew he would care?

He raced after her and had nearly caught up when she dodged through a doorway. Jamming his foot in the opening, he pushed into the room, then jerked her around to face him.

It was her, all right. She might have pulled her hair into a ruthless knot, but her cap did not begin to conceal its blazing auburn. Green eyes glared at him. No one else's had such clear color. All the old pain roared to life, choking him with remembered fury. How dared she return to taunt him?

"Alice Walford. It really is you. I thought you went to America, or was that another of your lies?"

"*My* lies?" She slapped his hands away, anger darkening those remarkable eyes. "How dare you blame me for your own perfidy? I thought you despicable before, but this takes the cake. Was it a wager? How much did you win for my kisses?"

"What?" Shock befuddled his mind. He loomed closer, trying to intimidate her into silence. "I can't believe even you could twist the truth so badly. How can you live with yourself?"

She glared. "I knew you were a cad, but I never thought your cruelty could extend this far. Have you no honor?"

He hardly heard her through the buzzing in his ears. How many times had he wished she had chosen someone else for her holiday flirtation? How many nights had he lain awake fighting his hunger for her? "What do you know of honor? You could at least have told me you were leaving the country."

"How? You had already jilted me before Papa decided to go." Her eyes hardened. "Not that it would have made a difference."

Of course not. She had deliberately used him. But her earlier words suddenly penetrated his mind. "*Jilted?* You know very well I had no choice, Alice."

"Mrs. McDougal," she corrected him stonily.

He flinched. Somehow he had never pictured her married. Was she up here visiting her children? Pain nearly doubled him over. "Since when?"

"I married Malcolm aboard the ship that took us both to America," she said, chin held high. "Not that it's any of your business. There was no need to attack. I can hardly reveal your sins without calling my judgment into question for believing you."

"That's not what—" The pain exploding through her eyes paralyzed his voice.

"So I feared, but you'll not deceive me again, sir. I am not available for sport. If you'll excuse me?"

Before he could respond, she was out the door. By the time he managed to follow, she was gone.

Alice ducked into the tiny room she shared with Miss Parkenson, governess to one of the Mason cousins—with over two hundred guests visiting Blatchford, space was at a premium. She was lucky. The lady's maids were packed four to a bed in spaces

smaller than this. Lower servants shared pallets in one
of the attics.

Why had Jeremy arrived at precisely the instant she
had been reeling with memories of Josh? At any other
time, she could have melted away without notice. But
back-to-back shocks had made her clumsy.

She cursed under her breath.

His face looked much the same, though his body
had filled out, broadening his shoulders. His hair still
had a mind of its own, waving wildly around his ears
and neck. His eyes had been hard today, but she knew
they could soften with warmth—and with passion.

She shivered. *Damn him.* And damn her for still caring for him, despite everything. Malcolm had been a
dear friend and a considerate husband, but he had
never elicited the wild emotion Jeremy could raise
with a single glance. And that had been good, she reminded herself sharply. He had protected her, physi-
cally and emotionally. Never in a million years would
he have hurt her.

Memories assailed her. Jeremy had callously used
her, his betrayal tearing her heart asunder, destroying
her will to live. Such cruelty was unforgivable.

Don't ever forget, she reminded herself again. *Ban-
ish any sign of weakness.* His sudden appearance had
thrown her off balance, though she had quickly recovered, despite his unexpected fury—but she would not
think about that. Her real danger did not come from
him. It was in her. His touch still filled her with heat—
and joy.

To protect herself, she must remember the pain, remember the agony, remember that black moment when
she had been poised to throw herself overboard and
end it all. She could not survive a repetition of the past.

Tears stung her eyes, but she forced them back. *I need your calm, Malcolm.* She shuddered, but picturing his solidity soon brought her emotions under control. Dearest Malcolm. He had prevented her from jumping, then allowed her to cry out her distress on his shoulder. Under his quiet probing, she had bared the whole story. No one else knew about Jeremy, but Malcolm had caught her at a vulnerable moment. And he had understood her despair, for he had been trying to recover from his own blackness.

But Malcolm was gone, and she knew Jeremy all too well. Her words had raised questions, so he would confront her again and again until he found satisfactory answers. He could charm the birds off the trees. Would he convince her that his desertion had been her fault?

She shivered.

For her own protection, she could not afford to lose her heart a second time. Never again would she ignore the gulf that separated them—a gulf far wider than it had been ten years ago. Governesses could not look to earls' sons for anything but dalliance—not even younger sons. She must not forget that truth. Avoiding him was the only way to retain her sanity.

Jeremy returned to the schoolroom, though he barely registered the children's exuberance. He listened to their tales with a corner of his mind and promised to join them on various expeditions, but most of his thoughts were mired in shock.

Mrs. McDougal.

He shivered.

Married aboard ship.

Had she cared so little that she could turn to another

within a month of leaving? His heart recoiled at the thought, yet he could hardly ignore the evidence. She had told him none of her plans, had left without a word, had immediately married another. Just as Elizabeth had done five years later. What was wrong with him that he commanded no allegiance—or even respect—from those he loved?

And now she had returned to England. Was her husband with her? Her children?

Stupid questions. *I am not available for sport.* Why else had she been in the schoolroom?

He glanced around as Harry handed him a ball, wondering which youngsters might be hers. Half a dozen were strangers, though that was not unusual. He knew most of the Caristoke relatives, but he had never bothered to seek out the more distant Mason connections—except Alice.

So which ones were hers? A girl in the corner shared her coloring. Another had her delicate build, promising to grow just as tall and slender.

He grimaced, realizing the futility of the exercise. That last one was at least twelve years old. Any of the Masons were likely to resemble her since she had inherited many of the family features—as would half of the Caristokes. He had no way of knowing whether hers were even in this room. Children occupied this entire wing.

Giving up, he tackled his brother's twins, tickling them into giggling balls. A dozen others joined the melee, shrieking with laughter as they rolled across the floor. But his mind remained on Alice.

In retrospect, his behavior had been abominable. Anger had blinded him from the moment he recognized her. His words had escaped without thought.

Even if every one of them had been true, manners condemned him for speaking them aloud. And some of them had been false.

He had done her an injustice, it seemed. For ten years he had assumed that she had led him on, knowing that she would be leaving the country within a fortnight. Once she disappeared, he had suppressed all thought of her, never checking to see when the trip had been arranged.

Pride. His had taken a beating, so he had lashed out without thought or logic.

You had already jilted me before Papa decided to go.

If that was true, he owed her an apology. After breakfast, the party would gather greenery. He must make peace with her. Christmas was a season for good will. Arguments—or even avoiding each other in the drawing room—would draw notice, leading to the exposure of a past neither wanted to reveal.

He headed for the breakfast room.

"You look recovered," said George, meeting him on the stairs.

It took him a moment to recall his journey. "Completely."

"Hungry?"

"Starving."

George laughed.

"I ran into Mrs. McDougal in the schoolroom. When did she return to England?" he asked lightly.

George looked surprised, then sighed. "I forgot you wouldn't know. You didn't come up here last summer."

He shrugged. Estate problems had kept him in Sussex. He rarely came to Northumberland more than once a year anyway. Most of his family spent the Season in London. That and Christmas kept them in touch.

"She turned up at Walford a little over a year ago," said George. "Though she didn't get much of a welcome, since her grandmother had died back in 1811." He shook his head. "Sir Edward has never forgiven her father, but he let her stay for the holidays before turning her off. She came here, and Agnes took her on as governess. She had references from a Boston family."

A governess. But he still owed her an apology. "Rough life. I wonder what happened to her own family."

George shrugged. "Her husband is dead, but I don't know how or when. She doesn't talk about America."

Jeremy fell silent. If Alice wasn't talking, then the story must be bad. She had always been open—something he should have remembered sooner. Only a disaster would close her off. What had she suffered?

But George had saved him from a faux pas. Asking after her family would be a mistake. And now he knew she would not appear for meals.

The breakfast room was nearly full. By the time he had filled a plate, the only seat left was next to Victoria.

"Good morning," she said, smiling. "Your journey must have been difficult. You arrived quite late."

Warning sounded in his head. She was keeping track of his whereabouts.

He had not yet decided what to do about her. Battling yesterday's storm had left him lethargic. His meeting with Alice had added to his mental confusion, distorting his impressions, and making intelligent decisions impossible.

He hid a grimace. It wasn't Victoria's fault that his mood was black today. But until he decided whether to make an offer, he must tread very warily.

"We got in about midnight. And you?"

"Two days ago. I was disappointed that you were not already here."

This time the implication was clear. She wanted an offer, and he could hardly blame her. Her father had died two years earlier, leaving her mother in financial difficulty. That had never bothered him, but it put pressure on her to secure her future. So he had to make up his mind. Today. It wasn't fair to keep her hanging.

"I was visiting friends."

Her smile wavered. "What activities can we expect during the holiday?"

"The usual. Since we have snow this year, that will include sledding, skating, and sleigh rides for those so inclined. With luck, we will have more outings than last year—it rained the entire time, or seemed to. The children nearly drove us to Bedlam before the weather eased."

"Will you be sleighing?" This smile was openly flirtatious.

"I don't, as a rule." Not caring how he sounded, he focused on cutting his ham.

The last time he had gone sleighing had been with Alice. Memories of those days still brought pain. Which gave him another reason to apologize. Perhaps making peace with her would ease his own heart. Once he closed the door on the past, he could decide what to do about Victoria.

"Lady Blatchford led us on a tour of the house yesterday. It is a fascinating place," she continued brightly.

"Did she include the secret passage?"

Her eyes widened, but she shook her head. "Where does it lead?"

"Which one? I know of half a dozen, though the

exact locations were lost for nearly a century. Rufton, Hartford, and I discovered them the summer we were twelve."

He chuckled at the memory. Thomas, now Lord Hartford, had used the secret passages to impersonate the legendary Blatchford ghost, popping out so suddenly that he had scared George's sister Agnes into a swoon. They trotted out reminders whenever she grew too haughty.

How did Agnes treat Alice? He frowned. Agnes had a long history of castigating servants. Did Alice satisfy, or was this post her latest trial in an unhappy life?

What had happened in America?

She had been so beautiful that Christmas. He had known her for years, of course, though never well. Technically, she had still been in the schoolroom, for she had not yet staged a formal come-out, but many boundaries relaxed during the holidays. She had even been included in the ball.

He nearly groaned at the memory of her kisses, at the way her body had fit so perfectly against his own, at the breathtaking smiles she had bestowed only on him. She had seemed perfect, sharing even his thoughts.

"I beg your pardon," he said to Victoria, suddenly realizing that she was waiting for an answer to another question.

"I merely wondered if you were joining the search for greenery." Pique sharpened her tone, flaying his conscience. If he wasn't careful, the decision would be taken out of his hands. No woman would tolerate being ignored.

"Forgive me. I am not quite recovered from a gruel-

ing journey," he lied. "But tradition requires every able-bodied guest to join the expedition."

She relaxed.

3

An hour later, Jeremy pushed his way through the crowd, looking for Alice. It seemed a hopeless task. More than a hundred adults were already gathered in the hall. He didn't try to count the children. The mass of people had spilled into adjacent rooms.

"Jeremy!" boomed a voice in his ear, diverting him from his quest. "So you finally made it."

"Last night." Roger Caristoke was a distant cousin closer to his father's age than his own. He worked as steward for Sir Edward Walford, Alice's uncle. Just the person he wanted to see. "I ran into Mrs. McDougal in the nursery this morning. Is it true that Walford disowned her?"

Roger nodded. "For all practical purposes. He wants no reminder of her father. That last quarrel caused too much trouble."

Jeremy raised his brows as the company trooped down the steps and headed for the lake. "What tale is this?"

"Mrs. McDougal's father?"

"Exactly. I knew that he had taken his family to America, but no one mentioned a quarrel."

"It happened about the time old Pembroke died, so I doubt you would have known. Alfred managed Sir Edward's second estate, you might recall. But the brothers had frequent arguments over procedure. Alfred was a proponent of change while Sir Edward prefers tradi-

tion." His voice revealed some of his own frustration, for he was in a similar situation.

"Sorry to hear that."

"We manage to compromise," he said dryly. "But I never understood why Alfred was running Tower House. The brothers had not gotten on even as children. And that worsened after Alfred's marriage."

Jeremy raised his brows.

"Sir Edward considers himself superior to Alfred—an opinion that was hard to justify once Alfred married into Blatchford's family. His repeated invitations here and to Pembroke Park stuck in Edward's craw, so he found fault with everything Alfred did."

"Jealousy?"

"Exactly. The title is Edward's only claim to fame. Few would heed him without it. Alfred often swore he would move to America if Edward didn't quit meddling, but few took it seriously—until ten years ago. No one knows exactly what happened, but one of their periodic arguments took a vicious turn. Edward wound up unconscious, with a broken arm and severe bruises. Alfred and his family disappeared before dawn."

Jeremy shivered. "Fleeing retribution?"

"Or delivering it before leaving the country. At least one servant swears that Alfred attacked because Edward had assaulted one of his tenants—Sir Edward has a medieval view of landowner rights, especially when it comes to pretty girls. But no one really knows. Sir Edward swore vengeance on the entire family. When Mrs. McDougal returned, he allowed her to stay only because he was entertaining influential guests. He threw her out the moment they left."

Jeremy made a mental note to find Roger a better position, for his stronger ties to the aristocracy made

his situation worse than Alfred's had been. Turning the conversation to more pleasant topics, he mulled Roger's information.

Alice had claimed that her father's decision to leave the country had been unexpected. He had to believe her, which meant that his condemnation had been unwarranted. Had he sought to assuage his pain by casting blame elsewhere? How juvenile.

If only he had known she was going. They still would have parted, but at least he could have bidden her farewell. She had felt jilted, which must have hurt badly. He definitely owed her that apology.

Leaving Roger, he worked his way toward the back of the crowd. Unless she had changed drastically, she would be hiding out there. But within moments, Victoria grabbed his arm, demanding his support down a slippery slope and asking questions about this relative or that. Her flirtatious chatter annoyed him, as did her efforts to become separated from the group. By the time he was free of her, he was nearly ready to abandon his tentative courtship. He didn't like pushy females.

Alice stayed well to the rear as the party set out to gather greens. A ridiculous surge of loneliness engulfed her, making her frown. Why should she feel lonely when people jostled her from all sides?

But a moment's thought solved the conundrum. She no longer fit into the world of the Masons. Accepting a post as governess placed a wall between her and the others. She had not noticed it until now only because the children usually kept her too busy.

But that was no longer true. Today they were reveling in adult attention. William rode atop Lord West-

lake's shoulders. Michael was already tossing snow-balls at his uncles. Elizabeth chattered with her mother.

Which left her alone—and far too aware of another figure striding toward the lake. Despite the mass of humanity that separated them, she knew exactly where Jeremy was—and with whom. Miss Havershoal clung to his arm. As they reached the foot of the hill, she slipped, flinging herself against him with a girlish shriek.

Pretense, of course, but he didn't seem to mind.

And why should he? He was poised to wed the girl. Alice had to admit that they made a charming couple. Miss Havershoal was beautiful, her blond hair and peachy complexion providing a perfect foil for his golden brown. Her breeding was good, her manners faultless, and no one knew anything derogatory about her character.

Deliberately turning away, she concentrated on the job at hand. Which trees would yield the best greens? How much could she cut before one of the children demanded attention? She hoped one would arrive soon, though that was unlikely. With two uncles to play with and parents to watch their antics, they would not need her.

Elizabeth was already clipping holly, her father's leather gloves protecting her from thorns. Michael sat on Rufton's shoulder so he could reach the best branches. William squealed as Frank dumped snow on his head.

Watching all that affection was bittersweet. She missed her own family. Accepting that loss had been far harder than taking a post as a governess. Never again would she play with Josh, teach him, feel his

childish hugs. She could no longer look forward to watching him grow, crying at his wedding, receiving visits from grandchildren.

And just as well, whispered her conscience. *You are unworthy of such happiness.*

"Alice Walford!" exclaimed a voice. "I haven't seen you in years."

"Ten years," she confirmed, turning to face one of her cousins. "Though one would never guess it to look at you. I swear you must still be seventeen."

Sylvia giggled. "Flatterer. Three children put that to the lie."

"Who did you wed? You were making sheep's eyes at Cousin Harold the last time I saw you."

"Richard Caristoke—Sir Reginald's youngest."

So here was yet another tie between the two families. Richard had missed that last Christmas. As secretary to a government official, he had no time to journey all the way to Northumberland. Sylvia must have met him again during the Season.

She listened to tales of Sylvia's children, surprised that they raised neither envy nor pain in her heart. Either she was finally getting over Josh's death, or Sylvia's warmth overwhelmed everyone in the vicinity.

"Are those yours?" Alice asked, nodding toward Sir Reginald.

Sylvia laughed. "They do love their grandfather." Three youngsters were happily burying the man in a snowdrift. "Do you remember the year we attacked Lord Rufton?"

"And then discovered he had half a dozen friends to defend him."

"But we had nearly twenty on our side."

"Which is why we managed to bury them."

"I'll never forget how they retaliated."

Alice shook her head. The boys had lured the girls into the ancient tower, locked them in, then terrorized them with ghostly noises and spectral manifestations. Only afterward did she learn that a secret passage had allowed them to enter and leave unseen.

That was the Christmas she had formed her first *tendre* for Jeremy. He had been fifteen.

Sylvia giggled, recalling other incidents from the past. Alice basked in her amity for several minutes before Sylvia's children called her away to witness some daring feat. It had been years since she had been treated as an equal. Even the other governesses were wary of her, unsure whether she was one of them or one of the family.

Her plunge back into loneliness was bleaker than ever, but she shrugged it off. It did no good to dwell on a life that no longer existed. To keep her mind occupied, she joined a group of children who were building snowmen. It didn't take long before their ranks swelled.

Elizabeth tugged on her skirts. "Judith says she's way too old to build snowmen," she reported, her bottom lip trembling. "Am I too old?"

Judith was twelve—and was so anxious to grow up that she distanced herself from anything the younger children enjoyed.

"I'll tell you a secret, Elizabeth," Alice whispered in her ear. "You are never too old to have fun. I built snowmen in this very park when I was seventeen, and I built them in America when I was three-and-twenty."

Both memories hurt, though less than usual. Perhaps the renewed sparkle in Elizabeth's eyes assuaged her

discomfort. Or maybe facing Jeremy had been good for her.

He had been shocked at her accusations. That reaction could not have been faked. Every vestige of color had drained from his face as he choked *jilted?* Was there more to the story than she had known? Maybe his words of love had been true.

But such thinking was dangerous. She could not risk loving him again, especially when he was poised to wed another.

Answering Elizabeth's questions about winter in America kept her thoughts occupied. And though she had not willingly discussed her life there since returning to England, the pain was mild. Closing the circle had touched her frozen heart with warmth as this familiar trek to gather greens recalled the love and excitement that had permeated the holidays in her youth. Anything that offset the barrenness of more recent years was welcome.

"Yes, it got very cold where we lived," she confirmed. "With deep snow. Christmas in Boston is celebrated much like it is here, but on the frontier, it is not a season for parties. Most people do not have family nearby. Winter travel is nearly impossible, and even church is held only when the circuit preacher comes through."

"But doesn't God punish you for not attending weekly services?" asked Elizabeth hesitantly.

"God knows what is possible and what is not," she said gently. "We said our prayers each day, just as you do. And we rejoiced when the preacher arrived."

Her answers were simplistic, of course, due as much to the Season as to the age of her audience. Informal gatherings had occurred more frequently as the popu-

lation grew. But discussing the hardships of the frontier would dampen their joy in the holidays. As it was, Elizabeth was shocked to learn that the wilderness had no holly.

Boston society kept the English Christmas traditions alive, just as they clung to many other English customs. It set them apart from the country folk, many of whom were descended from Puritans and still condemned the pagan influences found in the traditional celebrations. Neither attitude affected the frontier. Life was simply too hard to waste time on tomfoolery.

But she kept her recital light, describing brilliant red birds with cocky crests that brightened snowy winter days; friendly black-capped chickadees, similar to English willow tits, that had foraged for seeds in her flower plot; pretty black-and-white animals rather like cats, who sprayed a foul-smelling liquid if annoyed; and the herd of deer that always wintered near their cabin.

While they talked, they built a snowman. Judith was gazing longingly in their direction. The girl wanted to join the fun, but couldn't let go of her pride long enough to admit she had been wrong.

Elizabeth fetched her parents so they could admire her creation. Alice was looking for another activity when a voice sounded just behind her.

"Walk to the lake with me, Mrs. McDougal."

"Why?" she demanded, facing Jeremy. "I need to watch the children."

"They are fine—and busy. You could disappear for hours and no one would notice."

It was true—at least until it was time to put William down for his nap. A glance showed that George was

helping Michael untangle a branch of mistletoe from a shrub.

"Come with me, Alice," said Jeremy again. "I owe you an apology, and I would rather forgo the audience."

"Very well." If he realized that his anger had been unwarranted, he would not leave her alone until she accepted his apology, so she had no choice. But once they clarified the confusion of ten years ago, they would go their separate ways. Surely, she could tolerate five minutes at his side.

She headed for the lake, refusing his proffered arm. Snow covered much of the surface, but a portion of the skating cove had been swept clean. Hills rose on the other side, their frosted trees glistening in the sunlight.

Jeremy stepped in front of her, blocking the view. "I should have asked what happened instead of throwing accusations at your head this morning, but you caught me by surprise. I meant every word I spoke to you all those years ago, so it hurt when you disappeared without warning."

She raised her brows. "I would have expected tales of Father's confrontation with Uncle Edward to keep the neighborhood entertained for months. The servants reported that Uncle suffered a broken arm and that a suspicious fire consumed the stables."

"I knew none of it."

He looked sincere, not that it mattered. Too much water had flowed under the bridge for it to make a difference. Yet curiosity prompted her own questions.

"If you meant your words, why did you leave so suddenly?"

He sighed. "Surely, you knew about my grandfather."

His grandfather? Had the old earl forbidden further contact? It was a possibility she had never considered, but Jeremy had been dependent on the man for his allowance, so he would have been susceptible to pressure.

"I waited at the folly until after dark, but you never came," she admitted. "I could hardly ask where you were without revealing our assignation, but I overheard one of the grooms say that you had left the day before. He didn't mention why. The most obvious conclusion was that you had finished with me and moved on. Within the hour, Father announced our departure. We were gone by morning."

He passed a hand over his eyes. "How you must hate me. I returned from our last meeting to learn that my grandfather had fallen gravely ill. He had gone to York after Twelfth Night, and with the weather so bad, it had taken the messenger more than two days to reach us. Fearing it was already too late, my parents left immediately. I followed the moment I heard. I should have told you, but fear drove all else from my mind. Not until I arrived in York did I think to send word. When my groom reported that you were gone, it was a greater blow than Grandfather's death."

"If he knew we were gone, he should have known why."

"You knew I was gone, yet didn't know why. He never asked."

She kept her face rigid, though his words softened her heart. So it had been no more than a comedy of errors.

Jeremy turned away to stare across the ice. "Knowing how anxious I was, he returned immediately to York. The shock nearly killed me."

His statement recalled that black night aboard ship. She cringed.

"All I could do was try to get on with my life, so I left for Oxford," he continued. "And I spent that summer with Thomas. It was nearly a year before I came north again."

Another layer of ice melted from around her heart, but she refused to relax. It was time to leave, before her control slipped. " 'Twas fate, then. And just as well. I apologize for cursing you all these years, and I wish you good fortune in the future."

"Not yet, Alice." She hadn't taken two steps before he blocked her way. "Have you forgotten that we are betrothed?"

Alarm exploded through her head. "That was naught but childish foolishness," she reminded him. "And negated by my marriage in any event."

"I loved you. Can you honestly say you did not love me?"

"Jeremy—" She bit her lip until she could steady her voice. "Whatever we felt ten years ago is irrelevant. We were young—little more than children. We let a holiday flirtation get out of hand, but it could never have led to marriage. We were too far apart in station, and you were still in school. They would not have allowed it."

"I could have talked them around."

"That is beside the point." She interrupted him, desperate to keep distance between them lest he inflict further pain. "We cannot return to the past."

"True, but we *can* look to the future."

Her jaw hardened. Was this a quixotic way to atone for abandoning her? He didn't understand the agony

his words already caused. She had to drive him away. Succumbing to temptation would destroy them both.

"Don't try to resurrect the past, Jeremy. Marriage would never have worked. I only accepted you because I was desperate to escape from home. Father had been growing stranger for some time. Both he and my brother wanted to throw off Uncle Edward's dominance, often threatening to drag us off to America. The idea terrified me, so I jumped at the chance for security." Somehow she kept her voice cool, twisting truths without a qualm. She had accepted him out of love, of course. But she could not wed him now. Causing him a little pain was better than revealing a truth that would devastate them both.

"Yet you went with them in the end."

"What choice did I have? Uncle would never have taken me in. Blatchford might have allowed me to stay, but only if Father had asked. You know that girls have no control over their lives. Besides, once you jilted me, there was no reason to stay."

"I didn't—"

"True, but I didn't know that then."

"So you married McDougal. Was that an escape as well?"

"In part."

Pain flashed in his eyes.

She turned away. Studying his face might explain this new pain, but it would also expose her own thoughts. He had always been good at reading her, and she could feel her control slipping.

He paced to the shore and back. "Did you love him?"

"He was a good man."

"But he is gone, and we are no longer children. There is nothing to bar reinstating our betrothal."

Pain clenched her heart. He didn't believe her. Even claiming to have used him hadn't swayed him. *Stubborn idiot. Now what?* "You are forgetting Miss Havershoal."

"What?"

"Do not treat me like a fool. Everyone expects you to wed her."

His eyes widened. "Who is *everyone*?"

"Your brothers and sisters, according to their governesses. Your hosts. Probably most of the other guests. The only disagreement is whether you will make the announcement at tomorrow's ball or on Twelfth Night."

"They are wrong. I have no intention of offering for her. She is a nice enough girl, but not for me."

"Then why is she hanging on your arm?"

"It is true that I escorted her several times last Season," he admitted, his eyes darkening in anger. "But no more than half a dozen other gentlemen did. And you must know that she is only one of many unattached females invited this year. Blatchford wants George to marry and secure the succession. There is only one lady I want, and that's you."

Perversely, her opposition had made him dig in his heels. Perhaps reason would work. Somehow, she must convince him to leave her alone. "You are dreaming, Jeremy. Your parents would have been appalled at a match ten years ago, for we were too far apart even then. That is now worse. Earls' sons do not wed governesses. Nor do they wed women whose experiences make them unfit for society."

"You have always put more space between us than

is really there," he said with a sigh. "You once claimed that your father would never approve my suit."

"Which was entirely true."

He glared.

"Think. No caring father would have accepted your suit. You were a nineteen-year-old younger son without prospects. How could you have supported a wife?"

"My uncle left me an estate and fortune."

"When?"

His shoulders sagged. "Eight years ago."

"Did you expect it?"

He reluctantly shook his head.

"You see? I spoke the truth." She turned to leave. "And I still do. I appreciate the chance to straighten out our misunderstanding, but further conversation is pointless."

"Hardly. I want you."

She backed away, fearing his intensity. He didn't know what he was saying. "No, Jeremy. Leave me alone. For once, will you listen to me? I am not available for dalliance, and I am unsuited for any higher position. I can no longer fit into English society."

"You have always underrated yourself, Alice."

Her temper shattered. "Damn you! Quit living in the past! *You don't know me!* Forget that schoolroom chit you courted ten years ago. You can't begin to imagine the life I have led since then. I am not even suited to be a governess." Which was true. Anyone who studied her past would never trust her with their children.

"I don't believe that, Alice. Whatever hardships you endured have not changed the essential you."

"Hah! Such drivel seeks to hide pity. Don't subject me to that." She leaned wearily against a tree. *Dear God, make him go away.*

"What happened?"

His implacable will was terrifying, but other memories steadied her. Patience had never been his forte. He would lose interest if she stood firm. "Alice Walford is dead. Accept it and get on with your life."

"What happened, Alice?"

The quiet question tore at her heart. He sounded concerned, even supportive, but only because he didn't understand. And she couldn't explain. She would rather return to their mutual misunderstanding than reveal the truth. He would hate her. And that was something she could not endure.

Forcing her face into a stoic mask, she turned to meet his eyes. They bore into hers, demanding answers she could not provide.

"You don't want to know," she vowed. "Remember our holiday diversion with fondness if you must, but that girl is dead. Her grave lies on the banks of the Maumee River."

She left him standing on the shore. A circuitous route offered time to fight back her tears before she had to face anyone else. This was not the time to indulge in emotion. She had a job to do.

But it took several minutes to regain her composure. *Nothing to bar reinstating our betrothal.* He was Satan incarnate, dangling temptation before her eyes. But it was impossible.

Would she never be free? She stared at her hands, able to make out every callus, every scar, even through the gloves. Hands that had built a home and harvested fields, healed the sick and buried the dead, done a thousand and one chores every day that he could never imagine. These hands had condemned her to hell. How many penalties were left to pay?

Joining the group around the fire, she lifted her voice in a familiar carol that brought tears to her eyes. For her, peace on earth was an unattainable illusion.

Jeremy frowned as he watched her leave. He shouldn't have teased her, especially after she had resolved his turmoil so easily.

Her assumption that he would wed Victoria had cleared his confusion. What he still felt for Alice was far stronger than any emotion Victoria raised. No woman deserved a husband who wanted another. At the first opportunity, he would tell Victoria that he was not interested. The decision thrust her from his mind.

Dear Alice. Her suffering was obvious, the pain in her eyes filling him with a burning desire to assuage it. Whether she accepted him or not, he must do that much for her.

Could he convince her to wed him? Instinct shouted that she had been lying to keep him at a distance, an idea supported by her unwillingness to look him in the eyes. They had always been able to read each other's faces. It was a memory that fury and pain had suppressed after her disappearance.

Her stubbornness certainly hadn't mellowed in the last decade. But she *had* changed. At seventeen, she had laughed and teased, her eyes always sparkling with mischief. Now she was quiet, solemn, staid—and very unhappy. Did she ever smile? He couldn't tell. Their two meetings had been laced with anger and recrimination. But he doubted that she did. Her mouth had fallen into a permanent frown—suitable for a governess, he supposed, but it did not resemble the Alice he remembered.

So what had happened? No one but Alice knew, and

she would not reveal it even to him. Her reluctance made a difficult task seem impossible, giving him no place to start. How could he fix a problem he didn't understand?

Sighing, he helped Miss Wallace load greens into the wagon. She was one of Lady Blatchford's protégées. Spreading his attentions evenly among them would protect Victoria's reputation when he failed to come up to scratch.

From the wagon, he headed for the fire, where he joined Miss Higgins in singing carols. Warm cider removed the bite from the morning air. Squealing children added to the holiday spirit. But he had trouble feeling festive.

Something had scarred Alice beyond the events he knew about—abandonment by the man she had loved, leaving for America, marriage to a near stranger, her husband's death.

The Maumee River . . . Was that where she had lived? The name sounded familiar, but he could not recall why.

He had studied America in recent years. Now that his anger had dissipated, he could admit that learning about her new country had been a way to stay in touch with her memory. But all his books were at home, so he couldn't check out her hint.

She was making snow angels—and demonstrating that she hadn't lost her touch with children. Why did she have none of her own? Had her marriage proved barren? And where was the rest of her family? She had returned alone to England. Why?

Alice concentrated fiercely on her charges, fearful that her control would snap if she allowed her mind to

wander. After four years, she should be used to suppressing the past, but Jeremy's questions made it harder than ever.

And making snow angels was a poor choice of activities, recalling the day she had taught Josh. She was returning to the fire when Duncan Mason joined her.

"Welcome home," he said in greeting. "We've missed you. Nobody else tells such good stories."

She laughed. Duncan had been thirteen when she'd left, one of a group of cousins she had often entertained with ghost stories. "Surely, you could have asked Rufton. I learned most of my tales from him."

"But he rarely visited the children's wing."

"Nor would I have," she pointed out. "Had I stayed, I would have made my bows the following spring. I might never have spent another Christmas here."

He laughed. "I doubt that. Masons always return. And you would have called on us. Christmas is a time to relive one's youth—except for poor Rufton," he added, nodding to where that gentleman stood in close conversation with Miss Havershoal. "Blatchford presses harder each year."

"I thought she was slated for Jeremy Caristoke." She had to work to keep her voice steady, which annoyed her. Jeremy had denied the connection, but she had assumed he was teasing. His family had never been delusional. If they expected a betrothal, then he was all but committed.

Christmas is a time to relive one's youth.

She hoped he had not fallen into that trap. They had no future together. Jilting Miss Havershoal so he could renew their flirtation would hurt an innocent girl, leaving him disappointed and possibly discredited, and add to her load of guilt. She didn't need that.

Duncan snorted. "Hardly. She's another of Lady Blatchford's candidates. Caristoke joined her court last Season, but he was no more serious about her than any of his previous inamoratas. He enjoys escorting the ladies, but few believe he will ever marry."

Alice turned the subject as the company tramped back to the house. Duncan's attention tugged at her. Here was another who was treating her as family rather than employee. The seasonal blurring of boundaries made it difficult to remember her place.

And that continued when she carried William upstairs for a nap. She had hardly tucked him into bed when the other governesses all but pushed her downstairs so she could help with the decorating. They, too, claimed that she was family.

The servants had piled the greens in the great hall. Michael helped his father hang apples. Elizabeth worked on kissing boughs under her mother's instruction. Alice joined a group weaving evergreen ropes.

Conversation buzzed around her. People raced in and out, whisking away the finished ropes to hang on mantels, walls, and banisters. Others carried off kissing boughs and bunches of mistletoe. Blatchford decorated every public area, from the smallest sitting room to the great hall, where the Christmas ball would be held.

"Alice Walford," exclaimed a man, sitting at her side. "I only just heard of your return."

"Mrs. McDougal." His face was familiar, but she couldn't recall his name beyond recognizing him as a Mason. That stocky build and square jaw were unmistakable.

"You don't remember me." He sounded chagrined.

"It's been a long time," she reminded him.

He nodded. "Allan Mason."

"The vicar's son." She smiled. "How is he?"

"He died last year."

"My condolences."

"It was for the best. He had been ailing for years. I have the living now."

"You?" She laughed. "I have trouble imagining you as a vicar. Aren't you the lad who led a midnight foray onto snow-encrusted battlements?"

"You do remember me. Not one of my better ideas. But I saved you from falling."

"After making me slip to begin with." She had been eight that Christmas. "I hope your punishment was suitably severe."

"A caning and an exorbitant amount of Latin translation." He made a face.

For the next half hour, they enjoyed a nostalgic review of childhood Christmases. But his repeated commiseration over her widowhood made her wary, and when he decried the difficulty of doing parish work without a wife, she decided that he had an ulterior motive for seeking her out. He was not the least confused about her position. A governess could make an admirable vicar's wife—and many would welcome the improvement in their lives.

But not this governess. Leading the conversation onto neutral topics, she pondered his timing. Was approaching her his idea? Or had someone noted Jeremy's interest? Linking her with Allan would keep her away from Jeremy, prevent him from making a cake of himself over a mere governess, and preserve his courtship of Miss Havershoal.

She was interested in neither of them. Finishing the rope, she excused herself to check on her charges.

Both were happily helping their parents, which would give her a chance to slip upstairs.

Two minutes later, she swore under her breath. Escape from the great hall was impossible. People were pouring through the entrance, ready for another Blatchford tradition—the raising of the largest kissing bough. Rufton would have the honor this year, and it looked like Jeremy was going to hold the ladder for him.

She worked her way around the periphery of the crowd, trying to keep from being swept away. It was slow going. Laughter soon signaled that the kissing bough was in use. She caught a glimpse of Jeremy and Miss Havershoal in a passionate embrace and turned away to hide her pain.

She should be feeling relieved, she reminded herself. He had believed her after all—which confirmed that his offer had arisen from pity. Now that she had turned him down, he was concluding his rightful business. She wished him luck—or would as soon as she got her emotions under control.

In the meantime, she would avoid him.

Jeremy dutifully laughed at his uncle's latest tale, wishing he had a few minutes alone to plan his next move with Alice. But like every other gentleman in the house, he was climbing ladders to hang garlands, apples, and kissing boughs as fast as the women could fashion them. Blatchford was enormous. The quantity of decorations they managed to hang every year amazed him, as did Lady Blatchford's ability to organize it all.

But they were finally done. He held the ladder in the

great hall while George attached the largest bough to a chandelier.

"Try it out, Caristoke," called someone from the crowd—probably his brother Harold. He gritted his teeth.

But raillery was part of the Season. "Why not?" he called back before realizing that the nearest lady was Victoria. *Damn!* It was too late to back down. He swept her into a dramatic kiss, feeling not the slightest spark from her willing embrace.

Devil take Harold! He hated being pushed. Unless he turned this into a game, he would find himself backed into a corner.

"Who's next?" he called, laughing. Making an even greater show, he kissed Miss Higgins, Miss Wallace, then his cousin Emily.

"Whew!" He furiously fanned his face. "I need air. George's turn." Shoving his friend into position, he turned to leave—and spotted Alice heading for the door.

Recklessness overcame caution as laughter erupted behind him. This chance was too good to pass up. As usual, a sprig of mistletoe was attached to the doorjamb. He rapidly worked his way through the crowd.

"Ahah! Caught me another one," he murmured when he reached her side.

But his grin died the instant his lips touched hers. *Oh, God!* Sparks exploded through every part of his body. Heat pooled in his groin, recalling countless dreams that had tormented his nights. Nothing had affected him like this in years.

They fit together even better than before. And despite her words by the lake, she was not indifferent.

She shuddered as his arms closed around her. Tremors dug her fingers into his waist.

"Allie," he whispered into her mouth, but she pulled away with a soft cry.

"Don't," she begged. "Your teasing will ruin my reputation and cost me my job."

For a moment he had forgotten everything, wiping the last ten years from his mind. But she was right. Until he convinced her to accept him, she was a governess. Despite the easing of social boundaries during the holiday season, overt attention would ruin her. Her status as a Mason would count for little if her honor was called into question.

Somehow he pulled himself together and grinned at those nearby. "This one works, too." He must not have held her too long because no one seemed shocked. Fleeing the ballroom, he sought the sanctuary of his room.

Allie. She hadn't changed where it counted. Somehow he must convince her of that. But it would be difficult. She had been right to suspect his motives.

He frowned over that confrontation by the lake. Until he had faced her, he had not planned to renew his offer. He had teasingly reminded her of their betrothal only to keep her from running away, then persisted in an effort to counter the devastation he saw in her eyes.

But her pain ran far deeper than their ancient parting, and the years had made him doubt his impressions. Did she still care? Could he read her face as before? Ten years was a long time.

Now doubt had fled. Her response to his kiss was unmistakable. He ran his fingers through his hair.

No wonder he had failed to find a wife. None of the ladies he had courted raised even a fraction of the heat that Allie could generate with a single glance. She was

the woman he wanted, the woman he needed if he was to find happiness.

But it wouldn't be easy. She was as stubborn as a mule when she got an idea in her head. It had been hard enough to convince her to accept him the first time. Even then she had insisted that she was not good enough for him. Now it would be worse.

George rapped on the door, letting himself in without waiting for an invitation.

"Would you care to explain that scene with Mrs. McDougal?" he demanded.

"Did I make a cake of myself?"

He sighed. "No. I doubt anyone noticed except Miss Havershoal. I had just finished bussing her—had to do every one of the chits to keep any of them from getting ideas. When you grabbed Mrs. McDougal, Victoria stiffened. That was no Christmas kiss, Jeremy. Do I have to warn Agnes that you are stalking her governess?"

"Yes . . . no . . . I don't know." He paced the room in silence for several minutes, trying to decide how much to tell George. "What do you know about her years in America?"

"No more than I already told you. She married. Her husband died. She worked as a governess in Boston for two years. When the war ended, she returned to England. Why?"

"She accepted me ten years ago, though her father fled to America before I could speak with him. My feelings haven't changed, but she won't give me the time of day now. Something happened over there."

George collapsed into a chair, shaking his head in shock. "Ten years ago? You were only nineteen."

"I know how old I was."

"But—"

"I never told you because she disappeared before we could make it official, and the circumstances made me wonder if she'd been playing me for a fool." He explained their mutual confusion. "But that no longer matters. I can't lose her again. I love her as much as before—perhaps more."

"She doesn't act as if she agrees with you," he said quietly.

"She does. She was just as affected by that kiss as I was, but she has some bee in her bonnet about being unacceptable—and not just because she is working for Agnes. I've got to find out what happened. The details don't matter, but how am I to convince her of that if I don't know what they are?"

"So what do you want me to do?"

"Find out what Agnes knows. And spread the word that Miss Havershoal is one of your mother's protégées."

He laughed. "Dear Mother. She never gives up. But I refuse to get married until I find someone I love."

"Thomas has had a profound influence on both of us. At least you understand my position."

"I hope you haven't pushed the Havershoal thing too far."

Jeremy shook his head. "I haven't seen her since the end of the Season. I've hardly spoken to her here, and we're in your house. She can't realistically expect anything."

He nodded. "I'll talk to Agnes, and perhaps I can find someone to distract Miss Havershoal."

4

After dinner, Alice brought the children to the great hall for the lighting of the Yule log. The men had gone in search of it once the decorating was finished— though *search* was a euphemism these days. The log had been chosen months ago, cut, then left in the forest to dry so it would burn well. But tradition was served.

Again, the children joined their parents and uncles, leaving her at loose ends. In Boston she had always slipped away during Christmas festivities, grateful that she did not have to stay with her charges. But that was impossible here. Where could she go? Memories clung to every room, leaving her as uncomfortable alone as she was in company.

"You are Louisa Walford's chit, aren't you?" demanded a voice at her elbow. "Went to America, as I recall."

"That's right, Uncle Horace." He was another relative. She couldn't recall the exact connection, but everyone called him Uncle. He had been ancient ten years ago, so she was surprised he still lived.

"How are Louisa and your father?"

"Gone," she said, repeating the lie she had told Uncle Edward. It was the only reason he had allowed her to cross his threshold. And it might even be true. She had not heard a word from them since they had parted ten years earlier.

Rufton distracted them as he carried in shards from the previous year's Yule log. Blatchford carefully arranged them around the new one. Oohs and ahs reverberated as the flames caught hold.

"Rascals," chuckled a gentleman Alice didn't recog-

nize. Half a dozen youngsters were climbing on the
end of the log that protruded into the room.

"But enjoying themselves," she murmured.

"Just as you did," said Uncle Horace.

"Me?" She tried to sound horrified, but couldn't re-
press a grin.

"You. One year you rode that log like a horse. Another, it became battlements in a war with your
cousins."

"Ah, yes. The war year." She actually giggled. "The
boys wanted me to be a damsel in distress, but I insisted on fighting the attackers." The Caristoke boys
had kidnapped her from the Masons, forcing them to
stage a rescue. Her cooperation with the supposed
enemy had started a new battle. She had been six or
seven at the time.

He laughed. "You always were an intrepid miss. But
I can top that story. My cousins and I managed to
sneak in loads of snowballs and drew up battle lines on
either side of the log. That was one escapade that was
not well received."

"And rightly so. You probably lost some poor governess her job. How old were you?"

"Maybe nine. But no one else was blamed. Everyone knows how easy it is for a determined child to slip
away during these house parties."

She could feel a blush staining her cheeks, for she
had often slipped away to meet Jeremy. Seeing him
again had recalled the wonder of those days. And Horace's tales proved that part of her was inextricably
woven into the Mason family tapestry, anchoring her
to a tradition that stretched centuries into the past. Another layer of ice melted from around her heart.

Excusing herself, she blinked back tears. Uncle Hor-

ace weighed family ties before position. His affection recalled the love and security she had enjoyed in her youth. Was the gulf between herself and Jeremy narrower than she had thought?

But that was a dangerous idea, for it raised hope that could never be fulfilled. Even if she remained a Mason, her sins formed a barrier between her and the world. Crossing it was impossible.

Prickles slithered across her neck.

Jeremy was searching for her. Her awareness was as acute as ever. She always knew where he was, and with whom. Tensing, she hid in an alcove until Pembroke waylaid him.

Jeremy slid into the pew beside his brother. Services were usually enjoyable, but tonight he could not keep his mind on the vicar's words.

His eyes kept straying to Alice, who shared the Westlake pew. She was quietly rocking William to sleep, leaving Michael and Elizabeth to their parents' attentions.

He had hoped to find her in the great hall, but when he finally caught sight of her, she was too far away. Even in the jovial atmosphere after lighting the Yule log, he had been unable to approach her. Every time he moved, someone stopped him to talk.

As promised, George had spoken to Agnes, learning only that Alice's parents had also died—which explained why she had returned to England. But no one knew how, where, or even when.

And he would have to be careful how he approached her, for George's questions had raised Agnes's suspicions. If he jeopardized Alice's position, she would have a real grievance. But returning to secret assigna-

tions made him feel unclean. It would have been better to have courted her openly that year. Yet he had been embarrassed by the depth of his emotions, and he had wanted to savor the wonder of her love away from the joshing of his friends.

What an idiot he had been.

His mood deteriorated when the vicar's eyes strayed toward Alice for the fourth time in as many minutes. Allan had been with her in the great hall that afternoon. Everyone knew he was looking for a wife. His sister had helped their father with the parish work, but she had recently wed. Would he have to vanquish another suitor as well as Alice's stubbornness? In her present odd humor, she might believe that a vicar was more suitable than an earl's son.

The service finally ended. The younger people always walked to the church, so only a little maneuvering brought him to her side. George carried William, leaving her unencumbered.

"Let me escort you home," he said, stopping in front of her so that the Westlakes drew apart. She could not refuse his arm without causing a scene. Slowing his steps soon dropped them behind the crowd.

"Shouldn't you be escorting Miss Havershoal?" she asked as they turned down the lane to Blatchford.

"I told you I wasn't interested in her," he reminded her softly.

"That's not what it looked like this afternoon."

He frowned, then shook his head in chagrin. "That was just the usual foolishness under the kissing bough, and she was only one of several. I made sure it meant nothing. Giving her ideas would be cruel, for I will not wed where I do not love. You are the one who taught me that I am capable of love, Allie. And Thomas has

shown me how rewarding a marriage can be when love is present. Do you remember him?"

"Of course. Black hair, green eyes, always flirting."

"That's Thomas. He had become London's most lovable rake before he settled down, and my godson promises to be just like his father."

She laughed, sending shivers down his back—and warming his heart. It was the first time he had heard her laugh since her return.

"Allie, you still affect me like no other woman I know. If you no longer care, I will accept it—but not until I understand why you are refusing me."

"A governess is far too low for an earl's son," she said primly.

"Fustian! That is a meaningless excuse. Even were I my father's heir, it would mean nothing. But I am far lower than that. My brothers have produced six sons already, so I'm in no danger of getting the title. And I don't care what your circumstances are at the moment; you are granddaughter to a baronet and cousin to an earl. That is more than adequate for a rascally third son."

"Rascally?"

"Bad choice of words. I never followed Thomas's path. Nor was I a jokester like my brother-in-law. Have you met Wormsley?"

She shook her head.

"He looks and sounds like an undertaker—long face, solemn countenance, deep voice. Always wears black. Many of his pranks involved coffins."

She laughed, so he related one of the more repeatable escapades. "Thomas was the larger-than-life rakehell; George is known for sober responsibility; both are well-known Corinthians. In comparison, I seem a light-

weight, for I prefer art and music, though Thomas has turned me into an acceptable equestrian."

"Stop it, Jeremy. This discussion is pointless. Your interests and reputation are not the issue. My character is lacking, and my training is unsuited for the life you would offer."

"Why? I know your character, Allie. It is everything I want in a wife. You are everything I want."

"Believe me, Jeremy. If there were any hope of a future, I would explore it. But there is not. I can only repeat what I told you this afternoon. You no longer know me. How could you? Events have molded both of us into new people, moving us along different paths. The girl you knew is long gone. The woman she became can never be yours."

"I don't believe you."

"Quit beating a dead horse. It's hopeless."

"Nothing is hopeless, especially at Christmas. Didn't you listen, to the vicar tonight? This season celebrates the birth of Christ, whose coming offered each of us a second chance at life."

"Not everyone," she said sadly, raising enough fear to choke him. "Some things can never be forgiven. Put the past behind you, Jeremy. If you cannot love Miss Havershoal, then find another. But not me. Never me."

She turned her head away, refusing to say more. Her lips formed a thin line that might have masked anything from minor irritation to excruciating agony. *Stubborn wench!* He ground his teeth in frustration.

"You aren't entertaining a *tendre* for our good vicar, are you?" he demanded finally.

"No. I am even less worthy of him."

"The vicar is more worthy than I am?" He swung her around to face him.

"Let it go, Jeremy. Please? This discussion is pointless."

"Never. I may not know what troubles you, but nothing could make you unworthy to be my wife. And you still care."

"I can't."

"You do, and I'll prove it."

Sliding his other arm about her shoulders, he pulled her into a kiss. This time he had no audience, allowing him to savor her, coax her, lose himself in her. Heat and need exploded between them.

She moaned, opening her mouth to his invasion. He had to lock his knees to keep from collapsing at her response. This was not the innocent kiss of first love, but a mature exchange, full of desire and longing. And her need was as great as his. Her love remained as hot.

Pressing closer, he devoured her mouth. A corner of his mind cursed the heavy cloaks that protected them from the cold, cursed the snow that kept him from dragging her to the ground. He wanted her with a ferocity he had never experienced. She belonged to him and to no other.

"Allie," he gasped. Another deep kiss had her melting against him. He wanted nothing more than to carry her to his bed, but he reined in his control. He could not dishonor her so. First, he must convince her to wed him.

But the moment his grasp loosened, she spun away, breathing heavily. "I can't," she sobbed. "I truly cannot. Don't torture me like this, Jeremy. If you care at all, leave me alone."

"Why?" he demanded, fisting his hands to keep from touching her again. Her eyes were full of panic.

"I am not even suited to be a governess," she cried. "How can I possibly be worthy of you?"

"I don't believe that," he began, but she backed away.

"Believe it!" she spat. "I killed my son." She stumbled toward Blatchford, tears running down her face.

Jeremy stared after her. Dear God, what kind of hell had she been living in? He didn't for a moment believe her. He knew her too well. Not only was she incapable of cold-blooded murder, she had always been harder on herself than on others, demanding a higher standard of behavior and condemning herself if she failed to meet it. She had once accepted the blame when Frank Mason had lamed her horse, yet all she had done was give him permission to ride it.

So what had happened?

And where? Unless she was exaggerating even more than usual, the incident must have occurred in a remote area. She could never have found a post in Boston if she had been involved in anything unsavory. Which brought him back to the Maumee.

He still couldn't recall why he knew the name, but she and her husband had probably lived there. They had produced a son—he suppressed a stab of pain—but something had left both husband and son dead. Alice blamed herself.

He turned his feet toward the house. Convincing her to tell him the details would require a very delicate touch. But he had to do it. She would be free of pain only after he convinced her that she was exaggerating. And she would never consider his suit until she was free of pain. Refusing him was additional self-punishment.

It would be impossible to see her before morning, for she would be shut in her room by now. How would she spend Christmas? Her charges would be with their par-

ents. Would she remain in the children's wing or enjoy the company of her unattached relatives?

He didn't know. Nor could he find out from the various cousins with whom he passed the remainder of the evening. Perhaps he could have learned more if he had asked direct questions, but he could not link his name to hers just yet.

Miss Havershoal was being properly entertained, he noted, watching George smoothly direct a progression of relatives in her direction. He was doing the same for all the unattached guests.

Alice returned to the house through a side door and sought an empty room where she could control her nerves. Why did she have to work for the Westlakes? A family of cold strangers would have been far better—like the one she had served in Boston, where the children's constant questions had kept unwanted memories at bay, and no one had treated her as an equal.

Dear Lord! Every time Jeremy touched her, the pain grew worse. She wanted him more than ever. If only she had kept the children nearby as a buffer. He could not have kissed her. Nor could he have badgered her.

Damn that kiss! The memory would keep her sleepless for weeks to come. As would imagination. He had changed in ten years. There was nothing tentative about his embrace now. He knew exactly what he was doing and how to force her response. She had been unable to hide her need—or her continued love. Finally, her desperation had grown so great that she had resorted to shock. It was her only means of escape.

Had she succeeded in driving him away? Surely, he could not love an admitted killer. But her heart knew that it was not over, would never be until she told him

everything. Only the full truth would end this farce. Watching his heart turn cold and his eyes fill with hatred was the next penalty she must pay.

So be it. Somehow, she would survive.

5

Alice tossed all night, Jeremy's questions torturing her mind just as his touch had tortured her body. At least she did not have to attend to the children today, she thought before sleep finally claimed her at dawn.

But older pains soon woke her. It was Christmas morning. The day she confronted the worst agony of all.

Josh!

Sighing, she knuckled the sleep from her eyes and stared out the window. Snow still blanketed the park, pristine except for the few places where the children had disturbed it.

For ten years she had hated Christmas, enduring it through a haze of guilt, grief, and heart-wrenching pain. It always emphasized her loneliness, for she had no one to share it with—no family, no friends, no child. Even Malcolm was gone. Not that he would have celebrated Christmas. That was not his way.

But he had been a good man, and she had never regretted wedding him. Perhaps if she could have loved him, she would have felt better. But despite a comfortable friendship, her heart had never been his.

He had been a hard worker, devoted to her and Josh. But he had also been an austere Scotsman who decried English rituals. She could still weep that Josh had missed the warmth and love of the holidays. Of everything they had given up, that had seemed the worst.

Frowning, she squinted against the dazzle of sunlight

on snow. The pain was duller. Sylvia, Duncan, Uncle Horace—even Allan—had demonstrated that she was no longer alone. She was alive and healthy, with a roof over her head, food in her stomach, and a position that allowed her to retain her dignity. And her family would continue to support her.

A hawk plunged into the snow and came up with a mouse.

Yet life wasn't that simple, she reminded herself, no matter what Jeremy claimed. Though only seven-and-twenty, her experiences on the American frontier made her feel fifty—and gave them even less in common than they had had ten years ago.

On that thought, she turned her back on the window and gasped. A package lay on the washstand, its tag bearing her name. She recognized the hand.

"Damn him," she whispered, grateful that Miss Parkenson had arisen early.

The package was not well wrapped. When she lifted it, an amethyst brooch fell out.

"Double damn him."

She knew the piece. It had been her grandmother's and had fastened her cloak the last time she had seen him.

This cannot be considered a gift, read the note tied to the clasp, *for I am merely returning your property. Cherish it, as I have.*

"Why are you doing this to me?" she wailed. "Are you trying to hurt me?" He was succeeding. The memories unrolled despite every effort to stifle them.

They had met on the edge of Pembroke Park, their first assignation since Christmas at Blatchford. A storm had driven them into an abandoned cottage. He had

slipped the brooch into his pocket for safekeeping while he kissed her senseless.

That had been the day he had finally persuaded her to accept his proposal. Both knew that convincing their parents would be difficult. His youth and limited prospects were against him. Her modest origins did not help. He had promised to meet her the following afternoon to decide when and how to proceed. By then, it had been late afternoon, and in her haste, she had forgotten the brooch.

She had never seen him again.

Now the amethyst sparkled through a sheen of tears. Not only had he kept it, he must carry it with him. There was no way he could have sent for it.

"Damn you, Jeremy."

Half an hour later, she had calmed enough to leave her room, but not until she escaped outside without meeting Jeremy did she truly relax. They must talk, and this time she must tell him everything, but first she had to assert better control over her emotions. With luck, she could postpone the final confrontation until Boxing Day. Too many activities filled Christmas. They would not find time to slip away.

The first was the children's party. He was there, of course, but they were both too busy to speak. The younger adults always helped with the games. Older ones came to watch and remember their own Christmas triumphs.

Jeremy was organizing the older children's activities, which kept him in the far end of the room, away from where she worked with the smaller ones. But even staying apart did not hold memory at bay, especially when Michael pulled at her skirt.

"Look at Uncle Frank!" Rufton was tying Frank's

ankle to a female cousin's for a three-legged race—a
favorite among the girls because the only way to main-
tain balance was to wrap arms around each other's
waists.

A wave of heat made her stumble.

She had partnered Jeremy in this race. They had not
won—in fact, they had fallen three times—but afterward, he had refused to leave her side, much to her delight. Her long *tendre* had made his attentions
welcome.

She sighed. They had met often after that. Only
George and Thomas had noticed, but they had assumed
that he was merely amusing himself. That had made it
easy to believe the worst of him after he disappeared.

Falling in love had been inevitable. Jeremy had been
so different from the other young men she knew, especially from her brother and cousins. He had always allowed the younger children to tag along, welcoming
them in his games and protecting them from being bul-
lied by the older boys. Once he turned his full attention
on her, she had given up her heart without a qualm.

Children squealed as the three-legged race got under
way. Judith had insisted on joining this event. She was
paired with a sixteen-year-old cousin, but her excitement turned to childish wails when he tripped her, letting Frank and his partner win. Judith's haughtiness had
not endeared her to those she sought to impress.

"Snapdragon!" shouted someone as the footmen
began drawing draperies and extinguishing most of the
candles. Others carried in huge bowls of fruit drenched
in flaming brandy.

"You have to be quick," Elizabeth reminded Michael
as they crowded around one of the tables. With so many
children present, half a dozen bowls were set up.

Michael glared. "I know that."

Alice hid a smile, then caught sight of Jeremy, who was helping one of his nieces. He was so good with children. It was a shame he had none of his own. But perhaps he could settle down once he accepted that she was truly ineligible.

A child yelped.

"He was greedy," chortled Michael. "If you take more than one, the dragon will bite." He demonstrated his skill by swooping in to grab a treat.

"Very good," Alice told him, then snatched one for William.

"Why can't I do it myself?" demanded William, sucking on his fruit.

"Next year," she promised.

"Who wants to go sledding?" George's voice silenced further questions.

Sledding followed the party whenever there was snow. She soon found herself atop the longest run, helping an uncle keep order and making sure that each slider was securely seated before pushing off. Others were stationed at the bottom, digging children out of snowdrifts and sending the sleds back up for the next ride.

Shrieks marked each precipitous descent. Those waiting in line amused themselves by pelting one another with snowballs. The adults joined in the game, ignoring snow that trickled down collars and into boots.

The afternoon was the most enjoyable she had spent in years. The family's love wrapped around her, warming her heart and lightening her spirits. She felt like a child again—which wasn't like her. She had always faced trouble head-on, admitted fault, and accepted the consequences.

Yet now she was wishing for the moon. The *what ifs* that had kept her awake most of the night returned, playing tag through her mind. What if Jeremy's grandfather had died a week later, or her father had not called on Uncle Edward that day, or she had thrown herself on Blatchford's mercy instead of fleeing with her family? What if she had moved to Boston after Malcolm's death, or had remained at Sarah's house, or had locked—

"Will you join me for the last trip?"

His voice nearly sent her tumbling over the edge of the hill. She had no idea how long she had been staring sightlessly toward the fire where servants warmed chocolate for the revelers.

Her hand clutched her throat as she turned to face Jeremy, embarrassed that they now stood alone on the crest. The children had gone. Only one sled remained.

"Sit in front, Allie," he ordered softly. "It's quicker than walking."

The invitation revived more memories—a dozen laughing rides down this very hill, clasped tight against his chest. They had slipped away while everyone else built snow castles. Their last run had overturned into a drift—not entirely by accident, she realized through more mature eyes—where he had kissed her until she thought the snow must melt from the heat.

He gently unclasped her fingers from the neck of her cloak, smiling at the amethyst.

"Back where it belongs."

"Thank you for returning it." She paused uncertainly. "I cannot believe you had it with you."

"I have wanted to return it for ten years, Allie. Thank God I finally got the opportunity."

"So you carry it just in case you might run into a girl

who left for America ten years ago?" Skepticism burned off the last of her embarrassment.

"Not entirely. Despite my anger over your departure, I never forgot what we had together. I kept the brooch as a reminder to accept no less. I have wanted to marry for a long time, but no one else ever measured up."

She had no response to that, so she cautiously took her place on the sled. Jeremy sat behind her, pulling her against him.

"I've always loved sledding," he murmured, sliding his hand across her stomach and tightening his thighs around her hips.

"Has your steering improved?" she asked lightly.

"Yes, alas." He pushed off.

The hill was steep and contained enough bumps to give a thrilling ride. She couldn't help herself. A shriek of pleasure escaped the first time a sudden drop sent her heart into her throat.

"Relax." He leaned over her shoulder, his warm breath tickling her ear even as the wind blew faster against her face.

She did. Exhilaration drove away memories and deadened thought of the future. All that mattered was the moment—speeding downhill in the arms of the man she loved.

His heels dug in so they halted behind a clump of bushes.

"Don't spoil it," she begged, clasping his hand.

He rested his head atop hers. She didn't know how long they sat there—five minutes? ten?—but they were the most precious minutes of her life. Just sitting, absorbing the warmth of his body pressed into her back, basking in the illusion of safety provided by his arms.

The harsh cry of a bird broke the spell.

"I must get back," she said, pushing away from him. "The children will have returned by now."

"Come along, then." Pulling her to her feet, he escorted her to the house.

6

Jeremy checked the folds of his cravat one last time before going down to the ball—and Alice.

He let out a sigh. He had wanted to talk with her earlier—had even deliberately stopped the sled out of sight where he could steal a kiss—but in the end he had allowed her to remain silent. And that had been good.

She had enjoyed the afternoon. Every time he had looked her way—and he had done so often—she had been relaxed and smiling. He doubted that she had done either for a very long time.

This had been the ideal place for them to meet again. A holiday at Blatchford must remind her of how it had been before—and could be again if she were not so stubborn. He would take every bit of help he could get.

Would it have made a difference if his grandfather had not fallen ill at precisely that time? If he had met her as planned, could he have kept her with him when her family left? The question had tormented him since he had learned of her father's flight.

Yet the answer was not clear. Many hurdles had stood in their way. He had been barely nineteen that Christmas. Marrying would have forced him out of school, for Oxford allowed only single students. They would have had to live at Pembroke. Even an increased allowance would not have supported an independent existence.

His youthful boasting aside, he doubted he could

have talked their parents into it. Would he have developed any of his current interests without Oxford and his years in London? What about friends? Following such different paths would have pulled them apart.

From the perspective of a nine-and-twenty-year-old, marriage at nineteen seemed absurd—which made his courtship appear sordid in retrospect. No wonder she had believed that he had abandoned her.

Perhaps they had been lucky that fate had divided them. In the interim, he had learned patience, responsibility, and how to enjoy small pleasures—like the minutes he had spent just holding her.

But however impossible marriage had been, his feelings had been true. He had loved her—and still did. Fate had separated them, but it had now brought them back together. Did that mean their union was ordained?

He snorted, striding out of his room. He was beginning to sound like his youngest sister. She had a long history of gullibility, including a prank George had played on her ten years ago.

His chuckles floated down the hallway. George had found the holiday boring once Jeremy abandoned him, so he had amused himself by spinning tales to Jeremy's young sisters. One had embellished the old myth that animals talked on Christmas Eve. Upon returning from church, the girls had slipped into the stable to see if it were true, and had overheard a shockingly lewd—though thankfully obfuscated—exchange between two sheep and a goat.

But George had received his comeuppance, choking on a biscuit when the girls repeated portions of the dialogue in the drawing room and asked what the words meant. Perhaps now he would reveal what his punishment had been . . .

But this sidetracking was getting him nowhere. He must press Allie for the truth. If anyone was unworthy, it was he. His behavior had been anything but gentlemanly. Secret assignations were unacceptable. Even at nineteen, he had known better.

The great hall was filled with candlelight, music, and the crackle of a wood fire. Wassail, evergreens, apples and spices, and the sweet smell of the Yule log wove the unique scent of Christmas. Dancers twirled through a waltz. Others gathered in brightly colored groups to laugh, talk, and toast each other and the holiday.

He led out an aunt, a cousin, Miss Wallace, and his youngest sister. Only then did he offer his arm to Miss Havershoal.

"I have seen little of you since arriving," she said as the country dance brought them together.

"That is hardly surprising. This is always a large house party."

"I see." She paused, then met his eyes squarely. "We were not invited at your request, then."

He had been searching for a way to introduce this very topic. His prepared lie was close enough to the truth to cause her no pain, and he would be glad to have the conversation finished. "Perhaps your name was mentioned by my father, or it may have been included by Lady Blatchford. Both Rufton and myself are under pressure to wed, but I have met no one in London who stirs my soul."

"You are looking for love." It was not a question.

He nodded.

"I wish you luck. And thank you for being frank."

The dance parted them. When the steps brought them back together, she slipped into light social chatter, giv-

ing no sign that her affections had been engaged. Thank God.

He danced the next set with another cousin. Only then did he turn to Alice.

Alice had mixed feelings about attending the Christmas ball. The family's warmth would make returning to her governess's duties harder. Then there was Jeremy. She did not wish to confront him tonight, but she could not avoid the ball without insult. Her compromise was a seat sheltered by potted palms, where she could exchange gossip with other governesses without being seen by the company.

Yet her cousins refused to leave her alone. Duncan and Allan danced with her. Uncle Horace sought her out for chatter. Even Lord Westlake treated her as family tonight, followed by Frank Mason. They had often played in the nursery when they were children.

"It's been a while, Cousin," he said as they began a country dance.

"As I recall, you pushed me into a snowdrift the last time I was here."

"Surely not!" He sounded scandalized, but ruined it by breaking into a laugh. "You screamed even louder than I'd hoped."

"And enjoyed it rather more than I should have," she shot back, grinning.

"Ah, but you retaliated by revealing the kiss I stole from Charlotte Caristoke."

"That's what you get for not doing it under a kissing bough. You were quite a scamp. Not nearly as serious as your brother."

"George?" He gaped. "Didn't you know that he was behind that talking animals caper?"

"Really? How did I miss so delicious an *on-dit*?" She knew, of course. She had been meeting Jeremy instead of drinking tea in the drawing room that afternoon, and she had paid little attention to the tale later on. Her mother had scolded her for missing tea, but the woman's pique had been tempered with relief that her innocent daughter had been spared such scandalous tales.

"I suspect he was bored. His closest friend had been ignoring him." Frank reddened, suddenly recalling that she was responsible for Jeremy's defection.

She turned the conversation to family news—marriages, births, deaths. Ten years of gossip easily filled the rest of the set.

Frank had hardly returned her to her corner when Jeremy appeared, hand outstretched. "May I have the next set?"

It was a supper dance and a waltz.

"Surely you waltz," he said softly, noting her reluctance. "How else could you teach your charges?"

It wasn't her skill that she doubted, but her ability to remain aloof. Yet refusing would create a scene. "Not well. You should partner someone more adept."

"But I want to waltz with you."

She sighed. "Did you command the others to dance with me?"

"No. You should know your family better than that," he chided her. "Blood counts far more than fortune or status. The Masons and Caristokes have that much in common. No matter where you go or what you do, you will always belong here."

She stifled the warmth, as she had done earlier. The sentiment was nice, but every rule had its exceptions. If they knew everything, they would not welcome her

back. Her crimes were unforgivable, especially in one so distantly related.

"You don't believe me," he murmured. "But you'll find it is true. Accept it. Let them remove some of the burdens from your shoulders."

"They already have," she quipped lightly. "How else could I have landed this position with only a reference from an unknown American that I could easily have written myself."

"Did you?" His eyes showed he was teasing, but the question wasn't funny.

"No." Her voice hardened, forbidding further probing.

They danced in silence for several minutes—dangerously. The lack of conversation focused her mind on the heat of his hand at her waist, the brush of his leg against hers on the turns, the spicy scent he had always worn. He was an excellent dancer, far better than she. And he used that expertise, deliberately forcing her to feel him, to remember all too clearly the way his hands had once caressed her, excited her, disrobed her . . .

Yet she reveled in his touch. No matter how painful the next days and weeks became, she would not regret it.

"We need to talk, Allie," he said as the music drew to a close. "Seriously talk. About everything. Will you come with me?" Couples already were moving toward the supper room.

So much for postponing the confrontation. "Very well. But you can only hurt yourself by insisting."

He led her to a morning room on the other side of the house, using a spill to light a lamp and several candles. It was unlikely that anyone would interrupt them.

"I want the whole story this time, Allie. All the whys and wherefores. Don't put me off by making shocking

statements and walking out. I don't believe you are a cold-blooded killer."

"Cold-blooded? No. But a killer nonetheless. My son is dead because of my negligence. An innocent child. That is not an act you can forgive, no matter what the circumstances."

"Try me, Allie." He leaned a shoulder against the fireplace. "My love is stronger than you suppose. And I know you better than you want to believe. You have always been too hard on yourself. I have heard of the Maumee River. It was the line of retreat Tecumseh followed when he withdrew his warriors into Canada. Were you caught up in that unpleasantness?"

"No, that occurred farther west. As did the attacks on settlers."

"Then what happened?"

She swallowed. Ten years ago she had sworn never to see him again. Four years ago she had renewed that vow. But circumstances had driven her back to England. She had feared when she stepped off the ship that this day would come. And what more fitting time to tell the tale than the anniversary of Josh's death. So she was prepared—she hoped.

Fumbling with suddenly clumsy fingers, she drew open her reticule and pulled out a miniature. Taking a deep breath, she handed it over. "My family."

Jeremy stared at the portrait, drawing nearer the lamp to make out the details.

"Oh, God," he whispered, not wanting to believe his eyes. But the truth was too obvious. The artist had been talented, capturing a perfect likeness of all three subjects.

An unsmiling Alice sat in a chair, her hair flaming like the sun, her green eyes brighter than any emerald. Her husband stood half behind her, his stocky body ra-

diating strength despite his lack of height, his iron gray hair still holding a few strands of red, his eyes a lighter green. A boy stood beside her, McDougal's arm draped lovingly across his shoulder.

His heart skipped a beat. The lad was tall and slender, staring straight ahead through rich brown eyes that matched his cap of riotous curls.

"No," he gasped as the miniature slipped from trembling fingers and crashed to the carpet.

"Yes," she confirmed, voice cracking. "Dearest Josh. I loved him more than life itself—because he was yours."

"Why did you never tell me?" His voice broke.

"Think, Jeremy. I was gone two days after the rain drove us into that cottage. I did not even begin to suspect until weeks later, and then only because Malcolm made me face it. He had fathered three children with his first wife, and his sisters had produced a dozen more, so he knew the signs. The voyage was rough enough that I had assumed I was suffering from seasickness."

He tried to pull her into his arms, but she stepped aside.

"Don't, Jeremy. This is no time for lovemaking. Have you forgotten why we are here? You may have fathered him, but I killed him. Your son."

He flinched. "Start at the beginning, Allie." Picking up the miniature, he gazed into eyes that mirrored his own. Tears spilled down his cheeks.

"Malcolm made me face the truth. I was carrying your child with no way of reaching you and no hope you would want me back if I did."

"How—"

She raised a hand to stop his words. "I know you had asked me to wed you, but within the hour, you were gone without a word. You were barely nineteen—an

age at which pranks and wagers are common. Women may wed that young, but men rarely do. What else was I to believe?"

"Heedless youth," he said with a sigh. "If only I had sent a message before I rode out. But I could think of nothing but Grandfather."

"And by the time you did, I was gone," she finished for him. "We already agreed that fate was at work. Accept it. I was in the middle of the Atlantic with no possibility of escape. The thought of facing my parents terrified me, and not only from shame. Father had been short-tempered for months, but his fight with Uncle Edward changed him. He seemed to be teetering on the brink of insanity. I dreaded pushing him over, so when Malcolm offered an alternative, I accepted."

"Marriage."

She nodded. "He needed a wife, having lost his family to cholera the year before. I desperately needed a husband, and we were already friends. He confronted my father. I never asked what he said, but I doubt it was the truth." She shrugged. "The captain married us that night. We landed a week later and immediately parted from my family, so there were no questions of Josh's parentage."

"Malcolm sounds a good man."

"He was. I wish I could have loved him. He deserved so much more."

"So you joined him on the frontier."

"And that was ultimately our undoing." This time, her shrug turned to shivers. Tears sparkled in her eyes.

Jeremy laid the miniature aside. "What happened, Allie?"

She paced the room. "Six years later, Malcolm was kicked by a horse. We tried everything to get the wound

to heal, including several remedies I had learned from the local Indians, but it festered, eventually killing him. If only I had sold out then and returned to Boston! But I didn't. I should have at least hired someone to work on the farm."

"Don't dwell on it," he urged softly.

She ignored him. "I was too busy to watch Josh. He helped a little, but mostly he ran wild while I worked in fields or cut wood to see us through the winter."

"What happened, Allie?" He was growing impatient at how she skirted the subject, and he didn't want to hear how hard she had worked to stay alive.

"A young couple had settled upriver from us. They sent for me on Christmas Eve. Sarah had gone into labor, and I was the only one they could reach—the weather was filthy, snow and wind making travel nearly impossible."

He exhaled, carefully schooling his features to hide his shock. He had not considered the deprivation she had faced on the frontier. How had she survived without servants, without doctors, without shops to supply what she needed? How had she dealt with storms like the one he had battled only two days ago?

Her pacing feet picked up speed. "It was a difficult labor, made worse because the babe was positioned badly, but she made it. Her son was born on Christmas morning. The storm had moved on, leaving a foot of snow behind. I should have stayed, of course, at least long enough to get a few hours of sleep. But I had planned a real Christmas for Josh, and I did not want him to miss it. I forgot that he had slept all night."

He could no longer remain aloof. She was shaking so violently that she could barely stand. Placing his hands

on her shoulders, he drew her close. "What happened, Allie?"

"We opened gifts and played games. I taught him how to make snow angels. We built a snowman. But when we returned to the house, I fell asleep. Dear God, I fell asleep. There was no one to look after him, but I fell asleep."

"Allie?"

She shuddered. "It was dark when I woke up. Josh wasn't in the house. I hadn't even locked the door, Jeremy. How stupid could I be? I hadn't locked the damned door!"

"Easy, Allie."

Her shaking grew worse. "I found him in the barn. He probably climbed into the loft to see the litter of kittens we'd found the week before. But he must have slipped and landed on his head. His body was already cold. If only I'd put that ladder away. I always took it down. Why didn't I do it that time?" Her voice broke.

"Cry it out, Allie," he said softly, pulling her head against his shoulder. So much pain—and on Christmas Day. Within hours of bringing a life into the world, her own had shattered. How had she survived?

He blinked back his own tears. Such a simple thing. She was so caring, thinking nothing of exhausting herself to help others. If this had happened to anyone else, she would have absolved them of guilt, yet she could not forgive herself.

"You are not to blame," he said when her tears finally slowed. "It was an accident, Allie. It could have happened at any time to any person. One of Father's grooms fell to his death just last year. Sleeping did not cause it. Even the ladder is not responsible. Boys are al-

ways climbing things—especially when something interesting is at the top."

"But I was his mother. I should—"

He covered her lips. "Perhaps you could have caught him had you been there. But he might well have fallen the next day. Or the day after that. His death was tragic, but not your fault." He stared into her eyes. "Even the door was not your fault. Are you sure it was unlocked?"

Shock widened her eyes. Obviously, she had never questioned her guilt.

He smiled. "How old was he, Allie?"

"S-six."

"More than capable of unlocking a door. And smart enough to hide the evidence of his disobedience. God knows, I did things like that often enough as a boy. The activities just beyond reach are always more interesting than those at hand."

"But—"

"It was a tragic accident. No more. I deeply regret not knowing my son, but I will never blame you for his death. I love you, Alice Walford McDougal. You have done nothing wrong. Quit punishing yourself and go ahead with your life."

"You're serious."

"Utterly." He tugged her to the window. "See that, Allie? It's the Christmas star, a promise of hope and forgiveness. Nothing is beyond redemption. We have our second chance, love. Accept it. You are the warmest, most caring person I know. Intelligent, strong—a far better person than I."

She was shaking her head. "I can't believe you don't hate me. I killed your son."

"No. Fate killed Josh. The same fate that has kept us apart. Someday, I want to hear all about him, but for

now, I have you, and I have no intention of losing you again. You belong in my arms."

"Do I?"

"You do indeed." He kissed her long and deeply.

Warmth flowed from his lips to hers, filling the empty spaces that had ached so long in her breast. His words reverberated through her mind, healing the wounds tragedy had left. She felt reborn.

His hands slid down to pull her closer. She twined her arms around his neck. Wonder at his forgiveness gave way to powerful heat and excitement as her love burst forth. He was hers. Forever. She was free. *Thank you.*

"I love you," she murmured as his lips trailed across her face. New shivers danced along her skin when he nipped at her ear.

He grinned. "I could kiss you all night, but we must finish our business before we can think of pleasure. There's a little matter of a betrothal that has dragged on for ten years. Don't you think it's time we scheduled the wedding?"

"Yes." His brown curls felt even softer than she remembered. He trembled as she pulled his head down for another kiss. "I missed you so much."

He groaned. "Business, love. What will it be? Banns, a special license, or a quick trip to Scotland? I've often wished we had done that the last time."

"Banns. We don't need to raise questions. My background will cause scandal enough."

"So be it." He nipped her nose, grinning. "But it's going to be a long three weeks."

The Christmas star winked as he lowered his head to seal their bargain.

The Christmas Ornament
by Carla Kelly

It happened over tea in October, 1815, tea in London with an old friend who required few conversational preliminaries, beyond the observation that Napoleon was at long last taking a sea voyage to St. Helena, and the weather was unusually pleasant for fall.

"Excellent tarts, by the way, Lord Waverly," Sir Waldo Hannaford said, eyeing the table again. "Prune centers?"

"Yes, indeed, Sir Waldo," the older man replied. "Did'ye ever think a purgative could be so tasty?"

Sir Waldo didn't, of course. There was a time when he would have eyed the tarts with a fair amount of suspicion. But he was older now, and willing to indulge in something that might smooth out the effect of too much dinner last night at his daughter Louisa's house. He ate another, then settled himself before the fire, sharing the footstool with his older neighbor from Woodcote, Lord Waverly of Enderfield.

"Gilbert, I have something to ask you," he began after a long moment's thought.

"Ask away, Waldo. The only thing I have ever held back from you is the location of my favorite trout stream in Scotland."

It was a joke of long standing between the two, and

they both chuckled, then settled back into the comfort they were born to. "Gilbert, I have a daughter," Sir Waldo announced at last.

"I believe you have three," the marquess replied, a smile playing around his lips.

"Indeed, I have. One is married and lives here in London as you well know, and the other followed her laird to Inverness, where, incidentally, he has an excellent trout stream on his estate."

Lord Waverly clapped his hands and then rested them on his comfortable expanse of waistcoat. "Good for you! And there is little Olivia, if I am not mistaken."

"Indeed there is, my friend, except that little Olivia grew up."

Lord Waverly looked at him over his spectacles, his eyes bright. "Did she do that, too? Children have that knack, haven't they?"

Sir Waldo nodded, pleased at his friend's good nature. "She is eighteen this month, and preparing for a come-out."

"Lord help us! Eighteen! I remember when Jemmy aided and abetted in pulling out two of her baby teeth. Eighteen, you say? A come-out?"

"That is the plan, except that Lady Hannaford and I are not so certain that a come-out is quite the thing for Olivia." He leaned forward to explain himself better. "Martha is determined that Olivia should marry within the district, because she cannot bear to see her last chick fly from the nest." He looked down at his hands, wondering how to say this. "I am not so certain that Olivia would be happy with what she would find here on the Marriage Mart, anyway."

"Picky?" Lord Waverly asked.

"No. Rather too intelligent for her own good," Sir

Waldo stated, crossing his fingers that such an admission would not lower him in his neighbor's esteem.

He wasn't sure. Lord Waverly frowned and contemplated the sweets again. "I have one of those," he said.

"A prune tart?" Sir Waldo asked, following the direction of his host's gaze.

"No, no! A son too smart for his own good." He scowled at the dessert tray and motioned for the footman to remove it. "You cannot guess what he is studying now."

Sir Waldo couldn't. He had endured a year's incarceration at Magdalen College until his father was kind enough to die and provide a ready-made excuse to return home to run the estate. He had never found scholarship to his taste. "No, I cannot imagine," he said.

"He watches people move!"

"No!"

"Yes! He sketches all their motions and tries to figure out ways for them to do their tasks more efficiently." Lord Waverly made a face and moved closer. "He even attends autopsies here at London Hospital to study muscles."

"No!"

"The double firsts were bad enough, but Jemmy knows so much now that I have a hard time talking to him. He is a don at All Souls and he actually has students who write down every pearl of wisdom that issues from his overheated mind! I call it ungentlemanly, and so I tell him, but he just laughs . . ." He lowered his voice. ". . . and ruffles my hair. The tall take liberties," he concluded.

A gloomy silence settled over the sitting room; a log dropped in the fireplace. "Is he attached to a female?"

Sir Waldo asked, his voice more tentative, considering his friend's obvious irritation.

"Lord, no! He is twenty-eight and I despair—positively despair—of grandchildren."

This was obviously a sore topic with Lord Waverly, because it propelled him out of his chair to pace the room. "Since he has a fortune in his own right from his dear mama, I cannot compel him to find a wife by threatening to hang onto his quarterly allowance." He stopped in front of Sir Waldo, his hands out, the picture of frustration. "And even if he had only a small stipend, he is so frugal he would make do all year, and then probably invest the residue!" He put down his hands. "I'll wager that half our friends would wish for problems like this from the fruit of their loins." He sighed. "Truth to tell, there is a sweetness to his nature that always quells me when I think I will pick a fight with him. So would he be your perfect son-in-law?" Lord Waverly sat down heavily in his chair and stared into the fire.

"I believe he would be." Sir Waldo pulled his chair closer to his old friend. "I want someone who will be kind to Olivia, keep her in the vicinity, and not mind if she reads books."

"That would be James," Lord Waverly agreed. "Such a union might even produce grandchildren eventually." He was silent a moment, staring into the fire, then looked at his old friend. "He is also mortally shy. How do you propose to bring this about?"

"I'm going to ask him," Sir Waldo said. "You know I am not a fancy speaker. I'll put it to him straight out."

"You're going to propose to my son?" Lord Waverly could not help smiling.

"H'mm, I suppose I am," Sir Waldo agreed, struck

by the thought. He picked up his glass. "What would you say to an engagement by Christmas?"

Without a word, his friend picked up his own glass, and they drank together.

It was one thing to laugh about a proposal with an old friend, Sir Waldo discovered, but quite another to actually put the suggestion into motion. Even the harvest scenery between London and Oxford failed to rouse his interest as he contemplated the next step. My older daughters would call me the rankest meddler, he thought as he stared out the window. They would point out how well they did on the Marriage Mart, and assure me and their mama that Olivia would find a man on her own.

But will she? he thought, far from the first time. Even the vicar, who was not given to either reflection or observation, noted once that Olivia "looks at me as though I don't quite measure up." I should never had indulged her whim for scholarship, Sir Waldo told himself, again not for the first time. Who would have known she would outshine everyone in the family, with the possible exception of her oldest brother, Charles? She is too smart for her own good. And probably at the mercy of fortune hunters, considering her trusting disposition. That causes me worry, he thought.

God be praised that at least she was not difficult to look at, although no beauty, he knew. Still, even there, Olivia was a true original. She had the correct posture and deep-bosomed loveliness of her mother and sisters, but she was only a dab of a thing. "I hope James Enders has not grown too much since last I saw him," he said to his reflection in the carriage window. "He could be intimidating to a chit like Olivia."

He knew Olivia's hair was hopeless, red like his own, though darker, but with the added defect of curling like paper corkscrews that pop from a magician's box when the lid is removed. It wasn't a matter of taming the wild mop, but rather forcing it into submission. Olivia did not help the matter much, he reminded himself, not when she dragged it all on top of her head into a silly topknot. Well, not precisely silly, he reconsidered, smiling at the thought. I call it fetching, in a funny kind of way, even if her mama despairs. She is interesting to look at, he concluded, possibly even memorable. But a beauty? Alas, no.

He sat back, smiling at the thought of his daughter, thinking of her quick step, her outright laugh, and her absorption in books. "It is this way, I should tell you, James Enders," he rehearsed in the carriage as the Oxford spires appeared on the horizon and the land began to slope toward the River Isis. "An estate agent once told me that even the most oddly arranged house can find a buyer. It just takes the one person who happens to be the right buyer."

Even his admitted lack of scholarship never quite prepared Sir Waldo for Oxford. Whatever his inward turmoil, he took the time to admire the loveliness of Magdalen Tower, smile at the architectural eccentricity of the Radcliffe Camera, and listen as Great Tom tolled the hour from The House. Olivia should be here, he mused, and then chuckled at the impossibility.

In his own year at Magdalen, he had passed All Souls numerous times, and never without a sense of awe, knowing that it housed the brightest among them, those who were finished with undergraduate years and embarked upon more study, a thing Sir Waldo could never

imagine. He addressed the porter at All Souls and asked him to locate Lord Crandall.

"Ye timed it right, sir," the man informed him. "We are almost at Evensong, so the tutorials are over. I'll have him here directly, if you would wish to wait in the foyer."

Sir Waldo did not wish to wait there, not when the quad beckoned, with its trees of fall colors. Christmas is coming, he thought, looking at the late afternoon sky. I wonder what my dear wife will tell me that she wants me to surprise her with on Christmas morning? I shall have to ask her soon, he mused.

The day was cool, but the sun had warmed the stones in the quad. Flowers close to the warmth of the wall still bloomed. He heard footsteps and looked up to see Lord Crandall approaching him. He was content to stand slightly in the shadow of the corridor and watch the man come closer.

James Enders—Viscount Lord Crandall from one of the family's various honors—wore his black scholar's robe, which the wind picked up and made him seem larger than life for a moment. Sir Waldo smiled to notice that Lord Crandall's hair, dark like his own father's years ago, looked no tidier than Olivia's. Hair must be a nuisance to the brightest among us, he could only conclude. Louisa's and Mary's hair was always in place, and not even a loving father could overlook their lack of book wit.

He had not seen Lord Crandall since the death of his second son, Timothy, seven years before, killed in the retreat from Corunna and buried with all military honor in the Hannaford vault. James, an undergraduate at New College then, had attended the obsequies, his face serious, his eyes troubled. And I never invited him

back, Sir Waldo thought with a pang. I was always afraid to see him again, because he was so closely allied with Tim. I may not have been fair to any of us. I wonder, first of all, if I owe him an apology?

James was even taller than before, with that purposeful stride of all Enders men. Not a lollygagger in the bunch, Sir Waldo thought, as he gazed with something close to fondness on his dead son's friend. Big hands and big feet and a wide mouth, he observed. The Almighty was generous in all ways to that particular twig on the branch of the human family. None of them handsome, but they do have an air.

And then he was standing in front of Sir Waldo, his hand extended. Wordlessly, Sir Waldo came forward, then found himself caught in a bear hug of an embrace, something he had not anticipated, but which he found gratifying in the extreme. And then what would the young man do but take his hand and kiss it? Sir Waldo felt tears start in his eyes. What is it about you Enders? he asked himself as he allowed his hand to be kissed and then held. Such a gesture would seem strange indeed from another, but from James it seemed so fitting as to make him grateful he had come here, no matter the outcome.

"You have been too long away, Jemmy," he said simply. "Or I have."

"No matter," the viscount replied. "There's hardly a rip in the world that can't be mended. Come inside with me, and I'll send my man for beer and cheese."

Soon Sir Waldo was seated, warm and comfortable, in what must be Lord Crandall's favorite chair, all rump-sprung and soft, while his host sat cross-legged on a shabby rug in front of the fire, toasting cheese. "I suppose I should serve you something better than

cheese and beer," he said, turning the fork with a certain flair that told Sir Waldo volumes about his young friend's dining habits. "I like it, though, and suppose that others should, too." He deposited the cheese on a plate next to a slice of toast and handed it to Sir Waldo. "And excuse me, sir, but Madeira is for old men."

Sir Waldo took the plate, relishing the fragrance of the cheese. "This is the perfect antidote to last night's dinner," he said. It was good, he decided, and as plain and ordinary-seeming as the man sitting on the floor.

"You've been dining in London, I'll wager," James said. "Visiting Louisa?"

"Indeed, yes," he said. "I have left Lady Hannaford there." He lowered his voice. "Louisa has just been through a confinement and finds her mother's presence. to be a comfort, even if this is our fifth grandchild. A son again, Louisa's third."

"Congratulations, sir," James said. He forked another wedge of cheese onto Sir Waldo's plate, and nodded for his man to pour the beer. He turned his attention to the fireplace again. "And the rest of your family? What do you hear from Charles?"

"Still in Paris, and hoping—along with all Europe, I believe—that this Second Treaty of Paris will put a period to French trouble."

He fell silent then, thinking of his second son, dead at Corruna, who would be alive yet if Napoleon had not adventured where he was not wanted. To his gratification, James seemed to understand his silence. He leaned back and touched Sir Waldo's leg, giving it a little shake. The gesture was as intimate as his earlier kiss, and Sir Waldo's heart was full. This is the only man for my beloved Olivia, he told himself.

"I miss Tim," James said simply. "I am twenty-eight,

dear sir, and I look in the mirror and see lines and wrinkles that were not there a year ago. But Tim is forever twenty-one and young."

"So he is," Sir Waldo managed to say. He took a deep drink from the mug in his hand. I cannot fault his ale, he thought. He may live like a student still, but he knows his victuals.

"We have all been too long from each other," James said after a bite of cheese and a quaff of his own. "I did not come around because I did not wish to give you added pain."

Straightforward like all the Enders, eh? Sir Waldo thought. You say what you think, rather like Olivia, and somehow, it is the right thing. "There was a time," he began, but could not continue. They ate in silence then, raising their glasses in tribute to the one who was not there. In his own book of life, Sir Waldo felt a page turn.

"Charles hopes to be home for Christmas," he said, handing his plate to the valet. "Louisa and her family, too, if she and the baby are strong enough to travel."

"How nice for you," James said. "I suppose I will go to London and Papa, although it would be nice to see Charles."

He waited then, expectant without appearing nosy, for Sir Waldo to explain his visit. Sir Waldo hesitated. As right as he is for Olivia, I have no business pronouncing this scheme I hatched, he thought. I could merely say something about wanting to see him after all these years, and it would be right enough. I could extend one of those meaningless invitations to visit us for Christmas and leave it at that. He sighed. And I could throw Olivia onto the Marriage Mart with all the other hopeful girls and pray that one man in ten thousand will

see and understand her special qualities, and even love her for them. Or I could speak. He cleared his throat.

"Jemmy, I have a daughter," he began.

"I believe you have three, sir," James said with a smile. He raised his knees and rested his arms on them, his eyes on Sir Waldo's face. "Has Lady Hannaford ever forgiven Tim and me for assisting in the removal of Olivia's two front teeth?"

Sir Waldo laughed, and his young friend joined in. "Oh, they were due out, lad! The only thing Martha took exception to was when Tim taught Olivia to spit through the vacant space. I believe you were blameless in that."

"Actually, yes." He grinned. "How nice to have a pure heart for once."

How good to talk about Tim! "Jemmy, you are an antidote," he said simply. "I don't know when Tim was ever in more trouble. Olivia was six then?"

"I believe she was," James agreed. "Tim and I were almost eighteen and should have known better. How is Olivia?"

"She is planning for a come-out this spring," Sir Waldo said. "Martha and I have been long away from London, but Louisa is all eagerness to do this thing for her little sister."

"She is eighteen," James said, more a statement than a question.

"Or as near as." Sir Waldo paused again. I could still stop here, he reflected. Who is to say that my darling girl will not find the best man on her own? He frowned. And who is to say that she will? "Jemmy, I want to talk to you about Olivia." He glanced over his shoulder at the valet, and James nodded to the man. Sir Waldo

heard the door close quietly. "I want to find her a good husband, but I have certain requirements."

Sir Waldo went to sleep that night in his own bed, a happy man, a father with a clear conscience. I have explained to Lord Crandall my concerns for my dear daughter, he thought, warned him that she is often nose-deep in books, mentioned her considerable fortune in passing, not overlooked a single freckle or her unruly hair, and stressed her clear-eyed way of doing things. He smiled in the darkness. I have told Jemmy of his own father's wish to see him married and setting up his nursery, and reminded him of the duty he owes there, and he took it without a murmur. Possibly I am trafficking on his own tenderness for Tim, and the sweetness of Jemmy's own nature. The word love never came up, but kindness did. I am a happy man.

He composed himself for sleep, thankful to be in his own bed, but restless without Martha nearby. I will leave it to James Enders to fill in the details. He knows his duty to his own family, and my personal interests to this little sister of his great good friend. Sir Waldo smiled into the darkness. One can hope for love, too. Stranger things have happened.

It took until the middle of November for James Enders to nerve himself to consider the next step—his step—in Sir Waldo's plan. When he should have been concentrating on student recitations in tutorials, his fertile brain was taxing itself with a plan of his own. He had earlier congratulated himself that while he had agreed to actively consider little Olivia Hannaford—great gadfreys, was she *old* enough for a man's bed?—as a partner in marriage, the matter was not chipped

onto an obelisk somewhere. I can certainly take a month to visit Enderfield, he reasoned. If she takes my fancy, I can pursue the matter.

How, he had no idea, not one. True, his undergraduate days had not been without occasional visits to discreet women, and there was even one term when he was certain he was besotted with an opera dancer; the occasions passed, as do all the storms of youth. He had gone to Almack's like the proper gentleman he was, bowed and danced, and carried on what light conversation he possessed, which was precious little. These females do not wish to know of autopsies, and quivering muscles of rats, and the beauty of motion, and the people who perform the world's labor, he decided, after one particularly profitless evening several years before. He would not thought it possible for a living woman's eyes to glaze over while he talked, but after that evening, he did not doubt it again. He never returned to Almack's.

He knew he wanted a wife. Enough of his friends were walking arm in arm with pretty things that bore their name and children. Despite the concentration of hours and hours of rational scholarship, he found himself longing late at night, or at odd moments in the day, to reach for something besides another pillow, or a second book off the shelf. "I want a wife," he declared out loud.

"My lord, we all do," said his student, grinning in spite of himself.

"Forgive that, Walters. I received a wedding announcement from a friend today, and the matter was on my brain," he lied. "Now, where were we?"

"I was describing the function of the female pelvic floor," the student said.

James had the good grace to laugh. "Walters, that accounts for it! Do proceed, and I will remember my manners."

He delayed in suggesting to his father that they return to Enderfield for Christmas, partly out of stubbornness, and partly from a certain delicate shyness that he knew was part of his nature, and which irritated him from time to time.

He did bring up the matter during dinner after one of his visits to London University. *I wonder if fricassee of liver was the right choice tonight,* he asked himself. *I have been wrist deep in a hip reduction all afternoon, and this looks very like.* He pushed away the plate. "Papa, let us go home for Christmas," he suggested.

The sentence had barely left his mouth when his father declared that it as a capital idea. "I am perfectly at liberty to go as soon as you wish, son," he said. He frowned at his own plate. "Ah, Jemmy, we have been so long away that things are probably shabby there. I wonder . . . do you think . . . do we dare impose on Sir Waldo to loan us Olivia to offer suggestions on refurbishment? If she is anything like her mother, she has some skills along those lines."

It was a wonderful suggestion, and James leaped on it. Only after he was lying in bed that night did he wonder if Sir Waldo had been discussing intimate matters with his own father. It seemed unlikely, considering his father's somewhat formal demeanor, and Sir Waldo's easygoing nature. *Merely a coincidence,* he told himself. And that probably accounted for his dream of dissecting fricassee while Sir Waldo smiled benignly from a scat in the surgeon's gallery. At least he did not dream about Olivia; those dreams left him a trifle embarrassed with himself.

There is something about Sir Waldo's suggestion that is doing strange things to me, he thought the next afternoon as he walked from the Camera back to All Souls. Is the world in a conspiracy? Only moments ago among the books, he had chanced upon one of his brightest pupils and surprised himself by suggesting that they end the tutorial a week ahead of the Christmas holidays. He knew the lad—so intense, so eager to learn—would object, but he had not been prepared for the swiftness of his acquiescence.

"You don't mind?" James had inquired in all amazement.

"I'll bear the strain, Lord Crandall," was the reply, given in such a serious tone that James could not be sure if he was being quizzed. Students today are certainly more subtly layered than I ever was, he thought as he nodded and left the Camera.

He surprised himself further by his own heated argument with his valet that night as the poor man attempted to pack his clothing for the return to Enderfield. James knew that his was a mild disposition, absentminded even, in all areas outside of his studies, and he disconcerted himself with the vehemence he directed toward his own shabby shirts and collars. Mason, ever the soul of rectitude, was finally driven to say in clipped tones, "My lord, if you will not go to a tailor, the result is what is laid before you!"

"You could have insisted more strenuously," James countered, but he knew his argument was weak at best. The valet only tightened his lips and maintained a stony silence that persisted throughout the remainder of the evening. I have been more pointedly ignored only by cats, James thought as he went to a cold bed unencumbered by the usual solace of a warming pan. I can only

hope that Mason's miff wears off before he brings me shaving water with ice chunks in the morning.

To his great relief, the shaving water was hot. Mason unbent long enough to inform his master that he had taken the liberty of writing to Lord Crandall's London tailor to request an audience the next afternoon. "My lord, you are going to London anyway to retrieve your father," Mason reminded him. James thought it prudent not to argue.

Two days later, he sent Mason to Kent and his own relatives for Christmas. Having discharged all London duties, James and Lord Waverly traveled back along the same road through mud and sleet, stopping ten miles shy of Oxford at the village of Woodcote. On the advice of his father's butler, they dined at the inn while the family servants rode ahead to reconnoiter at Enderfield. "For while I suspect that the Carvers have been adequate caretakers, one cannot assume that the chimneys are drawing properly, or that the beds are made," the butler warned.

They tarried long enough over dinner for the butler to work any number of miracles. When they arrived at Enderfield, long after all light was gone from the sky, fires were in the hearths, holland covers removed from the major rooms, and beds made. James strolled with his father through the gallery to gaze upon any number of Enders ancestors a trifle dusty in their frames, but none the worse for neglect.

"It is a little shabby," Lord Waverly admitted, stopping before the portrait of his lovely wife, dead since James's days at New College.

"Mama is not shabby," James contradicted.

"No, indeed," his father agreed. "She never was." After a moment's contemplation, he set them both in

motion again. "But we can certainly refurbish her house before she looks down on us from whatever celestial sphere she graces and despairs over husband and son!"

I am here to claim a wife who will turn this into a home again, James told himself as they proceeded toward the bedroom wing and slumber. Mama would have liked that, Papa will be ecstatic, Sir Waldo suggested it, Tim would have approved, and I think it must be a good idea if everyone feels that way. As he composed himself for sleep that night in his old chamber, James wondered if anyone had ever asked Olivia.

Over eggs and bacon the next morning, he knew that it was not a question to put to Olivia, or to any female probably. One does one's duty, he thought, even if the nuts and bolts of the matter are less discussed between men and women than Watt's steam engine or Lavoisier's treatise on the properties of oxygen. And, he reflected, gentlewomen seem to have a knack for knowing. We assume the rightness of marriage, and if some among us need prodding . . . He took his cup and saucer and stood gazing out the French doors that would have been open in the summer, giving onto the small breakfast terrace. In some matters, I am a slow learner.

It was good to be home, he decided as he leaned against the door frame. The snow had stopped, and the sky was so blue that he squinted. The trees were bare of leaves now, and he could easily see Sir Waldo's property, the house substantial as Enderfield, if not quite so large. He thought of Tim and his youth, which suddenly seemed so long ago.

He knew it was a simple matter to pay a morning call on the Hannafords, but by the time he worked up his

nerve the next day, it was afternoon, and really too late for such a call of courtesy. "They will think I am finagling a dinner invitation," he explained to his father.

"You used to do that," Lord Waverly pointed out.

"And Tim was my excuse, sir. I have none now, beyond a desire to see the family," he said. "Maybe tomorrow."

He never did pay a courtesy call to the Hannafords that week, choosing instead to organize his notes for lectures after the holidays were over, and reread Ketchum's paper on motion. His father had a mild sore throat so they did not attend church. By the next week, he realized that he had waited too long to make a casual visit and might as well give it up as a hopeless case and return to Oxford. Some men are not destined to marry, he told himself; perhaps I am one of them.

James wondered how to broach the matter to his father, who seemed content to regard him with a certain fondness and continue his own career in front of the fireplace, reading when he felt like it, and dozing when he did not. Papa is glad to be here, James thought. He would be disappointed if I suggested that we return to London for Christmas. James decided that he would find stationery in the book room and write Sir Waldo a letter, telling him to choose another son-in-law who was not too shy to pay an initial morning call.

He was in the hallway, heading for the book room with the firmest of intentions, when someone knocked on the door. He knew that his father had gone out earlier to walk among the shrubbery and breathe deep of the brisk air, so he hurried to open it, waving away the footman. He opened the door and there stood Olivia Hannaford.

He knew he would be surprised the first time he saw

her—if he saw her—because at their last meeting at Tim's funeral she was only eleven years old. Time does things, he thought as he looked upon her loveliness.

He remembered her from her childhood, but even then, he was not prepared for that certain something about her that he, the most eloquent of men on paper and in lecture hall, was totally unable to explain. Sir Waldo was so right; I have never seen anyone like this, he thought.

There she stood, not greatly taller than he recalled from their last meeting, but so different. She wore a heavy grey cloak with the hood up, but her marvelous hair threatened to spill out of its boundaries. Wonderful, impudent hair, he thought, entranced by the curls. She was covered completely by the cloak, but her shape was a graceful outline. Time, which had done nothing to ameliorate her hair, had managed to subdue her freckles. They were the palest marks now, and completely bewitching. Great God in heaven, what a woman this is, he reflected.

"I wish you would ask me in," she said. "My feet are cold. Jemmy, that wreath has to go."

He smiled and motioned her forward. "Miss Hannaford, excuse my bad manners. Come in, please. What wreath?"

She stopped right in the doorway and stared at him, then turned pointedly to look at the door directly next to him. "That one you are almost leaning upon. And please do not call me Miss Hannaford. I have always been Olivia to you, except when I was Oblivious, or Ollie, or . . . what was that other name Tim hatched?"

He thought a moment, resisting the urge to shake his head because he knew his brains would fall out and

drop onto the floor at her feet. "I believe it was just plain Livy."

"You're too kind," she said with a smile of her own. "I believe it was Liver." She held out her hand to him. "Livy will do, unless you are determined to be formal."

She wore gloves, of course, and as he took her hand, he wondered how human bones could feel so delicate. I will have to take such good care of all this magnificence, he told himself, then said without another moment's thought, "Olivia, you have superior bones."

What just came out of my mouth? he asked himself in stupefied amazement. Good God, but she will think I am crazy, he thought, then blundered on. "I mean . . . oh, hang it, I have seen a lot of bones in autopsies, but none of them ever felt like yours."

Open mouthed in total shock or wonder (he wasn't sure which), her hand still in his, she stared at him.

"I mean . . ." he began lamely, and stopped. Shut up, James, he thought. And let go of the nice lady's hand. There's a good man. Step away slowly and maybe she will think you are harmless. No quick motions. If she slaps you or faints at your feet, it will be only what you deserve.

To his surprise, she did neither. While she did carefully remove her fingers from his grasp, she merely stepped back and shook her head. "Mama would say you have not changed an iota, Jemmy," she told him.

"I probably have not," he agreed. "Olivia, please come in. I promise to remove the wreath."

"And I will make you another one," she said, stepping inside and looking around. "Oh, it has changed here."

I suppose it has, he thought to himself as the butler took her cloak. We have stayed away since Mama died,

and I fear that our neglect shows. He took a deep breath. "What would you do with the place, Livy?" he asked.

"Paint it and put on new wall covering, and send the crocodiles packing," she said promptly, pointing to the chaise with the reptilian limbs, a remnant of an earlier remodeling, modish after Napoleon's plunge into Egypt.

"And go to the warehouses in London for new furniture?" he suggested, walking with her toward the sitting room.

She shook her head. "First, I would go into your attics and see what is there." She stopped. "Are you planning to marry and bring a viscountess here?"

He almost winced. "I suppose I am," he managed to say.

"I would not have thought you would ever leave All Souls," she said as they moved into the sitting room. "Papa tells me that you are doing great things there."

"I like to think so," he said, hoping for a touch of modesty, where he felt only embarrassment, and the surest conviction that she would think him strange, indeed, if he explained his study.

"What, for instance?" she asked.

"I doubt it would interest you," he replied.

Lord Crandall prided himself on the sensitive side of his nature, but he winced again at the expression that came into Olivia's eyes after his bumbling statement. It was as though he had blown out a candle inside her.

"Perhaps not," she said, her voice as nicely modulated as before, but with something less in it, he thought, some overtone that seemed to bank the fire he had noticed when he opened the door on her loveliness.

To his dismay, no amount of small talk seemed to

bring about any recovery. Gracefully, she accepted his offer to pour the tea when it came, and she certainly held up her end of the inconsequentials that both of them seemed to be uttering. A man more shallow would have not noticed a thing, but James knew he had blundered, and the deuce of it was, he was not entirely sure how.

After she left, he took the wreath off the front door and stood for a long time gazing into the mirror in the entrance hall, wondering how it was that a man such as he should be permitted to roam free in England without a restraint around his neck. He was still standing there, heaping all sorts of abuse on himself, when his father returned from his stroll through the shrubbery.

"Did I see little Olivia walking home?" he asked.

"You did," James replied. He turned to look at his father. "Papa, what do you see when you look at me?"

His father frowned and stood a moment in contemplation. "Someone pleasant to look at, a little shabby at the elbows, perhaps, and possibly too tall for some doorways." He shrugged. "Other than that, I can see no glaring defects."

James groaned. "They don't show until I open my mouth, Papa! Do you know . . . can you imagine . . . what I said to Miss Hannaford?"

He felt no relief when Lord Waverly smiled back, the picture of patriarchal serenity. "Oh, something inane about pretty ankles or her tiny waist? I am at a loss, son. Do enlighten me."

"I could not see her ankles. She was wearing boots!" James said, then felt his face grow hot. "I took her hand . . ." It was so stupid that he closed his eyes and rushed out the rest of the sentence. ". . . and I told her

that I have felt many bones from autopsies, but none as nice as hers! Shoot me now, will you?"

Lord Waverly laughed, which sank James further. "It would be a mercy killing, but I cannot think this county's coroner would overlook it." He took James's hand in his own. "Nice bones, son. And that froze her completely?"

"Well, no, it did not, now that you mention it," James said, a little surprised at his own density. "Actually, she went all quiet after she asked what I was doing at All Souls, and I said it would not interest her."

A thoughtful look on his face, his father released James's hand and linked elbows with him, as though to stir him from further self-criticism at the mirror. "Did it occur to you, son, that she might be interested?"

"The thought never crossed my mind," James said frankly. "I have mentioned it to other ladies, and heaven knows, they did not care."

"Perhaps Olivia does." Lord Waverly nodded to the butler. "Withers, do bring me tea, and something rather more strong for Lord Crandall." He patted the seat beside him on the sofa. "James, if she is interested in what you are studying, you are certainly at liberty to tell her. Surely, it is not a secret." He leaned closer. "I would be the only man admitting it if I were to assure you that I know what a woman thinks. It is a mystery, indeed, and that is all I know, even after nearly sixty years of sharing this planet with creatures of the fair sex."

One could grow bitter with the lack of good advice I have received from this father, James thought as they went to the Hannafords' the following night to dinner. And the deuce of it is, I tell the man I am in despair, and he just smiles.

They could have taken the carriage, but Lord Waverly had suggested that they walk, which pleased James. He had a dislike of sitting in overheated rooms and was in no hurry to arrive at the Hannafords'. At All Souls it would be cheese and bread, biscuits with sprinkled sugar and cinnamon, and the window open just enough to make the beer lively. He sighed. Perhaps marriage would be a drawback. Be she ever so complacent, no wife would tolerate such a menu, or winter's chill in her sitting room. I doubt she would allow me to hang my clothing on doorknobs, either, even though it is such a convenience when I am late for tutorials.

"Papa, how do I know if she is the right one?" he asked suddenly as they crossed to the side door on the Hannafords' terrace, where they always entered.

"You listen with all your heart to what she says," Lord Waverly told him. He put his hand on James's shoulder and gave it a shake. "Pray you are not so scientific to overlook that kind of heart."

Pray I am not, he thought as he knocked on the door.

If Olivia had been beautiful last week, with her hair wild, and her cloak snowy, she was incomparable this night, James decided as he sat across from her at the table. His momentary disappointment at not being seated next to her was quickly assuaged by watching her animated good cheer from the stuffed haddock to the almond crescents. Although she was a small woman, she ate well, with none of the finicky, die-away airs of ladies of fashion. He noticed that she did turn down the stewed pigeon, a particular favorite of his, and promptly decided that should she consent to be his wife, he would not miss it too much if it never appeared on their dinner table.

He carried on as brisk a conversation as was his na-

ture, which allowed him ample time to admire Olivia Hannaford some more. Her hair was but partly tamed, a halo of dark bronze ringlets that bobbed when she laughed. I wonder how she brushes that mop, he thought. I wonder if she would let me try. The thought so unnerved him that he performed a juggling act with the brussels sprouts that nearly saw the entire bowl slide into Lady Hannaford's lap when he passed it to her.

James knew he should be making brilliant conversation, but nothing witty sprang into his brain, that brain so extravagantly admired at All Souls, and even, if he could believe the chancellor, at London Hospital now.

Conversation wasn't essential, anyway. From dinners past, he knew that Lady Hannaford could be relied upon to furnish all the words he lacked. She did not disappoint him, at least, until the pudding, when the subject of Charles in Paris surfaced.

"Lord Crandall, it is the drollest thing possible, but what do you think Charles is bringing with him from Paris?" she asked him.

If he remembered Charles—and he did—there was no danger that whatever the Hannaford's eldest child was bearing home would be in bad taste. "Brandy for your cellar, mum?" he suggested, aware that Olivia was watching her mother, a frown on her face.

To his discomfort, Lady Hannaford laughed. "No, indeed, James!" she declared, touching his arm, "although Livy declares she will lock herself in the cellar!"

"Mother," Olivia said, and there was no mistaking the distress in her eyes. She said no more, and James thought that wise of her, considering that Lady Han-

naford never turned loose of a good tale, once launched
upon it.

"Charles is bringing home a fellow diplomatist, with
the whole intent of fixing Livy's approval! I knew you
would be amused!"

He was not, but he managed a weak smile at his hostess. He made some inane comment, but it was forgotten the moment it left his lips, when she continued.

"Peter Winston, Lord D'Urst. Perhaps you know
him? I believe he was at some college or other at Oxford."

Only by serious discipline did James keep from
groaning out loud. Peter Winston? he asked himself.
Peter Winston? Oh, why not just blend Apollo for
looks, Croesus for wealth, and Solomon for his brain
box? "Yes, I know him," he said, hoping that his tone
of resignation would be taken for a certain languid
sangfroid. "He was two years my senior at New College. He is coming for Christmas?" He hoped he did
not sound too forlorn.

"The very man. Charles tells us that Lord D'Urst has
expressed a real interest in Livy, and all from seeing her
miniature that Charles carries about with him," Lady
Hannaford said. "Imagine that!"

He chose not to imagine anything; the reality of Peter
Winston was daunting enough. "I had thought him to be
married long since," he said. Damn the man, he
thought. Too many single gentlemen roaming loose in
England are a menace to society. "Wasn't he engaged
before? Indeed, I am almost certain of it."

"So Charles wrote us, but apparently Lord D'Urst
called it off because . . ." Lady Hannaford leaned closer
to him. ". . . the lady was insufficiently intelligent!
Claims he wants a wife with brains." She beamed

across the table at her daughter. "Between you and me . . ." And the vicar, two old maids, Sir Waldo, my father, and your aunt at table, he thought glumly. ". . . we will be saving the expense of a come-out for Livy in the spring!" Lady Hannaford concluded in triumph. She blew a kiss to her daughter as the footman removed her plate. "And here I feared that your brains would be a detriment, my little love. How silly I am!"

He could not dispute her silliness, and felt only gratitude when she turned to the vicar to continue her conversation with him. *I wonder why Sir Waldo went to all that trouble of securing my consent to pursue Olivia,* he asked himself, as he stared down with considerable distaste at the blancmange before him. *He could have saved himself the trouble, apparently.*

He put that very question to his host when they strolled to the sitting room an hour later, after brandy, which gave him a headache. The other men had gone ahead, and it gave James some wintry solace to realize that Sir Waldo wanted to speak to him. He slowed his steps.

"Jemmy, I had no idea this was afoot," he said, his voice low. "Probably the fault is mine. I must have lamented one letter too often about my fears for Olivia."

"And Charles is never slow," James finished for him when he fell silent.

"You're not going to give up even before you begin, are you?" Sir Waldo asked, his eyes anxious.

It is not a matter of giving up, he wanted to tell the man. *I know Lord D'Urst, and I could never measure up. It certainly isn't too late to return to London, where Papa and I have spent every Christmas since Mama died.* "Sir Waldo, he is an excellent man, and I know

none of you will be disappointed," he said, hoping it would be explanation enough. "Olivia cannot help but be impressed."

Sir Waldo was silent a moment, walking slowly with his chin sunk onto his chest. "You are the one, laddie," he insisted, as the butler opened the door to the sitting room. "I just know you are. Say you won't give up yet, and for God's sake, begin!"

Sir Waldo spoke in a whisper, but James could not overlook his intensity. *And I have always known you as such an easy-going fellow,* he thought in wonder. "I will," he said, the words surprised right out of him.

"Tonight," Sir Waldo said, and to James's ears, it was not a question.

"Very well."

Resolution, he told himself, but still he hesitated in the doorway. He could see that his father had been captured for hard duty at the whist table with Lady Hannaford and her maiden aunts. Olivia had seated herself close to the fire, her embroidery stand in front of her. James did not think she was aware of him, but as he watched her, he smiled to see her slide a footstool toward the chair next to her.

If ever a man needed an invitation, he thought. Taking his courage in hand, he sat down beside her and propped up his feet. He hoped he looked more relaxed than he felt, but after only a few moments of sitting beside Olivia Hannaford, he began to feel burdens he had been hitherto unaware of roll from his broad shoulders. *This is odd,* he told himself, risking a glance in her direction.

She wasn't doing anything in particular to put him at ease, just leaning forward slightly, her attention on her handiwork; she hummed under her breath. He took a

deep breath, and then a smaller, more discreet one as he enjoyed the faintest fragrance of almond. She had a slight smile on her face. There is just something about you, he decided, then opened his mouth before he thought.

"Miss Hannaford, you smell remarkably like a biscuit."

He cringed inwardly, but the fear quickly passed when she pushed the needle in the linen and leaned just a little in his direction. "You have found me out, my lord," she whispered. "I spent too long below stairs before dinner. Extract of almond covers a multitude of sins, I have discovered." To his utter delight, she smiled at him. "Perhaps I could recommend it to you after autopsies."

He laughed softly, not wishing to attract anyone's attention, put at ease by her commonsense air. "I might just go to the apothecary's for a bottle of my own." He cleared his throat. "Let me apologize for my artless declarations of last week. I am only grateful that you did not summon the constable to have me bound, trussed, and admitted to the nearest lunatic asylum."

"Oh, no," she assured him. She resumed her work at the frame. "You and Tim hatched enough schemes that I would be a silly sister indeed if I allowed comments about autopsies to throw me over." She put down the needle again and looked at her hands. "Just tell me that you did not mean that my digits are bony."

"No, Olivia. I should have said bonnie instead of bony." Well, that was good, he told himself, when she laughed, colored up so prettily, and returned her attention to her embroidery. In another twelve or fifteen years, I might even be clever around women. Why, by then, Olivia and Pete Winston will have been married a

dozen years at least, and have three or four children. I wonder if I could hire a Sicilian to kill the man? Or one of Napoleon's out-of-work Imperial Guards?

The thought so absurd made him smile. He stretched out further in the chair and put his hands behind his head, content to gaze into the flames and breathe deep of almond extract from the Hannaford kitchen as it wonderfully scented Olivia's hands and neck.

"And now you are smiling," she began.

"I was thinking of homicide this time," he said. To his relief, Olivia only laughed.

He glanced at Sir Waldo, seated beside the vicar, who was using his Sunday gestures, but saying something about "bits of bone and muscle," and "just wait till spring at Newmarket." It cannot be a sermon, James realized. The man is far too animated to be discussing something from Holy Writ. Perhaps if he preached from the starting gates, we would be more entertained, of a Sabbath.

As James watched his host, Sir Waldo made a shooing motion with his hands, as though to hurry him along. "Resolve," James said.

"Beg pardon?" Olivia asked, her eyes still on her work.

Had he spoken out loud? "Resolve, my dear, resolve," he stammered, buying a moment. "I am resolved to do something about shabby appearances and out-of-date furnishings."

She looked at him, narrowing her eyes as though she were actually contemplating his person. "I do not think your coat is so old, Lord Crandall."

"I mean the house, Olivia," he told her, even as he resolved to seek out his tailor when he returned to Oxford. "Mama's crocodile chaise still leers at us from the

sitting room, and the draperies have more dust on them than the pyramids."

"Oh, dear! That was a fashion several years ago, wasn't it?" she asked.

"Dust is always fashionable in my chamber at All Souls," he joked.

To his distress or delight—he wasn't sure which—she jabbed the needle into the fabric and pushed away the hoop this time. "Sir, I mean the crocodile chaise!" she declared, speaking with some emphasis, even as she kept her voice low. "You mean this, and I mean that, and we are ever at cross comments. If you do not say what you mean, how will we ever manage when . . ." She stopped and turned quite red, to his greater amazement.

"When what?" he asked, more curious now than surprised at her unexpected vehemence.

"Oh, nothing!"

She looked so adorably confused and off balance somehow that he surprised himself by taking her hand. "My declaration is this then, in plain terms, Miss Olivia Hannaford—"

He could not continue, because she had turned quite pale at his words and was gripping his fingers so hard that he winced. He peered closer. "Olivia, are you breathing? I wish you would."

The moment passed. She took a deep breath and relaxed her tenacious grip. "It is this," he continued, not certain anymore. "Our house is shabby from neglect and needs the critical eye of a female. Will you come over tomorrow morning, walk through my house with me, and give me advice on what to do about it, short of a bonfire?"

She seemed relieved at his question; he could almost

feel her sigh. "Of course I will do that." She pulled her fingers away and looked beyond him across the room. "Oh, my. Mother is either exercising her fingers from too much discard at the whist table, or she wishes me to see about tea. Do excuse me, Lord Crandall."

She rose gracefully, quite herself again, and left him there with only the scent of almond extract for company. Women are strange, he thought. Thank goodness that men have no truck with subterfuge. He sat there peacefully enough, admiring Olivia's handiwork on the embroidery hoop. She returned in a moment with tea for them both, and seated herself behind the hoop.

"Nice work," he said after a sip.

"I like embroidery," she replied, her attention on the hoop again. "What a good thing that is, considering that I will have a lifetime of it."

"What, no ambition?" he teased, and was astounded when she took a long look at him, then rose and left the room. Too embarrassed to look at anyone in the suddenly silent parlor, James sat staring into the flames until what seemed like four centuries later when his father tapped him on the shoulder and said that it was time to go home.

He spent a completely sleepless night, certain that she would not show up in the morning, and equally positive that he would never see her again. The thought numbed him and set him pacing about, berating himself. All I do is apologize to her, he thought. Charles and Peter Winston are due to arrive any day. It is not a matter of fixing my interest with Olivia Hannaford before the competition shows up—I cannot even get beyond apology. Lord D'Urst will come as a great relief to Olivia.

Or so he reasoned at three-thirty in the morning.

Nothing had changed his opinion by breakfast, except that he had a great dread of spending one more day at Enderfield. After a long moment staring at breakfast on the sideboard, he turned on his heel and stalked to the library, where the furniture was comfortable and much more conducive to sulking. To avoid looking at the clock, he attempted to review his notes and then glance over his sketches. Easier said than done; he found himself mentally wagering how much time had passed before each glance at the clock.

By eleven of the clock, he decided that Olivia was not coming. And who can blame her? he berated himself. I, for one, would not. Resolutely he turned away from the clock and tried to absorb himself in his studies.

It must have worked. He was sitting at his desk, staring out the window and thinking about action and reaction, when he heard a discreet cough almost at his elbow. He jerked his head around, startled out of his contemplation, to see the butler.

"Beg pardon, my lord, but the Honorable Olivia Hannaford is here to see you. Sir, are you in?"

Oh, I am, Withers, he thought. He paused and counted to ten slowly, not wishing to give the impression of overeagerness. "Yes, I am. You may show her into the sitting room. I will be there in a moment."

When Withers left as quiet as he had come, James clapped his hands and stared at the ceiling. The Lord is good, he thought, and kind to fools this holiday season. He spent a moment before the mirror over the fireplace, and pronounced himself totally shabby, from his worn-out shirt (kept because it grew softer with each washing), to his corduroy vest (buttons long gone but a prized possession because the vest pockets held any

number of erasers and pencils), to his country leathers (comfortable beyond all reason, if not stylishly tight), to his shoes (at least they matched today). I could have combed my hair this morning, he told his reflection. Too bad that I did not.

Olivia, of course, looked as neat as a pin, dressed in a plain dark wool dress of no distinction, except that it reminded him how womanly she had become since the day eleven years ago when he and Tim had pulled out her two loose teeth. Merciful Father, that hair! he thought as he stood in the door of the sitting room, admiring her.

She was not watching him, but eyeing the crocodile chaise. "Ugly, isn't it?" he said when he had had enough of gazing.

She turned around to smile at him. "Actually, my lord, it is so stupendously, marvelously horrible that I confess I like it. Give it to me for Christmas, will you?"

"Absolutely, and up to half my kingdom, as well," he told her, meaning each word.

She laughed, and he felt in his heart that for some unknown reason, he was quite forgiven for his thoughtlessness of last night. "The chaise will be enough, my lord. I will have to keep it in my room, else Mama's pug will go into spasms. Well, are you ready to begin?"

Begin what? he thought wildly. Is this some carte blanche to pull you onto my lap and make little corkscrews out of your hair, and maybe see where it leads? Not even the Lord is that merciful at Christmas.

"Looking at your rooms, Lord Crandall," she reminded him, which only made him realize that he must have been staring at her like a Bedlam inmate.

"Oh, yes, yes indeed," he said. "Let us attempt the west wing, Olivia. It's the newer part of the house." He

held his breath, but she made no comment on his use of her first name.

To reach the wing, they crossed through the gallery with its walls of Waverlys and Crandalls looking down, some single portraits and others surrounded by handsome wives and numerous progeny. It had never occurred to him before how fecund a family he came from, and he was glad that the woman beside him could not read his thoughts. Olivia seemed content to stop, gaze, and stroll beside him. "Do you suppose the children played ball in here when the day was stormy?" she asked as they stood before one portrait.

He had never thought of such a thing, which his own mother would never have allowed, even if he had possessed brothers and sisters. "Would you permit it?" he asked.

"Of course," she answered promptly, "after I had removed vases and other breakable items. What a wonderful room for blind man's buff."

It was a pretty thought, and it made him smile, thinking of Olivia playing in here with their children. Oh, Lord, that is a reach, he acknowledged. Here I am thinking of reproduction, when I should be grateful she is still speaking to me this morning. And why she is still speaking to me . . . I do not precisely understand the reason.

There were ten sleeping chambers in the west wing, and Olivia went through them all, making notes on the tablet she carried, but spending more time looking out the windows. "Your view is so much better than ours," she told him when he joined her at the window. "Perhaps it is the slightly higher elevation."

He uttered some monosyllable. Then they continued to another room where she admired the view of bare trees and snow-covered ground, and he admired her. If

I could think of something brilliant to say, I would, he told himself, and then spoke anyway, as though his brain had no connection to what came from his mouth. "Olivia, I was so rude to you last night. Why did you come today?" James winced as soon as he said it, alarmed with himself, but to his unspeakable relief, Olivia seemed unfazed by his plain speaking.

She sat in the chair by the window. "I said that I would," she replied simply, "but we must get one thing straight: just because I enjoy needlework does not mean that I have no ambition. What it means is that I am a woman."

She turned her attention to the view outside the window again, but he sensed there was more. It was his turn to speak, as clearly as though she had told him to, and he knew in his bones that what he said would be the most important words of his life.

He wanted to give the matter weighty consideration, but there she was, looking at him, expecting some comment. "Do you mind so much?" he asked instead.

He quietly sighed when she smiled at him. "Sometimes I do, Lord Crandall," she told him. "Do you remember how I cried when you and Tim left for New College?"

He had forgotten, but now he sat on the bed, recalling her distress all those years ago, and how exasperated Tim was. "I seem to remember some rather caustic comments from your brother about watering-pot sisters," he said, then stopped, struck by a thought so startling that he almost—but not quite—rejected it. "But you weren't crying because you were going to miss him, were you?"

Olivia shook her head, rose gracefully, and headed for the door. She turned the page on her tablet. "Two

more rooms, my lord, and then I should be going. I cried because I knew I would never be allowed to go to college. I do believe this wonderful hall suffers from no more malignancy than the need for paint."

Clearly, she did not wish to disclose any more of herself to him. As he followed her into the next room, and then the one after, he knew he had been granted—for whatever reason—some tiny glimpse into her most private corner. Papa says I should listen to what she tells me, James thought as they finished in the last room and she handed him her list of suggestions. She kept her own counsel as they retraced their steps through the gallery, and he thought through his conversations with her.

There was nothing to keep her in the house one more moment, he knew, as she made her way toward the entrance, and he had the dismal sense that he had failed her again. Oh, God, what is she telling me? he asked in desperation.

And then he knew, as plainly as though his own personal guardian angel—which he most certainly did not believe in, thank you—had tapped him on the shoulder and slipped him a handwritten note from the Lord Himself. "Hold on there with that cloak, Withers," he said to the butler, who was waiting in the entranceway. "Olivia, when you asked me last week just what I was doing at All Souls, you meant it, didn't you?" He knew from the way her gaze deepened that he had finally said the right thing.

"I meant it," she assured him.

He took a deep breath. "I am studying time and motion, Olivia, and how the efficient use of the latter increases the former." He was afraid to look at her, afraid that he would see polite boredom overtake her features,

which up to now were animated. "The applications are of enormous importance . . ." He took another breath then plunged on. ". . . in factories."

"I imagine they would be," she said with scarcely a moment's hesitation. "If time and motion equal efficiency, then efficiency equals increased revenue, does it not?"

It did, but no woman had ever mentioned it to him before. Only the sternest handle on his emotions prevented him from picking up Olivia and planting a kiss on her forehead. "Correct, Olivia," he replied in what he hoped was a detached, professiorial tone. "There is a professor at Harvard College in Massachusetts who is analyzing the motions of mill girls at a textile factory in Lowell. He has written a treatise on the subject."

The next logical step was to ask her if she would care to read the paper. He hesitated, thinking of his own friends, fellow scholars at All Souls, who had laughed and turned away when offered the paper. "It can be as dry as . . ." He stopped, humbled almost to his knees by the trust on Olivia's face. *How strange that she should look at me like that, when I only want to spare her the tedium of Charles Ketchum's paper, for tedious it is, at first glimpse. And here you are, loveliest of creatures, looking at me as though this matters to you.* "Would you like to read Ketchum's paper?" he asked, his voice low, not sure if he was offering her the driest bone in scholarship, or a little glimpse of himself—take it or leave it—that he had never shared before.

"I would like above all to read it," she replied.

"Don't move," he ordered. He ran down the hall to the book room and snatched the paper from his desk, hurrying back, out of breath, afraid that great good sense would have taken over and she would be gone.

She stood precisely where he had left her, except that she was smiling at him. "I did not move," she assured him. He took her by the arm to prevent any possible escape and walked her to the library, where only hours before he had stewed, despaired, and cursed his own ineptitude and paced the floor.

"I think I have quite worn it out with reading," he said as he handed her the document. "Do have a seat."

She sat on the sofa, her eyes on the paper. In another moment, he could have turned in circles, barked, and scratched himself, for all the attention she paid him. As he watched in amazement, Olivia drew up her legs and made herself comfortable, her eyes focused on the close-written pages before her. He had the good sense to leave her in peace.

When luncheon came, he made an effort to tempt her with food, but she shook her head and waved him away. He did leave a tray within reach, noting to his amusement that every now and then her fingers would range across the plate without her eyes leaving the paper. He could have fed her cotton wadding.

He knew the paper was long and involved, and he was not surprised when she propped a pillow behind her head and settled down in more comfort with her knees drawn up. He laughed to himself and sat in a chair just out of her vision, content to watch.

He woke later that afternoon to find himself covered with the light blanket that his father often used in the library. Olivia, sitting straight and proper now, watched him, her excitement visible even in the way she sat forward on the edge of the sofa.

"I thought you would never wake up," she said when he opened his eyes and looked around in surprise. "Oh, I covered you. Lord Crandall, you looked so tired."

That is only because I was up all night, worrying about whether I would see you again, he thought, touched to his soul. Fuddled with sleep as he was, he could tell that only a lifetime's training in manners held her in check. "Well, what do you think?" he asked, acutely aware as he looked at her that probably not many men ever asked such a question of a woman.

She leaped off the couch as though springs released her and pulled up a footstool to sit close beside him. "Do you *know* what this says?" she demanded, gesturing at the paper held so tight in her grip. She colored up then in a most adorable way. "Of course you know what it says! I am silly. Oh, my, it is all about value and work and time."

"And efficiency," he added.

She looked at the paper in her hands. "It is all so simple," she told him. "Are all great ideas so simple?"

"Most of them, I think. Someone puts forth a theory and the rest of us just slap our foreheads and say, 'I could have done that.'"

She nodded, so serious that he almost smiled. "Do you have your own ideas about what Mr. Ketchum has written?" she asked.

No, he decided as he leaned closer to Olivia, this woman must never be thrown into Almack's, where ladies are only ornaments. Sir Waldo, you were so right to put us together. "Yes, I have my own thoughts on what Ketchum has postulated. I have even begun a paper in response to his. Would you . . ."

"Above all things," she interrupted. "Only let me borrow it, and I will return it tomorrow."

He stood up. "It's still a work in progress. If you have any suggestions," he began, then stopped. That is too much to ask, he thought. And yet . . . "I will enter-

tain any and all suggestions from you for the improvement of my paper," he told her. I love this woman's laugh, he thought. He held out his hand to her and helped her up from the footstool. "And now I suppose your mama will be wondering if I have abducted you. Come with me, and I will fetch my paper."

She walked with him to the book room and took the paper from him with great seriousness. "I will guard it with my life," she assured him.

"See that you do," he said, his smile concealed in the face of her solemnity. "Heaven knows there are legions of road agents between my house and yours. Probably even Mohicans, and each one desperate for that treatise."

She claimed her cloak from Withers this time, and let him put it about her shoulders. "Oh, drat," she said under her breath as James opened the door for her. She looked at him. "I suppose we must go into your attics tomorrow and look at musty old furniture, when I would much rather talk about your paper."

"We could leave the crocodile chaise and the campaign beds where they are for another season," he suggested.

"We daren't, not when I have selected colors for the walls that will never match Egyptian flora and fauna." She held out her hand to him. "But we will be fast in the attics and efficient enough even for Mr. Ketchum!"

Not too fast, he thought. One can overdo the value of efficiency. He took her hand. "Olivia, you are completely remarkable," he said.

"I am nothing of the sort," she said, then made a face. "Please don't laugh, but I used to wish and wish that I could be at New College with you and Tim."

Laughter was the furthest thing from his mind.

"What would you have studied?" he asked, conscious that her hand was still gripped tight in his.

She stared at him. "Do you seriously wish to know?" she asked after looking around to make sure that no one eavesdropped.

"Above all things."

She sighed and released his hand. "Lovely, lovely geometry," she confided almost into his ear, her voice low. "I used to do Tim's papers for him when you two attended school at the vicar's. Oh, I confess it; I have *ideas* about geometry."

With a shout of laughter he grabbed her by the shoulders and planted a loud smack of a kiss upon her forehead. "And here I thought I knew everything about Tim! Do you know that the vicar never could understand why he did so well on the work from home, and so poorly on examinations!"

"Now you know!" With a smile, Olivia gathered her cloak tighter around her and rolled up his paper to fit into her reticule. "Tomorrow, sir!"

He knew tomorrow would not come soon enough. Over dinner that night, he confided to his father what he had done. "She promised to read my paper and offer any suggestions," he said. He shook his head as Withers came round again with the dish of stewed haricots.

"Suppose she actually has suggestions?" his father asked.

"I will take them, of course!" he declared. "You know how atrocious my spelling is. I confess to less uniformity than is commonly allowed."

"So you do, if that is all she wishes to change," Lord Waverly murmured, with enough hesitation in his voice to make James wonder.

He did not wonder long. When he composed himself

for sleep that night—and it came sooner than usual, because of his little sleep the night before—his heart was pure, his mind clear of everything except his love for Olivia. *After Christmas I shall engage an estate agent to find me a house in Oxford,* was his final thought before he slept.

He was impatient for her to arrive in the morning, so eager was he to see her again. *Confess it, James,* he told himself as he stood at the window. *You crave her praise and adulation.*

He wondered at her tardiness as the clock's hands moved so slowly. *Charles and Lord D'Urst must have arrived,* he thought with a pang. *How I wish Pete Winston had been set upon by brigands between here and Paris! Lord, I must look like a two-year-old here at the window,* he told himself. *It is a wonder I have not mashed my face against the glass.*

And then he saw her, hurrying along the lane with that peculiar bounce to her step that he found so endearing. He looked closer and laughed out loud. The day was warm for December, and she had not felt the need to cover her head. Her hair was as he remembered it from years past, gathered into that funny topknot that she resorted to when time and curls thwarted her. *Will it seem odd when someday soon I ask a portraitist to commit that casual look to canvas? Olivia is my Christmas ornament, my funny little mantelpiece decoration.*

While he had far too many manners to actually shove the footman aside, James opened the door for his sweet thing, and found himself almost taken aback by the liveliness that seemed to career about in the entrance hall, once she was in it. *She is a life force all by herself,* he thought in wonder.

"Mama says I should be locked in my room and fed

bread and water through the keyhole for going any-where looking like this," she apologized by way of greeting. "Lord Crandall, there are mornings when this trial of mine that sits atop my head absolutely defeats me."

"I think it is charming," he told her.

She made a face at him, and only the sternest kind of discipline kept him from sweeping her into his arms for a kiss from which she—or he—would never recover. "You used to make fun of it," she reminded him.

He put his hand to his heart as though she had stabbed him, and was rewarded with that laugh he so longed to hear. "My dear Olivia, I am a mature man now," he said. "I would never tease you."

"Then you will never be much fun!" She made a pre-tense of trying to reclaim her cloak from the footman, who was watching the exchange with an expression close to delight.

"Well, I will only tease you now and then," he said, wondering in the deepest corner of his heart if she had already consented somehow to a lifetime of his com-pany. When did this happen, he asked himself in bliss that was close cousin to reverence. Is there something understood? Or better yet, is there something *I* don't understand?

"I would have come sooner, but I wanted to finish these," she said as she held out a sheet of paper to him. "I could hardly pry them loose from Papa at breakfast, he was enjoying them so much."

As a smile spread across his face, he stared down at the little figures Olivia has sketched. She had taken his stupid stick figures that accompanied his treatise and turned them into clever drawings. Olivia's dainty lady of pen and ink, looking remarkably like her, stooped

and bent and lifted across the page, perfectly illustrating the motion he had tried to duplicate with his own crude efforts. He laughed out loud at the last figure on the page, which was turned out, hands on hips, facing him. It was Olivia herself in miniature, down to the top-knot.

"My dear, these are charming," he said. "Please say you will permit me to use them instead of my own apologies for figures."

"They are yours," she assured him. With the same enthusiasm, she handed him his paper. "Lord Crandall, I so enjoyed reading your treatise! Mr. Ketchum himself will be completely impressed. I am certain he will want you to brave an Atlantic passage and lecture at Harvard!"

He smiled at her with what he hoped looked like modesty. "I wanted to share it with you. Any corrections?" he asked. "I never could spell."

"I can't either," she confessed. With a grin that made her look like a child again, she handed him several sheets of paper, closely written. "What I did was correct your argument beginning on page ten. Right there," she said, coming closer to ruffle through the pages of the treatise in his hand. "Somehow, you lost the gist of the argument. See. Right there. You pick it up again on page twelve, but something had to be done about ten and eleven. It took me the better part of the night, but I couldn't stop until the logic was right."

Dumbfounded, he stared down at both sheafs of paper as though they writhed and hissed at him. "There was nothing wrong with my reasoning," he said, trying to keep his voice calm.

"Not up until page ten," she told him, her eyes narrowing slightly as he watched her face. "It was the only

place where you lost the thread, Lord Crandall, and I knew you would want it back."

"Oh, you did," he said. "That was a bit presumptuous of you, wasn't it?"

As irritated as he was, if he could have taken back his words and swallowed them whole, he would have. To his dismay, her eyes widened, and then she stepped back until she was no longer peering over his arm to look at the paper he held. "You did say that I could make corrections, did you not?" she asked. "You didn't mean it?"

"I thought . . . spelling . . . grammar . . ." He paused, confused, and waved her paper in her direction. "I didn't think you would ever . . ." Words failed him, but not long enough. "This won't do, Olivia."

She stepped back, her eyes shocked, as though he had suddenly reached out and cuffed her. Sick at heart, not sure if he was angrier with her or with himself, he watched as she visibly swallowed words on the brink of speech, drew herself up a little taller, and then seemed to retreat within herself. She looked at him, then managed a smile. "I am sorry," she said, her voice so low he almost leaned closer to hear her, except that he was angry, and would not. "I should not have presumed that you meant what you said."

He felt her softly spoken words like a shot to the heart, like an indictment, like a blue-covered subpoena slapped into his hand by a grinning summons server. "Well, I . . ." he began. "Olivia, I . . ."

To his everlasting shame, she put her hand on his arm. There was nothing in her eyes but contrition. "Do forgive me," she said. "You are welcome to the drawings. You can use the other pages to start a fire in the book room, Lord Crandall. My cloak, please."

He watched in stupefaction as Olivia accepted her cloak from the footman, who stood carved in marble. "Perhaps we can look at the attics tomorrow, my lord," she told him as she stood by the door. "Perhaps you will not be so angry with me." And she was gone. Transfixed, he stared at the closed door, then down at the papers in his hands.

"Will there be anything else, my lord?" the footman asked, his tone detached and entirely proper. To James's sensitive ears, it sounded perilously close to reproach.

"No. Go away."

"Very well, sir."

He stood in the entrance hall fully five more minutes, his mind in a perfect tumult. How dare she presume to correct my work? he asked himself. I have been at this for four years, and she only just read it last night! Amazing cheek for a girl, I would say.

It wasn't enough to think it. In a rage, he stormed down the hall to the library and threw open the door, startling his father from somnolence. He paced up and down, venting his displeasure, throwing his arms about, until finally he paused before the fireplace. "I think the flames are the only fitting venue for such impudence, Papa!" he declared. "Who does she think she is? I ask you!" Breathing heavy from his indignation, he glared at his father.

"Yes, indeed," his parent said from the depths of his favorite chair. "After all, son, you have double firsts from Oxford and everyone sings your praises now at London Hospital. What presumption from a mere chit! By all means, throw the wretched thing on the fire."

It was said so quietly, which was not unusual, James knew. His father was ever the best and calmest of men.

He frowned and stared at Olivia's paper, crumpled now in his fist. Slowly, he straightened the paper against his thigh, hardly aware of what he was doing.

"Son, you alone know how hard you have worked on this paper." It was a statement and James could only nod in agreement, glad that his father understood his position. I knew he would see it my way, he thought.

Lord Waverly got himself up and held out his hand for the paper. "You are certainly justified in your anger, lad, but maybe you might wish to consider one thing."

"I doubt it."

His father shrugged. "Or possibly not. I have observed Olivia Hannaford for years, Jemmy, and I always come away with one nagging suspicion."

"That she is an impertinent baggage?" James asked.

"No, actually," his father said, his tone almost apologetic. "I am probably wrong—your own irritation at her meddling will bear me out, most likely—but I have often suspected that she is even more intelligent than you are."

James sucked in his breath as his father took the pages from him and set them on the table by his chair. "Perhaps you could just look them over, when you feel less miffed. Excuse me now, son. I think I will have a walk. The air is a little stale in here, wouldn't you agree?"

After the door closed quietly, James threw himself into the chair his father had vacated and stared into the flames. He closed his eyes, seeing Olivia again, her expression so hurt, and then so calm, as though she was determined not to let his petulance matter to her. The thought made him wince. I love her and want her, he thought as his anger cooled. She will have to learn that

there are areas where I am her superior, and that is all there is to it.

He sat in the chair for over an hour until his mind was finally at peace again. I think she will be inclined to forgive me, he told himself. I mean, she did not scream and shout. As I have done, he thought next, then writhed inside. He reached for the paper. "I suppose I can at least read the thing," he muttered out loud. "Olivia Hannaford, I would like to know how you think you can do this better."

He read her addition once, set it down, then picked it up and read it again. A third reading followed, and hard upon its heels, a fourth. When he finished the pages, he closed his eyes and gently banged his head against the back of the chair. "James Enders, you are so far removed beyond a fool that there are no words to express such abysmal stupidity," he announced to the world at large. "Someone ought to use you for a bad example in cautionary tales."

He looked at the page before him, dismayed as it began to blur and swim before his eyes. "My love, you are absolutely right," he said. "I lost the argument, and you found it, corrected it, and strengthened it."

It was the last thing he wanted to do, but he stood up, walked to the fireplace, and took a long look at himself in the mirror. James, are you so arrogant and sure of your own scholarship? he asked himself. You claim to be a modern man. If this is so, how could you ride so roughshod over Olivia Hannaford? You claim to be in such sympathy with her because she has been denied the education lavished so freely upon you. You are a hypocrite.

He did not like what gazed back at him in the mirror. Without stopping for his coat, he went outside and

found his father in the shrubbery beside the house. "Father, I read Olivia's addition, and it is a masterpiece. She was completely right."

His father nodded serenely, but offered no advice.

"I wish you would tell me what to do," James said, the words torn from him.

"I did, son," his father replied. "It's the only advice any man needs with a woman. Weren't you listening to me, either?"

James stopped his pacing about, looked at his father, and thought a moment. "You told me to listen to what she says, didn't you? That's it?"

"That's it. The corollary ought to be obvious to you, son. Take her seriously as you would any man. If she gives you sound advice, take it."

He was right, of course, without question. Only *now* I am listening, James thought ruefully. "Where did you learn this?" he asked.

"From your mother."

It took him the better part of the afternoon to work up the courage to go to the Hannafords' estate. He had vowed earlier that he would never apologize again to Olivia, and here he was, with the biggest apology of all. He stopped several times on the short walk, struck all over again by the notion that even though he had been wickedly, perversely unkind, Olivia would probably smooth it over and accept his mumblings with far more kindness than he deserved. I have bumbled about in her life for only two weeks now, so I know that it cannot be love on her part, he told himself. Of course, *I* love her, but surely that is different.

Why it should be different was his next thought. I want to wed her and bed her and breed with her, and

enjoy her company and that of our children, he thought, stopping again. And now there is this added dimension of her excellent mind, which, if I am far luckier than I deserve, she will give to me—no, share with me—as freely as her body. I wonder if she feels that way about me?

His heart sank as he walked up the lane to the Hannafords' estate. All mud-spattered, a traveling coach was stopped at the entrance, luggage still strapped on top. Pete Winston, could you not have waited another week? he asked himself in real irritation when he recognized the coat of arms on the door. Whatever Olivia thinks of me, she may find you far less trouble.

The butler showed him into the sitting room, where Charles and Lord D'Urst were standing, Charles with his arm about his sister, and Sir Waldo and Lady Hannaford close by. To his everlasting relief, Olivia came forward and took his hand. "How good of you to come, Lord Crandall," she said, as pleasant as though they had parted on the best of terms. "I knew you would be eager to see Lord D'Urst." She grinned at him in that heart-stopping way only she possessed. "And of course, old Charlie."

Wishing Lord D'Urst someplace due east of Madagascar, he shook hands with the man, and clapped old Charlie on the back, mouthing some inanity about what a pleasure it was to see them both. They carried on a stupid conversation, and then all paused to pass smiles around again.

Lord, but I am as insipid as everyone else, he thought, then took Olivia's arm. She had not left his side in the whole meaningless exchange, and this gave him some heart. "Sir Waldo, do allow me to borrow your daughter for a moment or two."

Sir Waldo beamed at him. "Did'ye like her little cartoons?"

"I did, sir. They were splendid." So far, so good, he thought, except that Lord D'Urst was frowning at him and trying hard not to look at Olivia's arm linked through his. "In fact, it is that paper I wish to discuss just briefly, if you can spare her." Make this good, he told himself, noting that Olivia's arm gently resting in his had stiffened at his words. "Pete. Charlie. I know you have just arrived. Do not let me keep you from the removal of your traveling cases from the carriage. Olivia, take me to the library."

Without a word she ushered him from the room; to his utter relief, no one followed them. She led him to the library, not looking at him, but not pulling away from his arm, either. "You didn't need to bring back the sorry thing," she told him when he closed the door behind them. "The fire would do."

Now or never, he thought. He pulled her into his arms and hugged her as hard as he could. With a sigh, she clasped her hands together around his back, as though she did not wish him ever to depart from the circle of their embrace. "You do forgive me," she said finally, her words muffled against his waistcoat.

He sighed and pulled her away to look into her eyes. "No, Olivia," he corrected her. "Do you forgive *me*? I was so entirely wrong about your corrections, and I am thoroughly ashamed of my hypocrisy."

"Done, then," she said softly.

It was the perfect moment to sweep her into his arms again and kiss her, but he was reticent at so bold a step, and merely stood looking down at her. How do shy men ever marry and breed? he asked himself in some despair.

Olivia solved his problem by putting her hands on his shoulders and standing on tiptoe to kiss him on the lips. He knew what to do after that, and he did it, without any demur from the object of his admiration. He would like to have done more, but the wingéd harpy of good manners clattered into the room and flopped down to roost on his shoulder just as he was about to run his hand across Olivia's magnificent backside. "Goodness. What got into me?" he said instead as he released his grip.

That was not precisely true. It was Olivia who was gripping him. With what he liked to think of as reluctance, she let go of his neck. "Do you know, James, there is one other place—on page twenty, I think—where the argument strays again," she whispered. To his ears it was an endearment of provocative proportions.

"I will look at it when I go home, my dear," he told her. "Thank you, Olivia." He wondered if it was proper to thank a woman for a kiss, but he knew that he was thanking her for forgiving him so freely.

She must have known, as well. To his heart's everlasting ease, Olivia placed her hand on his chest. "I only wanted to do what I felt was right," she said.

"You did," he assured her. He took her hand and kissed her fingers. "When you come tomorrow for the attic expedition, we will spend more time in the book room. I want to share the conclusion of the paper with you. And please call me James. Everyone else calls me Jemmy, but I want you to call me James."

She blushed quite becomingly, which made him smile. "Very well, James. I will see you tomorrow."

"Happy Christmas," he murmured after she left the room. He went to the mirror to straighten his neckcloth

and allow his high color to recede. "Olivia, do you suffer all fools gladly, or just me?" It was a good question, and it carried him down the hall and out the front door.

The sun was setting. He stood a moment in quiet contemplation on the front steps, breathing deep of winter and smelling snow on the way. As he watched, Lord D'Urst joined him. "Nice night, isn't it, Pete?" he asked, full of charity in this most charitable of seasons.

Lord D'Urst shrugged. "I thought you and your father generally spent Christmas in London," he said, turning to admire the same sunset.

"And I thought you had gotten married a year ago," James commented.

Lord D'Urst waited a moment to reply. "So that's it?" he asked, but it was more of a statement. "Silly me. I was certain you had given your soul to All Souls." He smiled at his own witticism.

"Not entirely, it would seem," James replied, unruffled.

They remained silent another moment, then the front door opened and Olivia joined them. "I do not know why Mama has not invited you to dinner, James," she said.

Lord D'Urst laughed. "She is afraid he will amaze us with his scholarship, and we will quite forget to eat! That's it, isn't it, Jemmy?"

Ah, the Lord D'Urst I know and love, James thought. He can make his barbs sound funny, and no one is the wiser. He smiled. "I'm certain, rather, that she is dismayed at my frayed waistcoat and shirt almost out at the elbow." There, Pete. I beat you to it. "She fears I will put diners off their feed."

Lord D'Urst only looked him over. "I would have thought it was because your hair is uncombed." He

leaned companionably close to Olivia. "Do you know, Miss Hannaford, that we in the upper form used to wager the times in one term that Jemmy would remember he had hair and comb it?"

To his dismay, Olivia put her hand to her mouth, but was unable to entirely stifle her own laughter. His spirits rose a notch when she touched his arm. "We don't mind here at Hannaford, my lord."

Take that, Pete, he thought. I don't notice her touching *your* arm. "Olivia appreciates the finer things," he said, knowing that it did not sound at all clever, but pleased because she beamed at him.

They started down the steps together, Lord D'Urst taking the moment to inform Olivia that he needed to retrieve his document case from the post chaise. "Treaty making is tedious business, my dear Miss Hannaford," he said. He sighed. "Of course, one must make sacrifices for the good of one's nation."

Well, rally and jab, James thought, knowing that he could be magnanimous. I will yield the field tonight, Pete, but then again, she won't be accompanying *you* to my attic tomorrow. He nodded to Olivia and continued down the steps with Lord D'Urst.

He thought he knew the steps well, considering the years and years that he and Tim had pounded up and down them, but to his chagrin, pain, and amazement, he took a wrong step, then another. Quicker than a snap of the fingers, he found himself on his back, his ankle on fire, staring up at Pete Winston. "Gadfreys, man, did you trip over your feet?" Pete was asking him.

He would liked to have answered, but all he could do was wheeze and wish for his air to return. Olivia hurried down the steps and threw herself beside him. "James! Can you breathe?" All he could do was shake

his head and look behind her at Lord D'Urst, who was grinning now.

She helped him into a sitting position and called for the footman. "It's my ankle," he managed to say. "I think it's broken."

"Lord D'Urst, do help the footman get him inside," Olivia pleaded.

"I have a better idea," D'Urst said. "Since my traveling carriage is right here, the footman and I can pop him into it and take him home. You'd prefer that, wouldn't you, James? I mean, just look at you!"

"You're so kind to think of that," Olivia said.

"It's nothing, my dear," Lord D'Urst replied. "Give us a hand now, lad."

Lord D'Urst helped him into the carriage, but not without crowding his ankle hard against the carriage door, which made James yelp in pain. He was almost too embarrassed to look out the window, but at least he was rewarded by the anxious look on Olivia's face when he did.

"I'll be over first thing tomorrow," she told him. "Pray your ankle is not broken!"

"*We'll* be over first thing," Lord D'Urst amended. "In fact, I will come along with you now, Jemmy. Miss Hannaford, he has always required looking after, but perhaps you don't know that. Buck up, Jemmy. This shouldn't slow you down beyond a month or two."

They made the short trip in silence. James shut his eyes against the pain and breathed as shallowly as he could at every jar of the carriage. Lord D'Urst reached out to steady him several times, but he only managed to shove his hand against the offending ankle. "That is really swelling prodigiously," he said.

"Well, don't sound too happy about it," James said,

gritting his teeth. He waited for the wave of pain to sub-
side. "Why do I have the feeling that you pushed me?"

"I would never!" Lord D'Urst declared, his eyes
wide. He laughed and gave James's ankle a squeeze.
"Jemmy, dear boy, I would never have to resort to low
tactics. You're just clumsy."

Perhaps he was. It was not a calming reflection, he
decided. Lord D'Urst, all sympathy and concern to
Lord Waverly, deposited James in his chamber and left,
after promising to come tomorrow with Olivia Hannaford. He sweated and suffered through a visit from
the surgeon, who poked and prodded, and pronounced
the ankle unbroken. Mr. Walton was kind enough to
wipe off his face and then peer at him with the sympathy of ten. "Lord Crandall, an actual fracture would feel
better than this nasty wrench." He pointed his finger at
James. "You are to stay entirely off that leg for at least
two weeks. I will even insist that two footmen carry
you to the commode, when nature calls."

"Oh, Lord! Not that!"

Mr. Walton only smiled at his anguish. "Now, now,
Lord Crandall! Your own father tells me how you long
for solitude to work on dissertations. Now you will
have solitude to your heart's content! Good night now,
Lord Crandall. Take these powders every four hours,
keep the ankle elevated and cool, and let me know if
anything changes."

Nothing will change, James thought wearily as his
father walked the surgeon downstairs. I will eat my
Christmas pudding with a book propped open beside
me, as I usually do; Olivia will drop by until Lord
D'Urst becomes more interesting; my ankle will heal
eventually; and I will return to Oxford without my
Christmas ornament.

After a sleepless night that the powders did nothing to improve, he felt no better in the morning. He waved away food; the pain in his leg only added to the queasiness in his stomach. He lay in bed completely frustrated and hardly able to bear the agony of even a light coverlet on his ankle.

Olivia arrived early, as she had promised, with Lord D'Urst in tow, wearing his sympathy like a pose. The portrait of boredom, he stared out the window on the falling snow while Olivia sat beside James. He was too gone with pain to say anything. And what good would it do? he asked himself in perfect misery. Pete will overhear everything I try to say to this wonderful creature, and I have no clever repartee, even in the best of times, which this is definitely not. He could only gaze at Olivia in mute appeal.

She surprised him by lifting the cover off the end of his bed to look at his wounded ankle. When she put her hand near to touch it, he flinched. "Poor dear," she murmured. "I have not touched it, and you cannot even bear the thought."

"Jemmy, have a little heart!" Lord D'Urst admonished in a most rallying tone.

If he had felt better, James would have relished the glare she gave the man. "James, you need some help," she told him.

He could not deny it. "My father has sent for Mr. Walter again."

She nodded and looked around the room. "That is what I need," she said.

He tried to follow her gaze, but he was lying flat on his back. He heard her by his desk, and then Lord D'Urst laughing. She returned with his woven waste basket, empty now, and folded a towel inside it. "I don't

mean to hurt you," as he told him as she carefully raised his leg, then rested his foot and ankle inside the basket. "There now." She felt his other leg. "You're cold, but with the weight gone now, I can add a blanket or two."

"Foot of the bed," he said, shivering from the pain she had caused, even as he appreciated her care. She opened the chest and extracted two blankets, covering him and tucking them in on all sides. He closed his eyes, enjoying the warmth and the relief of pressure on his ankle.

"Now I will wait for the doctor," she said, seating herself beside him again.

"Not necessary," he managed to say. "Perfectly all right."

"See there, my dear, even Jemmy says we can leave," Lord D'Urst said. "Jemmy, does your butler have a key to the attic?"

"I am waiting for the doctor," she repeated.

"My dear Olivia! You take too much upon yourself!" Lord D'Urst protested. "Surely the surgeon knows best."

"I am not convinced," she said quietly. "You may leave if you wish, my lord. James is no trouble to me."

Yes, leave, by all means, James thought. It hurt too much to turn his head, but he could hear Pete Winston huffing off to sit in the window seat. Olivia continued to hold his hand, stroking his wrist until he wanted to pull back the covers and usher her inside. I am three parts dead and she moves me, he thought simply. I astound myself.

When the doctor came, she took him immediately to task, mincing no words, overriding all his protests until the man appealed to James.

"Do what she says," he told the surgeon. "I trust her."

"Over my own judgment?" exclaimed the doctor.

"Over your own judgment."

With a great sigh, the doctor mixed more powders, then left the room without a word. When Olivia followed him into the hall to continue her argument, James couldn't help but think of a mother wren, fluttering and chattering at foes twenty times her size.

"She's certainly a managing little baggage," Lord D'Urst said from the window seat. "Charles never told me that about her."

"New to me, too," James said.

She returned to the room and quickly prepared another dose of powders. She put her arm under his head to raise him and whispered, "This is much stronger and will put you under for a while. James, Lord D'urst can help me locate the furniture in the attic."

He groaned, but not from pain this time. He closed his eyes and yielded himself without a murmur into the sweaty arms of Morpheus.

There he stayed, through several days that had no meaning to him. He was dimly aware of assistance to the commode from his footmen, and his father's presence now and then. Olivia came, he thought, because at least once there was a rustling of skirts and the faintest fragrance of almond extract.

And then one morning he woke to see snow falling. He lay as still as he could, unwilling to invite the stab of pain so familiar to him now. He lay on his back and watched the snow fall, feeling at peace with his body for the first time in days. On experiment, he moved his foot slightly and was rewarded with a dull throb, instead of shooting agony. "Well that is better," he said out loud.

"Eh?" Charles sat by his bed this time, his eyes on the book in his lap. "Are you in the land of the living again, Jemmy?"

"I could be," he said. "Give me a hand, Charlie, and help me sit up."

His friend obliged, and in a moment he was upright again, propped against the headboard with many pillows. He raised his knee slowly, anticipating the pain, and then relaxed when he discovered that pressure on his leg actually felt good now, from that angle. "I may live," he announced. He ran his hand over his chin. "Another week and I'll have a beard," he commented, pleased that he felt well enough to joke. "Charlie, did you get nominated to keep this morning's death watch?"

"Something like," he teased in turn. "We've all been drawing straws. The short straw loses and gets you." He patted James's shoulder. "Don't despair about the refurbishing you were attempting with Livy. She and Pete have been careering about the countryside from warehouse to warehouse, accumulating paint and wallpaper enough to redo Prinny's palace at Brighton."

"I'm delighted," he said with what he hoped resembled gratitude, even though he felt none.

"Knew you would be pleased, lad," Charles said. He leaned closer. "And I am pleased, as well. Your accident may have turned out to be just the thing to guarantee Olivia's attachment to Lord D'Urst, a thing *I* have been plotting for some time now. I suspected they were suited for each other. How gratifying to have one's efforts borne out."

James sighed. Charles looked at him in some consternation. "Are you certain you are feeling better?" he asked.

"Of course I am," he lied.

"I knew you would be pleased, considering how you and Tim—God bless his memory—used to practically share Livy as a little sister." Charles stood up. "Let me summon the watch from below stairs, Jemmy. You'd probably like a trip to the necessary, and maybe a shave. Some gruel or barley water?" he joked.

Slip some strychnine in my nourishing broth while you're at it, James thought. "Thank you, Charlie. I appreciate your ministrations and leave you at perfect liberty to return to Hannaford."

"Not so fast, James!" Charles said. He tugged on the bellpull, then sat down again. "Louisa showed up two nights ago—I suppose it was the day after your accident—and who should she have in tow besides children and husband?"

"I can't imagine," James said.

"Her stupid brother-in-law!" Charles declared. He made a face. "I think Papa has been telling the world of his concerns for Livy, and Louisa communicated them to Felix, who has somehow convinced himself that he will be the answer to Livy's prayers! You remember him, don't you? I'm quite happy to sit over here at Enderfield from Christmas Eve until Twelfth Night, with that lunatic loose at Hannaford, don't you know."

James nodded, feeling weaker by the moment. "Certainly Felix is my favorite man milliner and Bond Street beau! Charles, could you help me to lie down again? Perhaps I am hasty in sitting up."

Charles did help, smoothing down the covers with some of that same touch that Olivia possessed. "Lord, Jemmy, the worst of it is watching Pete and Felix glare at each other and dog poor Livy from room to room,"

he said as the footman came into the room. "If she can escape, I'll send her your way."

That vague promise was his only consolation as the day wore on. *I can understand Olivia's desperation to avoid Felix at all cost,* James told himself, when she did not materialize. *He will make Peter seem all the more palatable. And what female would not be impressed by a diplomatist who has been everywhere from glittering St. Petersburg to backwater Washington, D.C.?* Wearily, he waved away his father's efforts to administer more powders. *I have an entire new wardrobe on order in London, but it would never impress Olivia,* he told himself. *The moment I hang clothes on my frame, they wrinkle. Dust balls see me coming and climb aboard for the ride. I look in the mirror, and my hair tangles. And now I am too clumsy to negotiate stairs I know as well as the ones here at Enderfield. I am probably even a threat to national security.*

If he could not walk at present, James discovered how effortless it was to spend a day pacing up and down in his mind, wondering if a cloister in the French Alps would take a Protestant, or if only felons were allowed to go to Sydney or Melbourne. His heart bruised more surely than his ankle, he knew he could not bear to be the recipient of a wedding invitation from Olivia Hannaford.

He drifted in and out of sleep as the afternoon waned, not caring much whether he lived or died. He told himself that he was cured of love, until he woke as someone lighted the branch of candles by his bed, and he opened his eyes to look upon Olivia.

"James," was all she said as she took his hand and held it. After a long moment in which he was certain he was holding his breath, she brushed the hair from his

forehead and leaned her cheek against his for the smallest moment. "It is so blissfully peaceful here."

"How did you manage to escape?" he asked, wishing that she would stay close to him, even as she returned to her chair.

"Felix exhausted himself playing jackstraws with my nephew David and had to lie down." She looked beyond him to some blank space on the wall. "Lord D'Urst has closeted himself with my father and mother." She sighed, and with a visible effort, returned her gaze to him. "He has declared himself, James. He promises me exotic locales and libraries galore and tutors."

"For geometry?" he asked, not trusting himself to say more.

She shook her head. "I mentioned geometry to him, and he laughed." Olivia was careful to avoid his eyes. "He says it is wonderful that I am so smart, but thinks that a female should be more interested in poetry and Shakespeare. I do like them," she added hastily. "Don't think me ungrateful." She ran her finger along the stripe in the blanket. "He wants to shape my learning. He says that he wants his children to be raised by an intelligent woman. Not *our* children, but *his* children. Mama tells me that Lord D'Urst is all a woman could wish for, and it is a good offer."

"Your father? What does he think?"

She hesitated. "I cannot tell. He became so quiet when I told him of Lord D'Urst's offer. Mama says he's just melancholy because I am his youngest child. What do you think?"

"It probably is a good offer," he said after excruciating thought. He gritted his teeth and raised himself up on his elbow. "You know how much you enjoy schol-

arship. Here is a grand opportunity, even if it must be Shakespeare instead of Euclid." What puny words, he thought. I love her beyond all measure, but what could she possibly see in me? Sir Waldo, you were wrong.

She said nothing for a long while, returning her gaze to the distance. Her wordless indictment smote his heart. He wanted to reach for her hand, to tell her of his love and beg her patience with the foolishness of the male sex in general and him in particular. He closed his eyes instead. When he opened them, she was on her feet and looking down at him with an expression of real sorrow. "Lord D'Urst says he even knows of a *maison de coiffure* where they will tame my hair." She fingered a curl that had declared its independence from the bun low on her neck. "Right up until he said it, I thought I wanted that, too."

To his total misery, she kissed his forehead and went to the door. "Lord D'Urst says that I am a work in progress. Do you see that when you look at me?"

"Sometimes," he said. "I must be honest."

"Do you know what I see when I think of you?" she asked suddenly, the words coming out with some force.

He shook his head, almost afraid of the intensity in her voice.

"I see a good man, not a brain or a title, or a double first. Just a good man. 'night, James."

He cried himself to sleep, something he had not done since the death of his mother. He was sick to his soul, and the pain far exceeded the throb in his ankle. Just what is any man after in a wife? he asked himself. As he lay still finally, exhausted by his tears, it occurred to him that he could pinpoint the moment he fell in love with Olivia Hannaford. He closed his eyes to see the moment again, to watch her striding along the lane be-

tween the two houses, her topknot bouncing about, the picture of energy and endless fun. It had nothing to do with her scholarship, or whatever potential she represented, he decided, but only the breadth and depth of her. Olivia just *is*, he knew now, and when she is, I am.

He roused from melancholy long enough to share dinner with his father, who ate from a tray in the sickroom. "I trust you will not mind, son, but Lord Nuttall has invited me to play whist tonight."

"On Christmas Eve, Papa?" James asked, amused, in spite of himself.

Lord Waverly laughed. "It is the proclivity of two old widowers to entertain each other as we choose, son! I am only an estate away, should any crisis strike."

It already has, James thought. "Very well, sir. Let me wish you Happy Christmas now, for I plan to be asleep before you return."

He had asked the footman to gather up his treatise from the book room and bring it to him when he heard a firm knock on the front door. When his heart leaped into his throat, he reminded himself that Olivia never knocked with such firmness. All the same, he sat up and ran his fingers through his hair. The door opened. "Oh, it is you, Peter," he said, unable to hide his disappointment.

Dressed in his overcoat and wearing a natty beaver hat that just shrieked Continental good taste, Lord D'Urst made himself at home—except that to James's eyes, he did not look comfortable. When he did not say anything, James spoke. "Are you on your way to Christmas services with the Hannafords?"

"I am, James, and that is why I have come."

Lord D'Urst stared down at the floor as though expecting to see a message written on the carpet. James

peered at him in some surprise. I could almost suspect contrition, he thought, or at least a near relative to it. "Pete?"

Lord D'Urst looked up, roused from whatever reverie he had permitted himself. "I don't go to church often, Jemmy, but own to a certain squeamishness about a subject sitting somewhat sore on me." He cleared his throat. "I did push you on the steps, and I wanted to apologize." He sat on the edge of his chair, as though in a hurry to end such self-reflection. "I had no idea you would fetch such a sprain, but, Jemmy, I wanted time to court Olivia, because for some reason I cannot fathom, she seemed to favor you. I hope you'll be understanding."

James could think of nothing to say.

"She is all magnificence," Lord D'Urst continued, his eyes lively. "And so charming! When I think of what I can make of her, I am almost bereft of speech."

"What you can make of her? I do not understand."

"Jemmy, sometimes you are so simple! What man could resist to tinker with such a female?"

I could now, he thought. "Have you made her an offer?" he asked.

"Yes."

"And . . . and did she accept you?"

Lord D'Urst smiled. "She said she would let me know tomorrow. I am ready for the best news." He reached into his pocket and pulled out an elegant case. "What do you think of this?" He touched the clasp and revealed a single ruby on a gold chain.

"Beautiful," James said, and he almost meant it.

"I have written this note, and I will give it to her first thing. I'll own that you are good with a phrase. What do

you think of this?" he asked, handing a sheet of paper to James.

James read the little note, gulped, and read it again, his spirits rising. " 'My beloved, you are my Christmas ornament, my own pretty bauble. Peter.' " He let his breath out slowly. "Precisely the right words, Pete. I couldn't possibly have said it better." He returned the note, willing his hand not to shake.

"Yes, I thought it would be the right touch," Lord D'Urst said modestly. "She is a pretty bauble, isn't she?"

She is, if that is all you see, James thought. "She certainly is. I don't know that I feel full of forgiveness for this thick ankle, Pete, but I do know that you'll get what you deserve tomorrow."

"No hard feelings, Jemmy?"

"Not one."

He could hardly wait for Peter Winston to quit the room. He broke into a sweat that left him trembling, but he managed to hobble to his bookshelf and retrieve a dusty volume. He shivered in his nightshirt, but sat at his desk a long moment, staring at Euclid's theorems, before he dipped his pen in the inkwell. " 'I am no great shakes at mathematics, Olivia,' " he wrote on the fly-leaf. " 'Between us, I believe one plus one equals one. Somehow, it equals two as well. Marry me?' "

He wrapped the geometry text in brown paper discarded from another book, tied it with string, and wrote in big letters on the outside, OPEN AFTER LORD D'URST'S GIFT. His heart peaceful, he summoned his footman, let the man help him to bed, then told him to take the package to Hannaford. He went to sleep then and dreamed of pleasant doings.

He woke early, refreshed and hungry for the first

time in a week. Even his father was surprised at the prodigious breakfast he packed away. "Now, Father, if you would help me to the window seat, I am expecting a visitor."

"Olivia?" his father asked, his expression full of concern.

"If I am supremely lucky, and I wager I will be."

What a sunny Christmas day, he thought as he leaned back against the pillow his father had thoughtfully provided. The blanket was warm against his bare legs. He needed a shave, and he had spilt porridge on his night-shirt, but he didn't think Olivia would mind.

"If I recall Tim's habits from earlier days, you Hannafords will eat breakfast first, and then open presents," he announced to the winter birds that fluttered around the suet ball outside his window. He made himself comfortable, reached for his treatise, and turned to page twenty, where Olivia said he had lost the drift of the argument again. He found the spot and was beginning a correction when he saw Lord D'Urst's traveling carriage moving at a rapid pace down the road. "Oh, God, Thou art kind to sinners and foolish men on this Your day," he prayed out loud. No matter that he understood anatomy; his heart was so high in his throat that he knew if he opened his mouth, it would flop into his hand. He swallowed mightily and then almost shuddered with delight at his next sight from the window.

Olivia hurried down the lane. She had not taken the time to do her hair, and it perched in his favorite top-knot. He peered closer, noting his book clutched to her breast. He held his breath as she stopped and stared at his house for the longest time. To his everlasting joy, she began to run. With a wince and a gasp, he hobbled back to bed. In another moment he heard light steps on

the stairs, and then Olivia threw open the door and practically catapulted herself into the room. Without a word, he pulled back the covers. "Just look out for my ankle," he warned as she threw off her cloak and lay down beside him.

She kissed him, and he quit worrying about his ankle. "Yes, I will marry you," she said when he let her up for air.

"I take it you said no to Lord D'Urst," he said, pillowing her head on his arm.

She raised up to look at him, indignant. "He had the nerve to write that I was his Christmas ornament! Can you imagine such a thing?"

He could, and did, then tucked the words away, never to be used again. She pillowed her head on his chest. "And then I opened your package. Thank you, my love, from the bottom of my heart."

"That was what did it?" he asked, relishing the warmth of her.

She laughed and touched his face. "No! Well, it helped, but I had resolved to marry you weeks ago, James Enders."

He stared at her in surprise. "Even when I was bumbling, and erring, and apologizing around the clock?"

She nodded, burrowing herself in closer to him. "Before that. I have a confession to make. Before you arrived, Papa took me aside and told me that he thought you would make an excellent husband. He said that you were coming home for Christmas to make me an offer, and that I should accept it, as you were the best possible choice for me."

James could only gape. "Even when I was looking like your worst nightmare?"

"I own you did strain it, James," she agreed, her

breath soft on his neck. She kissed his ear. "I trust my father; I always have. He told me that you would do, and I trusted him until I could see for myself that he was right."

Sir Waldo, I will be a most grateful son-in-law, he thought as his heart filled with love for his neighbor. He held Olivia close. "You realize, of course, that it would be easier to marry Peter."

She nodded and looked at him, and he could see how serious she was. "That occurred to me as I was walking over here, love, and I had to stop and think a moment," she told him. "How simple it would be to let someone take charge of my life! But you will not do that, will you? That's a little scary, James. Are all women loved so much, or only a privileged few?"

"Your life is your own, Olivia," he whispered in her ear. "All I ask is that you share it with me and our children. I will protect you and shelter you, but before God, I will not try to change you."

There were tears in her eyes now. "And it will be the same with me. I love you." She kissed him thoroughly.

This is a better cure than powders, he told himself when he could think again. "I'm not so certain I will be up to cutting much of a dash in a wedding dance, Olivia, unless you prefer a lengthy engagement."

She shook her head. "We should wait only just long enough for the crisis to pass at my house; that is all."

"Crisis?" he asked. "I take it your mother is not too excited about this turn of events." He kissed her. "Face it, Olivia, you are marrying a shagbag, instead of an elegant diplomatist."

She turned her lively eyes on him. "Oh, the crisis is much more diverting, James. What should my nephew David do this morning but throw out spots! Louisa is

certain it is chicken pox. Those tidings of great joy sent her stupid brother-in-law Felix into a dither from which I am certain he will never recover. Charles is still laughing about it." She gasped then and put her hand to her mouth. "Lord D'Urst doesn't even know about this! Should Papa write and tell him? Suppose he breaks out in spots in Paris at the treaty table?"

"Our elegant Lord D'Urst?" James said. "Such a crisis! Oh, I wish it did not hurt to laugh!"

Olivia's eyes opened wider still. "Do you suppose du Plessis or Louis the Eighteenth have had the chicken pox?" She started to laugh. "Oh, my, what a Christmas gift that will be!"

It required no real imagination to pick up the thread of her thoughts. He settled himself more comfortably on his back and tightened his arm around his darling, who gratified him by resting her head upon his chest and putting her arm across him in a gesture he could only call possessive. "Think of it, my love: the source of contagion will be traced to Lord D'Urst, and there will be diplomatic reprisals of the worst kind. He will be sent in disgrace to . . . to . . . oh, what is the dreariest capital imaginable? Perhaps Washington, D.C., where the politickers conspire and duel with one another. What do you think, lovely lady?"

She was far too silent. He glanced down at her, snuggled so peacefully within the circle of his arm, and chuckled to himself to notice how even her breathing was. Oh, so you have also discovered what an exhausting business love can be? he thought. He kissed the top of her head. "Olivia?"

"I was just thinking," she defended herself, her voice drowsy. "Only a ninny would sleep at a time like this."

"And what were you thinking?" He had made a

pleasant discovery of his own: he never would have thought that such wondrous hair could be so soft. He kissed her head again.

"I was merely enjoying the oddest phenomenon, James," she told him. "How is it possible that when I am lying here with you, I have the feeling that no one in the world has ever experienced such wonder?"

He laughed. "Do you think this is worth a scientific study?"

He felt her laughter, even though he did not hear it. "I think not, my love," she told him, "although I do anticipate any number of excellent collaborations with you." She sighed. "James, for being no Christmas for you, and a worrisome one for me, this is the best Christmas."

How peaceful this is, he thought as his eyes started to close. I could tell you that scientists should not deal in absolutes at this stage of the hypothesis, particularly since I have the wonderful suspicion that our Christmases will only get better each year. "I love you, Olivia," he said instead, and he knew with a conviction that left him almost breathless, that this was an indisputable absolute.

The Hounds of Heaven
by Edith Layton

The only home they'd ever known had been in their mother's belly. After that, there'd been heaps of rags or piles of straw in various cellars or alleys, a different place every other day. She'd been a conscientious mother, but a restless one. She'd painstakingly carried her litter from place to place, as though something had been pursuing her, or she'd been in pursuit of something. The pups grew and thrived. But then one morning, they opened their eyes to find they were alone.

They played together for a while, slept, looked for food when they woke again, and then played some more. That soon palled as hunger grew. They whined and nuzzled each other, and something very like panic began to form in their unformed minds. One howled and startled itself and the others by the sound. But they waited. Waiting is one of the things dogs do best.

Something more important than hunger finally moved them on. They cocked their heads as though listening to a far-off whistle. And then they left their snug nest and staggered out into the world to discover their fates. Which might have been dire, or at least less interesting, at any other time. But Christmas was coming, and that was a magical time, even in London, even

for dogs, and especially for them, for they each had a destiny to fulfill.

One headed east, to Newgate Prison, another took a wobbly but certain tack to the west, where the finer homes and establishments were. One made straight—with a few minor corrections caused by interesting cats and terrifying horses—toward the outer regions of the city where the old North Wall once stood. One headed toward the park near the palace. Two played together until one knew it had to wander toward the scents of Petticoat Lane.

The other made its way to an alley near St. James's Street, where it sat, and scratched, and whined, and made a sad little orbit, circling itself a few times until it lay down, nose to tail. That felt a little better, because its nose was warmed and it smelled dog, but it was only itself. It whimpered. It was alone, and alone is the worst thing a dog knows. It waited, though it was growing cold and frightening. It didn't know what it was waiting for, but would wait until it did. However long that took.

". . . And since Christmas is coming, and a New Year approaches," the gentleman concluded, "with house parties and celebrations and family all together, I thought this would be a good time to ask, a better time to resolve things, and the best time to announce it. And so?"

". . . and so," the young woman said nervously. She knew what she had to say next, but her resolve faltered as she gazed at him.

He stood before her, a proprietary smile already on his shapely mouth, anticipating her answer. He hadn't much doubt of it. She couldn't blame him. Who would

refuse an offer of marriage from Lord Thadeus Rose, the flower—as everyone jested—of British bachelorhood?

But so he was, mind, body, and considerable fortune. His face was extraordinarily handsome, the best of his well-documented Viking, Norman, and Celtic ancestries combined to make it so. The nose might be a trifle long, but he was a man, after all, and it balanced his face, countering the positive beauty of that clear white complexion, and the long azure eyes. He had thick, straight guinea gold hair, was broad-shouldered but lean, of a decent height, with a trim body and an easy captivating smile.

There was nothing about the physical man to displease any female; his fortune and breeding were enough to give any matchmaking mama heart palpitations. Clever enough to entertain society hostess or wallflower, skilled enough at riding, driving, and sparring to please any gentleman, and wise enough to know all of that—in short, he was absolute perfection on the marriage mart. He knew that too.

He continued to smile at her. He was pleased with his choice, even more pleased at how dumbfounded she seemed now that he'd declared it. It was nice to be appreciated, and he basked in the moment. He'd chosen well. He congratulated himself.

She was dark to his light, her curly ebony hair and dazzling light gray eyes were a vivid contrast to him. He liked the thought of dark and light combined. Small and shapely, her skin was lily fair, her plump pink mouth was very like the proverbial rosebud, and he'd never heard anything foolish or spiteful coming from it. Instead, she made jests, and good ones, too. And spoke a great deal of good sense.

She was possessed of a tidy dowry and an unexceptional family. One-and-twenty, his junior by six years. The perfect age for him now that he'd decided it was time to set up his nursery. She wasn't a dewy miss, apt to make social blunders, or giggle, or be flustered by a salty jest like the other young creatures presented this Season. She wasn't precisely on the shelf, either. Because of one thing or another, a doting family, a disinclination to leave the nest, she hadn't been brought to London before. All to the good. She was old enough to be socially adept, young enough to be flexible, and new to everyone in Town. She was only minor gentry from Devon, that was true, and he could have had any titled lady. But he'd decided on her.

She'd make him happy, give him lovely children, compliment him in many ways. His bride, he thought, smiling the more, realizing she was still stunned by his question. She shouldn't have been. He hadn't spoken to her father first, but they were a modern pair. He'd made his intentions clear enough though. Hadn't they driven out together more than half a dozen times? And danced together at every soirée for the past month, with him taking her in to dinner at each one? There was that evening at the theater, the other one at the opera.

And hadn't he kissed her to distraction just last week, behind an arbor at the masquerade? That set the seal on it. His wife. He liked the idea and could hardly wait for the reality. But he realized he might have to wait a deal longer for her answer today.

"My dear . . ." he prompted, smiling wider, "and so?"

She knew what she had to do—it just wasn't easy. She gazed at the merriment in that handsome face and

sighed. In the late afternoon sunlight she could see the beginnings of gingery gold stubble on that firm jaw. It made her shiver, just looking at it, remembering the feel of it under her fingertips, against her own cheek . . . Masculine, so intelligent, witty, rich and . . . She shook herself. It was the "and" she had to deal with.

He had every reason to be smiling, she thought with sinking heart. Hadn't she let him kiss her senseless just last week? Not senseless, just the reverse—he'd awakened each and every one of them. He'd kissed her witless, though. That kiss had deprived her of reason, for then there'd been another and another, until he'd been the one to stop, draw back, drop his wonderful hands, shudder, and say huskily and somewhat incoherently, "Enough . . . for now . . . but soon," showing he was as moved as she was.

So now, as expected, he was doing the correct thing. But so was she, she remembered. She steeled herself, then spoke at last.

"Thank you for asking, I am honored, I truly am, Thadeus," she said, gazing down at her tightly clenched hands, "But it won't do. I can't."

"Because I didn't go down to one knee?" he joked, thinking it was a jest. "Think of the damage to my britches, my dear. And my dignity. Come, Helena, you don't seriously want me to grovel at your feet, do you? We've both seen too many farces for that, I think."

She held her hands more tightly together. "I mean, it won't do at all, for us, I mean to say."

He stopped contemplating the delightful curve of her breasts and frowned as he looked up to her face. She was very white, nervous, and upset. But so now was he beginning to be. "Do you think you might be a

bit more explicit about what you mean to say then?" he asked a trifle impatiently.

"I mean . . . I expect something other from marriage than you do, and there it is, and that's why there's an end to it," she said quickly. She turned from him and paced a step or two. She shook her head, setting her inky ringlets to trembling. "I know I oughtn't to have kissed you like that," she went on. "I knew it, but I did it because I so wanted to know . . . But even so, now that I do, it doesn't make any difference. I suppose it does, it makes it harder, and worse, but so it would in future, so better to have it done with now," she muttered, taking an agitated turn before facing him again.

"The thing of it is, Thadeus, that I take marriage very seriously. And I expect you don't. And so in future I'd be hurt, and because I know my temper—be sure, I'd make sure you were, too. It would be dreadful and so . . ."

"And so *what are you talking about*?" he demanded, losing his own temper, which was shocking because he couldn't recall the last time he had.

"You wouldn't be faithful to me, and well I know it," she said staunchly, "and so do you, if you think on. It would be terrible."

"Well . . . but . . . What are you talking about?" he asked a bit more weakly, because he began to suspect he knew. "You're talking about years and years from now," he rallied. "Who can say what will happen then?"

"Well, you should be able to, at least about that." She drew herself up. "But in your set . . . Well, I have eyes and ears, and I don't hold with such and never will. So there you are; it cannot be."

"Oh. Rumor and innuendo," he said with relief, "of

course, gossip runs rampant in our set. Note I say *ours*, for you're not an aborigine, you know, my dear. You know how these things are. And who is to say how you'll feel in a few years, with a few children behind us? And I growing boring and stodgy and stupid in your eyes, as I hear all husbands tend to do." He smiled tenderly.

Her face grew tight. "*I* am to say, my lord, that's who's to say, because I do know. I could never betray you, you see. It's not how I was raised, nor how I think or feel. I'd be crushed if you betrayed me. But you see, I fear you will. What's more, I fear you already know you will. Even here, even now."

"Why the devil are you bringing up what *might* happen?" he asked angrily, because he'd no answer for that. He was going to marry, yes, of course. But that didn't mean he was planning to die, as a man, even so. "Who can say what may be?"

"You can and you won't. As I suspected," she said, her eyes filling with tears.

"Ah. And what made you suspect that?" he asked, calming himself, understanding, wondering what envious scandalmonger had gotten her ear. If he could talk her round any spiteful gossip, the crisis would be over and they'd get on with their lives together. "Gossip about my amours? But my dear, I am a man, and such things happen, and that's the past."

"I'm talking about the future," she said miserably.

"Oh," he said a little self-consciously, wondering which of his friends needed their necks wrung, which of his enemies had spied him out . . . Not that he'd been particularly secretive about his latest opera dancer, damn it, he belatedly realized with chagrin. "Well, you needn't fret about that. It may be so in the

present, I know, but believe me, it's already the past. It was only a bachelor's folly, signifying nothing, I promise, not to me, nor to her. It's over, or will be in an hour. And at that, I doubt she'll remember me more than a day. I've already forgotten her. Better?"

"Oh," she said softly, as a tear escaped and began a sparkling run down her cheek. "No, it's not that."

"Then, what?" he asked in exasperation. "Who said anything to undermine my suit? At least, let me defend myself."

"No one said anything." She sighed, and seeing his confusion, blurted, "No one had to! And it isn't your past, or even the present, but our future I worry about. Don't you see? I had only to open my eyes fully, and look at your parents, no further than that, and remember that the apple seldom falls far from the tree."

"My *parents*?" he asked, taken aback.

"Of course." She sniffed. "Everyone knows they haven't lived together for years. Or, at least, they live together, but in such a huge house and in such state that they never are together in any other way. That's no secret. Your mama is with Bingham now. There's never an occasion when they aren't together—it's a known fact. And your father, well, there's always someone new. Now they're all talking about the widow he's seeing, because she's not very high *ton*, but even so . . ."

She never knew a man's ears could turn red, but he'd grown so white-faced, they were startling by contrast. That fine, firm mouth became a thin line, his eyes blazed. But he took a deep breath and held it, thinking quickly. It was common knowledge after all. Who didn't know about his parents and their so flexible marriage vows? But who didn't know that wasn't unusual for

persons of their station? And who dared question it?
Still, she was the woman he most wanted to marry.

"But my parents wed because of their families," he
said carefully, truthfully, "I marry to please myself."

"But will you follow their example?" she asked anxiously.

Enough was enough. My lord Rose was not used to
criticism, much less being questioned, and certainly
not to being denied.

"My parents," he said with obviously terrible restraint, "are adults who mind their own business and
have no one to answer to, thank God, but themselves."

"Well, of course," she said, "but the fact is that they
don't honor their marriage vows, and they don't care
who knows. And so then I suppose it's only natural
you'd think that was the way to go on. I'm only saying
it isn't the way I would, or could, or care to try."

"I see!" he said icily, because he did, and there was
no denying it. He decided to change the subject instantly. "And you think your other beaux would be
more faithful?"

She put her head to the side, adorable in her confusion, or so he thought, wanting to sweep her into his
arms and have done with this dickering. "Other beaux?
I don't know," she said in bewilderment, "for I've no
others."

"O-ho. So Matthews and Carlton, and my lords
Fitzhugh and Dunn are not suitors? That would surprise them, I think."

"Oh, I meant, no suitors I was considering," she explained. "That is—that was—only you."

"So you chose to play with them, and break their
hearts?"

"You know I wouldn't, and couldn't," she said on a

little laugh, "because they're only playing at being suitors themselves. No heart is engaged. That's the problem here, too, I believe," she added sadly.

"No heart? I asked you to marry me. What is it you want of me?" he asked, "a solemn vow of complete obedience, utter loyalty, entire faithfulness?" His voice grew mocking, "A promise to be at your side every moment, through every indisposition, every fit of temper, every peculiar start, as though I were welded there, will I nil I, throughout eternity, come what may?"

"That *is* what the marriage vow entails," she said softly.

His lips grew tighter. "So literal then, are we?" he said nastily, "and I suppose, after taking that vow, you'd never argue with me, dispute my opinion, try to get your own way in anything?"

"Oh no, that's not what I meant—"

"Ah, I see," he said with a sort of cold jubilation, since she'd fallen right into his trap, "so the vow would apply only to me, is that it? You want *me* to be the one who is utterly loyal, never doubting, never questioning, never straying, whatever your temper, lavishly love on you whilst obedient to your every whim and least command? I tell you, my dear, what you want is not a husband. Oh, no. What you want is a dog! Which I am not."

He stalked to the door. She'd refused him! She'd *refused* him? And all because he wouldn't grovel and promise not to stray—in future years so far away he couldn't calculate them? He could scarcely believe it, but he couldn't believe she'd any other reason to refuse him either. She looked genuinely regretful. And still tempting, still adorable. But he noted she didn't

try to stop him from leaving. He was staggered, vexed, and confused. But not without armor.

He turned to fire one last shot at her. "I give you good day, my dear, and only pause to suggest you not be so liberal with your kisses in the future if you've no intention of following through on them. For that, I think, makes you little better than the female I return to now. She, at least, expects nothing from me but myself."

She straightened her spine. "Yourself—*and* her room, board, and a new ruby necklace, or so I heard!" she said with some spirit.

He colored, bowed jerkily, and left immediately.

She was very glad to have got in that parting riposte. Before she started crying, at least, she thought as she burst into tears. Because he *could* have said he'd try. That, at least. She didn't know if it would have made any difference, but to know that he never even considered trying, even for her sake, was unendurable. Not that it would have been endurable if he'd tried fidelity and failed.

She supposed he was honest. She supposed she was lucky to know now, and not in that inevitable *then*. But if she was, she didn't know why she felt as though she'd a paving stone on her chest and a hole big as one in her heart. Because he'd gone, and she didn't know how it could have been any other way, given who she was, who he was, what they were—oh, damn, damn, damn.

My lord Rose, finding himself still the flower of British bachelorhood, and likely to remain so for some time now, stalked into his favorite club. He sat for a few moments, arose, and stalked out again. He strode

to another club he sometimes honored with his presence, and strode out again five minutes later.

He visited his fencing master, stripped to his shirtsleeves, and engaged his opponent. He was told to put up his sword until he could get his mind in control of it. He'd have skewered or struck any other man who told him that. But though he was in a vile taking, he knew truth when he heard it. He nodded, shrugged into his jacket again, and stormed out.

The retired prizefighter he visited next, who usually sparred with him of an afternoon, showed him the door upon seeing my lord's expression at his door.

By the time he finally got to his own apartments, after insulting several friends, making some new enemies, and reducing his bird-brained mistress to tears because of the way he railed at her for only trying to do her best at the only thing she knew, because of the way she was doing it—heartlessly, soulessly, and lovelessly of course—he was already the latest talk of the town.

He was sunk in a chair in his study, glowering at his boots, when he wasn't staring at the wall, swallowing his finest wine as if it were ditchwater, when his man announced his first visitors, aquiver with curiosity.

"How are you, Thad, old fellow?" Jack Peacock, an old classmate and famous rattle, asked immediately, noting the usually collected golden gentleman was frayed and frazzled-looking.

"Under the weather, eh?" asked the Baron Barlow, a gossip who was such a fixture at every fashionable party it was said that the caterers delivered him along with the ice for the punch.

"Some problem we may be able to help with?" Lord Fitzhugh asked smoothly, hopefully.

They arranged themselves on chairs around his chair, like watchers at a deathbed, awaiting his answer.

"I will survive," Thadeus said, looking at them curiously, since they were not in the habit of calling on him. "To what do I owe this honor, gentlemen?"

"Oh," the baron said ingenuously, "nothing particular, just wishful of knowing how you were going on . . ."

They sat in silence, as their host seemed in no hurry to ask further.

"Ah. Erm. So you offered for her?" the baron, unable to take silence for more than sixty seconds, asked.

"How discreet," Thadeus answered slowly, looking from one avid face to the other. "I suppose I ought to save myself the effort of playacting and asking how you know?"

"Oh, but it's common knowledge," the baron said. "We'd all been waiting to hear the news and discover what day you've set. But then when we heard where you went this morning, and how sour you were when you left, we supposed there might be some hitch in the wedding plans. Since that's hardly possible, we thought we'd come to find out what else was amiss."

"How very kind of you," Thadeus said in such a knowing way they all squirmed. "But yes, I offered, she refused me, and there's an end to it."

"Refused you? Never say!" the baron exclaimed.

"What folly!" Lord Fitzhugh said gleefully.

"Has the chit run mad?" Jack Peacock asked. "Why you two were . . . That is to say . . . well, the girl's dicked in the nob and no mistake!"

"Not at all," Thadeus said with a sudden, singularly sweet smile that reminded his interrogators why he was the catch of the Season, and every other one as

well. "She was right. And now, as I said, let's have an end to this, my friends, shall we?"

Since they knew none of them actually qualified as "friends," and that my lord's moods were as mercurial as his smiles were sweet, and further, that his voice had an edge to it they didn't wish to test because of his fame with saber and pistols, they quickly agreed. After a few desultory comments about the weather and a poor attempt at making conversation out of guesses as to the weather for the coming Christmas season, they left as quickly as they'd come. Not only was their host in a chancy mood, they couldn't wait to spread the news.

And so it will be all over London by nightfall—which was quickly coming, Thadeus thought wearily. He could sit and stew, and let them think he was sulking. Which he was. Or take his sulk for an airing.

He didn't care what people thought of him, he told himself as he walked to the hall. Nor did he care what they said, he decided as he called for his coat and hat. He was not such a paltry creature of fashion, after all, he thought as he strode out into the night, determined to show all London that my lord Rose did not care.

He cared even less several hours later. Although it was possible he might have if he could have. But it was difficult to get his mind fixed on any one thing after swallowing as much as he had tonight. A man who'd drunk as much water as he had wine would have been intoxicated. And he'd avoided water at all costs. He'd toasted one and all with champagne at a dinner with friends and partaken of a nice port after, with many a chuckle as he'd raised his glass, jesting, "Any port in a storm." Making fun of himself? That would show them

how much he cared, he'd thought, and downed the drink. And the next, and next.

Another bottle was drained at the gaming establishment he found himself at after that, and he was almost sure he'd broached one more at the amusing place he'd gone to next. Although for the life of him, he couldn't remember where or what that was now, or why he'd found it so amusing. Somewhere along the way he'd lost his friends, as well as his sense of direction. He found himself alone in the night, on some street or other. It was clearly time to go home. If he could only remember how to get there.

First, he'd had to discover where he was. If he could get the sidewalk to stop lurching, and his stomach to stop noticing it, he might be able to do that. He peered into the empty darkness of the deserted street. His head whirled, his eyes blurred, and in some still sane small part of his brain he was deeply ashamed and disgusted with himself. He hadn't been so disguised since the first year at school when he'd finished those secret bottles with his new friends urging him on—only to realize they were not friends but upper classmen, after he'd done it.

He'd been sick for two days that time. He felt sicker now—because he was a grown man and had acted like a damned fool. In that same untouched part of his brain he knew it was also beyond folly for a well-dressed man to be staggering around the streets of London alone, in the dark of the small hours of the night, and near an alley. *An alley?*

There was the sound of running boot steps before he heard a thunderclap and felt it pound against his head. Lightning shivered across his eyes, but he felt no rain. He sank into complete darkness.

*   *   *

He was wakened by a kiss—a soft, warm, velvety kiss, on his very lips—a light damp breath of a kiss, a shy maiden's touch that was followed by another. Lord Rose forced open his eyes, winced at the shock of the pain in his head, then raised his hand to feel that aching head, feeling sticky wetness on that hand and another kiss on his lips. He dimly realized he was on his back in an alley, had been attacked, and was now being kissed, being . . . He shot up to a sitting position in spite of the pain. Not a kiss—a lapping. Something was trying to eat him! *Rats!* was all he could think in inchoate horror as he scrabbled backward on his bottom, wildly searching for a weapon.

He grasped at nothing and turned to face his foes. Because if a man had no weapon in hand, his fist was one, and sick as he was, he would not be attacked by vermin. However, even London didn't have rats that big—with such big, sad eyes. He lowered his hand as the dimmed echo of light from the gaslights outside the alley showed the pain in those large dark eyes to be almost equal to his own. Seeing the dawning recognition in his own eyes, the mouth that had been lapping at him fell open, a pink tongue lolled, and somewhere behind that black blurry mound, a furry tail started beating against the ground.

A dog. Or rather, the beginnings of one, because large as it was, even in the darkling light Thadeus could see it was clearly not yet fully a dog at all. Just an enormous sad-eyed, droop-eared puppy, delighted to find company in the alley tonight.

"Enough," Thadeus groaned, and was horrified at the pain in his voice and his head. The dog obediently sat back, its tail still drumming on the ground, watch-

ing to see what this new friend would do next. Thadeus felt for his wallet and groaned again. Gone, along with his watch, his hat, and walking stick. Well, he thought as best he could with his throbbing head, at least he still had his boots, his jacket . . .

A darker shadow suddenly fell over his shadowy retreat. He looked up to see the silhouette of a large man looming in the entrance to the alley. He could use some help and opened his mouth to ask for it—and realized that if the intruder meant to help he'd have done so by now. A jackal come to grab what spoils his original attackers had not taken? *Damn*, Thadeus thought, he was as feeble as a kitten, and without a weapon. He tried to struggle to his feet, but only gained his knees.

"Well, are you just going to stand and stare? Give me a hand," he commanded, realizing the only weapons he had now were his very consciousness and his voice of authority. But that voice came out shockingly weak.

"'ad an accident?" the voice asked with more calculation than sympathy.

"No, I sleep in alleys," Thadeus said with as much sarcasm as he could muster. "Come, man, give me a hand, I say!"

"Oh, I will, I will," the man said with innuendo, as he edged slowly closer, "and mebbe y'll gimme yer boots and yer fine jacket fer me pains, eh?"

Well, there was nothing for it but to fight as best he could. If for no other reason than the justice in it, Thadeus thought with resolve, trying to haul himself upright before he was knocked down again. But his head swam, and there was a terrible buzzing in his ears. It seemed to come from within his head and from the alley itself. He looked down. The little black crea-

ture at his feet was fairly vibrating with snarl. A low, deep, threatening growl that seemed to come from a much larger chest than the one the nascent dog possessed was thrumming through the alley. It was amazing.

Thadeus stared in astonishment. The intruder hesitated.

"Good boy!" Thadeus whispered loudly to his unlikely protector, "now, go for the throat, as I taught you, Titan, my lad."

The "Titan" came from memories of a ferocious mastiff a neighbor had owned, the inspiration, from sheer desperation. But the intruder paused. The growling grew in volume. And then, in a blink, the man at the front of the alley vanished, and could be heard running off down the cobbles.

It might have been the clink of an ash can a street away that disturbed the dreaming night and set his would-be attacker to flight, Thadeus thought, sinking back to a knee. Or the little creature next to him. He gave a pat to the silky head, grateful for whatever it had been. He was less so when he tried to rise again. But it was folly to remain where he was. He staggered to his feet, gripping a wall for purchase, and inched his way out of the alley and back into the world. He wandered a few feet before he doubled over and relieved himself of the dinner he'd had and the wine he'd imbibed. Then, at last, more sober, and sorry for it, he set off toward his town house as the night sky blurred toward a bleak winter's dawn.

He hadn't gone three streets when he finally heard the soft puffing behind him. He spun around. He had a small, square, furry shadow. The black puppy was waddling three paces in back of him as though he were

pulling it on an invisible leash. The dawning light showed the beast was the size of a substantial Christmas turkey, and covered with fluffy black fur, except for a thin white triangle on its broad head, four white socks, and a medallion of white on its plump breast that shone in the night like the fading bone white moon above them. A patch of white ornamented the tip of the too long tail, like a fifth white stocking. The animal rocked back and sat, tongue lolling, when it saw its new friend paused before it.

"Coming with me? Well, I suppose you deserve it," Thadeus said more reasonably than he felt, because he'd still a great deal of alcohol in his thinking.

And so, when my lord Rose's man woke, wrapped a robe about himself, and opened the door at dawn, he saw his master swaying on his feet, tattered, torn, bloodied, but unbowed. Or at least, only bowing slightly, more a listing, really, as he told the other servants later, and bearing in his arms, an enormous black puppy.

"No," my lord said when the servant tried to remove his burden. The burden had something to say, too, a thing that sounded most unpuppylike, and set the hackles on the valet's neck up. He drew back.

That seemed to please the pair in the doorway. "We should like to go to bed now," my lord said with painstaking care, "if you would be so kind as to show us where it is?"

She must have been better than he remembered, Thadeus thought drowsily, feeling the warm supple body pressed against his. Odd, that, he thought as he sighed, deep in his bed, half asleep still, but feeling unusually solaced, oddly content. Because he usually

didn't stay the night with his women. He'd found what was entrancing at midnight was less so in the cold light of morning, and generally avoided actually sleeping with the females he bedded. But this one! She lay curled in his arms, and when he moved, she moaned, stretching with pleasure.

He bent his head to nibble her neck. And tasted warm fur. He blinked. It was not unpleasant. But it was not a woman. Or a human . . . he hoped. And then he remembered, and lay back, chuckling. It woke his companion, and the puppy sprang up, delighted. It romped on his chest and buried its nose in his neck and was thrown back and sprang back, and the two of them tussled in my lord Rose's feather bed like boys, or newlyweds, until the elder of the pair remembered such things as fleas. He sat up and frowned at his new friend, who sat back on its plump haunches, looking eager, alert to whatever new game this enchanting new master had in mind.

He'd awakened with worse companions, Thadeus decided, eyeing the animal carefully. It was bigger by day than he'd thought it had been last night. But it looked clean; in fact, in the bright morning light it seemed glossy as any thoroughbred. It was gleaming black, its white and rust markings fresh and clear as new paint. There was some rust on the muzzle and two rust eyebrows that wigwagged its thoughts like sema-phore flags as it regarded Thadeus one way and then the other, waiting for new sport. And it was astonish-ingly fat. A clean, plump, sweet-smelling puppy from out of an alley? But who would have thought to find a lean, sweet-smelling lord in an alley? he thought on another chuckle.

It was a delightful animal. He'd find it a good home.

Christmas was coming; it would look well with a red ribband around its neck. Better than he looked, at any rate, he thought ruefully, when he rose with difficulty and made his way to his looking glass. The sight of his face brought back all his memories, and the gladsome feelings the dog had inspired faded like the mists of sleep. The deep melancholy her answer had given him returned to him with his senses—and was replaced by the deeper outrage about it. He was himself again.

"You wished the beast to remain with you," his valet said as he entered the room, bearing shaving materials and some linen for the wound on his lordship's bruised head.

"Likely I did," Thadeus agreed. "No harm done. I quite like the fellow, and he seems free of such irritants as fleas *and* gossip, which is more than I can say of most of my acquaintances these days." He sat in a chair by the window and let his valet inspect his wound. "I was set upon by footpads last night, and little as he is, this gallant creature was the only one to defend me from more, and perhaps more serious damage. A valiant fellow. I think my nephew Richard would like him. He's out of apron strings by now; there's nothing like the friendship of a boy and his dog. I'll give him this jolly fellow for Christmas, I believe."

Thadeus paused, wincing at the touch of cold water on his wound.

"You'll give him this jolly bitch for Christmas, you mean to say," his valet said.

His master jumped, but not because of his ministrations. *"No!"* he said, gazing at the dog as though it had somehow betrayed him.

"I assure you, my lord, yes."

"Well, then . . ." Thadeus said hesitantly, looking at

the puppy, who promptly rolled over on her back on the coverlet, waving all paws in the air like a dying spider, proving his valet right in his appraisal.

It would be the devil getting rid of a female, Thadeus thought. But wasn't that always the case? He grinned. It would be a change at that, since a female had just rid herself of him. He frowned, wishing he hadn't remembered. Helena had black hair, too. She, too, was pretty, charming, sweet, and friendly—or had been until he told her he wanted her, and then she'd turned on him.

"No wonder they call them that," he muttered to himself, eyeing the puppy whose sex vexed him so.

His valet understood the oblique reference better than his employer could have guessed. He'd heard about his lordship's disappointment yesterday at the hands of the dark lady he desired. Indeed, who had not? But to agree would be presumptuous. To disagree, untrue. He said nothing. Instead, with sympathy he dared not speak, and the expertise he was paid for, he silently proceeded to shave his suddenly silent employer.

He was too pale, and there were shadows under his eyes, but in all, it could be worse, and almost had been, Thadeus thought when his valet was done. The thing to do, he decided, eyeing his restored self in his mirror, was to go forward and never look back, just as his father always said. Thinking of his father reminded him of his recent disappointment. Bedamned to it, and her, he thought savagely. Bedeviled, he dressed. When he was done, he whistled to his puppy, causing her drooping ears to move forward as she sat up and stared at him. He studied her.

"The creature must have a bladder like a camel," he

told his valet. "There's not a damp spot on my bed, or the floor. It's a poor reward for such forbearance to keep her in such straits. Get a collar and a lead and have Willis walk her, and after breakfast I'll see to finding her a proper home."

The valet nodded and left the room, returning with a large young footman.

"No collars nor leads in the kitchen, my lord," Willis said, grinning at the puppy, "but here's a collar we fashioned from a coach whip, and I got a length of rope. 'Twill do for now. Would you look at her?" he crooned, approaching the puppy. "Fat as a stoat and so bright-eyed. I love dogs, I do, my lord, had a pack of them at home, didn't I? Come to Willis, little girl, and we'll have a look around the park together, won't we?"

The puppy sat up so sharply her white breast poked out till she looked like a pouter pigeon strutting on a windowsill of a May morning. As Willis neared, she stood, and drew back, her rump in the air, her foreparts lowering. The low growl that had saved his lordship in the night vibrated through his bedchamber now. Willis came nearer. The growl changed to a frenzy of yaps as she backed up on the bed. He reached for her. She snapped.

"Never you mind, my lord," Willis said as he edged around toward her, "got baby teeth, just like little needles, they are, but they won't do no lasting harm. Here, c'mere girl."

"No," Thadeus said. He approached the puppy and bent to her. She stopped barking, licked his hand, and then retreated behind it, looking out at Willis warily. Thadeus was amused, and secretly a little flattered by her obvious preference for him. *Well, clunch, but she*

knows you, after all, he told himself, refusing to take it as a compliment.

"Such a fuss," he told the puppy. "But you know? A brisk walk before breakfast only sharpens the appetite, and after last evening, I do believe I could use that. So come along, Titan . . . Titania." She immediately tumbled off the bed to come to attention by his boots, as the valet and footman shook their heads in wonder.

My lord and his puppy bobbed down the avenues. She kept pace with him, and he slowed down for her, amused at the way she seemed to walk in several directions at once, her back end swaying while her head forged ahead. The streets of London were more crowded than usual. Christmas was coming. The shops were newly bedecked for the Season, with shoppers as well as the usual strollers taking advantage of the bright, cold day. There were almost as many taking advantage of sighting a newly rejected suitor, Thadeus thought gloomily, as one person of quality after another stopped to chat with him.

They asked about how he was keeping, they asked about his family. They asked about everything but what they both knew they were thinking about. And of course, they asked about the dog my lord was exercising.

"It's a surprise gift, for giving at Christmas," Thadeus said calmly whenever he was asked, which was at every other step. "I cannot tell you more for fear of ruining the surprise, of course," he added firmly, to end further questioning.

Except it didn't always work—at least with those anxious to mine more information to fuel more gossip.

"And just what sort of an animal is it?" one gentle-

man asked rudely, bringing up a quizzing glass to inspect Titania.

"My sort," Thadeus said casually. It was a deliberate
snub. But such a delicious one that it went from one
end of fashionable London to the other in a day.

"I see. Well, a fellow has to have a *some* sort of
companion, one supposes," his inquisitor countered
snidely, ending Thadeus's joy in the confrontation,
much less the day.

"I think," he told Willis when he returned to his
house shortly after, "that she could do with a bath. She
has no inhabitants that I can see, but I want her spotless to be sure. Can you see to it? She's a clever little
thing, walked at my side as though I'd trained her to it,
and seems to know what to do in a house. Go along,
Titania," he said, handing the lead to the footman with
such a winning smile it made Willis wish he could
scrub the pup white to please him, since black didn't
show up a good washing that well.

Thadeus sat down to his breakfast and found his
spirits, so artificially buoyed by the company of the
bouncing pup, were back in their rightful place again.
Now he remembered the previous evening in all its
ghastly detail. Now he noticed his head ached, from
within and without. He looked at his breakfast and felt
his stomach turn. He turned his mantel clock ticking,
and wondered just what he was going to do with the
rest of his life. Last evening's drunkenness, beating,
and robbery, were nothing to the insult his heart felt
now.

He'd never asked a female to wed him—he'd never
wanted to. He'd never expected anything but her delighted acceptance when he had. He'd never realized
any woman would want a man to offer more than he

had. And to want such a promise, at that! As though a man of any spirit could pledge such a thing. He supposed he was guilty of many things, but he would not lie. Not even if lying might have gained him everything he wanted in the world. Which, as it turned out, she'd been.

He felt angry and hurt in equal parts, and now a little guilt was creeping into the equation. She'd been distressed when she'd dismissed him. But damn it, she *had* dismissed him!

He ate slowly, and lightly, and had just put a dab of jam on his second bit of toast when his man appeared, looking distraught.

"She won't tolerate it, my lord," he said dramatically.

"It's her or us," Willis said at his shoulder, and from the amount of fur and soap on the men, it was obvious that it was her, by a long way.

"Oh, what a fuss about nothing," Thadeus said. Here was something he could do, at last.

And he did. As his servants stood back in awe, wondering how he'd turned the little lion into a lamb. Lord Thadeus Rose was soon up to his elbows in suds, scrubbing a subdued, almost pitiable puppy. He wondered how he'd done it, too. She licked his hand as often as the soap, and tolerated every indignity without so much as a whimper, lying tender and pliant in his hands.

He made it up to her by buying her a beautiful leather collar, a long lead, a ball, and a basket, so she could sleep by his bed until it was time to give her away. She showed her pleasure by fetching the ball and giving it back without a tooth mark, every time, no matter how far he flung it, and sleeping in his bed, so

he wouldn't pine for her in the night. It amused him. It delighted her. But Christmas was coming. And he looked for other delights. Because though it was charming, it wasn't enough for him. Not nearly. The dark lady he dreamed about each night not only had refused his hand, but she'd never lick his nose, even if she had accepted him.

He dreamed of human kisses and embraces, but sought no other, dog or human, because there was only one that would satisfy him now. He decided he'd get over it. He wondered if he would. He knew he'd have to, because a man without free will was like a dog without spirit, less than the lowest cur.

A week turned into two. He enjoyed Titania's company more than he could have believed. But as the holiday season approached, no matter how cunning the puppy, Thadeus's spirits lagged lower and lower.

He paid off his mistress. He stopped making his usual rounds during the day, lest his face or voice betray his feelings to his friends. He canceled his engagements most nights. Because the servants said the puppy cried when he left, howling like a banshee, inconsolable. He himself saw how reproachfully she gazed at him every time he put on his coat and went to the door. It gave him pause. It also gave him an excellent excuse to stay at home by his own hearth. She didn't even care to walk out with him when night fell, seeming more content to doze at his feet as he sat by the fireside. He did a deal of thinking there, realizing he'd never had much time for that before.

That staying home also helped him avoid curious stares was not being craven, he reasoned, because in this case it was the humane thing to do. There was an unexpected reward for his kindness. Because he didn't

go to soirees, musicales, or the theater, where he might see her, he didn't have to go through the whole tiresome charade of not caring. To his surprise, he didn't miss those entertainments. But damn—he missed her.

"Still, what does it profit a man to gain his heart's desire, if by so doing he loses his free will?" he asked Titania one evening as they both sat by the fire.

She sighed.

"Exactly so," he said, and stared into the fire.

It was a wrench, but it had to be done. Enough was enough. A dog was supposed to be man's constant companion, not the reverse. Besides, it wasn't fair to the animal.

"I'd have waited until Christmas," Thadeus told his older, and only, sister, "but I heard you're leaving London, and I won't see you then."

"Why ever not?" she asked. "Mama is off to Bath with Greenley, and Papa is taking *that* woman to Brighton, so if no one's back at the family house, there's no sense going there. A home Christmas is the best sort. So why not my home? You might think the countryside provincial, but we have such good friends there. And good times. Do come, it would be such fun!"

"I agree, a home Christmas is the best sort, so I'm staying here, in mine," he told her amiably.

"Not even going to Hay Hall? But I heard you've started fixing it up . . . oh."

"Yes," he said with a twisted smile, "so I'd begun to do. But as you—and the rest of the civilized world—know by now, my plans are changed. I've no desire to sit and enjoy my country house in solitary state, and

the sort of fellows I associate with would surely shock the neighborhood."

She put a hand on his and asked softly, "Then it's true, it's truly not to be? I thought it such a good match. She's charming, so bright and friendly, and you, so elusive all these years, seemed truly caught. I had hoped . . ."

"It's not to be. Thank you for caring, I'll do very well for myself here in London," he said briskly, and not just because it was a sore point for him.

It bothered him to see his sister sad. She was a creature of shifting humors and passions, but none of them cruel or dark or bad. Of all his relatives, he was proudest of this, his only sibling. The only complaint he had of her was that they hadn't the time to know each other when they were children, and now that she was having children of her own, their lives continued to pull them apart.

"But, Mama, and . . . *Greenley*, you say?" he asked. "What happened to Bingham?"

"He grew boring, Mama said. But I think it's really because he grew stout." She giggled.

"Clarissa . . ." He hesitated. "On that head—did it ever bother you that Mama and Papa have such a . . . flexible marriage?"

She grew grave again, though her voice was light. "Bother me? No. Say rather, distress, disturb, and sadden me. You know? I never thought to ask you the same question. I supposed it would be different for a lad. And since you were usually at school, I thought you wouldn't notice, or care. I did, and do. But," she said deliberately, "that is them, and it's not for me to judge them, is it? My life is not so. I made sure of that. My George doesn't look at another female, unless

she's got four legs, of course. He'd rather ogle a beautiful mare than any lady. Why do you think I keep him in the countryside so much?" She laughed, but then sobered and looked at him curiously. "Why? Was I wrong? Did the way Mama and Papa live bother you? Does it?"

"No, not at all," he said lightly. "In fact, I was ten before I noticed, and twelve before it occurred to me it was in any way strange." *And seven-and-twenty before anyone dared criticize it to my face,* he thought, but said instead, "So, what do you think of Richard's present?"

"She's adorable," his sister said doubtfully, "but so large. Richard is only just five years old. Isn't she a mite . . . oversized?"

"Nonsense," Thadeus said, looking at Titania.

She sat at his side, as usual. She wore a red bow on her collar. Her coat was glossy, her eyes bright, a perfect present for any boy. She'd outgrown her basket, true, and bid fair to be outgrowing his bed, too. Or at least, these nights, when she stretched, she seemed to take up a whole side of it. Her fur, which had been like a caterpillar's when they'd met, was now growing lustrous and long. And her teeth were loosening. Time to get her to her new home, he thought resolutely, past time to get on with his life. That life was going to be in gaming hells and at racetracks, brothels and boxing matches, at least for the foreseeable future. Dogs needed homes. He needed diversion.

"Well, then . . ." his sister said.

"There's no pedigree, of course, but a great deal of breeding, even so," he said. "She's an extraordinary animal. I've never seen the like in a dog her age. She doesn't chew anything but her own food. It's remark-

able, but true. She actually sleeps with her head on my boots sometimes, and doesn't so much as smudge their polish, except for her breath, which fogs them, I admit." He neglected to mention her habit of sharing his bed, because he was sure young Richard's wouldn't be big enough for the both of them.

Well, they'd sort that out, he thought, and hurried on, "She's perfectly suited to living in the house, town or country, since she never makes her dirt inside. Not once. It's positively unnatural, but there it is. She appears to have been born broken to the lead, as well. Doesn't pull or try to run away. Young as she is, she's protective. Perfect for accompanying Richard to the park, or for country rambles. If he's naughty, she's also the perfect companion to solace himself with when he's punished, since she seems preternaturally sensitive to human moods. In short, she's an absolute angel."

"So why then don't you keep her? You're proud as any new father," his sister said, laughing.

"*I*, with a dog? Can you see me taking her everywhere with me? No, it's not fair. A boy and a dog are a classic team, not a dog and a rather old boy. And you spend most of your time in the countryside. Dogs, boys, badgers, and rabbits are much better suited than gentlemen, dandies, and tulips of the *ton*, don't you agree?"

She laughed. "I see your point . . . but a *female* . . . ?"

"My dear! You're the last one to complain of that. Who's the one who's always going on about blue-stocking ideas? If you hadn't landed George, I think you'd be up on the barricades yourself," he twitted her, before she could protest that liking Miss Moore's

works and trying one's hand at a little poetry did not make a person a bluestocking.

"She's become attached to me, it's only natural," he went on, rising to his feet. "But Richard is a good lad, and she'll be a fine dog for him. I wouldn't give her to him else. I could have got him some high-bred creature, but I doubt he cares about that. Manners and temperament do matter, and I promise you, I couldn't do better by him. Or her. So, here's her lead, and here she is. Best I leave now so when Richard comes home from the park he'll find her here, and she'll see him without any distractions to mar their first meeting. Happy Christmas, dear Sister."

He left the house without looking back, even when he heard a piteous whine at his back. She'd grow accustomed, he told himself sternly, and so would he, in time.

"At least we can go to the theater," Helena's mother said, a little desperately. "You said you don't want to go home immediately. I suppose I can see the sense to that; nothing causes talk like a swift retreat. But Christmas is coming, everyone is going home, and so shall we. It will be spring before you see London again. One would think you'd want to do something besides sitting home sulking."

"By heaven!" her father said, forgetting to pretend to be reading the paper. "You were the one to turn him down, not the reverse! Why hide here in silence? What if you do run into him?"

"I don't wish to meet him and his new lady," Helena said stubbornly.

"I hadn't heard!" her mama gasped, growing pale. "So soon? Is he so fickle then?"

"Only trying to show he don't care," her father grumbled, picking up the paper again, so his distress wouldn't show.

"Neither." Helena sighed. "He goes everywhere with his dog these days." Both parents stared at her. "A *female* dog," she explained, "a bitch, in short, as everyone takes special care to note. And tell me. Oh, bother!" she said, rising to her feet, tears in her eyes. "Never was there a worse insult! So clever. So cruel. You know what they're saying? A thing some vicious gossip composed that everyone's quoting, as Angela took pains to tell Elizabeth when I was standing so close I had no choice but to hear it.

"Rose is blooming these days. And why not? One bitch overset him, so he took up with another, and now they can't be parted!" She quoted the remark with a twisted smile.

"The cad!" her father exclaimed.

"But it might not be his intent. Perhaps he's just lonely?" her mother said. "Whichever, your father is right. It's surely wrong for you to continue to hide. You'll only give credence to the gossip if you do. You must face the world and hold your head high again. Nothing will defuse such unkind gossip faster. Surely, you see that?"

Helena nodded, head down, heart heavy. She did see that. But she also saw his handsome face before her, waking and sleeping. He was the first man she'd ever loved. She'd come to London to please her parents, never thinking she could actually find a man she'd want to share her life, her body, and her soul. She knew no other way to love. She'd had infatuations and longings before, but they'd always faded on better acquaintance, long before they resolved themselves into

anything. She'd come to accept that she might never wed.

Then to find such a man in such a stunningly handsome form, in such high position, and seemingly as taken with her as she was with him? A viscount's son, an ornament of the *ton*? But it was neither his title nor his beauty that finally caught her heart and held it. They seemed to understand each other so well, laugh together so easily and so often about the same things. She'd found a soulmate as well as a man whose very presence set her pulses racing.

She'd been sure he was as good as he was clever, and that was saying so much! That showed how much she knew, she thought miserably. She'd heard about his set's attitudes toward fidelity. Then she heard about his parents. She'd *had* to ask him his expectations after they were married, even though she knew it might destroy her happiness. Better now than later, she'd thought. But then, she hadn't known how much it would hurt.

Bad enough she couldn't forget a word they'd spoken, and relived those three wondrous kisses so often it was as though they'd exchanged three hundred by now. Worse that she regretted her decision every minute, while knowing she'd been right in every other one. But now? For him to flaunt a cur as his new love and constant companion, in a fiendish ploy to set the Town talking about how little she'd mattered to him? She never thought he could be so cruel. But then, she'd obviously never known him. She'd only loved him.

She'd dreamed of going out and flaunting her disinterest just as he was doing. There were other men in London—he himself had said they were serious suitors. But she'd committed her heart, and it ruled her

head now. She'd go home and try to forget. If she couldn't, there were worse things than spinsterhood. But she couldn't think of anything worse than not seeing him again. Except perhaps, seeing him with another female he loved, human or beast.

But jealous of a *dog*?

Helena bit her lip. *No*, she decided. Her parents were right. She was no coward. Best face the beast, look it square in the eye, pat it on the head, smile, and say, "*Lovely animal. You two are* so *well suited. I cannot think of a better match, my lord.*" That would show him, and the world.

Well, even if she didn't say that, she could look as though she thought it. And then go home, alone, forever, but, at least, having shown she did not care.

"Mama," Helena said with resolve, "I believe you and Papa are right. At least about sitting at home. I'm tired of doing nothing. Who knows when I'll come back to London? We leave in a few days. I'd like to pass them shopping and seeing those things I might miss at home. Would you come with me?"

"There is nothing I'd like more!" her mother cried, elated. Her father smiled. They both knew there was something she'd like more. But they weren't thinking of miracles, even though Christmas was coming.

The gossips noted it. How could they not? Miss Helena Thatcher was seen everywhere these days. Shopping and sightseeing, at the theater, the opera, the ballet, and riding in the park. Strolling the avenues, going to teas, dancing at Almack's, and flirting outrageously. Buying Christmas presents, going to lectures, looking at ancient Greek marbles, and attending balls. She was seen doing almost everything a young female could do in London. Except for the one thing they were

all waiting for, her meeting up with her one-time suitor, Lord Thadeus Rose.

They were disappointed in that, but it wasn't to be helped. He was little in sight these days. At least, he wasn't to be found in any place she might be. It wasn't as though he was avoiding her, just pursuing different interests, now that he'd rid himself of the amusing dog. He seemed pleasant enough when spied at one of his clubs, or fencing, or sparring with other gentlemen. Or riding out at dawn, or gambling by night. Now that his dog was gone, so was he, at least from any place where there was the faintest possibility of meeting any respectable females.

The gossip veered to greener pastures, literally. The wealthy and titled were leaving for their country estates, leaving London to the working folk, the merchants, and the poor. And Christmas.

Thadeus was busy every moment of his waking day. He dined, he rode, he read, he played, he talked with his companions. Everyone thought Lord Rose was himself again, well over his disappointment in love, as well as that queer business with the puppy he'd sported all over London. He smiled, he laughed. His friends were pleased, his servants cheerful. He couldn't remember being so unhappy.

He missed her. And he missed her. And he couldn't do a damned thing about either of them. One was better off by herself, since she didn't want him as he was. And the other was better off with another, since he wasn't good enough for her. And sometimes, to his complete and utter misery, he couldn't rightly say which was true for which of them. *Damn females, anyway,* Thadeus thought, and knew he lied. It was him-

self he was damning, because for the first time in his life, he didn't know what to do.

And so, when his man brought him the note, he read it eagerly. He'd finally gotten the message he'd been half hoping for, and half dreading. Still, his spirits lifted, even though he knew they ought not. He left the breakfast table with his food untouched and went striding out the door.

"She won't eat a thing! The poor thing's pining away," his sister said as he walked in. "I waited for her to get used to us. But it's getting dangerous now, see for yourself. She can't live on air!"

The moment he walked in Titania's head came up. She rose from the basket by the hearth she'd been curled up in, nose to tail, day and night. She didn't run to greet him. She didn't leap in the air or jump at him as she always had, forcing him to tell her *"down!"* She didn't circle his legs, yapping and waggling her round bottom either. She couldn't.

She was so much thinner that he felt his breath catch. She came to him slowly, on shaky legs, her tail waving madly, as though it were an oar sitting the air to help steer her to him.

He dropped to one knee, disregarding his fine breeches, not thinking of anything, not feeling anything but sorrow and guilt. She put one paw on his knee, another on his chest, and looked him in the eye. He saw what he'd been missing there, and closed his own eyes against the knowledge of it, and also because grown gentlemen did not cry. And certainly not over a dog. He put his arms around her, and felt her every rib in her rib cage beneath that thick fur coat. She was so lean now he could feel her heart beating against his own, and just as rapidly. He stroked her sleek head,

then buried his head in her neck, as his sister looked away, mindful of his dignity, fumbling for her hand-kerchief.

"We tried, Thad," she said mistily, "we did try. We tempted her with fresh liver, and cooked fowl, beef broth, and even my favorite bonbons. But she ignored them all. She only lay there in a huddle, pining. At first, she was fine, but she kept watching the door. And then, when she didn't see you, she slowly stopped eat-ing and playing. She didn't even want to go out. It nearly broke Richard's heart. It did break mine. You must make room for her in your life. It would be inhu-mane for you not to do so. You are hers, and she is yours, and that is that!"

"Yes," he said hoarsely. "She is indeed, and so it will be."

They made sure she drank a bowl of broth before she left. She surprised them by gobbling a good bit of boiled chicken, too, though all the while she kept her eyes on Thadeus, as though fearful he'd disappear if she didn't. When he put on her lead and walked out with her, his sister's eyes filled with tears, because the dog almost pranced out the door. But so then, too, did her brother.

He was flattered, and appalled because he was. But in truth, he felt humbled and shocked by the dog's de-votion—and staggered at how the mere fact of her loy-alty gave him joy. She was only a dog. But it was an amazing tribute nonetheless. Since Helena had refused him, he'd entertained some doubts about himself, but now . . . how bad could he be if another creature needed him as much as food and water in order to live?

He would not question it further. Things seemed right again, Thadeus thought as he strolled down the

street, taking care to walk slowly so as not to tax Titania. Things seemed better than that. She was thin, but she'd fill out. She'd grown taller in the days since he'd left her; he'd be sure she grew wider, too. She was already brighter, and was clearly as delighted as he was to be out walking. And why not? Now he noticed it was a fine day.

The avenues were filled with merry people, the street vendors crying cakes and dolls, chestnuts and tin soldiers. Street musicians played hymns and carols. Snow was in the air, and so was Christmas.

Thadeus smiled down at Titania, trotting at his side. He could have sworn she gave him a doggy smile in return. He'd be a gentleman with a dog as constant companion, he decided. He'd set a new style, and if he didn't, welladay, who cared? He didn't realize he was grinning until he realized how all the passersby were smiling back at him. He tipped his hat and smiled widely, until he saw a pair of ladies up ahead pause and hesitate, as though reluctant to pass him. One tried to cross the street to avoid him. The other held her back. They argued briefly, then commenced walking toward him again.

Some females are afraid of dogs, he realized, even pups. He slowed his pace, reining Titania in a little, so she wouldn't terrorize them by her very presence. *Clunches,* he thought, as he prepared to pass them. Still, as he came abreast of them, he had a smile set on his lips and a quip at the ready—which stuttered and died on his lips. He stopped and stared. As did she.

But he hadn't remembered how smooth and white her skin was! And he'd quite forgotten how her nose turned up just a jot at the end. He thought he'd remembered those lustrous jet curls so well, but how

could he have forgotten how they shone blue black in the light? It seemed he'd also forgotten how those soft pink lips parted in surprise, though try as he might, he hadn't been able to forget how they tasted. And he'd never noticed how her gray eyes shone with silver in the sunlight. He couldn't look away.

Unfair, Helena thought in despair. His golden hair glowed in the light, his skin glowed, his azure eyes glowed, the man glowed so bright he shamed the sunlight and burned a hole clear through her heart. All her rehearsed quips were forgotten, all those killingly clever snubs she'd enacted in her mind in her every empty night. She dragged her eyes from him and finally looked at the dog he led—and sighed.

It was obviously only an awkward puppy, and a starved one at that, but so sweet-looking and gentle, with big dark eyes that looked as sad as she felt. The plume of a tail wagged as she stared at the animal. How could she say anything cutting or cruel about that?

Helena knelt, extending one gloved hand for it to sniff. Then she stroked the square head, wishing she could actually feel that soft fur against a bare hand, wishing she could say something, wishing she could look at him again. Her mother saved the moment.

"Good afternoon, my lord," she said. "How have you been keeping?"

"Well," she heard him say in that achingly familiar rich, deep voice, "tolerably well, ma'am, and you?"

They spoke about how well they felt, how well their respective families were, how well the world was, and then, after a pause, how adorable the puppy was. Helena said nothing. How could she? It was only a puppy, and perhaps he really liked it. Who would not? And so

what else could she say? She straightened. She held her hands together in her muff, yearning to pat the lovely dog again, yearning to say something intelligent, or cutting or vile, or anything to break this spell he had over her.

"This is my dog, Titania," he told her.

"She is lovely," Helena said, looking past his ear.

"I came by her quite by accident."

"A fortunate accident to be sure."

"So it was. She's very clever. I'd given her to my nephew, as a Christmas present. But she pined away for me. I've taken her back. I'll give him a spaniel, instead. I'll keep her. She's usually heavier, you see."

"Oh, I see."

"She will be again soon."

"That's good. She looks a trifle thin, to be sure."

"Well, so she is."

"So I see."

"Well. It grows late. I give you good day then," he finally said in a strained voice.

She nodded, her mother said good-bye, and they went on down the street.

But he was devastated. So was she. Her mother wisely said nothing, but her frown could have turned milk. Helena thought of all the things she could have said. As none sounded right, she thought it just as well that she'd not said one intelligent thing. Thadeus thought of everything he'd said, and realized he'd babbled, and was only glad he hadn't begged. One dog in the street was enough for her in one day, he thought bitterly. He went home. But Titania kept looking back after Helena until she'd entirely disappeared from sight.

That night Titania dined the way her namesake

might have done, on sweet nectars and rare treats from her master's own plate. She had a bit of tongue, a taste of honeyed sauce, a smidge of veal, and a chicken wing, carefully freed from the bone. Some cream for her coat, and a dab of butter for her own bones. And a lovely collop of beef, sent straight to her from Cook.

Her master drank some fine Canary, then a good Rhine wine, and then a bracing red, because by then he couldn't taste the difference between vinegar and burgundy and would have drunk either if they had alcohol in them. And still he went to bed too sober to suit himself. The only good thing in it was Titania, breathing soft, and lying as though clipped to his side through the night.

One day until Christmas, Thadeus thought wearily. The Town was emptying as fast as the old year was draining away. He should have been content to stay with Titania, but the memory of what else was lost with this old year haunted him now. He ate less and drank more, and stayed sober even so. He was restless and irritable, the more so when he realized he was pining for the heartless Helena as much as Titania had grieved for him. But he was not a dog, he told himself severely—hadn't he told her just that?

He was a popular fellow. There were many places he'd been invited to for the holiday. House parties in Kent and Oxford, Surrey and the Cotswolds, and a huge one in Scotland, to boot. Empty as it was of the *ton*, still London wasn't entirely deserted. He'd been invited to dinners here as well. But he didn't feel like good company, in any construction of the words.

He walked to his window and looked out. He could go to his house in the countryside and watch the snow

fall. Or stay here and do it more easily. He whistled up
Titania. She came bounding toward him in a bumbling
waddle.

"We may have put too much meat on your bones,
old girl," he told her, riffling the fur on her head. She
looked up at him adoringly. "A nice long walk then,"
he said, "just the thing to shake some ounces from you,
my plump pet, and to shake the blue devils from myself as well. And then a book by the fireside for me, a
fresh bone for you, a glass of wine, and a dish of milk,
and Happy Christmas to all, and there's an end to it."

But somehow, a recital of those agreeable plans only
depressed him more. So he put on her lead and took
her out into the last of the afternoon.

They walked a long way, along streets suddenly
cleared of traffic, with few pedestrians and almost no
horsemen. Carriages filled with families bound for
holiday meetings had long since trundled away. The
street vendors were gone, even the beggars had called
it a day, because it was the eve of Christmas Day, and
they, too, wanted time off to celebrate.

"And if a fellow has no one he chooses to be with,
he stays home by himself, I suppose. So isn't it lucky
we have each other?" he told Titania, since there was
no one around to note a gentleman talking to his dog.
Even if there were, where was the harm in that? People always spoke to their dogs, because they always
got the right answers from them, few arguments, and
no demands for promises.

As twilight came on, they continued to walk on. Past
the Park, to new streets. Because Titania seemed intent
on going down this avenue and then up another, taking
him for a walk for a change. He didn't mind. He wasn't
in the least tired, and didn't think he would be no mat-

ter how far they went this evening. He let her lead. He followed, lost in his own dark reflections again.

So when the dark shape suddenly came hurtling at them, he was unprepared. He belatedly gripped Titania's lead tight as he saw the other dog fly at them. But she stood firm until he had his balance back. Only then did she turn to the other dog, the one off-lead that had come bounding up to her. Thadeus gripped his walking stick, prepared to fight it off if it meant to do her an injury.

But then he paused, and blinked. The two dogs frolicked at his feet, and it looked like she was playing with her own shadow.

"Ho, Hercules!" a voice cried. A plainly dressed but amiable-looking young man carrying two heavy carpet bags came running down the street, calling as he ran, "Sorry, sir! He means no harm!"

When he reached Thadeus, he put down his bags. He looked at the dogs anxiously, adding breathlessly, "I didn't put on his lead. My hands were full, and Herk here, well he's a good lad and never leaves my side. Don't know what got into him . . . Don't worry, he's harmless, won't hurt you or your . . . well, would you look at that!"

"I am, and can scarcely believe it," Thadeus said.

Titania's shadow was a trifle larger than she was, he saw now, but there wasn't much to choose between them. Perhaps the white triangle on Titania's forehead was narrower than the other dog's. Maybe her ears were a bit shorter. But they were both black, with white markings, four white paws, a white tail tip mimicking a fifth, floppy ears, broad muzzles, and foolish rust eyebrows to show their every delighted thought. They looked like twins, in fact. Both were solid

doorstops of puppies, and what was more, they seemed to know each other. Seeing that, Thadeus grew nervous.

"Your dog," he said as the two dogs romped in a small circle in front of them. "May I ask where you purchased him?"

The amiable young man looked much less amiable now. He folded his arms on his broad chest, looking Thadeus up and down. "I didn't steal him, if that's what you're asking," he said with hostility. "You might say he found me. If he's yours, and you can prove he somehow escaped your house, why, I'll pay you for him in full, whatever the price, because he's beyond price to me."

"No, no, you misunderstand," Thadeus said with relief. "I wondered if you'd make the same claim yourself. You see, I found Titania, or rather, I suppose," he said with a grin, "she found me, too. How old is he?"

"I can't say," the young man said, relaxing a bit. "I found him some four weeks past. I thought him to be an infant that night, but he surprised me by morning's light. He acted so much older and grew apace. And look at him now. I judge he'll be about three months old come Christmas morning. Leastways, I'm celebrating his birthday then."

"Ah. Sounds very like Titania! I imagine they come from the same litter and were separated," Thadeus said. "What a nice Christmas treat for her. So she has a relative in Town!"

The young man laughed. "But only for now, because we're leaving this very night. He changed my fortunes for me, my Hercules did, and that's a fact. I took him in when I found him shivering on my doorstep. The best thing I ever did, for he's the best dog I ever knew,"

he said fondly, beaming down at his dog. "But as I watched him grow, I got to thinking, and I had to think fast, I can tell you. Well, you know. Because he grew an inch an hour, I think."

Both men looked at their dogs and beamed like proud fathers discussing their infant prodigies.

"London's no place for a dog like him, I told myself," the young man went on. "He was so unhappy being pent in my rooms with me of a night. Good as gold otherwise, but restless, and then depressed. Well, you know how they are."

"Actually," Thadeus said, "Titania is perfectly content to sit by my side every night."

"Not my lad," the young man said. "He ached to go out every evening. I work so hard each day I'd taken to having my dinner and going straight to bed when I got home. But he'd bring me his lead, drop it at my feet, and then just sit, staring. Pleading, like, though he never made a sound. It went to my heart, it did. You know those eyes of theirs. So I walked myself into the ground each night. But I'm an outdoor fellow, really, and it did me a world of good. I do my best thinking on my feet, and all that walking gave me time and to spare to do it."

"Passing strange," Thadeus commented. "If they weren't twins, I'd wonder if they were even the same sort of animal. It's just the reverse with us. I was in the habit of going out on the Town every night, and always had too much to do to think. Since I've had her, I've had more time to reflect. She likes sitting by the hearth. Sitting with her has shown me more than pictures in the fire."

"Well, my walks with Hercules changed me, too, to be sure," the young man said. "He needs more than

cobbles and pavements, thinks I, when I went out with
him night after night. He needs fields and meadows to
romp, like I had when I was young. It set me thinking,
all right. I'd left hearth and home against my parents'
wishes, for I was set on coming to London to make my
fortune. I did well, I suppose. But there wasn't much in
it besides the money. Because I missed family and old
friends. But I was too busy to see it. Or to be more honest, I was too set on making my fortune in order to
show that I could—the way I vowed that I would when
I left home. Before Hercules found me, that is to say.

"London's got enough blacksmiths to shoe an army.
But Tiddleford, well, they could use another, like my
da always said. I know he could use a hand, though
he's too proud to insist on it. Hercules set me thinking,
and Christmas set my feet on the right track. Tiddleford will suit the two of us down to the ground. Neither of us are City folk. And so we're off this very
night. I've seats on a coach leaving from the Bull and
Mouth. I even bought space for Hercules, since I won't
have him leaving my side no more than he will. If he
hadn't found me, I suppose I'd still be living alone,
counting my money, with my head up my own stubborn rump. Instead, we'll be home by the New Year,
and will stay for the rest of our years in peace and content, good Lord willing."

"Too bad for Titania, but good for you," Thadeus
said. "Here, my card. Drop me a note to tell me how
you two are getting on, for in truth, it's a wonderful
tale."

"So I will," the young man said, glancing at the card
before dropping it in his pocket. He bowed. "James
Bright's the name, my lord. But now, as for you? Has
your Titania changed your life for the better, too?"

Thadeus paused. The one thing he wanted most, the dog couldn't give him. But, in truth, she'd given him much. "I expect she has," he said slowly. "Companionship, laughter, and unswerving loyalty—I suppose a man can't ask for more from his pet."

"And love, don't forget love," the young man said. "For it's no little thing to know there's one soul in the world thinks the world of you, one who will never let you down, no matter what. It makes a man feel good about himself. There's nothing a fellow can't do, or won't do, with that kind of devotion to see him through. Even if it's only a dog's love, love's powerful stuff, to be sure."

". . . To be sure," Thadeus echoed.

"But our coach is leaving soon, so we can't tarry, much as I'd like to. Farewell, and well met," James Bright said with a small bow. He picked up his carpet bags and whistled. His dog stopped nuzzling Titania's ear. He left her at once and went to his master.

"Fare thee well," Thadeus said, and watched them walk off down the street together, Hercules bouncing along at his master's side, never once looking back.

Thadeus and Titania retraced their steps, walking more slowly now, since he was deep in thought. She ambled by his side, taking her time, letting him set the pace. And when, after several streets, he suddenly picked up his head and picked up the pace, changing direction, she jogged along with him, as eager as he to move on. He was practically running by the time he finally reached the house he made straight for. She galloped beside him all the way.

He bounded up the steps, relieved beyond belief to see the door knocker was still on the front door. Be-

cause he hadn't wanted to take his coach to find her, but would have, if he had to.

"Miss Helena," he breathlessly asked the footman who opened the door. "Is she still here, is she in?"

"I will see, sir," the fellow said nervously, because the caller was obviously a gentleman, but the family wasn't having company tonight. And gentlemen did not ordinarily show up uninvited on the front step on Christmas Eve, panting almost as hard as the great black beasts they had with them.

"Tell her it's Lord Rose," Thadeus said, "Lord Thadeus Rose who begs . . . yes," he said, hearing what he'd said and grinning, "Lord Thadeus Rose and his friend Titania, who beg the pleasure of her company, just for a moment, if she'd be so kind as to receive them."

She did receive them, but seemed almost as nervous as the footman had been. She'd been at the piano, singing some carols, making them sound like dirges, when the butler had come in, eyes dancing. All the family, servants included, knew why Miss hadn't had the heart to go home for the holiday.

Her mama heard about their unexpected caller and retreated immediately. "The dog will be chaperone enough," she said and laughed, excited as a child on Christmas morning, as she hurried her husband into the library to argue with him about the propriety of letting their daughter receive the young lord alone— giving her time to receive him alone, of course.

"I expect you wonder why I'm here," Thadeus said when he entered the room and saw Helena looking apprehensive—apprehensive and lovely. He gazed at her hungrily, adding, "At least you must be wondering why I've come so precipitously."

"Oh, no," Helena said, much more lightly than she felt, deciding not to take it seriously, since it might all be some sodden jest. She tried to discreetly scent the air for traces of spirits. "We were expecting carolers," she added, eyeing Titania, sitting at his feet. "Are you and your bear going to oblige us?"

He grinned. "Oh, my Titania? She's the reason I'm here."

"Oh," Helena said, and felt her heart squeeze. Drunk, and demented with it, and why hadn't she gone home instead of refining on that stricken look she'd thought she'd seen on his face that day they'd met again? Gone home instead of hoping, praying, waiting for a Christmas miracle that turned out to be a Christmas charade?

"But she doesn't sing. She only teaches," he said with such sincerity she wondered what it was he'd drunk that addled his wits and yet kept his voice so sane.

"You remember that day? Lord, I can't forget it," he said, "that day when you told me what you expected in a husband, and I so cavalierly told you to get a dog?"

She nodded, fascinated. That handsome face was intent, his eyes sincere. If this was a drunken stupor, God send that he remained always so stupefied.

"Instead," he said on a shrug, "I was the one to get a dog, or rather, a dog got me. I learned some things from her, Helena. What I said that day made *me* into what we think of when we call a man a 'dog.' But it wasn't at all a doglike thing to do. Dogs have purer souls. They love unconditionally. We call it 'doglike devotion.' But it's only love in its purest form."

His eyes grew grave. "Titania showed me what it's like to have another living creature love you to the

point that their own self is unimportant compared to your own. She'd die for me, and almost did. She's utterly faithful to me—I'm surer of that than I am of the sun rising tomorrow. And do you know? I found it's wonderful to be so loved. Such love warms you, supports you, makes you feel more deserving than you are. It came to me, belatedly, that if one could ever be so lucky as to be able to count on a human being one loved to return love to the same degree, it would be quite simply, heavenly."

All laughter left his face as he stared at her. "I wasn't willing to promise you that, because I never imagined it. My parents, as you so rightly noted, never taught me that by word or deed. They were themselves deprived of such a thing. Their marriage being an arrangement of money and properties, they never knew that bliss. And so they've one lover after another, and no fidelity except to their own passing desires. *That* is doglike, in the way we speak of such things. A passing meeting, a meeting of flesh, and then a scent on the wind, and a new desire to chase after.

"But fidelity . . . It took a dog to teach me that is the most human of emotions. The most noble and gratifying. And so I vow, Helena, that if you give me the chance to be so devoted to you, so I shall be. I don't want to go on comparing myself to a dog," he said on a little laugh that faded when she didn't respond in kind.

He continued, his face stark, his voice strained. "I only want to say that this simple creature taught me what I need, what I want, and what I sincerely hope I've not denied myself forever. I offer for you again, Helena," he said softly, "and again, not on bended

knee. But this time only because I don't want Titania to lick my face," he added with another hesitant smile.

She only stared. He went on, a little desperately, "I offer on whatever metaphorical knees you choose to imagine, though. I offered you love before. Now I offer that, plus my complete loyalty, my utter fidelity. You may grow old, you may grow monstrous stout— though I do wish you would not, at least not right away—you may grow gray as a goose, for all I care. I pledge I'll always be true to you.

" . . . As true as you are to me, of course," he said, noting her expression changing, his spirits rising. "I'm not so besotted as to be lost to all reason. Not when I've just come to my senses. No, if you chose to run off to Italy with our children's music master, I cannot promise you I will remain forever faith . . . Oh, my love . . ."

Helena broke from her disbelieving silence. She made a little choking sound, then cast herself into his arms. He gratefully received her. They kissed, then drew away and looked into each other's eyes, and kissed again. She tasted no spirits on his lips, nothing but his own sweet nectars. He was sober, she thought with delight. But when they kissed again, he became as drunk as she was on the pleasure of their kisses.

By the time her parents came into the room, loudly "harumphing" to spare them embarrassment, they'd recovered themselves enough to sit on a sofa, Titania at their feet, looking at each other with enormous spaniel eyes.

They made their announcement. Then there was much merriment, they drank a toast, and laughed a great deal, and set a date. At the last, when they stood together in the darkened hall, trying to say good night,

they whispered "Happy Christmas" to each other as they heard all the church bells of London tolling midnight and the new and glorious day. They parted with kisses and promises and avowals of love, and then reluctantly had actually to part, promising it wouldn't be for long. Never for long, ever again.

Helena danced to bed after he left, hugging her happiness close. When she finally laid her head on her pillow, her last conscious thought was of the jeweled collar she'd buy for Titania, man's best friend, and the best friend any girl ever had.

Her parents danced together, alone in the salon, until the last of the candles flickered and they saw a familiar, delicious glitter in each other's eyes.

Thadeus waltzed home with Titania, stopping to dance with her in the street. His servants were waiting for him; they worried about him these days. He told them the news. They were relieved and delighted. They saluted him and drank to his happiness. Then he waved them to their beds, and smiling, took himself off to his own bed, his head whirling with plans for his future, a future in which he'd knew he'd never be so alone again.

As he slept, and the moon rode across the sky toward a new Christmas morning, Titania slid from his bed to lie on the floor. It was cooler there, and suited her, and always had, and suddenly she no longer needed to remain glued to his side. She'd loved him, and still did, but now she didn't have to cling to him like a tick. Because now he knew—or so she felt. And it was all feelings and urgings and silent commands for her, built into her like thirst or hunger—until now. Now she was suddenly released.

When she got to the floor by the bed, she found the

most entrancing scent there, and it led her to one of his hastily discarded boots. It smelled divine. And tasted even better, especially the gold tassels on its side. She chewed with gusto. She'd wanted to do that for so long. Now she could. *He* wouldn't mind. *He'd* decide *he* needed a new pair anyway, and would shake a finger at her, and tell her not to do it again, and perhaps, she would not.

When she'd gnawed the boot sufficiently and reduced the tassel to satisfactorily tiny pieces, she laid her head on the remnants and closed her eyes. She was alone on the floor, but it was as if a soft, warm, gentle hand stroked over her fur. It warmed her to her very bones. She stretched out with pure contentment and sighed.

Good dog, she thought she heard, and why not? A good dog she was. Her job was done, and well done. She'd taught him the thing a dog knows best of all things. He'd learned. Now, at last, she could get on with the enthralling business of simply being a dog for the first time—and for the rest of her long, rich, and deliciously happy life.